Intermission

Intermission

Phyllis R. Dixon

www.kensingtonbooks.com

DAFINA BOOKS are published by

Kensington Publishing Corp.
119 West 40th Street
New York, NY 10018

All Kensington titles, imprints, and distributed lines are available at special quantity discounts for bulk purchases for sales promotion, premiums, fund-raising, and educational or institutional use.

Special book excerpts or customized printings can also be created to fit specific needs. For details, write or phone the office of the Kensington Sales Manager: Kensington Publishing Corp., 119 West 40th Street, New York, NY 10018. Attn. Sales Department. Phone: 1-800-221-2647.

The Dafina logo is a trademark of Kensington Publishing Corp.

ISBN: 978-1-4967-4311-4
First Trade Paperback Printing: August 2023

ISBN: 978-1-4967-4312-1 (e-book)
First Electronic Edition: August 2023

10 9 8 7 6 5 4 3 2 1

Printed in the United States of America

For my mother—she told me I could and so I did.

Acknowledgments

It has taken a long time to get here, but to quote the spiritual—*I wouldn't take nothing for my journey now*. This journey would not have been possible without the love and guidance of my mother and best friend, Maggie Jackson-Hale, and my father, Timothy Jackson, who always told me to go read a book whenever I said I was bored. Special appreciation goes to three people who started on this journey with me but are no longer here: Kevin Clark, Karen Dean, and Fitzgerald Dixon.

Sending a big thank you to my agent, Marlene Stringer, for her tenacity and for sharing my vision. I'm grateful to the Dafina/Kensington team, in particular Esi Sogah and John Scognamiglio for their editing assistance and overall enthusiasm. I'd like to thank Tanya Beckley, Tyler Brown, Tujuana Burt, Sheryl Dean, Clarence Hale, Arlender Jones, Crystal Maddox, Jackie Miller, Patricia Montgomery, Mary Randolph, Juel Richardson, Annie and Caesar Slade, Michael Stewart, Betty Washington, Sharon Williams, and my St. Andrew A.M.E. church family for their encouragement and support. I would also like to thank my children, Trey, Candace, and Lee, for taking this journey with me (not that they had much choice).

Intermission is about sisterhood, and I appreciate the steadfast support of my Delta Sigma Theta Sorority, Inc., sorors, especially Kappa Eta Chapter and Memphis Alumnae Chapter.

And I thank you, for taking time out of your own journey to read this book. I hope you find it time well spent.

The first to apologize is the bravest.
The first to forgive is the strongest.
The first to forget is the happiest.

—Author unknown

PROLOGUE

CLOSING NUMBER

The Diamonds returned to the stage for their second encore. The sold-out crowd remained on their feet, clapping and cheering. The girls were drenched with sweat, but Angel's waist-length curls remained in place and her makeup flawless, even though she sang lead on most songs. The audience response was such a rush, Doreen had been able to ignore the nagging voice in her head telling her it was time for a fix. Jade was blowing kisses and waving like Miss America. Even Carmen, who had to be cajoled back to the stage, was moved, and tears filled her glistening brown eyes. The Diamonds were not an overnight success, or a studio packaged group. They were four girls from Memphis who worked their way from a local teen talent show to this moment.

Their set had gone overtime, and the musicians were unplugging their instruments. Ray Nelson had surprised the girls when he interrupted what was supposed to be their last song. As the owner of Peak Records, he usually stayed in his seventh-floor office in downtown Memphis. But he had made a rare road appearance to present them their third gold record.

Jade hugged the plaque as tears streamed down her olive

cheeks. Doreen jumped up and down so, her boobs almost popped out of her tube top. Carmen was speechless and forgot her Valentino stilettos were killing her feet, as Jade gathered them all for a group hug. Angel stepped in front of Carmen, then hugged Ray and kissed him on the cheek, while posing for the photographer. Angel thanked the fans on behalf of the group. The girls performed fifteen more minutes, until the lights came up and they were forced to leave the stage.

The girls had performed hundreds of shows, but tonight they had an extra burst of energy, knowing this would be their last show until fall. Their grueling six-month tour was finally over. They were as enthusiastic and eager to please as they were in 1991, when the original Diamonds—Carmen Ellis, and her neighbors, Doreen and Sophia Frazier—won the station WDIZ teen talent show. Gloria, Carmen's mother, had signed them up, picked the songs, choreographed the steps, and directed rehearsals.

They had come a long way in six years. The Diamonds had a string of R and B hits and a couple of their songs had reached the pop chart top forty. But with their newest single, they were on the cusp of crossing over. Angel had insisted they get new management, and the change was already paying dividends. Meetings were scheduled to discuss a clothing brand and soda commercial, and Ray Nelson was negotiating with larger venues for their fall tour.

"That was great," Ray said, clapping as the girls came backstage. "Angel, you held that high note so long, I thought you were going to burst a blood vessel. And looks like those extra practices paid off, since Jade's two left feet finally mastered the step routine. Doreen, honey, I'm so proud of you. You've been able to stay clean. I knew you could do it, one day at a time. And Carmen, you've never sounded better. Your solo mesmerized the audience. Tonight was perfect—or as you young folks say, the bomb."

"Thanks, Ray," Carmen said, as she turned away from him and rolled her eyes.

"We have a few hours before the bus leaves. The band is headed to a party. Let's join them," Doreen said.

"No thanks," Carmen replied as she stepped out of her stilettos. "I'm hungry, sweaty, and tired. I'll meet you on the bus. Please be on time."

"Carmen's right. You should rest. You've only got a week to get ready for the Unity Festival in Durban. President Mandela is opening the festival. This will be major inter-national exposure," Ray said.

"When did this come up?" Carmen asked.

"Somebody canceled and the promoter called. Funny how a hit record changes things. 'Searchin' for the Right One' is racing up the charts," Ray said, while lighting a cigarette. "And get this, he's paying twice what we initially proposed. We're rescheduling your *Soul Train* and *MTV Jams* appearances. If you had shown up for mic-check, you would've heard my announcement."

"I have an announcement too," Carmen said, as she picked up her bags and slung her shoes over her shoulders. "I quit."

"Again?" Ray sighed and checked his pager. "I guess you didn't hear what I said about more money. You'll clear almost half a million dollars."

"And I guess you didn't hear what I said," Carmen fired back. "I quit."

"I know you're still upset, but you can't take what happened earlier personally. I think you'll feel differently once we get back to Memphis, relax and unwind for a few days."

"I give less than a damn what you think," Carmen snapped.

"You and I may not always agree, but isn't this what we've been working for?" Angel asked, as she flipped her hair over her shoulder. "Girl groups are hot right now—look at Destiny's Child. We're finally about to make some real money."

"Tonight was magical," Jade said, as she grabbed Carmen's hand. "Don't let a misunderstanding block—"

"I understand quite well," Carmen stated. "I understand treacherous, backstabbing bullshit when I see it."

"This is crazy. Musicians are updating charts, travel arrangements have been booked and wardrobe is expediting new costumes," Ray said, blowing smoke in the air. "The Diamonds are hotter than ever. Besides, I have a contract, and you gals owe me a lot of money. You think recording sessions, designer clothes, room service, hotels, and travel are free? I own your ungrateful ass. You can't quit."

Carmen waved his cigarette smoke away, stepped around him and said, "Watch me," then disappeared offstage.

ACT I

BACKGROUND MUSIC

CHAPTER I

CARMEN

Twenty years later...

Carmen placed the pineapple cake on the stand and licked icing from the spatula. It was Saturday morning, but her kitchen smelled like Sunday dinner. It seemed strange not to gather at her mother's house for the Fourth of July. Gloria always invited the neighbors and the celebration became a combined block party and family reunion. But over the last nine months, Carmen and her siblings had gradually moved more of Gloria's things to her house. So now, it was easier for Carmen to host the family.

While the other Diamonds splurged on drugs, clothes, cars, trips and more drugs, Carmen bought her mother a house and one of her own. Other than dusty gold records on the dining room wall, those houses were the only tangible evidence from her days in one of the hottest girl groups of the nineties. One of her proudest moments was handing her mother a deed stamped *paid* with her name *Gloria Mae Ellis* typed in the owner space. When her mother finally left her last husband, Carmen, her older sister Faye, and younger brother Sonny moved five times in two years, outrunning eviction notices. Gloria found a job at McDonald's and worked her way from fry cook to district manager. She also worked part-time at the radio station and sometimes sang with bands in Beale Street clubs. Carmen loved singing with the girls, but her goal was to make her mother's life easier, and ensure they never again had to worry about a roof over their heads.

Angel, Doreen, Jade, and Sophia begged her to party after shows, but Carmen preferred to read and hoarded her money. The girls said she squeezed a dollar so tight you could hear George Washington holler.

The subdivision was new when Carmen moved in twenty years ago, and the two-story colonial had seemed like a mansion. There were some newer features she wished she had, but her home had the most desirable trait of all—it was almost paid for. Between her music teacher salary, sporadic child support, and an occasional royalty check, she had managed to provide her children stability and security.

When people learned she had been a Diamond, they expected her to have a bankroll stashed away. But even though the Diamonds sold millions of records, when she left the group in 1997, Peak Records claimed the Diamonds owed the company money. Carmen sued for unpaid royalties, and they countersued for breach of contract. Lawsuits dragged on for years. They finally settled four years ago, and after taxes and legal fees, Carmen got forty thousand dollars— not the high six figures she expected. After a new roof, braces for both kids, and a splurge trip to Disney World, her windfall had dwindled to less than twenty thousand. Money she added to her children's college fund.

The oven had warmed the house, and Carmen cranked up the air conditioner. She had planned to bake last night, and not heat the kitchen today, but Nathan called and she decided the cake could wait. They went to get ice cream, then to Lake Park to watch fireworks, and then, went to make their own fireworks behind closed doors. The memory brought a contented smile, and she hummed an Aretha Franklin tune as she loaded the dishwasher. The back door opened and she looked up. "It's about time you got here. Oh," she said when she saw it wasn't David.

"You certainly aren't healthy for a girl's ego. Here, I had this in my freezer." Gloria handed her daughter a container of hogshead cheese, a dish saved for special occasions.

"Sorry, Mama. I was expecting David."

"I just talked to Faye. She said business was slow, so she let David go around ten. He was getting a haircut, then coming home."

"He knows the barbershop is packed on Saturday mornings, and the buses are slow," Carmen responded. "He asked to take my car; maybe I should've let him."

"He probably stopped by his little girlfriend's house. I'm sure he'll be here soon," Gloria said, as she sat down and pulled a rib from the pan.

"He'll get an earful from me when he does get here. David promised to help."

"You know," Gloria said, pointing the rib at her daughter, "If you had brought your fast tail home at a decent hour, you could've gotten an earlier start."

Carmen breathed deeply and ignored her mother's commentary on her private life. "I had planned on being outside, but it's starting to rain, so we'll all be inside, and the house is a mess."

"It's family. We're not guests. You're stressing over nothing," Gloria advised as she reached for the cake.

"You know you're not supposed to eat this," Carmen said, sliding the cake stand away from her mother.

"Living with you is like being in basic training. I checked my sugar, it's fine." Gloria was diabetic and had a stroke just before Christmas. The doctors said it was a light stroke, although it still sounded serious to Carmen. Thankfully, other than weight loss, she had minimal side effects, but she needed to start dialysis. Since Faye and her husband kept long hours at their florist shop, and her brother Sonny shared a small apartment with his newest girlfriend, they convinced her to stay with Carmen, at least until she adjusted to dialysis.

"David knows I'm going to fuss so he won't answer," Carmen said, calling him again.

"You're too hard on him. He's an A student, on the student council, basketball, and debate teams—and he has a job. Faye says he's one of her best workers," Gloria said. "Let him enjoy this time in his life. Hope should get out more too. She said she had to work today. That child has the rest of her life to work. She should be on the phone giggling about boys."

"Hope has enough time to worry about boys. I'm glad she wants to be independent and have her own money. And I don't want David thinking he can get by because he's cute and can bounce a basketball. I definitely don't want him living with me when he's thirty-five, like *some* people."

"Sonny has his own place now, and he'll have plenty of money when he gets his lawsuit settlement."

"He's been waiting on that settlement for years," Carmen said. "And he's moved in with his girlfriend. That's not the same thing. She could kick him out at any time. Then he'll be back at your house."

"I wouldn't mind. I don't like my house being empty. Sale papers and the Yellow Pages were sitting on my porch this morning, announcing to all thieves the house is empty. Folks these days will steal the butter off your bread. And the post office isn't forwarding all my mail. What if the sweepstakes prize patrol comes and I miss them?"

"Most of those so-called sweepstakes are scams. And insurance covers your stuff if there's a break-in."

"That stuff, as you call it, is priceless—all my pictures, my mother's dishes," Gloria said. "My album collection shouldn't be left in a hot house. Angel sent me designer shoes and hats from around the world. Heat isn't good for them either. And my fur is there. Angel gave it to me when I joined her at President Obama's inauguration. The more I think about it, the more I worry about my house," Gloria said. "I don't need to be babysat. I want to go home."

"I'll come to your next doctor visit and see what he says. And your house will be fine," Carmen insisted, as she pulled out the vacuum cleaner. "I doubt if a burglar wants old baby pictures, and Angela's hand-me-downs are as worthless and phony as she is."

"Don't start bad-mouthing Angel."

"Is it bad-mouthing if it's true?"

"I didn't raise you to be so judgmental," Gloria remarked with a sigh. "It's been years. You girls should settle your grudge."

"A grudge would be an upgrade, and I'm not wasting another second of my holiday talking about her," Carmen said. "Right now, I have a floor to vacuum."

"Do it tomorrow. Hope has been teaching me that new 'Cha Cha Slide Number Six,' and I plan to show you young folks a thing or two," Gloria said as she snapped her fingers, stepped from side to side and shimmied her ample behind. "Between dancing and folks tramping in dirt, it'll get dirty again anyhow."

"All right. Wallace finished the ribs and chicken this morning and said he would do the burgers and hot dogs this afternoon," Carmen said, as she texted her son again.

"He sure is persistent," Gloria said. "What's that song you girls sang, 'Searchin' for the Right One'? Well, you've been searching ten years, it's time to pull in your net. I don't know why you won't settle down with him."

"We're just friends," Carmen insisted.

"At forty, you can't waste time with friends," Gloria said, using her fingers to make air quotation marks. "No man is going to get up before dawn and barbeque for your family because he wants to be your friend."

"We don't click. Wallace is nice but…"

"Baby, nice comes home at night, nice pays the bills, and nice doesn't call you at the last minute for a booty call the night before a holiday. Nice spends the holiday with you."

"Mama, I don't appreciate your opinion on my relationship with Nathan."

When she started seeing Nathan, she had just ended a yearlong relationship. After yet another dating bust, she declared she was taking a break and Nathan was a cute diversion. But as weeks turned into months and now a couple years, he remained in her life—sort of. His job transferred to Atlanta. But his parents were still in Memphis, and he came back to town just enough to keep Carmen content. She didn't need or want a man underfoot twenty-four hours a day, seven days a week. His wife could worry about that.

"I know times change, but I don't think what you and that no-good Negro are doing can be called a relationship. If you lay down with dogs, you get up with fleas," Gloria said. "Wallace just needs fixing up. Get him to shave his head and stop those homemade haircuts, switch to contacts, and take him to a dermatologist. He'll start clicking then."

"Mama, me and my kids are fine. My bills are paid, and we're all healthy. Life is good."

"Then come back to Blessings. There are several single men in the choir. We've got some on the usher board too. Doreen always asks about you."

Carmen and Doreen were the only Diamonds still in Memphis. They lived less than fifteen miles apart, but rarely saw each other. After reminiscing about the old days, and sharing news about their children, they had little else to talk about. And eventually, Doreen would try to get her to come to church. Carmen grew up in church, but was now a CME member: Christmas, Mother's Day, and Easter.

"Where there are church men, there are church women, which equals drama. No, thank you." Carmen said.

"It's too late now, but you probably gave up on your marriage too soon. Vernon's doing so well, and you have two beautiful children. Men take longer to mature and settle down."

"You cannot be serious. We were married six years and that was five years too long. Correction—I was married six years. Vernon never honored his vows," Carmen said. "Why so much concern about marriage? I don't see you and Mr. Wilson rushing to the altar."

"We've been together five years, and like things the way they are. He's seventy-five, so my sixty-four makes me his PYT. And there's no Social Security or pension issues."

"Mama, I hate to burst your bubble, but I don't think you're what Michael Jackson had in mind when he sang that song," Carmen said, laughing. "And haven't you been sixty-four for a few years now?"

"You're missing my point," Gloria replied, waving her hand. "I worry about you. You're still young, and should be spending these years with some sexy, smart man who makes your toes curl and pampers you—not stuck in a hot kitchen baking cakes and washing dishes."

"Never thought I'd consider forty young. But since Mr. Sexy, Smart, Toe-Curler hasn't appeared, I'll hang with my family today," Carmen said. "And I'm going to beat you in spades."

"Child, I taught you to play spades. Go get dressed."

Carmen reluctantly left the vacuum cleaner and headed to her room. It wouldn't take long to dress. She wore minimal makeup on her youthful, sandy-colored face, and just needed to dab moisturizer on her edges. Last year, to commemorate her fortieth birthday, she had done the big chop, cutting the perm from her hair, and letting her hair loc. Gloria disliked the small twists, saying, "Those things look like worms." Her locs were now almost shoulder-length, and with added auburn highlights, even her mother thought they were becoming, especially when she flashed her dimpled smile.

Her closet was stuffed with clothes she couldn't wear. Size twelves, fourteens, and sixteens had been pushed to the back, and she refused to buy many clothes in a larger size as an incentive to lose weight. But it was July, and her New Year's resolution to lose weight was a distant memory. Life was too short to waste time counting calories and fat grams. Besides, Nathan loved her curves and even insisted she undress with the lights on—something she usually avoided.

Carmen had been a chubby baby with a round face and big cheeks. Growing up, she was called big-boned, healthy, or thick, and wore a C-cup bra in junior high school. She was a shorter, lighter-skinned version of her mother, and her weight was never an issue until she became a Diamond. The record company put her on weight loss programs and nagged her to slim down. When she left the group, she was free to eat whatever, whenever, and pounds accumulated on her five-foot three-inch frame. She lost weight a few years ago, but regained it when she quit smoking. She'd get serious about her diet when school started back and she wasn't home with the refrigerator all day.

She planned to wear white pants and a red-and-blue family reunion T-shirt. But the pants were too tight. She selected a pink sundress instead. Not patriotic, but it would camouflage her jiggly thighs, and be cooler than pants.

Her phone rang as she stepped into the shower. She didn't recognize the number, so she let it go to voice mail. She hummed a tune she planned to introduce to her class this fall. She was in such deep thought, she jumped when her mother opened the shower curtain.

"I've been calling you," Gloria stated. "Your phone kept ringing, so I answered it."

"I'm sure it could have waited," Carmen said.

Gloria handed her a towel. "It's David's friend, Julian Weaver, and he insists on speaking with you."

"I don't remember a Julian," Carmen said, as she took the phone. "Look, I have no time for games or excuses. Tell David to get on this phone right now—Car accident? Is he all right?"

Carmen was silent and the only sound was the shower spraying. She then stated, "I'll be right there."

"Well, what happened?" Gloria asked.

"He was in a car accident," Carmen said, while turning off the shower.

"Is he hurt? Is he in the hospital?"

"No."

"Praise God," Gloria said, and plopped on the bed. "From the look on your face I thought he was seriously hurt. Since you're not dressed, I'll go get him."

"I'll go, Mama."

"You stay here and greet your company. Besides, this is no time for an 'I told you so' lecture. What's Julian's address?"

"Julian is at the hospital. David is in jail."

CHAPTER 2

ANGEL

A smoky haze hung over Lake Michigan, as the last bright crimson fireworks trails dribbled to earth, then vanished. Angel drank the rest of her Dom Pérignon, blew out the magnolia scented candle, then carried the crystal flute inside. From her balcony, she could view the fireworks without the hassle of crowds. Today was officially Independence Day, but this was also her personal independence day. Most people make New Year's resolutions, but Angel couldn't wait until then. The ink was barely dry on the outrageous divorce settlement and Lorenzo, her newest ex-husband, was already engaged. Peak Records didn't renew her contract, even though they had made millions off of her. Her gynecologist told her she was in premenopause. And, according to Brooke Watson, her business manager, she was flirting with bankruptcy and needed to drastically cut expenses. Over the years, she paid a lawyer, agent, husbands, and business manager, yet she seemed to be the only one in financial straits. No more. Angel was making changes, starting today.

It was years since she'd been home on the Fourth of July. She told her agent she needed time off, but the truth was, she didn't accept the jobs offered. He wanted to book her at the Hard Rock Cafe in Madison, Wisconsin, but she told him it was an insult to play a small market on a major holiday. He told her he could get her a gig as the opening act for a comedian at a casino in Florida, and she insisted Angel Donovan was always the main attraction. He said she could be the closing act on an old school revue. She reminded him she refused to be classified as an oldies act. The only holiday job she'd booked was an appearance on an AIDS telethon, which was great exposure, but no pay. Her dissatisfaction grew the more she thought about it, and firing him had been her first act of independence today. She called and told him she was Angel Donovan, and if he couldn't find her suitable work, his services were no longer needed. Brooke could handle whatever little bit he was doing.

Angel relished the time off but wouldn't be spending it lounging. This would be her last holiday in Rose Manor, the lakefront estate she'd called home for almost fifteen years. She'd spent the day packing and purging, but stopped to watch the fireworks.

Brooke urged her to sell the house years ago, saying it was a drain on her finances and she didn't need so much space. But Rose Manor was Angel's reward for the traveling and butt-kissing she'd done to advance and sustain her career. When Peak Records moved their headquarters to Chicago, Angel happily left Memphis too, even though it meant leaving her daughter, Crystal, to be raised by her ex-husband as well as leaving her mom and dad. She received a big advance when she went solo, and began house hunting in Chicago. She wasn't looking for a large property, but when she saw Rose Manor featured in the Sunday paper, she wanted it. Rose Manor was a seven-thousand-square-foot mid-century modern house located on an acre near Lake Shore Drive. The gated entrance, circular driveway, mature elm trees, and meticulous landscaping reminded her of palaces in the fairy tales her mother read to her as a child. Before her health declined, her mother loved to visit and often marveled that her daughter was living the fairy-tale life she'd read to her. But last year she'd become combative and almost set the house on fire, so they moved her mother to a memory care facility. What a cruel twist of fate: Alzheimer's was robbing her mother of memories she had made possible.

When Lorenzo moved in, Angel agreed to a substantial remodel. She thought it was sweet that he wanted the house to have *their* stamp on it, not just hers. She didn't have time to work with the interior designers, so she let him oversee everything. The result was tremendous. Unfortunately, so was the remodeling bill.

The first Realtor suggested an insulting lowball asking price, and Angel didn't call her back. The second Realtor didn't last either. She signed a listing contract, but he wanted to stage the house, and said Angel's artwork was too personal. When he brought new artwork, Angel realized he meant her artwork was "too black," so she terminated the contract. The third Realtor was a better fit. Angel signed a contract and the house sold within six days. The buyer wanted to close by month's end, giving her four weeks to find a new place, pack, and move—not nearly enough time. But based on the mortgage company's letters, Angel knew she had no leverage to request more time. The mortgage company agreed to halt foreclosure proceedings when Brooke told them they had a buyer, but insisted there would be no more grace periods.

She stepped over boxes in her gourmet kitchen and searched through cabinets filled with expensive cookware and exotic spices. Cooking was not her forte, so she settled on peanut butter and jelly, which the cook kept on hand for when she brought her granddaughter to work.

Angel smiled as she recalled the peanut butter sandwiches her mother fixed for her school lunch. She wondered if her mother remembered those times. The sandwich was so tasty, she fixed another. This was vastly different from the dishes

Lorenzo prepared when he tested recipes for the restaurant he predicted "they" would open someday. The restaurant that had its grand opening on Memorial Day. The restaurant he'd built with her money.

It still made her furious to even think about him. After her third divorce, she vowed never to marry again. Lorenzo was ten years younger, and worked for a firm that catered one of her parties. They had an instant sexual attraction, quickly became friends with benefits, and he eventually moved in. He wasn't trying to be her manager, like her second and third husbands, and wasn't intimidated by her. Lorenzo didn't make her feel wicked because she was tenacious about her career and wasn't interested in making more babies. After three years together, he became husband number four. She thought she had finally found her soulmate, until she accidentally turned on the security camera app on her phone and saw him "entertaining" in her house while she was on tour.

When he requested a ridiculous settlement, she kicked herself for not getting a prenuptial agreement, as her attorney advised. They settled on two hundred thousand dollars to be paid in four installments. Brooke wanted her to refinance Rose Manor to pay for the settlement or set up smaller payments, but Angel refused. She wanted him out of her life as soon as possible. She planned to immerse herself in work to help make the payments. But there was no work.

Her phone rang and she saw it was her father. Her antenna went up since he rarely called after dark. "Hi, Daddy, is everything okay?"

"Hey baby girl. I was trying to text you to tell you your mother had a very good day, and I hit the wrong button. Sorry for calling so late."

"No need to apologize. I'm always glad to hear from you."

"Maybe Crystal's visit perked up your mother. And Crystal told me the good news."

"What good news?" Angel asked.

"That you're moving back home."

"I'm still thinking about it. I wish Crystal hadn't mentioned it to you." Angel was considering moving back to Memphis. Her hometown still loved everything connected to Peak Records and she'd be the big fish in the little pond. Another benefit: Rose Manor sales proceeds would stretch farther in Memphis. Also, she was an only child and her parents weren't getting any younger. The move made sense on paper, but she was still trying to convince her heart.

Angel loved Chicago and considered it home. It reminded her of New York, but better smelling, with more soul. It had an accessible lakefront, great museums, amazing pizza, and it was centrally located. It would be hard to go from the Magnificent Mile to a city whose signature store was a Bass Pro Shop.

"I'm thrilled you're considering it. I wish you could've come for the holiday. Your mother has had some really good days lately."

"Me too, Daddy. I wanted to come, but..."

"No need to explain. I know your business doesn't leave much time for family. I'm just glad to have my granddaughter close. We'll see you soon."

Angel didn't tell her father she couldn't find a decent holiday gig and was limiting personal travel to save money. Her father was her number one fan, and impressed whether his baby girl sang at Carnegie Hall or in the shower. But Angel didn't want to admit how far her star had fallen. Besides, this was just a temporary slump.

She slipped into silk pajamas and was channel surfing when a familiar tune caught her ear. It was the Heavyweight Band jamming at the Essence Festival. They had been on the same label as the Diamonds and toured together. There was Eric Hamilton, still singing lead. She recognized the bass guitarist and the drummer. The other members were new. In the post-concert interview, Eric announced the band was back together. He listed upcoming tour cities and encouraged fans to check their website and social media pages for updates.

She and Eric had a fling back in the day, and he was still fit and fine. The Heavyweights had several hits, but the members didn't own their masters and hadn't produced songs, so performing was the only way they made money. This was a lesson Angel learned late. The Diamonds also had a string of hits, and money flowed as long as they were out there singing. But when they stopped touring and their records stopped selling, the money train stopped too. She was lucky enough to have had a successful solo career. During her shows, fans always bombarded her with requests to sing Diamonds songs, which she usually rolled into an eight-minute medley. If people bought her solo records, some of which she cowrote, she made more money. There was renewed interest in 1990s neo-soul music. Commercials and ringtones, and artists from rap to country sampled the tunes, generating renewed cash flow for songwriters and record labels, but very little for the artists.

Then the idea hit her and she called Brooke. "Guess who I just saw?" she excitedly asked, oblivious to Brooke's groggy voice. "The Heavyweights are on national TV. We had as many hits as they did, and fans are always asking if the Diamonds are getting back together. Why can't we tour? Once those greedy record company executives see the ticket sales, they'll be begging to give me a record deal. Maybe I'll even record a song with the other Diamonds on my album."

"You're forgetting one little roadblock," Brooke said, in a sleepy tone. "You told me Carmen never accepted you in the group, and you're not too popular with Doreen either."

"True, we didn't part on the best terms. But that was immature drama. We haven't talked in ages and I'm sure everyone has mellowed by now. Besides, time has proven me right."

"I guess a reunion tour could work. Nostalgia sells. People love a comeback," Brooke said.

"*Comeback* sounds like we've been down and out, and *reunion* sounds old," Angel said, pushing hair out of her eyes. "Maybe *anniversary tour*—that sounds like a celebration."

"Call it what you want. More importantly, did you review the papers I emailed you?"

"That bankruptcy stuff? I told you, absolutely not. My name will not be associated with failure."

"It's a business strategy. You save your house, lower your alimony payments, reorganize your debts, and get a clean slate," Brooke explained. "Do you think 50 Cent was actually broke? And Donald Trump's companies declared bankruptcy six times."

"We both know there's a double standard. They're seen as shrewd businessmen. But what do they say about Toni Braxton or Dionne Warwick?" Angel asked.

"And since when does Angel Donovan care what people say?"

"I want people talking about this tour, not bankruptcy." Angel squinted to see the clock. "Look, I can't think about that now. Do you know what time it is? Call me tomorrow." Angel ended the call and plugged her phone back into the charger. She turned the television to the smooth jazz station on low volume for thirty minutes, slathered her stylist's conditioner on her hair, placed a cucumber gel mask over her eyelids, and began planning the Encore Tour.

CHAPTER 3

JADE

Jade Anderson placed three pancakes and two sausage links on her plate and put the rest in the microwave for Dawn. Just as she was about to sit, the doorbell chimed. When she looked through the peephole, she was surprised to see her son.

"Happy Fifth of July, Mom."

"Lance, what are you doing here?" she asked as she opened the door and hugged him.

"I got five days' leave, so I hit the road, and came to see my favorite girl," he said, tossing his Navy duffel bag on the floor. "You're just fixing breakfast? You and Dad must have had a busy night down at Seaside."

"I wish. It rained all day and we had monstrous thunderstorms. Then the power went out. After two hours in the dark, with noisy generators, I tried to get your father to close the restaurant early. But after last year's hurricanes, he's paranoid whenever there's bad weather. Power was on here, so I left him at Seaside, babysitting the freezers. I celebrated my Fourth of July with the Heavyweight Band on TV, then got under the covers with William Faulkner."

"Sounds boring," Lance said, while searching the refrigerator.

"Well, since you've dismissed my quiet holiday, what did you do to celebrate?"

"Some friends had a party. I left there, then drove here."

"I wish you'd told me you were coming," Jade said, shaking her head.

"Why? So you could tell me not to come, or to wait until morning?"

"That would've been safer. Especially since it was storming. But I remember those days. We'd perform until midnight, party until daybreak, then ride a bus to the next show."

Jade had fond memories of her Diamond days. The group was already successful, but record and concert ticket sales doubled after she joined. Some said her blue-eyed soul helped them cross over. Interviewers always asked, "What's it like to be the only white person in the group?" The first time she was asked that question, she told the reporter she was biracial, with Native American heritage. Ray Nelson pulled her aside after the interview and told her not to mention her biracial background. Sales would be greater if the public thought she was white. She wanted to reply, Why is it a big deal? It didn't matter when she was in foster care with black and Hispanic children. She was just another discarded child. And when they placed her with the Randolphs, a black family, race wasn't a consideration. The state was just glad to place another stray kid. But she complied and gave the standard answer—about not seeing color; music was universal; they were like sisters; blah, blah, blah. It sounded cheesy, but it was true. At least for Jade it was.

When she joined the Diamonds, she became the ultimate insider. For three years, she lived a dream. Money was no object. She hung out with A-list celebrities and visited places she'd only seen on TV. Unfortunately, the dream faded into a new reality. Angel and Carmen hardly spoke the last six months they were together, and Doreen had been too high to notice. Jade hoped things would get better, but they didn't and she was on her own again. However, she was now over eighteen, without the foster care safety net.

She had nothing to do with the breakup, but Peak Records demanded restitution for breach of contract and Jade walked away with only three thousand dollars. She sang backup briefly, until her boyfriend Brian, proposed. She wasn't living the jet-setting life, and rarely heard from her former group mates, but her sedate suburban life was stable and secure, and was her real dream come true.

"I can't picture you hanging out, Mom. You've got a bad back and can barely stay awake for the ten o'clock news."

"Hanging out was fun, but that was a lifetime ago."

"Me and Tiffany are out of the house, so you can have your life back. That's why I don't understand why you'd burden yourself with a foster child."

"Shh," Jade said, putting her finger to her lips, pointing to the bedroom hall. "Dawn might hear you. And she's not a burden. You've been blessed to have a stable, loving family. How do you think you'd feel if you had to go live with strangers because your parents couldn't or wouldn't take care of you? If there are children in the family, you feel like an outsider. If there aren't children, you feel like extra income. You're always on guard for boys, and men too, trying to molest you. You're always the new kid at school. Every school is doing something different, so you're behind and kids call you dumb. If something is misplaced, they accuse you of stealing," Jade dabbed at tears starting to form in her eyes.

"I know. I didn't mean it like that, Mom," Lance said, as he put his arm around his mother. "But you should get out and enjoy yourself before you get too old."

"You sound like I have one foot in the nursing home," Jade said, smiling and sniffling at the same time. "Someone gave me a home. It's my turn to give back."

"But Mom, you were a normal kid. I mean as normal as a foster kid can be. If you're going to give back, at least find someone who appreciates it."

"She appreciates it," Jade stated.

"Well, she has a funny way of showing it. Cussing at you and Dad, skipping school, and sneaking out of the house are not how you taught us to show gratitude."

"She's dealing with a lot. Sometimes I hated my mother for leaving me. When I was in Oklahoma, I hated being different and loathed the tribal traditions they practiced. Once I ran away, I resented most of the foster families, and got in fights all the time. Dawn acts tough to cover her hurt," Jade said.

"You rarely even raise your voice," Lance said, while picking up a sausage. "I can't picture you fighting anyone."

"People can be cruel, and even if they don't mean any harm, often say dumb things. I had wavy, jet-black hair, blue eyes, and olive skin. There wasn't a mixed race, Cherokee peer group for me to fit in, and kids would make racist Indian comments. I always felt picked on."

"Maybe a black family could better relate to her," Lance said.

"There's not exactly a waiting list for biracial teen foster children. Being willing and able are the primary qualifications."

"I guess you know what you're doing. I admire you for doing it, despite Dad's hesitancy."

"He doesn't mind," Jade said. Her husband had been reluctant, at best. He said this was just her reaction to being an empty nester. Jade promised their foster responsibilities wouldn't interfere with Seaside, and Brian relented. He and Dawn clashed from the beginning, but two years had passed, and Jade had brokered a fragile peace.

"Call your dad and let him know you're here."

"The storm must have been bad for him not to make it home," Lance said.

Jade walked to the window and opened the blinds. The bright sun gave no hint of treacherous storms the night before. In fact, last night hadn't been different from many other nights. Receipts were down, so Brian was working longer hours. When Seaside was open, he hovered over every detail. When it was closed, he claimed to be doing food prep, cleaning or paperwork. Jade spent most of her days there too, but left in time to meet Dawn when she got out of school. The storm had been a convenient excuse for him to stay out all night. But the sun was out today. She wondered what excuse he'd use tonight.

CHAPTER 4

DOREEN

Doreen lay on the chaise in her closet trying to decide what to wear. She woke up to killer cramps and was sluggish this morning. Her period was two weeks late and she dared hope she was finally pregnant. But her "monthly visitor," as her mother called it, was announcing its arrival.

"Hurry up, babe," James said, as he walked past her closet door. "I need to leave early, so you'll have to bring the kids with you. The twins are eating breakfast, and Paige is fooling with her hair."

"We won't be far behind you," Doreen promised.

Since it was a holiday, Blessings Tabernacle was holding one combined abbreviated service, instead of their usual two services. But even with the holiday, Blessings would be packed. James preached his first sermon fifteen years ago in a rented hotel meeting room, to thirty friends and relatives. Now Blessings Tabernacle had four thousand members, and had moved into a debt-free, thirty-thousand-square-foot facility last year.

She and James vowed to dismantle traditional rules and rituals that obscured the church's real purpose: to bring souls to Christ. Blessings Tabernacle had no dress code and members' garb ranged from jeans to the fancy dresses and hats

Carmen's mother wore. Blessings was a seven-day-a-week church. There was Bible study, midweek prayer, Zumba classes, two book clubs, youth and adult sports teams, Microsoft certification classes, and a food pantry. Their workout room rivaled any fitness center, and it was free. The church operated Sophia's day care, named in honor of Doreen's deceased sister. They weren't twins, but she didn't see how sisters could be any closer than she and Sophia had been. Songs, smells, and old TV shows still triggered memories, and Doreen was proud to fulfill her sister's dream of operating a day care center. She and James led marriage counseling sessions, and Blessings donated space to a drug rehab nonprofit—a service they were both passionate about.

Sixteen years ago, she and James had been rehab clients. Back when they were known as "Diamond and Gold," not Pastor and First Lady Golden. Unlike many of their contemporaries, including her sister Sophia, they conquered their addictions. That seemed a lifetime ago, and their old records, pictures, and awards were packed away. The only music from their R and B career James allowed played in the house was their Christmas album.

Doreen selected a yellow sundress and flat white sandals. Yellow complemented her Hershey chocolate-colored skin and since she wore conservative colors to work, she chose bright colors on the weekend.

The bank would be closed Monday, and most of her coworkers had taken off or worked a half-day on Friday. But she worked late to prepare for her upcoming presentation. Doreen was a vice president at Southern Federal Bank, a position that had taken her fifteen years to achieve. She was leading the community business initiative, or CBI project, as they called it. The mission was important to her, but she also believed this assignment would get her a long-sought promotion to senior management.

Doreen had started as a teller and was initially the breadwinner. When James went into ministry full time, he may have been a full-time minister, but he wasn't making full-time money. She took night classes at City College, eventually graduated, and was accepted into the bank's management trainee program. It had been a hard climb, but the hardest thing she'd ever done was to kick drugs. Since she'd achieved sobriety, she knew she could do anything—including make senior vice president.

"Babe, you look like you're going to a picnic," James said, when she emerged from her closet. "We're videotaping and yellow fades into our background. Find something red, white or blue to acknowledge the holiday and coordinate with my shirt."

Doreen thought the dress perfect for a sizzling summer day, but to appease James, changed into a blue-and-white dress. She ran her fingers through her layered pixie cut, dabbed ruby-red lipstick on her full lips, and was ready in five minutes.

She smiled and remembered her days with the Diamonds when they changed outfits three times during their ninety-minute performance. They practiced the wardrobe change until they could do it in two minutes. She missed her singing mates, and hated that so many of her memories were fuzzy due to drugs. For years they'd been inseparable. Now they rarely contacted each other. Angel, she could do without, but she missed Carmen and Jade. She made a mental note to call them tomorrow, as she took a last glance in the mirror and turned out the light.

By nine-thirty the first floor was full, and ushers directed people to the balcony. At ten o'clock, fireworks shone on the big screens. The praise team led the congregation in the hymn "Faith of our Fathers" then went right into "Celebrate" by Kool & the Gang. James delivered a brief but thought-provoking message about freedom based on scriptures from Psalms and Galatians. Three people joined the church and James congratulated them for claiming their true freedom. Before the benediction, James indicated he had an announcement.

"I realize I'm standing between you and your leftover ribs, so I will be brief. We know we can't be free without the love of Christ. But freedom also brings responsibilities, and one of our greatest responsibilities is to our children," James said, as he came from behind the pulpit. "God has blessed us and we must bless others. We plan to finally open Freedom Prep, offering an academically rigorous curriculum with an expectation of excellence. We should be ready to enroll students next year."

A chorus of "amens" rang out and the congregation applauded at the end of his remarks.

"I'm excited about what the Lord has in store for us. And Sister Golden is just as excited. To fulfill this vision, she's coming to work full-time in the ministry." James beckoned his wife to stand, as the congregation cheered.

Doreen stood and forced a smile on her face. Her eyes met James's and he blew her a kiss. Good thing he couldn't read her mind, she would have told him to keep it.

She loved her job, enjoyed helping her customers and building up her community. And, she proved she could do more than "hum a few notes and shake her behind," as her mother had referred to her singing career. James claimed he understood her zeal and was proud of her accomplishments. But she saw now he didn't understand, or he wouldn't have asked her to give it up. Giving up the Diamonds was sacrifice enough, not to mention everything else she had given up for him. Wasn't that enough?

ACT II

COMPLICATED MELODY

CHAPTER 5

CARMEN

Carmen had been in shock the last four days. She kept thinking someone would call and say this was all a terrible mistake. But the weekend passed and David remained behind bars. After speaking with Julian, Carmen left her mother to greet their guests, and raced to the county jail. She had to park three blocks away and walk in the sweltering hundred-degree heat. After waiting in the security line for thirty minutes, she still couldn't see her son, because she wasn't an approved visitor. Carmen took the application, went to the end of the security line, and completed it while in line. But the last item required was a color passport photo. Carmen hurriedly left to find a Walgreens. The sign said ONE HOUR PASSPORT PHOTOS, but apparently, no one told the employees, as Carmen waited almost two hours. She finally got the photo, headed back to the county jail, and got back in line. She turned in her form, then stood in the corner to wait, since there were no empty seats. After about fifteen minutes a guard approached her. "Ma'am, you can't loiter in here."

"Believe me," Carmen said, "I wouldn't be here if not necessary. I'm waiting for my inmate visitation approval."

"Someone should have explained the process to you. Approval takes two to three weeks, and you'll be notified by mail."

"What?" Carmen shrieked. "My son won't be here that long. This is all a misunderstanding."

"Of course it is," the guard said, touching Carmen's elbow. "But you still—"

"Don't patronize me," Carmen said, jerking her arm away. "My son is being treated like a criminal. I want to speak with the manager, or chief or whoever is in charge."

"Miss, I know this is stressful, but—"

"Know this. I'm not leaving without seeing my son," Carmen shouted.

A second guard walked over and said, "What's the problem?"

"There's been a huge mistake. My son has been arrested. I know everyone says their child is innocent, but David has done nothing. He's never been in trouble and—"

"Miss, if what you say is true, it will be sorted out at the arraignment."

"When is that?" Carmen asked.

"Since Monday is a holiday, it will be Tuesday," the second guard stated.

"Tuesday? You expect to keep my son locked up four days? The devil is a lie. I'm not leaving until I get some satisfaction," Carmen shouted and crossed her arms.

"We don't have time for this. Let's get her out of here," the first guard said, pulling out his handcuffs.

"Don't touch me," Carmen shouted hysterically. "This is how you treat innocent taxpayers? I pay your salary. You work for me. I want everyone's name."

"Please," the second guard said softly. "If you don't leave, we'll have to arrest you and charge you with disorderly conduct. That won't help your son."

"But I can't leave him here."

"Those are the rules," the second guard said. "Will you be okay? Is someone with you?"

Carmen shook her head. "I drove."

"I'll walk her to her car." The first guard shrugged and walked away.

She spent the rest of the weekend in her bedroom, barely ate, and didn't dress. Julian's mother called Monday morning to tell her their cousin was a lawyer and would represent the boys at the arraignment. They should be prepared to post bail of about five thousand dollars. Carmen was sure there would be no need for bail, once they realized their mistake, but followed her instructions anyway.

The arraignment was at ten o'clock, and Carmen, her mother, and sister, arrived an hour early. Gloria did her old lady act and got them to the front of the security line. Judge Gray's court was on the third floor and as soon as they stepped off the elevator, they were blinded by camera lights and bombarded by reporters with questions about her son's gang affiliation and how she felt about the police officer. Carmen was about to tell the reporters how wrong they were, but Faye and Gloria ushered her through the throng. In her Diamond days, she wore dark shades when she expected lots of cameras. But she was unprepared today.

The accident made the newspaper front page and was breaking news on all the local stations. David was at the bus stop when his friend Julian saw him and urged his cousin, the driver of the car he was riding in, to pick him up. Two blocks from David's house, the driver didn't hear the siren and T-boned a police car responding to a call. Julian and their friend Isaiah were on the passenger side, and sustained several glass cuts and were taken to the hospital. David and the driver weren't hurt. The officer on the passenger side suffered a few bruises, but the driving officer was in intensive care, clinging to life. Carmen felt bad for the officer and prayed for his recovery, but locking up her son wasn't going to help him get better. Once everyone heard David's explanation, this nightmare would be over. She hadn't eaten breakfast, and was sure whatever they served her son, if anything, was nasty. She planned to take everyone to the Pancake Shop when they got out of here.

They finally found David's attorney in the maze of people huddled in the hall. Carmen had questions, but by the time the attorney got off his phone, it was time to enter the courtroom. At ten o'clock, the bailiff entered and told everyone to rise for the judge's entrance. They sat through scores of cases and even had a lunch break.

It was after three o'clock when the bailiff called David's name. A lump rose in Carmen's throat when her baby shuffled into the courtroom, handcuffed and feet in chains. She fought the urge to vomit at the sight of her usually meticulously groomed son, with matted hair, in a baggy, orange, county-issued jumpsuit. His eyes were bloodshot red and puffy underneath, which meant his allergies were flaring up. She flashed David a quick smile and with her trembling hand, patted her heart in a show of solidarity. He barely nodded his head.

The bailiff stood in front of the judge and declared, "We now call, the State of Tennessee versus Isaiah Brown, David Vernon Payne, Julian Weaver, and Zamir Roberts." Those words sent chills down Carmen's arms. Short of sickness and death, this was a black mother's worst nightmare. She knew the disproportionate statistics regarding black boys in the criminal justice system. But that happened to others, not her son.

The judge stated the charges and asked the young men how they pled. They all responded "not guilty." The judge then stated, "Mr. Roberts, please step forward. You have been accused of driving under the influence, fleeing a law enforcement officer, possession of a stolen vehicle, possession of a controlled substance, reckless driving, driving without a license, and being a felon in possession of a firearm. Moreover, as you have broken the terms of your probation, bail is denied and you are immediately remanded to the West Tennessee Correctional Facility to serve the remainder of your sentence. The bailiff will remove the defendant.

"Mr. Brown, Mr. Payne, and Mr. Randall, please step forward. You are accused of vehicle theft, reckless endangerment, possession of stolen firearms, and possession of a controlled substance. Bail condition will be as follows: A two-hundred-thousand-dollar bond is assigned, to be supported by twenty thousand dollars in cash or property. Defendants' travel is restricted to the Sixth Circuit of the West Tennessee District and defendants must surrender travel documents and not seek or obtain any new or replacement travel documents while this criminal action is pending. Defendants will be subject to regular pretrial supervision. All bail conditions must be satisfied before the defendants' release." The judge then looked up from his computer and stated, "If you have satisfied the bail conditions, you must appear in court whenever you are directed to do so. If you fail to do so, you and any cosigners on your bond will be liable to the government for the full amount of the bond. Do you understand these conditions?"

David, Julian, and Isaiah said yes. Carmen was shell-shocked and her head spinning. She wanted to stand and interrupt like they did on *Perry Mason*: *This is a horrible mistake*. But her son was shuffling out of the courtroom, and the bailiff was calling the next case.

Carmen rushed to the attorney as soon as the proceedings were over. Isaiah and Julian's mothers were already speaking with him. "Miss Payne, as I was telling these ladies—"

"Stop right there. This is not a group case. My son was not involved in whatever the others were doing and I won't let you or this court railroad him," Carmen insisted, her voice quivering.

"Are you saying your son is better than mine?" Julian's

mother said. "We're doing you a favor. I didn't have to call you about an attorney. How ungrateful can you be?"

"If you want to do me a favor—"

"Ladies, please," Attorney Weaver interrupted. "Miss Payne, wait for me by the exit sign."

"I'm not going anywhere," Carmen stated. "This is ridiculous. David was simply in the wrong place at the wrong time. Why didn't you explain that?"

"Miss Payne, come sit down." He led her to a bench near the exit sign. "Your son is in a lot of trouble. I've asked the young men to consider a plea bargain."

"Are you crazy? My son is not guilty!" Carmen shouted. "Whatever happened to 'innocent until proven guilty'? And isn't two-hundred-thousand-dollars bail high for being a passenger in a car accident?"

"Please lower your voice," Attorney Weaver said, as the security guard looked up disapprovingly. "The judge is reacting to public outrage over gang-related violence and—"

"My son is not in a gang!" Carmen shouted. "He has a job. He's an honor student and attends Memphis Academy. He's on the track team, basketball team, and the debate team. He made a twenty-seven on his ACT and has been accepted at three colleges. He was with those boys because they were giving him a ride home from work."

"I must admit I didn't have that information."

"Well, now that you do, can't you get another hearing?" Carmen pleaded.

"Ma'am, it's not that easy."

"Look," Carmen said, while digging through her purse. "I'm not a freeloading relative. I can pay you. My son is not involved with gangs, guns, or drugs. I didn't even allow him to play with water pistols."

"I understand your frustration. But if I had a dollar for every mother who insisted her child was innocent, I'd be a rich man," he said, and stuffed papers and folders in his bag.

"If your son takes a plea deal right away, he'll get the lightest sentence. I'll argue these should be misdemeanor charges—"

"Plea deal? Absolutely not. He was working at my sister's flower shop when those boys stole the car. She's his alibi."

"That may be true, but relatives are rarely effective witnesses. Juries discount them as biased."

"Then get statements from the other boys. They'll verify that David was not with them when they took the car. Open-and-shut case," Carmen said.

"Ma'am, it's not that simple."

"Why not? David just needs to tell his side."

"With what you've told me, your son has a good chance of getting off. But it won't be easy. For the trial I can ask teachers to give character references and we can..."

"Trial? What about right now? I want my son released," Carmen demanded.

"The trial won't start until October or November at the earliest," the attorney stated.

"What now?" Carmen asked, in a quieter tone. "David can't stay in there until then."

"We could petition for another bail hearing. But it probably wouldn't get scheduled until late next month."

"David can't stay in jail until then. He has allergies and his gums will get infected if he doesn't use a Waterpik. He's in there with vicious, violent criminals," Carmen said, tears streaming down her cheeks.

"I'm sorry, Miss Payne. Unless you can get the money within twenty-four hours, I don't see an alternative."

"That's twenty thousand dollars. I can do a hardship withdrawal from my retirement account, but it takes several days."

"As I said, we can try to get a hearing to reduce the bail, but we probably couldn't get a date until late next month anyway. Time I spend working on bail is time I could be working on his case. I'm sorry, but I'm late to my next hearing. Call my office tomorrow and we'll put our heads together," he concluded, placing his card in her hand.

"Did you not hear me? My son is not spending another night here, and if you can't find a way to get him out, you are obviously not the attorney we need. You're fired."

"Whatever, lady," Attorney Weaver said. "This is the real world—not some TV show, where everything wraps up in forty minutes."

Faye and Gloria walked up as the attorney was leaving.

"We figured you wanted to speak privately to the lawyer. What did he say?" Faye asked.

"Nothing worth anything. He's talking like David is guilty. They're portraying him as a menacing gangbanger and assigned bail like he's some murderer. That shyster was totally incompetent. I've got to find someone else."

"I thought the court had to appoint you a lawyer," Gloria said.

"I've heard you shouldn't use court-appointed lawyers. They have too many cases and are underpaid," Faye said. "We should contact Al Sharpton. I bet he could get results."

"What can I do? Vernon is on a cruise and no help. I can't let my baby spend another night in there. Did you see him?" Carmen said in tears, while they walked down the hall.

"I'll contact your councilman. They don't show up until election time," Faye said. "They claim they're here to serve the people. It's time to start serving."

"I'm sure one of my club members can recommend someone," Gloria added.

"Summer is our slow season, but I can give you a few thousand," Faye said. "And I'll start a GoFundMe page."

"I can't wait for someone else to rescue my son. He can't stay in that hellhole."

"I have some money tucked away," Gloria added. "It's yours."

"I can't take your money, Mama. Your Social Security is barely enough for you to live on." They rode the elevator in silence, and when they were almost to the exit, Carmen went to the ladies' room. There were no windows in the courtroom or halls. But once she saw daylight, she couldn't bear to leave without her son. She stood over the sink, washing and rewashing her hands for several minutes.

Faye entered the ladies' room. "Carmen, we were getting worried."

"I need you and Mama to get an Uber," Carmen said, drying her hands. "If I hurry, I can get David out today. My son does not belong in jail and if I'm breathing, he will not suffer for something he didn't do. I'm going to the bail bondsman. I'm going to pledge my house."

CHAPTER 6

JADE

The security guard buzzed Jade in and she felt like she was entering a prison, rather than a high school. Buildings weren't on lockdown when her children were in school. In those days, between band practices, games, and PTA meetings, Jade was at the school almost daily. She was band booster club president and raised the most money ever, thanks to her old friend Angel Donovan, who donated items for an auction to raise money for new instruments. Lance was now a Navy seaman and Tiffany was a college sophomore, and the nature of her visits had changed.

When Jade entered the guidance counselor's office—her second meeting in two weeks—she knew why she'd been summoned when she saw the marijuana leaf on Dawn's T-shirt. Dawn left home with a black shirt but must have worn the T-shirt underneath. When Dawn brought it home from the mall, Jade had forbidden her from wearing it and told her to return it.

Now she knew how the Randolphs felt. Mr. and Mrs. Randolph were an older black couple who became her foster parents when she was fifteen. During her first year with them Jade had been rebellious, but they had been able to rein her in. She thought she could do the same for Dawn. Her children weren't angels, but they knew the rules and didn't step too far outside the boundaries. Jade felt her unstable childhood and success with her own children perfectly suited her to be a foster parent. Plus, with Lance and Tiffany gone, the house felt empty. Brian tried to dissuade her, saying they should enjoy this stage of their marriage and concentrate on running Seaside. But she was determined. At times like this, she wondered if maybe Brian was right.

The guidance counselor clicked on her computer, then looked up. "Miss Faber, so we meet again. Hello, Mrs. Anderson," she said, motioning for them to sit. "As you know, we have a relaxed dress code during summer school, but clothing with drug references remain forbidden."

"State guidelines are relaxing and pretty soon it'll be legal everywhere," Dawn argued. "It's just a shirt."

"The issue is not marijuana, but the principle of obeying authority. When you join the workforce or the military, there are certain things you can and cannot wear, do, or say," the guidance counselor lectured. "It's the same here. Summer school is voluntary, with a compressed schedule. There's no time or staff to deal with distractions. If you don't want to be here, you are not required to attend."

"Cool," Dawn said, sitting up in her chair.

"But if she doesn't get her English and history credits, she won't be classified as a senior," Jade stated.

"That's Miss Faber's choice," the guidance counselor said. "Your grades do not reflect your intelligence and you're doing yourself a disservice by displaying such poor conduct. I'm sure you're aware of college tuition grants and waivers available to you as a participant in the foster care system. It's a wonderful opportunity to create the type of future you want. But if you don't want to be here, I suggest you withdraw. Being suspended or expelled will look much worse on your record."

"I don't give a—"

"Dawn," Jade interrupted sternly, putting her hand on Dawn's arm. "We understand and thank you for your time. I assure you Dawn will not be any further trouble."

Neither spoke as they walked to the van. Other than Jade telling Dawn to put on her seat belt, they rode in silence until they were about four blocks away, then Jade pulled over and asked, "Do you understand the seriousness of this situation?"

"What's the big deal? States are legalizing weed every day. I bet that lame counselor was the main one getting high back then. Now she wants to act like it's a crime," Dawn said.

"What someone else did is not the issue. We're talking about you and your life. If you don't make up these credits, you'll be more than a year behind your grade level and they'll probably assign you to an alternative school."

"Cool. I'm older than most of the kids in my classes anyway."

"But if they take you out of this school, you'll have to leave us. Do you understand what I'm saying?" For the first time that afternoon, Jade thought she saw a flicker of light in Dawn's eyes.

"You'd be better off without me," Dawn said softly. "That would make your old man happy."

"You've been with us almost two years and we love you. Brian just doesn't understand what it's like growing up without parents. I was in your shoes. You've had bad breaks, but you can't let them define the rest of your life. You're an intelligent girl, and if you pass summer school, you can graduate next year with your class."

"Why do you care?"

"I care because I know how you feel. I hated school, but not graduating is one of the biggest regrets of my life," Jade admitted as she turned the air conditioner down a notch.

"It didn't seem to hurt you. You made big bucks in a singing group, then married a decent dude," Dawn said. "He may be an asshole, but at least he took care of you and his kids. You never had to work."

Jade didn't know how to explain the bucks weren't as big as people imagined, and being married to that asshole was work. But it was work she was glad to do. She had spent years in the foster care system and vowed one day she'd create and maintain her own family. She'd spent the last twenty years making that happen, and now she was determined that family would include Dawn. Dawn was a sore spot between her and her husband, but Jade felt she'd really gotten through to her today. She rarely opposed her husband, but they'd made a commitment to Dawn. Brian would have to get over it.

"There are three more weeks of summer school, and you need to pass those classes. Will you try?"

"Yeah, okay," Dawn mumbled. "I really hadn't thought about college. Was that lady right? You think I can go?"

"Absolutely. Anywhere in the state, almost for free. The better your ACT score, the more choices you'll have. We'll register you for a test prep class right away. And one more thing," Jade said, "Let's not refer to my husband as an asshole."

"Sure. He's a decent dude. I guess he can't help it." Dawn shrugged.

Jade wasn't sure that still wasn't an insult, but she smiled, gave Dawn a thumbs-up and headed home.

CHAPTER 7

DOREEN

Doreen stopped at the newsstand in the bank lobby and bought pumpkin seeds and the remaining copies of the weekly *Memphis Business Journal*. She and Mr. Thompson, the bank president, had been photographed at an event announcing the CBI project, and she wanted copies for the coffee table in the waiting area outside her office. The project's goal was to encourage and facilitate business growth in underdeveloped zip codes. The first deadline was September first—just three weeks away. She had submitted an outline to Mr. Thompson and he was so impressed he asked her to make the presentation at the upcoming board of directors meeting.

Her picture hadn't been in the paper since her days as a Diamond. The navy Chanel business suit, white ruffled blouse, and pearl teardrop earrings were far removed from the shoulder-length earrings and skintight, peekaboo outfits she wore back then. But she had to admit, the years had been kind. She had gained less than ten pounds and could still wear a size nine, sometimes a seven, depending on the designer. Thanks to weekly visits to her hairdresser, her permed hair always looked so perfect, people thought it was a weave. Her smooth, dark brown skin still glowed, and the rest of the world had caught on to the allure of large lips, which she had been ashamed of. She remembered wearing muted lipstick colors because she thought it made her lips look thinner. One evening before a show, Miss Glo gave her a tube of cherry red lipstick and insisted she wear it. "Show off those lips. You're hiding your best asset."

Miss Glo had been a cross between a mother and a favorite aunt. To hear her tell it, Doreen ran the bank. She didn't understand banks had layers of vice presidents and often gave titles instead of money. But with her own mother gone, it was comforting to have someone show that kind of love. Doreen made a mental note to give Miss Glo a newspaper the next time she saw her at church.

This was not a day for the beef stew she had left in the Crock-Pot this morning. She wanted to take the family to dinner and celebrate. She made reservations at one of their favorite restaurants, and tried to call her husband to inform him of her plans. Sister Mayes said he had been in a meeting all afternoon and offered to interrupt if it was an emergency, but otherwise he had asked her to hold all calls.

Doreen didn't remember him telling her about an afternoon meeting. She didn't like having to go through the secretary to talk to her husband, but he hadn't answered her texts and his phone went straight to voice mail.

Whatever highfalutin notions Doreen had about being a big-time mover and shaker were erased when she arrived home. Rain clouds seemed to have permanently settled over Memphis and accidents slowed her drive home. Then something was wrong with the gate at their subdivision entrance, and whipping rain rushed into her car as she repeatedly tried to input the entrance code. Once she got in, her remote wouldn't open the garage door, and she got further soaked when she dashed to the door. As she fumbled with her keys, she dropped the newspapers and the wind scattered them across the yard. The twins met her at the door, eager for her to settle their dispute with their big sister. Paige whined about being stuck in the house with her little brothers and told her version of events. Doreen took a deep breath and decided to postpone going out. She checked the Crock-Pot and whipped up cornbread muffins, prepared a salad, and chilled a bottle of sparkling grape juice. They would have to settle for a toast at home.

After dinner, Doreen helped the twins with their homework, then leafed through her CBI folder and made notes while they studied.

Since they didn't go out, Doreen brought the celebration to their bedroom suite. She placed a tray with sparkling grape juice, two wineglasses, and an ice bucket on the bathroom vanity. After a leisurely bubble bath, she put on one of her rarely-worn negligees under her favorite flannel housecoat. She was sitting in bed working on her laptop computer when James came in. "I thought the meeting would never end," he said and loosened his tie. "What's all that?" he asked, pointing to the papers spread across the bed.

"It's the CBI project I mentioned to you. For the next few months, I'll have a lot of extra work. We made the announcement last week at a press conference. My picture was in the paper," she said, as she turned her laptop off.

"How nice," James replied. "Reverend Baker had a heart attack."

"What? Oh, my goodness. Is he okay?"

"Yes, they think so. But his church won't be able to host the Sunday school convention. Bishop asked the Johnsons to take it, but his wife has surgery scheduled. So I told Bishop we could do it."

"Who is *we*?" Doreen asked.

"I know, I know—you're busy," James replied. "But we have a large, new space, which will work perfectly. I had it covered until Sister Dillon told us at the meeting her doctor is putting her on bed rest for the remainder of her pregnancy.

I need you to take over the Women's Guild until she's back on her feet."

"Did you hear what I said? My CBI project is starting. I can't take on anything right now."

"The convention starts in two weeks and you know the process. It'll be too disruptive to train someone else. I could ask Sister Rachel, but she does so much already. Her position as youth leader keeps her busy."

"James, I'm sorry about Reverend Baker's heart attack and Mrs. Johnson's surgery, but I don't have time now."

"I agreed to name someone else to work with our charter school committee, though you have perfect credentials for the job. I overlook your absences from Bible study and make your apologies for missing district meetings. But on this, there's no viable option. I need you."

"I just told you, I can't do it now," Doreen insisted, trying to control her voice level. "This project can lead to a promotion."

"A promotion? So you'll have even more responsibilities? I believe you've confused your priorities. Working is one thing. Forsaking your family and church is something else."

"I'm not forsaking anything," Doreen replied. "You weren't opposed to my working when I was paying all the bills."

"You're right. I've never forgotten those days and I vowed to make it up to you for sticking by me."

"Well, I need you to stick by me now," Doreen stressed. "President Thompson asked me to make a presentation at the next board meeting. This is a really big deal."

"You don't want me to stick by you. You want me to cosign what you're doing when you know I'm against this. I don't think you realize how many people depend on this ministry. Lives are at stake while you're running around fulfilling yourself. I can't believe you're being this selfish. A man wants a loving woman in his bed, not a workaholic. I'll sleep in the guest room, so you don't have to move your important papers."

Before Doreen could respond, he had left the room. She folded the one newspaper she had saved and put it in her nightstand drawer. Tears rolled down her cheeks, and she wasn't sure if they were from anger or hurt. She poured a glass of juice, changed into her faded cotton pajamas, and turned her laptop back on.

CHAPTER 8

ANGEL

Even after all these years, Mario's touch still did it for her. Angel instinctively closed her eyes. His fingertips on her skin were like raindrops on a parched desert. Her breathing eased and her toes curled in anticipation. No one compared to Mario. He mixed his own products and was one of the best hairdressers in town.

"I wish you'd let me loose on your hair," Mario said to Crystal, as he towel dried Angel's hair. "With your high cheekbones, a relaxer and chin-length bob with a few high-lights..."

"I don't do bobs," Crystal replied, as she stood in the doorway of her mother's en suite bathroom. "And I find nothing relaxing about burning and traumatizing my hair with chemicals that burn your scalp and pollute the water supply."

"Save your breath. Crystal is into the natural look," Angel declared.

"My products are organic and gentle on the scalp."

"I used your samples on Mother's hair the last time I was home. Her hair was easily detangled with minimal breakage, which is good since she won't sit long. You need to sell that stuff—not to me, of course," Angel said.

"I've only shared samples with a few clients. I don't want

anyone to steal my idea before I get it to market," Mario confided, while squirting conditioner from a blue bottle along Angel's hairline. "The secret to healthy and growing hair is to keep it from breaking."

"I'm not worried about my hair growing. I'm thinking of cutting it short," Crystal said.

"Don't do that. Men like long hair," Angel said.

"Then they should grow their own. I have better things to do with my time."

Angel turned to Mario and said, "A psychiatrist would diagnose her rejection of makeup and hair grooming as acting out abandonment issues and resentment toward me."

"Mother, it's not that deep. I don't reject hair grooming. My hair and skin are clean. What's the point of putting on all that stuff to look like someone you're not, so people can put on a phony act toward the phony you? You attended cosmetology school. Do your own hair. Think of the time you've wasted on hair and makeup."

"I don't mean to interrupt a mother-daughter bonding moment, but little girl, some folks *need* makeup," Mario said, as he searched his bag for his blow-dryer. He carried the tools of his trade in a black bag, like a doctor on a house call. When Angel's records were on the charts and she was selling out venues, Mario traveled with her. Her schedule had waned, but Mario remained a regular indulgence. Angel had skills from her hairdressing days and did her own hair on Mario's off weeks. But she relied on Mario for deep conditioning and color, especially since there were more gray strands lately.

"You look cute in your little Afro," Angel said, patting her daughter's hair. "When I was your age, the gel wrap was the thing, then bone straight weaves. I know natural hair is in now, but I don't feel right with my hair standing all over my head."

"Why can't you wear your hair the way you want? You don't have to follow the style others dictate. Do you," Crystal insisted.

"There wouldn't have been many people paying to see me with a nappy two-inch ponytail."

"You're messing with my livelihood, little girl," Mario said. "I'll thank you to keep your primitive hairstyling ideas to yourself."

"Mario is hilarious," Crystal said, when he left the room to take a phone call. "He said he's going to kidnap me next time he sees me and tame my hair."

"He's the best. My career has ebbed and flowed. Husbands have come and gone. But Mario has always been there, and I could count on my hair looking perfect."

"Nothing against Mario, but it's just hair, Mother. They're coming to *hear* you. If the music is right, you can be bald. And there's still no one who sounds better."

Angel's eyes watered as she squeezed her daughter's hand. "How did I get so lucky? I guess I owe your father for raising you so well."

"Don't give him all the credit. We're more alike than you think."

Angel and Preston were high school sweethearts. After graduation, Preston stepped into his father's mortuary and insurance business. Angel went to college in Nashville, but wasn't committed, and her grades showed it. She hated being broke, was homesick and missed Preston. When she came home for Christmas break, she announced she wasn't returning. She and Preston married on New Year's Eve and she enrolled in cosmetology school.

They had been married two years when she met James Golden at a Peak Records party. Her father-in-law was an early investor in the record company and had received an invitation. He gave it to his son, but Preston had to work at the last minute—you couldn't schedule dead bodies—and suggested Angel go without him.

Peak Records ruled the R and B charts when Angel was growing up and everyone in Memphis wanted to be connected to them. Angel hadn't been anywhere since Crystal was born four months earlier, and she was ready to release her groove from hibernation. She got her aunt Ivy to keep the baby and asked her cousin Margie to go with her. The party was at the Ritz-Carlton hotel and Angel marveled at the star-studded affair. Isaac Hayes, Mavis Staples, and a few members of the Bar-Kays were there. Even Al Green made an appearance. There was a live set by Booker T. & the M.G.s and M-Town performed their newest release.

She hadn't been out without Preston in a long time, but she felt freer than when he was there. He didn't like to dance and checked his watch the whole time they were out. She danced up an appetite and headed to the food line. James Golden was behind her, and heard her singing along with the Whitney Houston record. He said she sounded even better than she looked and handed her a business card. She showed it to her cousin when they were on their way home. "He said he's with Peak Records. They're looking for a singer, and I should come by tomorrow. What a tired pickup line."

"Angela, he really is with Peak Records."

"How do you know?"

"I have my sources. He's dating one of the Diamonds," Margie said.

"Really? He was following me all night, and didn't act like he's dating anyone."

"I don't know about all that, but I do know they're looking for a singer. There was an article in *Jet* magazine. Where have you been?"

"I've been doing hair and changing diapers from sunup to sundown," Angel said, carefully placing the business card in her pocket. "Do you think I have a chance?"

"You'll never know until you try. I'll go with you, just to be safe."

The next day, Angel and Margie went to the address on the card. James met them at the door and took them to the studio. She sang two songs, a cappella, for James. He made a few phone calls and within fifteen minutes she was singing for an audience of six, including majority owner Ray Nelson. Peak Records was one of the largest black-owned record labels in the country. Depending on who you talked to, he was an aggressive visionary, or an arrogant con artist.

Carmen and Doreen attended the impromptu audition. She was surprised how much younger they looked in person. Carmen asked what key she preferred and what her performing experience was and didn't seem pleased with Angel's responses. Angel couldn't read music and didn't know the key of A from Z. Her experience was limited to beauty pageants and school plays. Despite the audience, it was apparent only one person's opinion mattered, and Angel knew she had Ray's attention.

James thanked her, got her phone number, and said he would call. When he finally called, Preston almost blew the whole deal. She hadn't told him about her audition because she was certain it would come to nothing. Preston told James he had the wrong number because he asked for Angel. James misread her signature, but luckily she was in the room and intercepted the call. James said they wanted to make her an offer and to come to their lawyer's office on Monday.

Angel couldn't sleep the rest of the weekend. She arrived forty-five minutes early and had time to thumb through the *Ebony* and *Billboard* magazines on the table. She also had time to overhear a private conversation, when the secretary left her desk, but left the intercom on.

"James, this is bullshit and you know it," Carmen complained. "No one asked our opinion. Our records are starting to consistently chart. Did you discuss this with my mother?"

"This is what Ray wants. He's the boss," James replied. "He says Angel's soprano will give the Diamonds a fuller sound, but she's versatile and can sing other parts too."

"Ummm-hmmm," Doreen said. "It doesn't hurt that she's attractive, and I doubt she wore that tight dress by accident. What was your vote?"

"Ray's vote is the only one that counts. He's usually right, so just welcome her when she gets here. Trust me, it will be great," James said.

There was more conversation Angel couldn't distinguish, then Ray walked up.

"Promptness, something else I like," he stated as he escorted her into the office. "This move will put the Diamonds over the top. Don't know why I didn't think of it sooner. Our lawyers have prepared Angel's contract and we've scheduled a photo shoot for next week when Sophia returns. I hope everyone is ready to work," he stated, rubbing his hands together.

She didn't think twice about signing the contract, but did speak up about her name. "I'm so excited about this opportunity, but Mr. Nelson, my name is actually Angela."

"Angel has more pizzazz. Sign it both ways for now."

And with that, Angela became Angel of the Diamonds.

With Crystal in tow, Angel arrived early to rehearsals and was last to leave. Sophia was the friendliest, and eventually, Carmen and Doreen warmed up. The intense rehearsals melted away the baby fat and she weighed less than before her pregnancy. Ray engineered a makeover that included adding strawberry blonde highlights, and hair and eyelash extensions.

Preston was amused by his wife's new career, but demanded she quit once he realized it wasn't a passing phase. He said she was neglecting her family and musicians were poor role models for Crystal. But Angel insisted she could be a singer, wife, and mother. She was stunned when served with divorce papers. Preston told her she could leave, but she wasn't dragging their daughter up and down the highway, and he petitioned for full custody of Crystal. Angel contested the divorce, but the Diamonds were taking off and she kept missing court and mediation dates. She couldn't afford to pay a lawyer, establish a separate residence, and pay for childcare. Gloria sat her down and told her what she already knew. She had to choose. Angel dropped her countersuit and the court granted Preston full custody. For years, she resented him, but they had been able to put their differences behind them, and Crystal had grown into an amazing young lady.

"Wake up, sleeping beauty," Mario said, tapping Angel's shoulder. He took the perm rods out, carefully holding each ringlet as it fell. He sprayed Angel's hair then stepped back to admire his handiwork. "You are beautiful as always. My work here is done," he declared. "Crystal, would you be a dear and bring me something cool to drink?"

Mario looked down the hall after Crystal left the room, then closed the door. "Why Mario, after all these years, I never knew you had these feelings," Angel teased.

"You are beautiful, darling, but you know you're not my flavor," he said, with both hands on his hips. "I need to talk to you, and I didn't want your daughter to overhear us."

"What is it?"

"We go way back, so I'll be straight with you. I love you, boo, but I need to be paid."

"What are you talking about?" Angel asked as she admired her hair in the mirror.

"I haven't been paid since March."

"You can't be serious," Angel blurted as she swirled around in the chair. "Why didn't you tell me earlier?"

"I've mentioned it twice."

"I've made some changes and maybe there's been a mix-up in the transition."

"That's what you said before. I'm not pressuring you; I know how your business is," Mario said. "Up one year, down the next. You're still one of my favorite customers, and you can call me anytime. I'll do your hair for free, but I need to reserve Saturday mornings for paying customers. I hope you understand,"

"Of course I do. And I *am* a paying customer. I'll take care of this immediately. Leave a copy of the bill."

"Thanks, girlfriend," Mario said and hugged Angel. "See you in two weeks."

"Come walk me to the door, Miss Naturegirl," Mario said, as Crystal came to the top of the stairs. "I always need help finding my way out of this museum. I can't believe your mother is finally moving."

Mario had been kind, but she was still embarrassed. Although, he did owe his whole clientele to her. If she hadn't exposed him to the artists she knew, he'd still be doing retouches and haircuts in his mother's basement.

Her career was supporting everyone but her. Her songs were in commercials, but she didn't get a dime. She didn't own publishing on most of her songs, so royalties went to the songwriter and to Peak. Her songs were downloaded and streamed online and still played on the radio, but Peak didn't send any payments because they claimed to be still recouping her last advance.

Angel wondered if others weren't being paid. Her accountant had said she needed to cut back and she had, starting with him. She could go broke by herself and didn't need to pay someone to manage her into bankruptcy. Brooke was already her business manager and Angel wanted to be more involved in her finances anyway. She let her driver and cook go, cut her housekeeper and gardener back to once per week, and put her trainer and publicist on retainers rather than full salary. She'd made drastic cuts, but Mario was a necessity. The Rose Manor sale proceeds would tide her over for a while and once her plan was in place, money wouldn't be a problem. Like Scarlett O'Hara, she vowed to never have money woes again.

CHAPTER 9

CARMEN

It had been eight weeks, four days, and two hours since Carmen received the call that turned her family's life upside down. Now she was waiting for a call that would put things back in order. School had started, and they were trying to maintain a normal routine. But the accident and pending trial threatened them like a coiled snake under a bush. The daughter of one of Gloria's Sexy Seniors members had agreed to take David's case, and was presenting a motion to get David a separate trial. Carmen hated to miss the hearing, but the semester had just started, and she had already used two personal days. The attorney assured Carmen this was a formality and only attorneys and the judge spoke during these proceedings. David would be there but wouldn't be asked to speak. She promised to call Carmen as soon as it was over.

What could be taking so long? Carmen thought, after noting it was almost two o'clock. It was against school policy to take personal calls in the classroom, so she had turned her phone on vibrate, and skipped lunch so no one would see her using her phone when the attorney called. Finally, she saw the digital display light up. She quickly turned toward the window and answered.

"Miss Payne, I'm afraid things didn't go our way today."

"Hold on a minute," Carmen said. She left her students watching a video and asked Lynn Hodges, a teacher across the hall, to keep an eye on her class. "I had to get someplace where I can talk. Tell me what happened."

"The judge denied our motion to separate your son's case. And Miss Payne, I'm afraid I have more bad news. The judge assigned David's case is up for reelection and they usually rule more conservatively in election years. And just to be clear, if your son is found guilty, he could be facing five years."

"Five years! What did you tell them? I knew I should've been there."

"I didn't say anything. We'll have our chance to respond. This case is getting a lot of publicity. The district attorney's office wants to show they are being tough on crime."

"This isn't any old case. This is my son," Carmen said softly.

"Five years is a worst-case scenario and I will be doing all I can to ensure David is not an election year pawn. I need to see you and David as soon as possible. I know tomorrow is Saturday, but can you come to my office?"

"Yes, of course."

The school bell startled Carmen, who had spent the rest of seventh period in the teacher's lounge. She walked back to her classroom dazed from her phone call. Her students were filing out of the room. She had forgotten all about them.

"I was worried about you," Lynn said.

"Thanks for covering for me. I didn't think I'd be gone that long," Carmen said, and sat at her desk. "Everything is so messed up, and there doesn't seem to be anything I can do about it."

"I know this is a nightmare," Lynn said. "Just let me know when you need me to cover your class. I wish I could do more." Lynn Hodges taught band and music appreciation and accompanied Carmen's choirs during concerts. Lynn and Carmen both came to Fifth Street Middle School fifteen years ago. Lynn had been a ten-year veteran and helped Carmen navigate paperwork, budget realities, and discipline.

Now Carmen was the veteran helping new teachers, and she couldn't imagine doing anything else. She enjoyed broadening her students' musical palate. Students moaned at the beginning of each school year, when she told them they would learn chamber music, spirituals, and show tunes. But they perked up when she told them they'd get to meet Lightning, a popular rapper who was the son of Eric Hamilton, her former Peak Records label mate. Being a former Diamond still had privileges. They dated, but broke up when he got deep into drugs. He got himself together and was one of the few friends she had still in the industry. "Thanks, Lynn," Carmen said, as she began to collect sheet music and straighten chairs.

"Do that tomorrow. Let's get out of here."

"No, I'm going to stay a while and get myself together. Go on ahead."

"Are you sure?" Lynn asked.

"I'll be fine. Student progress reports are due Monday and I'd rather finish them now, then I won't have to work on them at home. I won't stay long. I promise."

Carmen shuffled and reshuffled papers, but she couldn't contain her tears any longer. They trickled on the paper and made puddles on her reports. The steel hands on the clock said five o'clock, and Carmen was still on her first stack of papers.

She heard a knock on her door. It was Gerald Wells, the school engineer. "Didn't mean to disturb you, Miss Payne. I let all my staff go and I was making the rounds to check their work. They said they cleaned all classrooms except yours."

"Don't worry about it, Mr. Wells. My room is fine."

"First of all, call me Gerald. Mr. Wells is my father. The room is fine, but what about you? You're the last one here."

"I've been better," she replied, self-consciously wiping her cheeks.

"I know you're worried about your son, but you still need to eat. Based on that mystery meat I scraped off the cafeteria floor, lunch wasn't too appetizing. Let me take you to dinner."

Carmen raised her eyebrows and cleared her throat. "Excuse me?" She had seen Gerald occasionally over the last few semesters. They had been cordial, but their conversations were usually brief.

"Forgive me if I'm being too personal," Gerald said. "I've been following the case on the news and this has to be stressful for you. Let me take you to dinner. Nothing fancy, but I know a great soul food restaurant not far from here. You probably haven't eaten a decent meal since this whole mess started with your son. You can't help him if you're sick."

"Well, I...uh..." Carmen stammered.

"No strings, just two hungry coworkers sharing a meal. My daughter was meeting me, but she's working late. My taste buds were all set for yams, fried catfish, and fried okra from Maggie's Kitchen. Have you been there?"

"No, I haven't," Carmen replied, as her grumbling stomach reminded her she had skipped lunch. "My daughter is spending the weekend with her father, and David's coach is having the team over for a lock-in tonight. Let me make a couple phone calls."

"Great. I need to sweep the gym and mop the boys' locker room again. Be back in about forty-five minutes." He waved and closed her classroom door.

What have I gotten myself into? Carmen thought. She pulled her compact out of her purse and checked her face. Her eyes were puffy from crying and her eyeliner was gone.

But Gerald was right. She couldn't afford to get sick now. A satisfying meal would hit the spot, and she didn't feel like cooking. Gerald would be pleasant company, but she didn't know if she would be. As hard as she tried, she couldn't get her mind off her earlier conversation with the attorney.

"I won't sugarcoat things. This is a difficult case. I've reassigned some cases so I can devote more time to your son. I will do my best."

I hope her best is good enough, Carmen thought as she turned her attention back to the stack of papers on her desk.

CHAPTER 10

DOREEN

Keys clanging on the floor awakened Doreen. "I'm sorry, baby," James said. "I was trying to slip in without waking you." He had left last night at ten-thirty after Sister Mayes called and said he needed to go to the hospital to see the Sanders family.

Doreen was worried about Officer Sanders, who was still in the hospital two months after the accident. He had suffered internal bleeding and been in a medically induced coma for two weeks. He was out of the coma, although still in intensive care. But she was also worried about her godson. David's case would be more difficult if Officer Sanders died. She prayed whatever had happened was a temporary setback. It seemed like she had just fallen asleep when James came in.

"That's okay. I should've been up an hour ago," Doreen said, as she checked the clock. "The kids are going to be late, and I have a meeting in forty minutes. How is Brother Sanders?"

"They did emergency surgery around midnight, and Sister Sanders fainted, so they admitted her for observation. But God is a healer and we must remain prayerful."

Doreen knew this was preacher-talk for "not good."

Earlier in his ministry she accompanied James on hospital visits. Sometimes she had to leave the room, so the patient wouldn't see her tears or hear the catch in her voice. Seeing and smelling so much sickness depressed her and made her stomach queasy. While her intentions were sincere, James finally told her she was about as uplifting as an undertaker. They agreed she would focus on other parts of their ministry.

"Why don't you sleep in today, honey?" Doreen asked. "Let the staff handle things. I can drop the kids off."

"I'm not sleepy. I'll drop the kids off, then go work out," James said. "But if you really want to be helpful, you can proofread the district report I sent you last week."

"I'm sorry. I completely forgot," Doreen said. "I'll skip lunch and review it, and email it to you this afternoon."

"Thanks," James said. "Good luck with your meeting. Keep praying for the Sanders, and don't forget the Women's Guild meeting this evening."

This was something else James had voluntold her for. Once this Women's Guild program was over, Doreen vowed to have a serious talk with her husband. She had suggested hiring a housekeeper several times, and James always shot down the idea. "You get off work at five o'clock. But you let them give you all those projects and you end up working late and you bring work home. You're too nice. You need to say 'no' sometimes. Besides, I don't want a stranger in our house, roaming through our things," he'd say.

James was a nontraditional preacher, but he was traditional at home. He never washed dishes or clothes. He was a good cook, but left the kitchen such a mess, Doreen didn't encourage him. So even if she got off at five o'clock, by the time she finished cooking, washing clothes, and checking homework the evening was over. She spent her weekends doing housework, grocery shopping, and Paige's hair. Whenever she suggested that he help more, James said he didn't have time. And when she mentioned hiring a housekeeper, he said if she spent more time on her real job—taking care of her family—they wouldn't need a housekeeper.

She knew plenty of preachers' wives with jobs and she didn't think she should have to consistently apologize, or work herself to a frazzle to prove her love of God or their church. But for now, she'd have to find a way to fit it all in.

CHAPTER 11

CARMEN

Carmen locked her classroom and went to the teachers' lounge, where there was a full-length mirror. She sprayed a light sheen on her hair and brushed her edges. She dabbed on plum crème lip gloss, added eyeliner and a dusting of eye shadow. She jazzed up the black pants and shell she had worn to work by tucking in the shirt and slipping on a chain belt. Carmen added a gold ruffled sweater jacket that covered her healthy backside, a black-and-gold onyx necklace and switched from small hoops to dangling earrings. She swapped flats for black, three-inch heels. Beautiful perfume on her wrists and cleavage completed the transformation from prim school-teacher to voluptuous vixen.

The building cleared out quickly on Fridays and almost everyone had rushed out as soon as the bell rang to get ready for the staff holiday party. Carmen chipped in when they asked for donations, but hadn't planned to attend.

Gerald Wells was pulling a garbage can to the dumpster, and did a double take when he saw Carmen strut toward her car. Since he rescued her from her classroom meltdown, they had talked several times and when Lynn insisted she attend a Thursday happy hour, she and Gerald ended up at the same table. He had helped her put holiday decorations in her classroom and brought her extra display panels, a precious commodity, thanks to budget cuts. Gerald whistled and waved as she crossed the parking lot. She did a curtsy and waved back.

Ordinarily, she would have stopped to chat, but not today. Nathan was in town. It was almost Thanksgiving, and they hadn't spent an evening together since the summer. This evening, they were meeting out in Millington at their favorite restaurant, then would see the new Eddie Murphy movie. He had made reservations at a hotel for them after the movie. Meeting at a hotel gave her a twinge of guilt. But since Gloria had moved in, Carmen's privacy had moved out. She would never be grown enough to bring men into the house with her mother there, even if it was her house.

Carmen arrived early and waited in the bar. She turned toward the door every time it opened, but there was no sign of Nathan. At five-thirty, she pulled out her phone to text him, but it was dead. She went to her car to charge her phone and called home to check on her daughter. "Hope, how's Mama?"

"She's okay. When she got in from dialysis, she wanted to take a nap. But I can wake her if you want me to."

"No, don't do that. If Mama is still sleep before you go to bed, make sure her alarm is set so she'll wake up and test her blood sugar. It can't drop too low. Call if you need me."

Hope's words lingered in her ears. *Gloria Mae Ellis napping on a Friday night?* That was unheard of. Her mother always had a card party or church revival to go to. They tried to convince their mother to switch from finger sticks to a digital glucose meter. The doctor said monitoring Gloria's blood sugar levels continuously would help prevent lows and spikes. But Gloria didn't trust computers and said she would not be hooked up to one. So all they could do was keep a close watch on her.

Carmen chided herself for worrying about things she

couldn't control. Tonight she was going to focus on having a good time. She saw Nathan pull into the parking lot and went to the door to meet him.

"I am so sorry, babe," he said, grabbing her hand and leading her to the parking lot. "My wife changed her mind at the last minute and she and the boys surprised me at my mother's. I'm not going to be able to get away like I thought. But I at least wanted to see you."

"That's disappointing," Carmen said. "Maybe tomorrow."

"Definitely tomorrow. I'll text you with details," Nathan said, as he pulled her to him. "You sure do look good. I've missed you."

"I've missed you too," Carmen replied.

"I guess I should get back to the house," Nathan said. "Stay sweet and save my loving."

All dressed up and nowhere to go—again, Carmen thought, as he drove off. She decided she could use a good laugh and went to the movie anyway.

Eddie Murphy and company were obviously funny because everyone around her was hysterical. But Carmen couldn't concentrate. Her thoughts went back two years to when she and Nathan met.

They were both guests at a wedding where the groom was Carmen's cousin and the bride was Nathan's cousin. Carmen was standing outside the banquet hall back door, smoking.

"May I join you?" Nathan asked. "We smokers are becoming an endangered species; we need to stick together."

"Be my guest," Carmen said, observing his model good looks. *I hope we're not related*, she thought.

They introduced themselves and talked like old friends between puffs. He was a project manager, with two boys and an estranged wife. He was in the middle of a nasty custody battle and not in a festive mood.

Carmen had just ended another drama-filled relationship,

and was not feeling the whole wedding and happily-ever-after mood either. Nathan and Carmen spent the rest of the evening together, and realized they had more in common than relationship cynicism. For the next three months they were inseparable and he had even given her a key to his apartment. But when Nathan's youngest son needed surgery, he moved back home. The move was to be until his son got better. His son recuperated, but rather than move out, he and his family moved to Atlanta.

Carmen knew what it was like to be married to a cheater, but each guy she dated seemed more trifling than the one before. Guys seemed to think sitting in front of her TV for hours was a date and expected sex if they bought her a hamburger. So when she saw his number, instead of blocking or ignoring it, she answered. She knew it was a cliché, but she was happier with part of him, than all of someone else. She knew they weren't a couple, but they had fun, he made her feel special, and she enjoyed his visits home to Memphis. Until recently, that had been enough.

Carmen didn't even realize the movie was over, until the lights were turned up. The theater was empty and the workers were sweeping and picking up garbage. *This is a pitiful night out on the town. It's only eight-thirty*, she thought. She had been looking forward to a night out and wasn't ready to go home. She didn't want to go to a club, and had already seen one movie. Then she remembered the school holiday party. Carmen didn't have a secret Santa gift, but she had contributed so she wouldn't be totally out of order.

She had to park several houses away and could hear the booming bass from the street. Carmen tried to enter unnoticed, but Lynn spotted her as soon as she stepped through the door. Everyone was doing the wobble and Lynn motioned for her to join them. Carmen had worn her cute heels, not her dancing shoes. *Shoot, I don't even have dancing shoes anymore*, she thought. But the beat was infectious, and

Carmen forgot about her bunion and found a spot among the pack of dancers. *Wouldn't Fifth Street Middle School students be surprised to see their boring teachers getting their groove on?* she thought and smiled. While smiling at her thoughts, her eyes met Gerald's, who smiled back.

She meant to look away, but couldn't. She had never seen him in civilian clothes. He usually wore khakis and a company T-shirt. The only hint of style at work was a monogrammed handkerchief hanging from his back pocket. Tonight he had on black Dockers, a tan Polo sweater that hugged what she could tell were impressive biceps, and shiny black Stacy Adams shoes.

The hostess turned up the lights as the song ended and announced this was a good time to sing Christmas songs.

"Hey Carmen, start us off," Lynn said. "Black Friday is coming up. Get us in the mood."

She began "Silent Night," and her rich alto was so mesmerizing, the others forgot to join in. Carmen rarely sang at school, unless she was in the background helping her students find the right pitch or alone in her classroom.

"I've always loved your voice," Gerald confessed as he handed her a cup of punch.

Lynn generated a fake cough and announced, "I think I'll get punch too." She winked at Carmen behind Gerald's back as she walked away.

"Don't admit you're a Diamonds fan. You'll be telling your age," she said.

"No, I'm not. Wait, let me clean that up. I don't mean I didn't like your records. I listen to you every day. Confession time: I linger in the hall when I clean up outside your classroom, just so I can hear you sing. You probably have the cleanest entry in the building."

"Thank you." The punch had ice in it, but Carmen felt her cheeks warm.

"Do you ever consider singing professionally again? It's a

shame to waste that beautiful voice on preteens who think Janet Jackson is old school."

The Diamonds were formed when Gloria, who was working at radio station WDIZ, entered Carmen, Doreen, and Sophia in a talent contest sponsored by the station. The grand prize was two hundred dollars with the winner chosen by audience response, à la the Apollo.

"Mama, you can't be serious. I can't sing in front of all those people," Carmen whined when her mother told her she had entered them in the talent show.

"Why not? You sing in church every Sunday."

"That's different. I know those people, and even if I sounded bad, they wouldn't boo me."

"That's why I entered your friends too. I already know what you girls can wear and what you'll sing," Gloria said, as she began searching through her album collection.

"But Mama..."

"I'll call their parents and get permission for them to stay here this weekend. We don't have much time."

Carmen knew once her mother made up her mind, that was it. That determination had gotten Gloria a recording contract at Stax Records, where she worked as a secretary and sang background for Isaac Hayes and Johnnie Taylor, and if you looked hard enough, you could see her on stage during the *Wattstax* concert finale. Gloria had been signed to a contract, but the company went bankrupt and so did Gloria's dreams of a recording career. She sometimes sat in for the weekend evening DJ on WDIZ, and when he moved, Gloria got the job. Listeners loved her stories about the Stax years, and she closed each show with "The Best Is Yet to Come."

Gloria bought black T-shirts and the girls hot-glued rhinestones down the seams of jeans they already owned. Gloria selected "My Baby Just Cares for Me" for them to sing. The girls were dismayed over Gloria's choice. "Mama, can't we sing something by Janet Jackson or Madonna?" Carmen asked. "No one has heard of this song."

"They'll hear it when you do it and they'll love it. Before Janet or Madonna, there was Nina Simone. You can't go wrong with a classic. It sounds good without music, but we'll add a trap beat to make it sound hip-hoppy. Trust me. It'll be great." The crowd loved the song and the girls came in second. When the announcer asked the group's name, *diamond* was the first thing that came to Gloria's mind. She had been up late the night before and watched *Gentlemen Prefer Blondes* while gluing rhinestones on the girls' shirts. Marilyn Monroe's "Diamonds Are a Girl's Best Friend," was still running across her mind. The girls were elated to win the second-place prize. They split two hundred dollars and each got a pager. But Gloria was not satisfied. "Second place is the first loser. My girls are the best," she stated.

Gloria became relentless in preparing "her" girls and they never lost again. She went through her Rolodex and lined up local and regional gigs, and then an audition at Peak Records. While Gloria was all in, the Fraziers did not approve of their daughters singing the devil's music. Doreen and Sophia knew their parents would disapprove, so they told them they were in the school glee club. They didn't learn the extent of their daughters' singing until church members congratulated them on their appearance at the Memphis in May festival. Gloria was able to smooth things over, promising to chaperone all performances, and Doreen and Sophia were allowed to stay in the group.

Carmen had heard adults who were in show business as children express resentment toward their parents for the demanding schedules and missed experiences. But Carmen never felt that way. They grumbled after hours of vocal and breathing exercises, walking with books on their head to improve their posture, and admonitions to stand up straight. But the work was paying off. Instead of dressing up for prom, she, Doreen, and Sophia got to dress up every week-end. Sophia did their hair and makeup and had them looking like cover girls. Each girl had a cell phone, when that was a big deal. They had even sung the national anthem at NBA and NFL games, and met a few players. They were only do-ing local and regional gigs, but they felt like celebrities.

By the time they auditioned for Peak Records, they were more than ready. Gloria had sent a demo, and Ray had been following them. He was just waiting for them to turn eighteen. Their first records didn't sell well, but again leave it to Gloria. She suggested another song none of them had ever heard, "Until It's Time for You to Go" by New Birth. They rearranged the beginning and it almost went gold. When Sophia held the high note at the end, crowds went wild.

Carmen's students had an idea she used to "be some-body," but they believed anything older than six or seven years was ancient history. They peppered her with questions. "What are you doing here? Are you rich? Do you know Angel Donovan?"

"That time almost seems like it happened to someone else," Carmen admitted while she ate a slice of fruitcake. "I couldn't imagine singing professionally again. Besides, my life has been full raising my children, and now my mother is living with me. Then just when I thought the kids were almost on their way, this nightmare happens with David. So don't stand close to me, this dark cloud over me may envelope you too."

"No more talk of dark clouds," Gerald said, as he set her cup on the table, then guided her to the dance floor. "What-ever problems you face when you leave here will be there whether you have fun tonight or not. So why not have fun? Let me see you shake what your mama gave you."

For the next four hours, she and Gerald rotated between dancing and playing bid whist. She had been the Diamonds' choreographer before they made enough money to hire one and still had a few moves. When they tired of dancing, they went to the dining room and joined the card players. They played so well together, others accused them of having a secret code.

Carmen and Gerald were two of the last ones to leave. "I can't believe it's after two o'clock," Carmen said.

"I guess it's true time flies when you're having fun," Gerald remarked.

"And I almost started not to come," Carmen confessed.

"I'm glad you did. We'll have to do this again sometime," Gerald said, while walking her to her car.

"Lynn missed her calling. She should plan more parties."

"We don't have to wait for Lynn to plan something. How about going to a movie tomorrow?"

Carmen was so surprised, she dropped her keys.

"I hope I wasn't too forward. I assumed you were unattached," Gerald said.

"I'm not attached," she said, as Nathan flashed across her mind.

"Good," he said, then took her keys and opened her car door. "Stay here and I'll pull up and follow you home."

"You don't have to do that," Carmen said, as she thought of all the times she and Nathan had parted ways at this time of the morning.

"I wouldn't feel right letting you drive alone at this time of night. Besides, this way I'll know where to pick you up tomorrow. I'll come around six."

It had been a long time since a man had come to her house to pick her up. On the rare occasion she was asked out, she preferred to drive, so she could leave if the date was a dud. Nathan either came over when he was in town, or they met somewhere.

"How about going to the new Eddie Murphy movie?" Gerald asked.

"I heard it's hilarious," Carmen said, not bothering to mention she had already seen it.

"Bet," Gerald said, giving her a thumbs-up. "Dinner and a movie. How does that sound?"

It sounded like a date.

CHAPTER 12

JADE

Jade rarely drove during rush hour anymore and had forgotten how congested Houston's morning traffic was. Brian was still in Louisiana, so she was opening Seaside. He had taken his mother to a funeral, and the day trip had turned into a two-night stay when his engine overheated.

Business was slow, so Jade went to Brian's office to study for the algebra portion of the GED test. Brian disapproved of her studying at the restaurant, saying it set a poor example for employees. But there were more than enough employees to handle the lunch rush, if it ever came. She moved the stack of mail on Brian's desk to the drawer, but noticed two letters from the bank and opened them. They were overdraft notices. An eighty-dollar check to Costco and a ninety-five-dollar check to a bread supplier were returned. *How in the world can we have less than two hundred dollars in the bank?* Jade wondered. She tried to transfer money from savings to the checking account, but didn't have the correct password, and couldn't get information when she called.

Jade left instructions with Rita, their assistant manager, and hurried to the bank. Brian would be upset if he knew she left during the lunch rush because he liked to keep an eye on the register. But he seemed impressed with Rita, and business was slow.

"You're sure your information is correct?" Jade asked the teller a fourth time.

"Yes, ma'am, I'm sure."

"Then I need a manager or the fraud department. My accounts have been hacked," Jade said. But the branch manager confirmed the teller's explanation. Their certificates of deposit had been redeemed and the bank had a hold on their savings account. Brian had redeemed the certificates three weeks ago and withdrawn thousands from the savings account. *What in the world could he have done with so much money?* Jade wondered. Miss Glo had advised her to always keep some money in her own name. Her stash had dwindled since Tiffany frequently needed money, but she transferred money from her personal account to cover the overdraft. She figured she could replace it when she found out what was going on.

She knew receipts were down because the city's flood control construction was taking longer than anticipated. Their business-interruption insurance claim was initially denied, but Brian had appealed and Jade thought everything was re-solved.

They opened Seaside seven years ago after Brian was laid off from his job as a dispatcher at the port. He was a good cook and since they had been successfully catering on the side, they decided the next step was a restaurant. They based the menu on Brian's Navy ports of call with a Cajun twist. Angel came to the grand opening and business took off. Business was so good, they were on an almost twenty-four-hour schedule with barely enough time to close, clean, prep, and reopen. Their location was near downtown and within two years, a new soccer stadium opened close by. Now the real estate alone was worth a million dollars so she couldn't imagine what Brian could have done with their money.

Jade returned to Seaside, but couldn't concentrate. Her thoughts kept returning to their bank accounts. Brian handled their finances but Jade knew what they had and where it was. Or at least she thought she did. She and Brian may not have had a perfect marriage, but he had always been responsible. It was one of the things that attracted her to him.

They met at O'Hare Airport. The Diamonds were headed to Los Angeles after two shows in Chicago. Brian was a Navy shipman returning to San Diego. The flight was delayed, and he and Jade began talking. When they finally boarded, Brian upgraded to first class, so he could sit next to her and he came to all their shows in California. For once, she had someone waiting for her backstage. The guys Jade met either thought they were jumping on a gravy train or wanted to add her to their collection. And she never felt like she was enough—not enough hips, boobs, or soul. Her discomfort with her Cherokee heritage made her grateful to Brian, who accepted her as she was. Brian thought her blue eyes and thick, wavy hair were exotic, and convinced her to stop dyeing her hair blond. Carmen and Doreen said he was controlling and didn't like him. Angel complained he was in the way and didn't trust him. But Jade was twenty and in love.

As far as Jade knew, most of her relatives remained in and around Dodge County, Oklahoma, on Cherokee nation land. Her mother had been a restless sixteen-year-old who ran off with a white truck driver passing through. Their fling didn't last long, and Jade's mom was left on her own with a baby in Tulsa. Her mother couldn't keep a job and they moved frequently. Her mother smoked weed daily, drank beer like water, and popped pills like candy. But Jade didn't feel neglected. She stayed home from school whenever she wanted and could have cookies and Kool-Aid for dinner. Oreos beat broccoli any day. When her mother was arrested for passing bad checks, Jade spent three months in foster care until her great-aunt found her and brought her back to Dodge County. She was with family, but always felt like a misfit. Her great-aunt died, and Jade went to live with her mother and new stepfather in Tulsa, who by then had two more children. But there were too many rules and it was difficult to make friends. There were white, black, and Hispanic kids at her new school, and she didn't fit in with any of them. She skipped school and ran away four times by the time she was fifteen. The last time she ran away, when child services brought her home, her mother had moved. Jade was placed in foster care and after stabbing one of her "big brothers" for attempting to rape her, she ran again. She went to the bus station and had enough money to ride as far as Memphis. After sleeping in the bus station a few nights, someone reported her to children's protective services and after a few group homes, she was placed with the Randolphs.

Mr. Randolph, who was a minister, was the first to praise her voice and insisted she join the youth choir. While working part-time as a waitress she was "discovered" when the waitstaff sang "Happy Birthday" to a group from Peak Records. She couldn't believe it when they invited her to audition. She was thrilled when they hired her as a background session singer and awestruck when she sat in with the Diamonds. Background singing was fun, and producers loved her five-octave range. It paid well, but the hours were erratic. Her restaurant job was stable and she didn't want to jeopardize it. When she explained this to Ray Nelson, he showed up the next day with a contract and told her she was being made a permanent member of the Diamonds. The Randolphs were disappointed she didn't finish high school. But she was aging out of the foster system and Peak Records was offering her independence and security. Jade promised to study with a tutor, but recording, touring, and partying became her priorities.

The Diamonds really were like family. They bickered,

but presented a united front to others. While Doreen was resentful that Jade replaced her sister, Jade was so humble and cheerful, they couldn't dislike her. Jade took the longest to learn routines, and the girls harassed her about it. But when Ray or anyone else expressed similar sentiments, Carmen, Doreen, and Angel defended her. And when a Peak secretary was too flirty with James, Carmen and Angel trapped her in the ladies' room, with Jade as lookout. Jade never knew what they did or said, but the secretary quit the next day. Their bond seemed unbreakable. But as suddenly as it started, her three-year Diamond career was over, and she was relegated to occasional background session work.

Angel's solo career took off. Doreen and James were in their own drug world and Carmen was a newlywed and not speaking to any of them. She bounced between Chicago and Memphis and spent some nights at Gloria's, but was basically a half-step away from being homeless. Shortly after the Diamonds broke up, Brian got orders to Germany, and he asked Jade to go with him. They got married in his hometown of Houston and Jade couldn't have been happier. Within nine months, she was in Germany with a husband and a baby. She finally had her own family. That was twenty years ago, and Brian had kept his promise to take care of her.

When he gets home, I'll calmly ask him what's happened to the money. Surely there is a valid explanation, she thought. *And it better be good.*

CHAPTER 13

DOREEN

The sweet smell of cloves met Doreen at the Maggie's Kitchen entrance as she arrived for a lunch meeting. The aroma reminded her of practicing at Carmen's house during the early Diamond days. Gloria's ham recipe included liberal doses of cloves and her thick ham sandwiches were an incentive for the girls to practice hard. Doreen had worked with the owners to get financing and their grilled ham and cheese sandwiches were her favorite menu item. Banks rarely loaned to new restaurants and Doreen had fought to get the loan approved.

She asked for a table in the back and waved to one of the owners behind the register. Doreen was sipping raspberry tea when she saw him. Seeing him triggered rage, hate, sadness, and hurt, all at once. As the waitress brought him to her table she wondered why she even agreed to meet him. She took a deep breath and said a quick prayer for strength.

"Hello, Doreen," he said as he sat across from her. "You haven't changed a bit."

"Lucas," Doreen said, with a slight nod of her head. "I have to be back at work in forty minutes, so let's not waste time with chitchat."

"Okay. I want to see my kids."

Doreen had planned to stay calm and get this over quickly. But he was starting with fighting words. "They aren't your kids. The court awarded them to James and me when you killed their mother and abandoned them."

"I did not kill Sophia. And I don't care what some white man's court says. They are my children," he stated, and picked up the menu.

"The judge was black. But you wouldn't know since you didn't bother to show up. You weren't interested then. Why the sudden fatherhood pangs? You must need money," Doreen said, as she pulled her checkbook from her purse. "I should have known you'd renege on our agreement one day. How much do you want now?"

"I don't want your money. I'm ashamed I ever took your money. I'm doing well now. I'm a partner in one of the largest black-owned real estate agencies in Chicago."

"How nice for you. So, what do you want?" As a Christian and the first lady, Doreen knew she should be pleased with the changes in Lucas's life. But his redemption was too late to save Sophia, and she blamed him for her sister's death. Doreen not only lost her sister, but her mother's illness had been exacerbated worrying about Sophia. Lucas had devastated her family once, she was not going to let him do it again.

"I told you, I want a relationship with my children. They'll be out for Christmas break in a couple weeks. I'll come visit for a few days and we can ease into it."

"Not happening," Doreen stated as she waved off the approaching waitress.

"I'm not asking for permission. My children have a right to know their father."

"They do know their father. James is the only father they know."

"Doreen, I didn't come down here to fight with you. I hoped we could work things out. This doesn't have to be ugly."

"You know what was ugly? Watching my sister struggle to raise three children on her own was ugly. Listening to her cry because you took her money to the dope house was ugly. Watching the pain on my mother's face whenever Sophia came around, looking a hot mess and begging for money was ugly."

"You introduced her to the pipe in the first place," Lucas said. "So don't act so self-righteous."

Lucas was right. Doreen began dabbling the first time they went on tour without Gloria. It was the thing to do. They partied after every show, and the measure of a good host or hostess was how much blow they provided. Sophia was hesitant, but Doreen coaxed her into trying it to control her weight.

Sophia may have started using after Doreen, but quickly surpassed her big sister and sunk further faster. Peak Records sent her to rehab, where she met Lucas. He had been a FedEx driver, and had an accident while on his route. He wasn't at fault, but the company still required him to take a drug test. He failed the test and the company sent him to rehab. Sophia and Lucas completed the program and upon release, went straight to the dope man. Sophia missed practices, lost too much weight, and became paranoid. When she jumped off stage and attacked a fan she said was laughing at her, Ray Nelson terminated her contract.

Doreen, Carmen, and Gloria pleaded with him to take her back. He agreed to let her do some background sessions, and said he'd consider reinstating her if that worked out. Sophia stayed with Doreen and James, and they stuck to her like white on rice for five days. Doreen screened her sister's calls, prepared her protein shakes, and they did vocal exercises. But on the sixth day, Doreen and James had appointments at the same time. When Doreen came home, Sophia was gone, and Sophia was a no-show to the session.

Doreen was so upset they didn't speak for three months. The next time they saw each other, Sophia was pregnant and living with Miss Glo. Pregnancy turned out to be the best motivation for Sophia, along with Miss Glo's tough love, nurturing, and companionship. Carmen got Sophia a job with the school district in the Head Start program. Sophia completed rehab, stayed clean throughout her pregnancy, and began taking classes to get certified to open a day care center. She loved working with the children, but there weren't any benefits and she couldn't afford child care, so she had to quit when Paige was born.

She moved back in with Lucas, saying she wanted them to be a family. Lucas was a functioning addict, but had never quit, and eventually lost his job. Doreen was still getting royalty checks, but they barely covered their rent. Motherhood was harder than Sophia imagined, and Paige was a colicky baby who was always crying. Sophia had tried to breastfeed, but she didn't produce enough milk, and Paige became underweight. Lucas had little time for these concerns. He and his friends were still partying and spending money they didn't have. Sophia's recovery was too fragile to withstand the pressures of new motherhood, financial insecurity, and constant contact with users. She eventually resumed her habit. Doreen was disappointed, but not surprised. She knew how hard it was to get and stay clean.

Doreen's experience made her a credible speaker when she recounted her winding road to recovery at Blessings' drug counseling sessions. She had told her story numerous times: *I don't have a hard-luck story. We weren't poor. My parents provided a loving home. I had no childhood trauma. I simply tried coke and I liked it. A lot. The cocaine high was glorious. I felt alert, confident, sexy, and full of energy. But that eventually gave way to feelings of paranoia, anxiety, and headaches. Not to mention staying broke, looking terrible, and hooking up with anyone who had a few rocks. I knew what it was doing to me, yet I couldn't put the pipe down. But I never realized what it was doing to my mother, until it was too late. I thought makeup, wigs, and flashy clothes were covering up my deterioration, but I was only fooling myself. And when my mother was diagnosed with advanced stage breast cancer, I was sitting by her bedside and in her faint voice she said, "I don't have much longer. Please find your sister, and both of you get off the dope." Then she closed her eyes. Machines started beeping and nurses rushed in. It gives me chills every time I think of it. Instead of me comforting her and making her illness easier, she was worried about me and my sister's addiction. Everyone's bottom is different, but that was mine. They were able to stabilize my mother, and she was able to be treated as an outpatient. James and I moved home to take care of her and she lived another two years. So thankfully, she did see me whole and clean before she died.*

Doreen knew she couldn't have quit if she wasn't ready. But she also knew, it would have been so much harder if James had been pulling at her, like Lucas had done to Doreen.

"James and I pleaded with her to stop, but you kept pulling at her."

"I've been through enough therapy and treatment programs to know only the user can stop the user. For years I blamed myself, which only led to more self-destructive behavior. It's about individual choices and responsibility. So don't brainwash my kids with that garbage. I went to Paige's school and she wouldn't even speak to me."

"You went to her school? How dare you go behind my back. I will have a restraining order placed on you," Doreen said, barely able to contain her fury. *The secretary makes me show ID and sign the log*, she thought. *Yet they give a stranger full access, on his say-so?*

"I don't want to hurt them, and I wasn't trying to kidnap

her. I just want to be part of their lives. Maybe they can visit me for spring break."

"You must be joking. Why would they want to spend a minute with the person who killed their mother?" Doreen asked.

"I did not kill Sophia and I hope you're not telling my children that lie."

"Forgive me. I guess I should say use, rob and desert. Is that better?" Doreen heard her voice rise and noticed other customers staring at them.

"Nothing you say will make me feel worse than I already do," Lucas confessed. "That's why I want to repair my relationship with them. You're a preacher's wife. Doesn't your church teach forgiveness and second chances?"

"The church also teaches people to get wisdom, and avoid confusion. And it would not be wise to disrupt the kids' lives when they are settled and thriving."

"Just because you can't have kids, don't try to take mine."

His words bore through her soul. She loved her niece and nephews more than anything, but still felt she had missed something by not bearing a child. People often commented that she was lucky. She got the kids without weight gain, labor pains, or stretch marks. They meant well, but Doreen resented the casual references to luck. People seemed to forget losing her sister, not luck, was the reason she had the kids.

"I'm sorry, I shouldn't have said that. Look, I hate what happened to Sophia. If I could redo things, I would. But I can't. So, I have to make the best of right now. I'm clean. I'm working. I have my own place and I want to see my kids. We can do this the easy way, or we can go to court. But I'm not going to let you keep me from them. I've already wasted too much time."

"What you are not going to do, is upset their lives, just because you feel ready to be a parent. You're ten years too late," Doreen stated.

"I'm their father. You can't take that from me."

"You sold your rights. Remember?" Doreen snapped back.

"Doreen, I promise you—"

"I am not interested in the lie you are getting ready to tell," Doreen said, as she sat back in her seat and crossed her arms. "This meeting is over."

Lucas placed a ten-dollar bill on the table. "You'll be hearing from my lawyer," he said, as he stood. "I'm staying at the Hilton near the Loop and I'll be here until Friday. Think about what I've said. Things get nastier once lawyers are involved."

Doreen sat at the table trying to regain her composure before returning to work. She remembered the day she brought the kids to her house. Sophia had called, said the kids were hungry, and asked to borrow some money. Doreen went to the grocery store, then to her sister's. She was appalled when she entered Sophia's apartment. Dirty dishes and roaches were everywhere. The twins were barefoot, wearing only soggy, sagging Pull-Ups. Paige had obviously dressed herself, because she had on a pink-and-orange floral tank top and red-and-blue–striped shorts, in January. Her hair was uncombed and her fingernails were black underneath.

"Where are your mother and Lucas?" Doreen asked. "And why aren't you in school?"

"Mommy's sleep and Daddy's gone. Can we go home with you, Auntie Doreen?" Paige pleaded with tears in her eyes. "Daddy took the TV again."

Doreen waded through fast-food containers and dirty clothes to the bedroom and turned on the light. Sophia stirred but didn't open her eyes. Doreen began shaking her.

"What's wrong with you?" she yelled. "How can you let your babies live this way?"

Sophia struggled to open her eyes, then smiled. "Hey, sis. I knew you'd come. Did you bring the money?"

"That's all you care about. Look at you. Your children are hungry and filthy, and you stink." Doreen's voice was stern, but she wanted to cry. This emaciated woman with rotting, yellow teeth and an ill-fitting wig was not her Sophia. The Sophia she had shared a bedroom with for more than half her life was a beautiful, voluptuous, germaphobe. They had even erected a clothesline to delineate their sides of the room. Sophia's was always neat and clean. Doreen hated it when their mother said, "You're the oldest, you should be setting an example for your sister." Doreen envied her sister's curves, acne-free skin, and long hair.

"If you came here to give me a lecture, no thank you. You weren't always Little Miss Perfect Holy Roller. Nobody could hit the pipe longer than you."

"You're right," Doreen said, searching for a clear spot on the bed to sit. "I haven't been perfect and I'm not perfect now. But I only hurt myself. If I was blessed with three beautiful babies, I would've straightened up sooner."

"And I'm going to straighten up too. I'm on the rehab center waiting list. They said they should have an opening next week," Sophia said, as she scratched beneath the cheap wig and pulled out a clump of straw-like hair.

"We have a rehab center at church. You can come right now."

"I don't want nobody preaching to me. Besides, I don't want to embarrass you and James. Once I get myself together, I'll come to your church."

"Sophia, you come to the Lord to get yourself together. Remember the song Mother sang, "Just as I Am"? The Lord is available now. We can't get ourselves together without him."

"There you go preaching to me," Sophia complained as

she sat up. "I told you I need a little money for rent and to get Pull-Ups, groceries, and stuff."

"I'll call the landlord tomorrow and I bought groceries. I'll bring them in," Doreen said, as she headed for the door.

"That's the least you can do," Sophia said. "You're staying in Mother and Daddy's house, but half of it's mine. So technically, you owe me rent money."

"Daddy worked too hard for me to let you turn their house into a drug den for you and Lucas."

"A judge would make you sell the house and split the money, or let me move in. But I wouldn't do you like that. I just need a few dollars," Sophia said, while lighting a cigarette. "I have a job interview tomorrow, but I don't have anything to wear."

"You can wear something of mine," Doreen said.

"You want me to beg?" Sophia snapped. "All right. I need money to get high. Are you satisfied? Lucas took his trifling ass to the grocery store with my EBT card three days ago and I haven't seen him since. I just need a little help. I'll repay you once I get on my feet."

These were excuses Doreen had heard numerous times before. When she was sympathetic, Sophia took advantage of her. When Doreen tried tough love, Sophia played the guilt card, asserting she only started to keep up with her big sister. She would tearfully promise to attend recovery meetings with Doreen, but right now she owed somebody money, or had a bill to pay, and Doreen fell for it every time.

"The best way for me to help is to cut you off. All I'm doing is enabling your addiction."

"I don't want to hear that crap," Sophia countered, while blowing cigarette smoke. "If James wasn't in good with Ray, they would have kicked your ass out of the group too. How well do you think you would have done if everyone turned on you—including your own sister?"

"Blame me if you want," Doreen said. "Whoever you blame, it's still up to you to change. But you have to hit bottom before that happens. And I will not let those kids hit bottom with you. They're coming home with me. You can come get them when you're serious about getting yourself together."

"You've always been jealous. My voice was better than yours and I had more boyfriends than you did. You should have stood up for me and not let them kick me out of the group."

Doreen began looking through dresser drawers for clothes for the children, but everything was dirty or too small. She removed the boys' smelly Pull-Ups and wrapped them in blankets. She found their shoes, but no socks. She took off her suede jacket and wrapped it around Paige.

"You can't take my kids," Sophia screamed. "Just because you can't have kids, you can't take mine."

Her words stung like a gut punch. Other than James, Sophia was the only person aware of her infertility issues. "You want me to take them or child protective services?" Doreen asked as she ushered the crying children through the door.

"Paige, come back here," Sophia yelled. "You can't do this, you sterile, two-faced bitch. I got rights."

"Stop embarrassing yourself and take your funky behind inside," Doreen demanded.

Neighbors were peeking down the hall as she left her sister's apartment. "You're doing the right thing, honey," an elderly woman who lived across the hall said. "I've been so worried about them babies. Sometimes she leaves them alone all night. I bring them over here when I hear them crying. I didn't have a number for none of her peoples, or I would have called you sooner."

Doreen thanked the woman and sprinted to her car. The

kids got inside, and she told Paige not to unlock the car. Doreen made three trips back upstairs with the groceries. She knocked on the door, but there was no answer.

"I'm leaving bags in the hall. Don't leave them out here unless you want them stolen," Doreen said.

"Kiss my ass, bitch," she heard Sophia yell.

"You used to have an ass, before you cracked it away," Doreen clapped back, as she rushed to her car. Her hands were shaking and her head was throbbing as she put the car in *drive*. Then she put the car back in *park*. She fished a business card out of her purse and wrote her cell, home and, church number on the back. Doreen went up the stairs one more time, and gave the neighbor the business card. She was pleased the grocery bags were gone.

Doreen went back to the car and turned the heat on high. She had tears in her eyes, but she knew she was doing the right thing. At least she thought she was. The next time she saw her sister was when she identified Sophia's body at the morgue. Sophia had indeed gone to rehab. The counselor called Doreen to schedule a family therapy session for the following Tuesday. But Doreen had forgotten about her accounting exam, and asked to move the meeting to Thursday. Sophia left the program that Tuesday night and was found dead the next day in an alley behind a known crack house. She'd been shot, but no one came forward with any details and no one was ever arrested. Lucas didn't even attend the funeral.

The first weeks after the funeral were rough. As bad a mother as Sophia was, her kids missed her. They were sad and confused, and never cried at the same time. It was months before she and James could reclaim their bed, since at least one child and sometimes all three slept with them.

Paige was struggling in school because Sophia didn't make her go. Doreen and James took turns helping her with flash cards and signed her up for an online tutoring program.

By the time the fall semester ended, she was reading on grade level and passing her classes.

For the first month, Doreen's world revolved around the boys' toilet habits. They were almost three years old and still wearing Pull-Ups. She had six weeks' family leave from the bank. The boys needed to be in day care before she returned to work, but a day care wouldn't accept them unless they were potty-trained. She read all she could on toilet training and got advice from Gloria. She tried bribes, punishment, having them mimic James, reading them books on the subject, and showing them videos about being "big boys." Lo and behold, one day everything clicked. She had been to the Grammys, the White House, and met Oprah Winfrey. But nothing was as exciting as the first day both boys went accident-free in big boy underwear.

To lessen the hurt of spending their first Christmas without their mother, she and James took the children to Disney World. But when they returned from Florida, they received a certified letter from children's protective services ordering them to present the children within twenty-four hours or be arrested for kidnapping. Lucas claimed she and James had interfered with his parental rights and taken the children out of state without his permission. Doreen couldn't believe the state was wasting taxpayer money on such non-sense. Obviously, the children were better off with her and James. The children were placed in foster care while their case worked its way through the system like molasses in winter.

She tried to work within the system, but when the state separated the children, Doreen took matters into her own hands. She told James of her plan and he said he didn't agree but wouldn't object. They were still living in her parents' house, but she took the money they were saving for a down payment, and got cash advances on their credit cards. She went to a lawyer and had papers drawn up. Then she called Lucas and told him she'd give him twelve thousand dollars to relinquish his parental rights. Her attorney had an envelope of cash for him and he had two days to go to his office and sign adoption papers. They went before a judge the next week and within ten days, she and James had an instant family.

Doreen and James had given them a stable home and Christian values. Paige was moody, but she was a good kid. And the twins lit up a room whenever they entered. If Lucas thought he was going to waltz in and take her children, as Miss Glo always said, *the devil is a lie*.

CHAPTER 14

ANGEL

After Rose Manor failed inspection, Angel lowered the price and got an "as is" offer. She wouldn't make much profit, but at least she could shed the smothering debt, and move on.

Angel spent days purging her closets. She gave Crystal first choice. Even natural girls like Versace and Givenchy. She rented a storage unit for stage gowns, furs, and couture outfits. She packed two trunks of jewelry, purses, and a sable cape for Miss Glo. Several boxes went to the women's shelter.

The next task was to cull her shoe collection. She stopped counting when she got to four hundred pair. She kept about forty and Brooke listed the rest on a resale website, netting fifteen thousand dollars. Brooke said she could have doubled her prices if she had identified herself as the seller. But Angel said that sounded desperate. Divas have pride.

She had hoped to rent a place with a Lake Michigan view, but the prices gave her sticker shock. Even when she expanded her neighborhood choices, the rents were unaffordable. As her move date got closer, she expanded her neighborhood choices again. Brooke finally found a condo in a newly renovated building in Hyde Park. When Brooke gave her the contract, she saw a familiar name.

"This says Nelson Properties. I know you didn't set me up to rent from Ray Nelson," Angel stated.

"Mr. Nelson's company redeveloped the property. Most of the units are already sold. Once they sell out—"

"Oh, hell no. How could you even consider such a thing?" Angel asked.

"Look, you need a place to stay. He has units available—a perfect solution."

"If not for him, I'd still be in Rose Manor. He slashed my income, so I can't afford my home, then I'm supposed to pay him to live somewhere else?"

"Angel, everything's new and it's a great deal. Not lakefront, but close enough."

"My records saved his company, then he tosses me aside like used concert tickets. If it wasn't for me, he probably wouldn't even own that building."

"Then why not enjoy the fruits of your labor? It's a twelve-month lease to own, at less than market rate. This gives you time to get back on your feet."

"I guess I don't have much choice," Angel replied as she crossed her arms. "Make sure my lawyer reviews everything." She wasn't crazy about renting from Ray Nelson, but it did give her one less thing to worry about. And renting her a condo was the least he could do considering the money she had made him.

Her move date was getting closer and she thought she was ready, until Brooke reminded her there were boxes in the attic. The first box was full of pictures. She wrinkled her nose at the picture on top, a still shot used for the cover of their *Wrong Number* album; their first album after Sophia left the group. They wore leopard bodysuits and four-inch heels. The girls had asymmetrical haircuts with a diamond pattern shaved into the side and Godiva bangs. Even Jade had spritzed her hair to achieve the stiff style popular among young black girls. *That cover was so tacky. The lighting was bad, the staging was amateurish, and the bodysuits were hideous,* Angel thought. Three years ago, a *Wrong Number* remake reached number one. The new group added rappers to the intro and sped up the tempo, but the backbeat was the same. She didn't usually perform Diamonds songs unless she had writing credit. But she didn't like their version and put the song back in her show, so people could hear how it was supposed to sound.

Going through old pictures inspired her. She had pictures of the group with then-president Bill Clinton at a fundraiser. Her two Grammy nomination announcements were at the bottom of the box. She didn't win, but really was honored to be nominated. These last few months had been a struggle, but she realized it was all part of an amazing journey. A journey she was determined to continue.

CHAPTER 15

CARMEN

Carmen went downstairs to check on the chicken and sweet potatoes she had put in the oven. She wouldn't be home when David got home from the gym, or Hope got off work, but at least she was leaving them a healthy meal. She and Gerald were going on an official date, not an impromptu Fifth Street Middle School staff gathering. Their previous attempts had been canceled due to his sore throat, then her last-minute union meeting, and most recently, an early-season ice storm.

With dinner taken care of, Carmen was leaving the kitchen when she heard a key in the door. "Mom, is my white blouse clean?" Hope asked as she blew in and opened the refrigerator.

"Hello to you too," Carmen said. "I thought you were working."

"Hey, Mom," Hope responded as she pecked her mother on the cheek. "I told you I was getting off early today. Remember, the choir is singing at the fall concert this evening? I told you about my solo. You forgot, didn't you? If it was David, you wouldn't have forgotten."

"You know I wouldn't miss your debut," Carmen said, thinking she needed to quickly text Gerald and cancel.

"It won't take me long to change," Hope said, with a much happier tone of voice.

"Hey, Mom," David said, as he came in the back door. "A silver car pulled in the driveway, a Corvette. Did Uncle Sonny get a new car?"

"I hope not. He owes me money," Carmen said, as she looked out the window and saw Gerald getting out of the car. "That's a friend of mine."

"What kind of friend?" David asked, with a raised eyebrow.

"A none-of-your-business type of friend," Carmen replied.

"What do you know about him? What kind of job does he have, that he drives that kind of ride?" David asked.

"Excuse you?" Carmen stated. "I believe I'm still the parent."

"All the more reason for me to check him out. Men like him take advantage of single mothers like you."

"He looks cool to me," Hope said.

"You haven't even met him. You can't judge someone by the car they drive," Carmen said, shaking her head.

"If there's nothing shady about him, why are we just meeting him?" David asked.

"It's nothing serious. We were just going to the—"

"I thought you said you didn't forget?" Hope accused. "So I guess you're not coming?"

"To quote Nettie from *The Color Purple*: *Nothing but death can keep me from it*," Carmen said. "David and I will both come."

"Who, me?" David said. "No, thank you."

"Hope attends your games, programs, and even some practices."

"Because those things are fun," David said. "Only parents and teachers enjoy sitting through boring school concerts."

"Nobody wants to see your big head anyway," Hope said, while punching her brother in the shoulder. "Let him stay here and do my chores. Get to mopping, mister."

"David needs to come. We haven't done much as a family lately," Carmen said.

"Are you sure, Mom? David can take me."

"I don't want to sit through some tired school program. I'd rather watch paint dry. Mom already said she's not going out," David said and left the room.

"And a minute ago you were whining about me not coming to your events," Carmen said.

"I didn't know you had a date, and he is kind of cute," Hope said, while peeking out the window. "I understand. It's not like you have a lot of guys coming to take you out."

"So you want your lonely, old, desperate mama to go because she might not get asked again?"

"That's not what I'm saying, Mom. You do so much for us. I'm glad you met a friend," she said, and winked at her mother. "I know it's hard to meet decent men at your age."

"And since when did you become a dating expert? And, what you know about a cute man? Child, go get ready," Carmen ordered.

Carmen opened the door before Gerald could ring the doorbell. "I have to take another rain check," she said. "My daughter's school concert is tonight. I'm sorry I didn't contact you sooner."

"Is it open to the public?" Gerald asked.

"Yes," Carmen answered.

"May I join you guys?"

"Uh, sure," Carmen stammered. "My daughter will be great, but I can't vouch for the other parts of the program."

"I work around young people all day, and I enjoy seeing them doing positive things. They need our support."

"You can't say I didn't warn you," Carmen said.

"There's one problem," Gerald said. "My car only seats two."

"We can take my car," Carmen said. "I'm sure Hope can get a ride home with one of her friends, then we can still go out."

David came back in the living room, as Hope walked down the stairs. "Gerald, I'd like you to meet my children, David and Hope," Carmen said, while getting her purse. "Mr. Wells is coming to the concert with us."

"I thought this was family only," David said.

"Well, that is, if it's okay with Hope?" Gerald asked.

"Sure. We get extra points for guests," Hope said. "Dad, Jaxon, and Sonya are coming."

Carmen kept smiling despite the nerve her daughter had hit. She had nothing against Vernon's children, but she didn't like her children being the "outside" kids. He had left their family and as far as she was concerned, he was the outsider.

"So are we ready?" Carmen asked.

"Let's go," David said, with a little more bass in his voice than usual. "We don't want to be late. The ladies can sit in the front seat."

Carmen had to chuckle at this six-foot man-child calling himself looking out for her. It was hard to believe eighteen years had passed. Her pregnancy announcement hadn't been enthusiastically received.

"Have you not heard of birth control?" Angel asked when Carmen announced her pregnancy at a rehearsal.

"That explains your sluggishness tonight," Jade said. "So what do you want to do?"

"What kind of question is that?" Doreen replied. "She wants to have her baby, and she wants me to be the god-mother."

The hardest part had been telling her mother. Legally,

Carmen was an adult, but she still lived at home and worried about her mother's response. Gloria had been disappointed when Faye got pregnant and left college. Carmen hated to disappoint her mother again, especially after all her hard work for the Diamonds. The girls agreed they would go with Carmen to tell her mother. When Carmen stalled and the other girls made small talk, Angel spoke up and announced, "Miss Glo, you're having another grandchild."

After what seemed like an eternity, Gloria hugged her daughter and said, "Faye has girls, maybe you'll have a boy. We're going to have the biggest baby shower Memphis has ever seen."

David had been a big baby, and the Diamonds, Gloria, and Vernon's people lavished him with love and attention. This foundation helped him grow from a precocious boy into a confident young man, with enough nerve to think he was chaperoning his mother. Carmen just shook her head and smiled, hoping this trial mess didn't kill that spirit.

CHAPTER 16

JADE

Jade turned off the OPEN sign, set the alarm, and locked the restaurant back door. On her way home, she practiced her conversation with Brian. They had spoken briefly last night, but this was a conversation she wanted to have in person. She couldn't imagine what had happened to their money and found no answers when she searched his desk drawers and files. Other than a splurge on a convertible Camaro when he turned forty, Brian was frugal.

She parked behind Brian's truck and noticed almost all the lights on in the house. Brian opened the door as soon as she reached the doorstep. "Am I glad to see you," he said, as he hugged her and pulled her inside.

The aroma of garlic and thyme filled the air and Jade figured Brian was experimenting with a new recipe. "Good evening, Mrs. Anderson. Have a seat," Brian said, while pulling out a chair for her.

"I'm glad you're in a pleasant mood," she responded. "We need to talk."

"You're right. You go first," Brian said.

"Our accounts are overdrawn. I thought it was an error, but I went to the bank and you've drained our accounts. What's going on?"

"City construction still has the parking blocked, and business has been down," Brian said.

"So, you spent all our savings?"

"Yes and no," Brian answered, while fishing two pot holders out of the drawer.

Jade moved the place setting to the side, set her elbow on the table and asked, "What does that mean?"

"I told you we were losing money."

"But you didn't stress the seriousness of it. You should have talked to me," Jade said.

"I tried."

"When, Brian?"

"I told you I didn't think we could afford to keep Tiffany at SMU."

"She's doing so well. If she transfers, she'll lose credits and take longer to graduate. That costs more in the long run."

"That's what you said when I told you, so I dropped it," Brian said. "Then later I told you I needed you to work more hours until things get better."

"But you know we can't leave Dawn alone after school."

"That's what you said then, so I made Rita full-time," Brian said, and turned off the oven.

"You're always bragging about the restaurant being worth a million dollars."

"The real estate isn't an ATM. Our loan matured, and our banker said they wouldn't renew it without more collateral or a principal reduction," Brian said, while taking French bread out of the oven. "I paid Tiffany's tuition and pledged the rest of the money as collateral so they'd renew our loan. When we repay the loan, the bank will release our money."

"That will take years. I've never questioned your handling of the money, but I don't think you should have done this without discussing it with me."

"I kept thinking things would improve and instead they kept getting worse," Brian said, as he filled her glass.

"So why are we drinking champagne if all our money is tied up? Did we win the lottery?" Jade asked.

"Not quite, but we do have a solution to our money woes," Brian announced while placing a hefty serving of shrimp étouffée on her plate.

"This smells heavenly, but you know I don't like to eat this late."

"Don't worry, I'll help you work it off," Brian said, with a wink. Then he pulled a legal-sized envelope from under the place mat and placed it in his wife's lap. "Here's the answer to our problems."

Jade looked at the Chicago return address and couldn't imagine what had her husband so excited. She pulled out the papers and moved her plate to the side, while Brian stood next to her with arms crossed. "Honey, I can't concentrate with you standing over me."

"Of course. Take your time."

Jade squinted to decipher the document, then retrieved her drugstore reading glasses from her purse.

Ten minutes later Brian burst back into the room. "What do you think? Isn't it great?"

"Angel is proposing a Diamonds reunion tour," Jade stated.

"I know," Brian said, as he refilled his glass.

"I saw her mention it in an interview, but I didn't think she was serious. Things ended so badly. There's no way the others will agree."

"Sure they will," Brian said. "It's already in the works. Details aren't finalized, but we're talking almost two hundred grand for a few weeks' work. And it'll be tax-free. Since Seaside lost money last year, we'll have a tax loss carry-forward to offset it against. Let's toast."

"You've talked to Angel?"

"I spoke with her manager. They want you to meet as soon as possible, with the goal of starting a fifteen-city tour in June."

"I can't go on a tour."

"What do you mean, you can't go on a tour?" Brian asked, as he drank more champagne.

"I'm not eighteen anymore. I have a family."

"Our children are grown, and I will be fine."

"What about Dawn?" Jade asked.

"What about her? School will be out. She'll be okay."

"You'll be working. What will she do all day?"

"We can find a camp. With the kind of money this tour will bring in, we can afford it."

"What seventeen-year-old wants to go to summer camp?"

"She can come work at Seaside."

"Brian, you know the foster agency will remove her if they find out I'm gone for an extended time. Miss Branch has been a lenient caseworker, but I don't think she'll bend the rules that much," Jade said, as she took off her glasses.

"Are you saying you're not going to do it?" Brian asked as he refilled his glass.

"I need to think about this."

"What's there to think about? You're always stressing the importance of family. Well, your family—your *real* family— needs that paycheck. We have a few holiday events coming up, but that money won't carry Seaside long. Our savings are tied up and Tiffany will need tuition in January. How do you propose we pay next year's tuition?"

"We'll think of something. What would we have done if this letter hadn't come?"

"I don't know," Brian said, as refilled his glass again.

"Honey, we'll manage. I'll work more hours at Seaside, or get a job. We can't jeopardize Dawn's placement with us. It would be devastating to move her now. She'll be a senior next year. Besides, I'm almost ready to take my GED test. If I take a break, I'll have to start all over."

"Let me get this straight. You're willing to pass up the opportunity to make *six figures* over the course of a few months, so you can babysit somebody's bastard child and so you can take some high school test nobody cares about?" Brian asked.

Jade pushed her chair back from the table. "I care, and don't say that about her. Is that what you think of me?"

"Don't twist my words. I know you're sensitive about your background, but you can't save the world. I don't think she even wants to be here. She's got a major attitude problem," Brian said, while spooning homemade dressing on their salads.

"I'm not trying to save the world. I guess I see myself in her. The attitude is a screen to shield her from more hurt."

"Well, right now, we need a screen to shield us from bankruptcy," Brian argued, while spreading healthy pats of butter on his bread. "Your family needs you, your real family. With your background, seems like your family would be your uppermost concern."

"But I feel like Dawn is our family too," Jade countered as she pushed her plate away.

Brian blew on, then ate, the heap of rice on his fork. With a mouthful of food, he stated, "Then it looks like you have a choice to make."

CHAPTER 17

DOREEN

Doreen stole glances at the envelope on the counter as she unloaded the dishwasher. For three weeks, she dreaded seeing the mail when she got home from work. Today, the letter finally came. The return address was a Chicago law firm, and Doreen wondered how much money Lucas had wasted on this nonsense.

She had worked late every night this week preparing for her board of directors presentation. Her preparation had paid off and the meeting couldn't have gone better if she had written the script. After the meeting, she shopped for Christmas presents, then headed home. Doreen was still basking in all the compliments she received, but that excitement evaporated when she saw the letter on the kitchen table. She pulled a casserole from the refrigerator and placed it in the oven, then picked up the dreaded envelope and walked as though she were headed to the gallows. She closed her bedroom door, then went in the bathroom, turned on the water, and closed that door. It was after office hours, but this call couldn't wait.

"Doreen, I won't say it's good to hear from you. If you're calling, things must not be going the way you had hoped," her attorney said.

"You're right. The letter came today. I haven't opened it

yet. I thought maybe it was better to act like I hadn't been informed. Will that stall things?"

"No. It's always better to have as much preparation time as possible."

"Then it's time to take the actions I spoke with you about," Doreen said.

"You want to have Lucas Powers investigated?"

"Yes. I doubt if everything is as rosy as he says."

"That can be expensive."

"I don't care, just get things started. I'll scan you a copy today and bring the original letter to your office Monday."

James was still at Blessings, preparing his sermon. Doreen usually didn't interrupt his study time, but he had insisted they face this together. Although, she wondered whose side James was on. When she first told him about Lucas, he got mad at her instead of Lucas. It upset her to think about it.

Tears ran down her cheeks and mascara ran into her eyes as she sped home from her encounter with Lucas. When she arrived home, she threw down her keys and ran into their bathroom.

"Doreen, honey, what is it?" James asked. "Are you all right?"

"You won't believe who I saw. Lucas called and wanted to meet with me. I met him this afternoon and he wants visitation with the kids. Can you believe him?"

"When did he call?" James asked.

"A few days ago."

"And you made an appointment to meet with him?"

"Yes. He asked to meet me for a few minutes," Doreen replied.

"And you set this meeting up and didn't tell me?"

"You've been so busy with the church and convention meetings, I thought I could take care of this without bothering you. I thought he would be begging for money like he did the last time he called."

"So, what did he say?" James asked as he closed their bedroom door.

"He lives in Chicago. He's working, he's clean, and he wants custody of the kids. He hasn't called, written, or sent a penny in years, and he has the nerve to ask for the kids, like they're clothes he forgot at the cleaners," Doreen said, while throwing her shoes in the closet.

"What did you say?" James asked.

"What do you think I said? I told him he lost his parental rights when he left them and their mother in an unheated apartment in the middle of winter, while he took the rent money to the crack house."

"I would have thought you'd say, meeting him was a mistake and you needed to talk to your husband. Then the three of us could discuss his petition."

"What is there to discuss?" Doreen asked. "We have adoption papers. He has no claim whatsoever."

"I don't know if he has a claim or not. We need a lawyer. That's why you should've notified me as soon as he called. We've counseled hundreds of couples with marital problems about the importance of communication. How could you not include me on something this important?"

"I told you, I thought it was a nuisance phone call and he'd go away."

"He may be more than a nuisance. Courts are more favorable toward biological fathers than they used to be."

"Even if the father is a drug addict and a bum?" Doreen asked.

"*Was*. Sounds like he's turned his life around."

"Maybe so, but he's ten years too late."

"Are you forgetting the lifestyle we lived?"

"No, but we only hurt ourselves. He had three children to consider."

"You may be judging him too harshly," James suggested.

"I know you're not on his side," Doreen said, in an accusatory tone.

"All I'm saying is we need professional help. Which is what I would have told you if you had come to me in the first place. He wasn't blessed to see the right road when we did, but let's not condemn him. Everyone criticizes brothers for not handling their business. When a brother tries to do the right thing, you won't give him a chance."

"Spare me the brother man blues. What about Sophia?" Doreen asked. "He contributed to her death as much as if he aimed and shot the gun. And now he wants to uproot our children? We have legal adoption papers, and this is their home. I won't let it happen."

"There you go again, talking that *I* stuff. You're not alone in this. You were wrong to meet him without me," James stated.

"So, you're going to hold that against me and side with Lucas?"

"I didn't say that. If he calls again, refer him to our lawyer and you are not to meet or speak with him again. Understand?"

Doreen nodded, but she didn't understand, and decided she would handle Lucas Powers herself. She would go along with James's plan, but just in case, she had her own plan.

"Well, it finally came today," Doreen said when James arrived home, about an hour later.

"What?" James asked.

"The letter from Lucas's attorney. You open it, I'm too nervous."

"I'm glad we're in this together now," James said. "Let's remember, the battle is the Lord's, and nothing will happen that isn't His will. The kids know we love them and have done our best for them. But ultimately, God knows what's best. We may not understand . . ."

"Baby, you know I love to hear you preach, but please, just open the envelope?" Doreen asked as she wrung her hands.

She paced a few steps while James tore open the envelope and began reading.

"Oh, oh," James said.

"What is it?" Doreen asked as she tried to read over his shoulder.

"I smell something burning."

"I forgot about the casserole," she blurted and dashed to the kitchen. She opened the stove and reached for the pan, but forgot to grab a pot holder and burned her fingers.

"Baby, you got yourself all worked up for nothing," James said, as he appeared in the doorway. "This letter isn't from Lucas. Here, see for yourself."

Doreen blew on her fingers and took the letter. She laughed out loud when she finished it. "Can you believe Angel wants to do a reunion tour?"

"She must be hurting for money," James said.

"That's so like Angel, to go through these formalities, rather than just calling."

"She could have saved attorney fees by finding out up front you're not interested. I never heard of anything so ridiculous."

"What's ridiculous about it?" Doreen asked.

"You still float my boat, but you ladies are—how should I say this without getting in trouble—rather mature to be prancing around on stage."

"I'm younger than Janet Jackson. She's performing and looks amazing."

"What about Carmen? She was heavy then; she's definitely too big now."

"Too big for what? Plus-size models are popular and curves are fashionable."

"It's only fashionable if you're selling something. Why are we discussing this anyway? Surely you aren't considering Angel's offer?"

"I don't know. I haven't had time to think about it."

"What is there to think about? You are the first lady of Blessings Tabernacle. You can't be shaking your booty talking about 'daddy come and get it.' Besides, I thought your banking career was so important. It's too important for you to join the ministry full-time, yet you can go on a cross-country junket."

"James, I'm not saying I'm going to accept Angel's offer. I'm just saying I'd like to think about it. What's wrong with that?"

"Okay, you think about it. I suppose it's flattering to consider recapturing your youth. I know you'll make the right decision," James said, as he kissed her cheek. "How long before dinner?"

The Diamonds had ended on such a sour note, she had never considered getting together again. But there were class reunions, family reunions, and team reunions. Why not a Diamonds reunion? Doreen knew it was only by God's grace she wasn't a statistic from the crack epidemic. She was always amazed when she ran across a picture or a YouTube clip of herself onstage, because she didn't remember half of her music career. The beginning had been so much fun. But eventually drugs became her priority, and the shows merely an interruption in her getting-high schedule. She had a diamond tattoo on her thigh she didn't even remember getting, which was just as well since needles terrified her.

With the benefit of age and sobriety, I could actually appreciate the experience this time, she thought. She couldn't possibly do anything until next summer, then the kids could come with her. Travel was educational and the kids would love it. Her CBI project would be running by then, so her workload would be less hectic. However, she did have another project she was working on. She expected to be very pregnant by summer. James was right. She couldn't possibly do a reunion tour, but it might be fun to see the girls again...

CHAPTER 18

CARMEN

The volume of traffic during school hours always amazed Carmen. The world of Fifth Street Middle School was so insulated, she forgot everyone wasn't confined from seven-thirty to three-thirty everyday. She had to leave school unexpectedly, even though she already had several absences. She had gotten this news at the last minute and was rushing.

Their attorney had withdrawn from the case because she was getting married and relocating. She assured them the new attorney, Jeff Peters, was skillful, and also committed to David. Carmen didn't like changing horses in midstream, especially when the horse had already been paid a hefty retainer—a retainer she had begged, borrowed, and pawned to get.

So far, Attorney Peters was living up to his hype. Thanks to his efforts, the judge waived David's travel restrictions so he could attend the regional debate workshop and tournament in Nashville. David's attorney called during her lunch period to tell her the news. So she had less than two hours to get home, pack a bag, and have it ready when David got out of school.

Hope was at school and Gloria was at dialysis. Once she finished packing, maybe she could find a few moments to

FaceTime Nathan. She had fallen asleep when he called the night before, and had forgotten to answer his text this morning. Carmen made it home, after stopping at every light, and was surprised when she saw Hope's backpack on the dining room table. Carmen yelled her daughter's name as she went upstairs. "What's going on?" Carmen asked, as she pushed Hope's door open.

"We had a half day. It's parent-teacher conference."

"Why didn't you remind me?" Carmen asked. "I never miss a conference."

"I gave you the papers. I figured you forgot. I know you're stressed about David and I didn't want to bother you."

Carmen took her daughter's hand and asked, "You're worried about me being stressed?"

"Well, aren't you?" Hope asked.

"That's not the point. You're my baby and I'm just as concerned about you as David. Let's finish this conversation while I pack a bag for David. Then we'll get our nails done and go eat."

David's bags smelled like a locker room, so Carmen asked Hope to look through her closet for a travel bag that wasn't too girly.

"I found a bag," Hope said, when she returned to David's room. "And I found these pictures. Who is this guy? You two look mighty cozy."

Carmen and Eric, from the Heavyweights, were posing under mistletoe at a Peak Records Christmas party. He had been her first love. She remembered her mother's warning not to trust musicians. But Peak Records was pretty incestuous, and everyone was pairing off. Doreen was dating James, and Sophia was dating another singer at the label. Even her mother was dating a company executive.

"And, Mom, look at this one. I can't believe Gram let you wear that."

Carmen smiled at the still shot used for the cover of their *Wrong Number* album. "I haven't seen this in ages," Carmen said and sat on the bed. This was their first album after Sophia had left the group. Carmen had been self-conscious in the leopard bodysuit Ray selected. They posed from shortest to tallest, with Carmen in front, and the others behind her standing on stacks of phone books. Even though she hadn't wanted to be out front, her body was banging back in the day. She had curves instead of rolls and the bodysuit hugged her in all the right places. The album cover had even been nominated for a Grammy in the best re-cording package category. Three years ago, a *Wrong Number* remake made the top ten. Her students were incredulous when she told them she was one of the songwriters and her group, the Diamonds, recorded it first. The remake included an introduction with rappers and she liked the faster tempo. Their hit meant increased royalty payments since she had partial writing credit. Her transmission had gone out and the check was right on time.

The girl in the picture was supposed to keep singing hits until she gave up her amazing career to stay home with her adoring husband and raise perfect babies. Grand juries, married men, and rolls around her stomach weren't in that plan.

"Those are some real hoochie-mama outfits. You won't even let me wear a halter top," Hope complained.

"When you get a record contract, you can wear a halter top," Carmen said. "I'm going to gather some snacks for David's trip, then I'll be ready to go." Her phone vibrated as she entered the kitchen.

"Hey girl, it's Doreen. Did you see the show yesterday?"

"What show?"

"*The Tonight Show*. Angel was a guest last night."

"I missed Her Highness," Carmen replied.

"She announced a twentieth-anniversary reunion of the Diamonds."

"Oh no, she didn't. How dare she make an announcement without talking to us. I don't care if she announced it to BET, CNN, and 60 *Minutes*. I told her hell would freeze over before I sang with her again and I haven't changed my mind."

"James and I are discussing what this could mean if I did the tour. Have you replied yet?"

"Replied to what?" Carmen asked.

"Didn't you get a FedEx from Angel?"

"I got an overnight letter from a Chicago law firm. I thought it was a bill collector and tossed it aside."

"You need to read it. It's a proposal from Angel. It's a hectic schedule, but it sounds like it could be fun. Angel said if all the original Diamonds weren't available, she was determined to bring this to the people, and had others available to step in."

"Angela is planning a Diamonds reunion without all the Diamonds? She should call it the cubic zirconias," Carmen quipped. "Can't we sue her for that?"

"I don't know. Angel usually gets what she wants."

"Well, not this time. She thinks she's a big star, but she wouldn't have been anything without us. We were supposed to be a trio until James unearthed her. Mama is usually right, but this was one time, I think I was right," Carmen said, as she remembered the day Angel became a Diamond.

Gloria had picked up Doreen and Sophia from their apartment, then treated them to shakes from Scoops, on their way to meeting with Ray Nelson. "Girls, I've got exciting news to share before rehearsal," Gloria announced when she pulled out of the drive-through.

"Remember that cute girl who auditioned a while back?" Gloria asked. "She's joining the group. Ray wants everyone at the studio."

"I knew something was fishy, with you taking us for shakes before a rehearsal," Carmen said.

"I didn't know we were looking for another singer," Doreen added from the back seat.

"We aren't," Carmen stated. "I say we vote. They can't make us add someone we don't even know."

"You haven't even heard the proposal," Gloria said.

"Let's look on the bright side," Sophia said. "I don't trust Mr. Nelson as far as I can throw him, but if they're adding someone, that means they believe in the Diamonds and will be backing us with more promotion and maybe increase our video budget."

"Will we have to split our money with her, or is Ray increasing our pay?" Carmen asked.

"I'm sure those are things we'll work out in the meeting," Gloria replied.

"Okay, listen," Carmen said and turned to face Doreen and Sophia in the back seat. "If we stick together, we should be able to overrule this. It's still *our* group."

"That's easy for you to say," Sophia said. "You're living with your mother. Me and Doreen got bills now." Their parents had tolerated their music career and late hours, but once they were both out of high school, they were expected to get real jobs or go to college. Sophia declared since they were making their own money, they should be able to run their own lives, and they were moving out. "Let's give her a chance."

"Sophia was Angel's main advocate, and how did she repay her—by getting her kicked out of the group," Doreen stated.

"We gave her a chance. Instead of being grateful, she connived her way into singing lead. Then she needed more attention, so she took Eric."

"Are you upset about her singing lead, or are you still mad about Eric?" Doreen asked. "Angel didn't force herself on him."

"She didn't try hard to avoid it."

"Forget about him," Doreen said. "Find the FedEx envelope and read the letter. She wants a response within thirty
days."

"I can give my response now. Maybe I could forgive her
for being a whorish wench, but after what she did to my
mother—no."

"Maybe she's changed. Read the letter."

"I know you believe in forgiveness, but I'm not there
yet. My mother's health, and David's case are already more
stress than I can handle," Carmen said, while adding two
bananas to David's snack bag.

"I was leery at first, but the longer I think about it, it
sounds like fun. And having a broader platform will help
David's case. When the public becomes aware of the
injustice, Spike Lee and Don Lemon will bring national
attention to David's case and the charges will be dropped.
Eric will see you on television. His unrequited passion will
be rekindled. He'll find out where our next show is, come
backstage with a five-karat engagement ring, and you two
will live happily ever after."

Carmen laughed despite her troubles. "I think you've
crossed the line from faith to fantasy."

"Good—you're laughing. I'm going to hang up on that
positive note. Read the letter."

"I'll try to find it, but like I said, the answer is no. Wait,
I'm changing my answer—and excuse me, First Lady, it's not
'no,' it's hell no!"

CHAPTER 19

ANGEL

The Diamonds achieved something few entertainers can claim: They went out on top. Their last album had four top-twenty songs, with "One More Song" used in a movie sound-track. Money was flowing like spilled sugar, and Ray moved the headquarters to Chicago. Ray said Memphis was too small and slow for the things he planned. He laid off most of the employees without much notice and headed north.

Angel had welcomed the change. It made her split with the Diamonds and Preston seamless. She loved Chicago's skyline and energy. Even the frigid winters didn't bother her. It gave her an excuse to buy furs.

Her first solo album went platinum and several com-peting record companies approached her. Some offered better terms and assured her they could find loopholes in her current contract. But Angel considered herself a key member of the Peak Records family. She was part of the Memphis core and she and Ray were a team. He spent more time at her place than he did at his own. He connected her with the best designers, sat in on her recording sessions, and made sure she didn't gain a pound. They weren't a forever couple, but they had an understanding, or so she thought. Part of the company remained in Memphis, so she didn't question his frequent trips back home. After a show in Louisville, she figured she was so close she would go home. She hadn't seen her daughter or parents in months and she could squeeze in a surprise visit with Ray.

But she was the one who was surprised. As the seventh-floor elevator door opened, she was greeted by a banner that read *Congratulations Mr. and Mrs. Nelson*. Most of the faces were new to her, but she recognized Ray, grinning like he'd won the lottery, with his arm around the wide waist of what was apparently his bride.

"Wow, news travels fast," Ray said, as he came to greet her. "We just got in from Vegas, and walked into this surprise. So glad you could come."

Angel smiled and congratulated the newlyweds. She held it together long enough to learn the new Mrs. Nelson was a nurse, who Ray met when his father had surgery. She appeared to be the epitome of the Southern, chicken-frying, Sunday-hat-wearing church lady. Everything Angel was not. Angel's divorce was barely final, and she and Ray had not discussed marriage. But this was still a betrayal and disrespect. And when he dared show up at her place in Chicago to resume their previous arrangement, she would not give him the satisfaction of crying or throwing a jealous tirade. She simply asked him to return her key and said she was also thinking of making changes and to expect a call from her lawyer.

At the time, she didn't even have a lawyer, having always used Peak's legal staff. That painful lesson taught her not to confuse attention with affection. Ray had been overseeing his latest investment, just as a trainer grooms their newest horse. It was business. Her new lawyer negotiated a higher royalty rate and she remained a Peak artist. But Ray sold controlling interest a few years ago and most of those remaining from the Memphis move were dismissed. This year it happened to her. When Angel called Ray to complain, he referred her to the employee relations department. So much for loyalty and allegiance.

But she wasn't relying on loyalty or sentiment today. Ray was a user, but he knew music, and would recognize a business opportunity. As Brooke said, "What good are connections if you don't use them?"

Angel smoothed her pencil skirt and refreshed her lip gloss before opening his door. "Angel, you are fine as ever," Ray said, rushing to meet her when she entered his office.

"Thanks," Angel said, as she leaned in for an air-kiss.

"I was so pleased when my secretary told me you were coming. You were pretty nasty the last time we spoke. I was giving you time to cool off before I called you. Is everything okay at the condo?"

"Everything is fine. I guess I should thank you, although that's the least you could do," Angel stated.

"Please know terminating your contract was not my decision. I wouldn't do that to my homegirl. This new generation has no sense of—"

"Ray, save it. I have a business proposition. My career is stuck and I—"

"You know how this business is. You're up, you're down, and when you least expect it, you're back up."

"I know about the highs and lows," Angel said, resisting the urge to roll her eyes. "And I also know the artist must be proactive and not leave their career to others."

"You've got me curious. What's your proposition?"

"A reunion tour. Fans always ask when the Diamonds are going to reunite."

"I tried to get you together for the Peak Records salute five years ago. Doreen wanted to include some ridiculous tribute to her sister, Jade's husband intercepted my calls and demanded an unreasonable amount of money, and Carmen wouldn't answer my calls. Besides, I thought you girls weren't speaking."

"I'll get the girls together," Angel said, crossing her legs. "I need you to line up sponsors and promotion."

"It's not that easy. Reunion tours are rarely successful, without some other hook," Ray said.

"Then why are you backing the Heavyweights tour?"

"It's different for guys. They can be bald, tottering on a cane with a watermelon gut, yet if they can still croon, ladies eat it up. But no one wants to see middle-aged women. People want to remember them as alluring young honeys."

"That's the most sexist thing I've ever heard," Angel said.

"I didn't make the rules," Ray said. "Here's what I can do. I can set up the tour and promote it, but you find the sponsors."

"If I could do that, I wouldn't need you."

"So, if I do this for you, what will you do for me?" Ray asked.

"I'm going to make you a lot of money, like I always have."

"What if I want something other than money?" Ray asked as he walked behind her chair and put his hands on her shoulders.

"Please. I'm not that desperate," she said, removing his hands.

"If I'm not mistaken, you came to see me."

"I came with a business proposition. I am not one of these young girls trying to catch a break," Angel said as she stood. "Let me tell you . . ."

"Time-out," Ray interrupted, throwing up both his hands. "You can't blame a guy for trying. Take it as a compliment."

"I'd be more flattered if you agreed to the tour."

"Like I said, I can set up the tour and promote it. I can get you on some dates with the Heavyweights. But you need to find sponsors to cover your costs."

"That's so tacky for me to be out there soliciting backers."

"Call yourself the executive producer. Movie guys do it all the time."

"Ray, you'd only have to make a few calls."

"That's the best I can do," he said, leaning back in his chair, with his hands behind his head. "Call me when you get more desperate."

Ray said he would set things up, but Angel knew she was on her own. She'd find the sponsors, arrange the dates, and promote it herself. *I'll cut out the middleman*, she thought. *Angel Donovan—executive producer—has a nice ring to it. Why didn't I think of it sooner?*

CHAPTER 20

CARMEN

Carmen was alone in the house and decided to do something she hadn't done in a long time. She went to her bedroom, locked the door, then pulled several shoeboxes from her closet, until she found the one she kept hidden in the back. After placing the box on her nightstand, she piled her pillows against the headboard for a backrest, sat on the bed, with the box in her lap, and opened it. There it was, just as she left it: a pack of Newports. She slowly unraveled the plastic string from the top of the pack and tapped out a cigarette. The pungent woody aroma jumped to her nostrils and even though it was past the expiration date, it seemed stronger than she remembered. Thinking about the smell, she got up, cracked a window, and turned on her ceiling fan. Carmen got back on the bed, then realized she didn't have a lighter. She got up again and searched her drawers and old purses. Her search yielded coins, mints, and old lipstick, but no lighter. She went to the kitchen and got matches from the junk drawer. She was almost to the stairs when her mother came in.

"Carmen, quick, turn on the news," Gloria said, as she picked up the remote control. "They're talking about the strike. They were streaming the news in the van."

Carmen stuffed the cigarette in her pocket, then watched the news report with her mother. "I can't believe the city won't budge on their offer."

"It's just as well. You could use some time off," Gloria said.

"It's not a vacation. I won't get paid, and when we do go back, there's twice as much work to do in less time. People say they want good schools, but they don't want to pay for them."

"Good thing you have the Diamonds tour to fall back on. The Lord does provide," Gloria declared.

"Surely the Lord will provide something else. I'm not interested in sentencing myself to time with Angela," Carmen said. "Besides, I am way out of shape."

"You and Gerald should walk the mall with me and Wilson. Three laps around the first floor is almost two miles. The new year is a good time to get these bodies in shape. And there are some really good sales."

"No thanks, Mama. Unless the sales are free, it's not in my budget."

"Who said anything about you spending money?" Gloria asked. "As you and Gerald walk, casually window-shop and mention how much you like this or that. I'll bet you can get him to buy you a little sumthin', sumthin'."

"Gerald and I are just friends," Carmen said, as she sat in the recliner and changed the channel.

"Still? You may be playing a little too hard to get. Don't let him get away. He's a keeper."

"Mama, you make him sound like a winning lottery ticket. We only went to a movie and he's not the last man in Memphis. I'll be fine." What her mother didn't know, was Carmen wasn't the only one in the Gerald Wells lottery. When they had gone to the movie, a lady who was with several other women, greeted Gerald and whispered something in his ear, oblivious to Carmen standing next to him.

She saw another woman arguing with him in the school parking lot, before getting back in her car and driving off. Even at Hope's concert, a *very* friendly lady, who had already spoken, came back and gave him her card. Whenever he stopped by her classroom, within a few minutes, the name Val would pop up on his phone. She knew from earlier conversations that wasn't his mother, sister, or daughter's name. He never offered an explanation and she didn't ask for one. Men brought drama, and she had enough to deal with.

"If not Gerald, then maybe you and that Eric Hamilton will rekindle things on the tour. I see him on TV. I'll bet he has lots of money," Gloria said.

"I know there's talk about climate change, but unless hell has frozen over, I am not working with Angela. Will you quit trying to pawn me off like an old spinster?" Carmen said, as she let the recliner back.

"I'm just looking out for you. That's my job. Gerald and the tour are a godsend, but you're as stubborn as the children of Israel."

"I wonder where it comes from," Carmen replied.

"Blame me if you want. I'm only trying to get you out of your way. Nothing wrong with making yourself available. Teaching is a noble profession, but there aren't many eligible bachelors walking around Fifth Street Middle. Someone is going to snap Gerald up if you don't," Gloria said. "I won't always be here. I want to see you secure and happy before I go."

"Don't talk like that, Mama. You're not going anywhere, anytime soon. I want to see me happy too, but I always strike out in the relationship department," Carmen said, shaking her head. "I don't know why black men are so contrary. Maybe I'll try a white man."

"You can try a purple man, they're all the same," Gloria said, with a dismissive wave.

"And how would you know this?"

"None of your business. And don't try to change the subject. You'd make money on the tour and you'd meet some men. That's a win-win," Gloria said, as she peeked through the curtains. "My ride's here. I'll see you in the morning."

"In the morning?" Carmen asked.

"I told you the Sexy Seniors are going to Hot Springs this weekend," Gloria said, pulling her packed rolling bag to the door.

"It's cold and raining. I hope you're wearing something other than those sandals. And isn't tomorrow your dialysis day?"

"I'll be okay," Gloria assured her.

"Wait a minute," Carmen said. "Isn't Mr. Wilson a member? I don't want any hanky-panky going on."

"Speak for yourself," Gloria said, as she winked at her daughter and walked out the door.

Carmen followed her mother to the door and put on the chain latch. She dug Angel's envelope out of the junk drawer, and found a pair of reading glasses. *Maybe I should at least see what I'm saying "no" to.*

CHAPTER 21

JADE

The Price Is Right theme song startled Jade. She didn't realize she had been sitting on the edge of the bed for two hours. Brian had stormed out after breakfast and made it clear what he wanted her to do. She hadn't moved since he left.

"Do you want to know what that girl just said to me?" Brian had asked.

Jade wanted to say "no." She knew from his tone, this wasn't going to be pleasant. Dawn could be disrespectful, but Jade didn't understand why Brian took things so personally. All teens were a challenge.

"She's got her music so loud, I can hear it all the way down the hall. I asked her to turn it down or put on her headphones, and she rolled her eyes at me, then slammed the door. I started to tell her not to slam my door, but I let it pass, showing more tolerance, as you suggested. I offered to take her to school since it's raining. Then when I went to her room to tell her to hurry up, she tells me she didn't ask me to take her in the first place. She walks past me and that Marquel dude picked her up. We told her not to associate with him. He is bad news. Obviously, what we say doesn't matter."

"I'll talk to her this afternoon," Jade promised.

"Why bother? We've given her too many second chances. I'm through."

"You're right. She must respect us and our rules," Jade said. "She can forget about going anywhere this weekend. Maybe she needs more household chores."

"Jade, you don't hear me. I said I'm through. We're through. We tried to provide a home for this kid. It's obvious she doesn't want it."

"Honey, let's..."

"No," Brian said, shaking his head. "Call the caseworker and tell her Dawn will be returning. Let's cut our losses and move on."

"She's not a car you return to the dealer. She's a person. She acts grown up, but she's still a child."

"Jade, she's not our child," Brian said softly. "It's not up to us to raise her."

"Then who will?" Jade asked.

"I don't know, but she's not our responsibility. I'm not arguing about it anymore. Call the caseworker. If you can't, I will. That one thousand dollars every month has come in handy, but it's not worth the aggravation."

"Is that what she is to you—extra income?" Jade asked.

"Of course not. I understand how important this is to you. We can still be foster parents. They told us in the orientation, every child doesn't fit every family. Let's ask for a different kid."

"Now you want to trade her in like a defective car?"

"Look, I'm not the bad guy because I want respect and peace in my house," Brian stated.

"But it's my house too. Let's try counseling again."

"I don't have time for counseling and you don't either. Seaside needs our full attention."

"You wouldn't say that if it were Lance or Tiffany."

"Lance and Tiffany would never talk to me the way she

does. I've got to go," Brian said, and grabbed his keys. "You call, or I will."

Jade was sitting in the same spot she was in when Brian left. He didn't understand and though he had tried, he needed to try harder. Jade decided to ask the caseworker to talk to Dawn, but sending her back was not an option. Then she remembered another option. Brian had accepted her decision not to join the Diamonds reunion tour, but he wasn't happy about it. Maybe she would reconsider. Brian's patience seemed to be waning just like their cash register receipts. She'd make a deal. She would do the Diamonds tour if he would let Dawn stay until she graduated. She'd work something out with Dawn and summer school and they would have to keep the caseworker from finding out. She turned the television off and went to the junk drawer to look for Angel's package. The Diamonds had given her a family once before. Maybe this time it could help save her family.

CHAPTER 22

CARMEN

As Carmen washed three, seldom-used wine goblets, she observed her mother sneak two brownies from the platter on the counter, wrap them in a paper towel, and slide them in her pocket. Just as she was about to confront Gloria, her sister came in with hot wings, nachos, and a fruit tray. Faye's husband, Mitchell, was out of town with his bowling league, and Gloria invited Faye to spend the night, saying she was looking forward to spending time with both her girls. Carmen had initially been irritated her mother hadn't checked with her first. But it was cold and rainy and she was looking forward to a fun family evening, with no talk of police or lawyers.

Carmen had bought enough junk food for a Super Bowl party, with Polish sausages, barbeque potato chips, corn chips and salsa, fried cheese sticks, pizza rolls, mini–ice-cream sandwiches, macadamia nut cookies, sangria, and Diet Dr Pepper on the menu. She had abandoned all pretense of dieting since she was losing weight due to David's legal nightmare. She knew she still needed to improve her eating habits. But not tonight.

David was putting his jacket on as Faye entered the

kitchen. "Going to watch the pay-per-view fight with Uncle Sonny," he said. "I'll catch you next time, Aunt Faye."

"Looks like it's a girls' night then. How's my favorite niece?"

"I'm leaving too," Hope said, as she grabbed a handful of potato chips. "I'm headed to a special choir rehearsal for the Black History Month program, and my ride should be here soon. I'll be glad when I get my license."

"Doesn't seem like you should be old enough to drive. We're getting old," Faye observed.

"*Mature* sounds better," Carmen said.

"I'm not old, so you can't be old," Gloria said, as she rose from the table and grabbed her purse.

"You're going out?" Carmen asked. "This shindig was your idea."

"I forgot, I'm sorry. Wilson and I are taking our mature selves to the lobster buffet at the casino. He has a two-for-one coupon that expires soon," Gloria explained as she walked out the door. "I don't feel much like playing, so we won't be late. Save me some wings."

"Since both of you have plans, I guess it will just be us," Carmen said. "We're going to stuff our faces, drink wine, and watch movies."

"You mean you don't have another date tonight?" Hope asked.

"Another date?" Faye asked.

"She didn't tell you? She went out twice last week," Hope tattled.

"You've been holding out on me. Who's this new boyfriend?"

"He's not a boyfriend. I'm too old for boyfriends anyway."

"Tell that to someone else," Faye said, as she turned to Hope. "Have you met him?"

"Yep. He came with her to my fall concert."

"Okay, he gets brownie points for that," Faye stated. "Where did you meet him?"

"He works at the school," Carmen said.

"Oh, a teacher. Sounds promising," Faye said, nodding her head approvingly.

"He's not a teacher," Carmen stated.

"Is he a guidance counselor?" Hope asked.

"No. He's on the school engineer staff."

"Really, Mom—the janitor?"

"I think he's the supervisor."

"Oh, excuse me, the head janitor," Hope quipped as she rolled her eyes.

"And what's wrong with being a janitor?" Carmen asked.

"Nothing, if that's the best you can do. But you're always telling us to go to college and get a good job. I didn't think you would settle for a janitor."

"I can't believe I'm raising a snob. As long as someone is kind and earns an honest living, that's what counts."

"Your mother is right," Faye said. "What a person does for a living does not define their character."

"I prefer a lawyer or banker with character, but I guess you lower your standards as you get older. At least he's got a nice car," Hope said, while grabbing her coat. "See you guys later."

Hope sprinted down the porch steps as Carmen waved to her girlfriend's mother. "Don't forget to keep something on your head," Carmen admonished. "It's just about cold enough to snow." Hope waved her hand without turning around. "What a blessing to be young and naïve. She'll learn, a single, straight black man with a job and his own place, is hard enough to come by," Carmen said, as she closed the door. "Prince Charming retired years ago. Adding more qualifications further dwindles the pool."

"So is that why you're settling for a married man?"

"Faye, if this is another lecture, save it. I've got enough problems, without you making jabs about Nathan." Gloria and Faye met Nathan when Carmen first began seeing him and he came over during a family gathering. They were noticeably cool toward him and had an intervention with Carmen as soon as he left.

"Did you know he's married?" Faye had asked.

"The devil is a lie," Gloria said. "I know I raised you better than that."

"Do you think he'd be hanging out over here if he was with his wife?" Carmen asked. "They're separated."

"And you believed him?" Faye asked.

"I know sometimes it's hard to resist an attentive, good-looking man," Gloria said. "But getting a divorce versus being divorced is the same as paying you back versus I'm going to pay you back. You can only spend one of them."

"That man isn't leaving his wife. His cousin goes to the same nail shop I do and she said—"

"Faye, I don't want to hear it," Carmen interrupted. "You handle your business and I'll handle mine."

"Okay, baby sister. Don't say we didn't warn you."

But, as Faye predicted, he reconciled with his wife. Months later, Faye casually mentioned that Nathan and his family were relocating to Atlanta. Carmen had already broken things off with him. But he did call whenever he came to town. Carmen saw no harm in it. He was just someone familiar to pass the time with.

"Who said anything about Nathan?" Faye asked while licking the honey-mustard hot wing sauce from her fingers. "I'm glad to hear you have a new boyfriend. I hope you checked this time to make sure he's not married."

"Gerald is a coworker. He's not my boyfriend, but for the record, he is single," Carmen said.

"Any man who works in a school should be good with kids. He sounds promising."

"I told you we aren't serious. Gerald Wells and I—"

"Wait a minute. Did you say Gerald Wells? Describe him to me."

"Why? You already have dirt on him?" Carmen asked.

"No, nothing like that. You say he's the janitor? Is his company Extreme Cleaning?"

"Now that you mention it, I think that's the company he works for. The district has outsourced so many jobs, sup-posedly to free up money for teachers. But we haven't seen it."

"Girl, forget all that. He doesn't work for them, he owns it."

"What are you talking about?" Carmen asked, as she poured another glass of sangria.

"Gerald Wells owns Extreme Cleaning and has a contract with the school district. We did floral centerpieces for his annual awards banquet. He has over one hundred employ-ees. He's loaded."

"Are you sure this is the same guy? If he's so rich, why is he cleaning toilets and floors?"

"You said he's not at your school every day. He probably wants to make sure his employees are doing their job. If folks don't know when the boss will show up, they tend to perform better. Isn't this him?" Faye asked, as she pulled up his company website on her phone.

"That's him," Carmen said. "But there's got to be another explanation..."

"It's about time you found somebody worth something. I know Mama liked him when she met him."

"They met when Gerald gave me a ride home when my car wouldn't start, and we arrived the same time as Mama's dialysis van. That's it."

"At least you know he has potential," Faye commented.

"Girl, please. He probably has women all over Memphis. I'm not trying to get involved with anybody right now."

"I'll admit, your dating choices have been questionable. But you can't cut yourself off completely. You'll never find anyone that way."

"I'm not looking. Besides, anybody single is gay, unemployed, crazy, or has baby-mama drama. And if they are halfway decent, they're certainly not interested in my two-hundred-pound behind."

"Don't be so sure. Gerald isn't hanging around your school just to ensure the floors are clean. And if you don't like Gerald, try a plus-sized dating website."

"So I can be scammed by some Nigerian hacker? No, thank you," Carmen replied. "Can we just watch the movie?"

"You mean watch the commercials," Faye said. "They seem longer than the movie. Don't you have Netflix or Hulu?"

"Nope. I've had to cut a lot of extra stuff now that I have a larger mortgage payment," Carmen said, as she headed to the kitchen. "I'm going to get some ice, you want something?"

"Wait. Look at this," Faye ordered, as she turned up the volume.

"This is News Channel Six with breaking news. After a long hospitalization, Officer Lawrence Sanders, injured last year in an accident with four reputed gang members, died this afternoon from injuries sustained in the accident. The district attorney vows to seek vehicular manslaughter charges against the gang members involved. More details at ten."

Chapter 23

DOREEN

Even though it was barely above freezing outside, Blessings' cafeteria was hot and Doreen fanned herself with the program. Blessings was hosting its annual Black History Month prayer breakfast and the room was full. With everyone dressed in African print garments, the room resembled the Zamunda scenes from *Coming to America*. The oldest person and the person with the most children and grandchildren present won prizes.

At times like this, Doreen missed her parents. Her father died shortly after she and her sister moved out, and she always felt guilty about it. Her mother died after witnessing the rise and fall of her career as Diamond and Gold. Mrs. Frazier never embraced her daughters' singing careers and said the girls were wasting their gifts and should be singing in church, or at least make a gospel record.

Today was especially hard because Doreen once again failed to get pregnant. Her doctor prescribed a new fertility drug and she even stopped working out, since she read vigorous exercise could interfere with fertility. Her period was five days late, and she just knew this time would be different. She sat near the sink and read the instructions, although she knew them by heart. Those three minutes seemed like thirty. She picked up the stick and saw two thin blue lines. One thick line and one thin line meant the test was positive. Doreen held the stick up to the window to ensure she was reading it correctly. Both lines still looked the same. No baby.

It's not fair, she thought, as she washed her hands. She and James had a stable, loving family and she couldn't understand why the Lord wouldn't want to bless them with their own child. She threw the test stick away when she heard James knocking.

"Are you okay?" he asked as he opened the bathroom door.

Doreen jumped, since she thought she had locked the door. As James's gaze went to the box in the garbage, she felt like a kid caught with their hand in the cookie jar.

"The test was negative and no lecture please," Doreen said, as she brushed past him.

"I wasn't going to lecture you, but I am worried. You're becoming obsessed with this baby thing. Why can't you be satisfied with the family we have?"

"I don't know," she said as tears rolled down her cheeks. "I love the kids, but I still want *our* child. Does that make me a bad person?"

"Of course not," James said, while dabbing her eyes with tissue.

"Sometimes I think God is punishing us for what we did."

"You can't focus on the past," James said.

"Don't you have regrets? Do you ever think about it?" Doreen asked.

"I used to. But I talk to people with a terminal diagnosis, or they're in danger of losing their house, or they've lost a spouse. We are so blessed. I can't help but be grateful. You did what you thought best," James advised.

"What do you mean, *I* did what *I* thought best?" Doreen asked with a tinge of anger. "I never would have done it if you hadn't practically forced me. Is that how you remember it, as something I did?"

"I try not to remember it at all. The Bible says God will throw our sins into the sea of forgetfulness, and we should do the same. Let's not rehash that old stuff."

It was easy for him to say, *let's not rehash it*, Doreen thought. He didn't carry around a useless womb. His emotions weren't tied to a monthly hormonal cycle, and the closer she got to forty, the more intense her mood swings became. God and James may have forgotten, but she hadn't. She remembered every detail.

Doreen had shown up late and high for a show at the Apollo, and James didn't come at all. The stage manager refused to let her go on, called a local drummer to replace James, and the girls performed without her. Ray was furious. He said promoters were demanding no-show clauses and threatening to cancel upcoming shows. He would smooth things over, but made them check into rehab.

They completed a twenty-one-day program and came out determined to stay clean. For future performances, Ray held Doreen and James's pay until the end of the tour, to prevent bingeing. In addition, their pay was cut to cover damages Peak Records had incurred. But what they thought was a temporary pay cut became permanent when Carmen quit a few months later.

James got a job as the afternoon DJ on an AM station and Doreen got a job as a bank teller. They were making poverty-level wages, but they were both clean and she couldn't have been happier. Leaving the industry was the best rehab.

One night, she had called James at work with a hint of good news, "Baby, eat light today. I'm preparing a special dinner."

"Forget cooking. I have something for us to celebrate too. We're going out."

"I thought we were sticking to our budget. Insurance is due this week."

"Okay, we'll stay home. I'll bring dinner." James came home with Red Lobster takeout and wine. Before Doreen could fuss about the expense, he made his announcement. "You can quit your job. I negotiated a contract with Peak Records."

"I didn't know you were talking to them. Carmen said she'd never come back. But I bet she will since Angel is gone. Are they replacing her, or will it be three of us, like before?"

"The contract isn't for the Diamonds. I called Ray a few weeks ago, and told him I had something for him. I sent a demo and he loved it," James said, as he opened the bottle and filled two paper cups. "You and I are going to record together."

"Really? Fooling around at home is one thing. Recording professionally is another. Besides, I'm already in a group."

"The Diamonds were great, but they're history. Angel has moved on, and you should too," James said.

"That's not fair to Carmen and Jade."

"I know they mean a lot to you, but there's no room for sentiment in this business. Besides, Carmen is the one who walked out," James said, pacing nervously. "Ray wants to meet with us next week. This is so great. Okay, I've jabbered enough. What's your good news?"

"We're going to have a baby," Doreen announced, with a big grin.

"Are you sure?"

"Yes, honey. I've already been to the doctor."

"I thought you were using birth control," James said, emptying his cup in three swallows.

"It's not foolproof, and that's not the reaction I was expecting."

"Timing's not good."

"Why not?" Doreen asked. "We're married and we're clean."

"But we'll be traveling. Ray already has tour ideas."

"The baby can come with us. People do it all the time," Doreen explained. "And what about your job at the radio station?"

"Why would I play other people's records, when I can record my own?"

"If that's what you want, okay. The baby and I will be fine," Doreen replied and began unloading the Red Lobster bag.

"Peak wants us both. They envision a routine like Sonny and Cher. They've looked at my songs and want to use them. They're my songs, but you're the face people know. It won't work without you," James said, while taking Doreen's hand.

"What are you saying, James? Are you saying I shouldn't have our baby?"

"Now isn't a good time."

"Because of the contract?"

"Because of the contract."

"And that's more important than our child?" Doreen asked, jerking her hand away.

"That's not what I'm saying. It's just..."

"I know exactly what you're saying, James, and I cannot believe your attitude."

"You don't understand what it's like, growing up without."

"Save the hard-luck stories. We didn't have a lot of money," Doreen said.

"You may not have had everything you wanted, but you had everything you needed. I never knew my father. I was thirteen when my mother died, and I was shipped down to Ace, Mississippi, to live with my grandmother. I adored Big Mama, but it was like stepping back in time. She cooked for a white family, walked to work, and brought me their son's hand-me-downs. Her house was on a dirt road and didn't even have a phone. Some days I didn't see or speak to anyone all day. She worked hard all her life, and one morning she just didn't wake up.

"I had aunts and uncles here and moved in with them, but they already had houses full of children. I was shuffled back and forth, and felt like a burden. I got a job at the Honey Pot washing dishes, as soon as I was old enough to work. The Heavyweights were starting out and played there a lot. One evening, their drummer didn't show up and they let me sit in. I was tall, so they thought I was older than I was. They were recording the next day and asked me to meet them at the Peak studio for the session. That's how I met Ray. I played on that session, and he hired me to do odd jobs. I was sixteen and I've been on my own ever since."

Doreen had heard this story before and knew in many ways her husband was still that anxious, lonely boy. But since his childhood had been so disjointed, she expected him to be excited about having his own children.

"I know you've heard all this before," James said excitedly, "but this is a once-in-a-lifetime opportunity to control our destiny."

"Explain the situation to Ray. What difference will a few months make?" Doreen pleaded.

"The deal is now, not in a few months," James said, kneeling in front of her, with his hands clasped in her lap. "In this business, a few months can be a lifetime."

"James, there's got to be another way," Doreen pleaded, shaking her head.

"Sweetheart, you know the road is no place for a baby. We're young. We can have lots of children. And I promise, we'll have enough money to spoil them rotten. Baby, it's up to you, and I know it's a sacrifice, but..."

"Shh," Doreen whispered, placing her index finger over

his lips. "Tell me about the contract." She forced a slight smile and listened, but didn't hear a word as she tried to process being heartbroken and mad at the same time. She was heartbroken about the baby, mad at James, and furious and disgusted with herself for not standing up to him. But she rationalized these were the sacrifices successful people made.

Most of James's predictions had come true. Diamond and Gold sold lots of records and made lots of money. They had a fan club, did a few network television guest appearances, and were even invited to Clive Davis's pre-Grammy party. However, with their new show, came their old so-called friends and their old habit. They promised each other they would only be recreational users this time. They quickly broke that promise and smoked and snorted up all the money they made. But the responsibility of serving as her mother's caregiver helped her approach rehab with a different mindset and commitment to getting clean. She and James combined Bible study with counseling and therapy, and were finally able to stay off drugs. Everything had happened as her husband predicted, except the part about lots of children. But it wasn't over yet. She was determined to choose their destiny, as James had promised. In fact, Destiny would be a pretty name for a girl...

ACT III

SAME OLD SONG

CHAPTER 24

CARMEN

Friday had finally come. The stretch between MLK Day and spring break always seemed extra-long. This week dragged due to miserable weather, state testing prep, and strike talk. And teaching hormonal middle school students that allegro, legato, and tremolo were musical terms and not Taco Bell menu items had worn Carmen out. Her plan was to make a quick trip to the bank, drive through Popeyes, then retreat to her bathtub with wine and Mary J.

She turned the key in the ignition, but the motor didn't turn over, even after several attempts. *Not today*, Carmen thought. She had one hour to get to the bank to make her mortgage payment. David's bond required mortgage payments to remain current, and today was the last of the month. Carmen had always paid her bills early and was proud of her 800 credit score. But now there was too much month at the end of her money. She called Lynn, who had left for the day, but agreed to come back for her. Carmen played solitaire on her phone while she waited, and jumped when there was a knock on her window.

"Gerald, you almost gave me a heart attack," she said breathlessly.

"Didn't mean to startle you. I noticed you just sitting here. Is everything okay?"

"My car won't start," Carmen said. "Lynn is coming to pick me up."

"Again? Maybe the battery needs a jump. Let me check."

I sure hope that's all it is, Carmen thought. She had no money for an expensive repair and definitely couldn't afford a new car.

Gerald pulled his Extreme Cleaning truck in front of her car and connected jumper cables. "It's not the battery," he stated, as he wiped his forehead with his handkerchief. "This is the second time in two weeks. I'll bet it's the alternator. I can get my mechanic to look at it."

"I'd appreciate that," Carmen said. "But I can't hang around right now. I need to run an errand before five o'clock. Lynn is coming to get me."

"I'm already here. Let me take you. I'll have my guy come get your car."

"Well," Carmen said, checking her watch. "If you don't mind, that would help a lot. I'll call Lynn."

They made it to the bank five minutes before closing. Carmen rushed to the door, but the security guard waved her away. She kept knocking, pointing to her watch, and saying words Gloria wouldn't approve of. Gerald came to the door and asked, "What's wrong?"

"I was here before five o'clock. You're my witness, but the lazy-ass workers won't let me in," Carmen shouted hysterically. "Isn't this illegal? I'm going to get the news stations out here. I cannot believe this bull—"

"Excuse me," Gerald said, as he stepped around her. He tapped on the door, waved, and like Moses parting the Red Sea, someone came and unlocked the door.

"Mr. Wells, you almost missed us. How are you doing?"

"Can't complain. How about you?" Gerald asked, as he stepped aside and motioned for Carmen to enter.

Carmen was so dumbfounded, she almost forgot what she came for. She was reminded of her Diamond days, when they were ushered beyond the velvet rope at any club they went to. She conducted her business, while stealing glances over her shoulder at Gerald, who was chatting with the manager. When she finished, the manager escorted them to the door, and Carmen was hoping he hadn't read her lips.

"Were you able to do what you needed?" Gerald asked, as he pulled out of the parking lot.

"Yes, thank you so much. I'm a little embarrassed, though."

"No big deal," Gerald said.

"Curiosity is killing me," Carmen said, as she turned to face him. "Is the manager your cousin or something?"

Gerald chuckled, then said, "Not a relative, but I do most of my banking at this branch."

"I do too, but they didn't open the door for me," Carmen said.

"I think they're more hospitable to their commercial customers. Between my payroll account, operating account, and personal accounts, they know me quite well. My secretary, Val, does most company transactions, but I remain involved."

"Payroll? You know, my sister said you owned the company. But I didn't believe her. And Val works for you?"

"Yes. Do you know her?" Gerald asked.

"Uh, no," Carmen stammered. "I'm embarrassed to confess this: I thought she was your girlfriend."

"I told you I'm not seeing anyone."

"You did, but guys always—"

"Look, judge me for me and not based on what other guys—whoever that is—do or don't do," Gerald said, a little irritated. "You don't have to snoop around or make assumptions. Ask me whatever you want to know."

"I'm sorry," Carmen said. "We're not dating or any-thing, so I didn't think—"

"So if we were dating, you'd be snooping through my phone and checking my odometer? Thanks for the warning."

"No, I would not," Carmen said with indignation. "I saw you arguing with your ex in the parking lot, and I couldn't figure out all these calls and texts."

"She was an ex, but not what you were thinking. She's an ex-employee with major issues. I even had to hire security to watch my offices."

"I didn't even know you had offices. Why didn't you tell me you owned the company?"

"You didn't ask."

"I'm impressed," Carmen said. "What other little sur-prises are you hiding?

"Stick around and find out," Gerald said.

CHAPTER 25

DOREEN

"How about going out for breakfast? We can drop the kids at school, get something to eat, then head to Blessings."

"I have a meeting this morning, But I'll be finished in plenty of time to get to the church," Doreen said, while putting the finishing touches on her makeup.

"You're working today?" James asked.

"Yes. This meeting was set up weeks ago. I told you what a coup it would be to get the Housing Foundation to participate in the CBI program. They're going to match all funds—"

"I rarely ask you to take off work, but today is different."

"You do funerals all the time while I'm at work. I doubt if anyone will even miss me."

"I'll miss you," James said.

"This meeting was scheduled weeks ago. If it were any other meeting, I'd reschedule."

"I guess Brother Sanders forgot to check your datebook before he died."

"That's not fair. I've worked hard on this proposal, and I'm the only female on the team. I know if I'm not there, one of the guys will take the credit, and it was my idea to start with."

"A man is dead and you're worried about office politics," James said, with an edge of disdain.

"I can do both. I'll be on time."

"On time is late. There will be lots of media and visitors. Never mind," James said. "I'll get Sister Mayes to assist."

"Honey, I'll be there. I won't let you down," Doreen said to the closing door.

The meeting with the Housing Foundation went well, and Doreen had just enough time to get to the funeral. As she was changing her shoes, her secretary announced she had a visitor.

"I really have to leave," Doreen said into the speakerphone. "Who is it?"

"It's your bestest friend in the whole wide world," a familiar voice said as Doreen's door opened.

"Carmen, it's great to see you, but I wish you'd called," Doreen said, as she hugged her. "I was just leaving."

"This is a business call. But it won't take long. Do you have a few minutes?"

"Just a couple," Doreen said, stealing a glance at the clock on her desk.

"These can't be the kids," Carmen said, picking up the picture frames on Doreen's desk. "They've gotten so big. And Paige looks just like her—Sophia."

"Yes, she does," Doreen said, and moved the folders and cold coffee to the side.

She knew Carmen hadn't meant any harm, but every now and then something reminded her that she wasn't the kids' biological mother. Her own baby would've been a teenager by now, and she often wondered what it would have looked like. What college would he or she be getting ready to attend? Did that abortion mess up her reproductive organs? Maybe if she'd had the first baby, she wouldn't have miscarried the others, she wouldn't have relapsed, she could have helped Sophia more, and her mother wouldn't have been as stressed and sick. She often thought maybe she worked so hard to ease the guilt she felt for those decisions. But Doreen knew these weren't productive thoughts and was usually able to redirect her musings—by working even harder. "I'm kind of in a hurry. What's going on? Have you heard from Angel?"

"No. This visit isn't about the Diamonds," Carmen said. "I'll get straight to the point. The police officer hurt when David was in the car with those boys has died."

"I know. He was a member of our church. I'm headed to his memorial service."

"His death elevates David's charges. I feel bad for the officer and his family, but this is basically a traffic accident. I'm not satisfied with David's attorney, and we're hiring someone else. I've gotten recommendations, but none of them come cheap. I need a loan."

"Home equity isn't my department, but I can start the application and make a few calls," Doreen said, while taking a notepad from her drawer.

"It's not a home equity loan."

"Then what were you planning to use as collateral?"

"Can't you make a loan without collateral?" Carmen asked.

"How much do you need?"

"No one will touch the case for less than fifty thousand, and they want half up front."

"Carmen, that's a lot of money. I really can't do anything without collateral," Doreen said.

"I own my car free and clear. It's worth around six thousand. That's more than ten percent."

Doreen shook her head. "I know you don't want to pledge your house, but that's the only..."

"It's pledged for David's bail," Carmen said. "You never make loans without collateral?"

"We do, but generally those borrowers keep substantial deposits in the bank. Maybe we can increase your credit card limit. I'll have to check your credit…"

"I'll save you the time," Carmen said, with a wave of her hand. "My score has dropped over two hundred points, since all this mess started. I don't guess you use an average."

"Afraid not," Doreen replied, returning the notepad to her drawer.

"I've banked here almost twenty years. Doesn't that count for something?"

"Of course, but the amount of your deposits is as important as the length of time."

"In other words, only people who don't need a loan, can get one."

"Carmen, I don't make the rules. You know I would help you if I could."

"I also know there are exceptions to every rule. What happened to, 'If you need me for anything—just ask?' –Well, I'm asking."

"If I could approve the loan, how would you repay it?"

"I can pledge my future royalty checks," Carmen answered.

"Unless your formula is different from mine, those checks are unpredictable. Maybe James and I can do something. Let me talk to him after the funeral. I really need to get going."

"Never mind," Carmen said, as she picked up her purse and stood. "After all I've done for you, I have never asked you for anything. When you smoked up all your money, who paid your rent? When your drunk ass woke up in a stranger's bed, who lied to James for you? Who got your car from the repo man—twice? I never expected anything in return because that's what friends do. But I'm not asking for me. I'm asking for David, your godson."

"Carmen, I know you're upset, but can you lower your voice?"

"I can do better. I'll leave."

"I'll call you later, we can—"

"Don't bother, First Lady Golden. So sorry to have disturbed you."

Doreen had never seen Blessings so crowded. Television station vans and police cars lined the street and the parking lot was full. She double-parked behind James since someone had parked in her reserved space. She darted in the side door and arrived in time for the family processional. Her usual spot had been taken, and Gloria signaled to another usher to bring her a chair. She smiled at her husband sitting in the pulpit and although he nodded, even from thirty feet, she could tell he was not pleased.

It seemed strange to see so many white people in the audience. *Too bad we only unite for tragic occasions*, she thought. Extra chairs had been placed in the aisles and people were standing in the back. The bishop read the opening scripture, and Sister Rachel sang a stirring solo. Officer Sanders's sister read a poem and sang "The Lord's Prayer." The funeral director closed the casket and ushers rushed to comfort the family as their wails of grief were no longer restrained. A deacon read the obituary, then introduced James.

A montage of Officer Sanders's life scrolled across the screen, and from the audience reaction to his cute baby pictures and Michael Jackson dance moves at his wedding, all eyes were on the video. But Doreen's eyes were on her husband as he approached the podium. Sister Rachel, who seemed to be wearing more makeup than she remembered, was two steps behind him and placed a glass of water and a handkerchief next to his Bible. James spoke from the book of Ecclesiastes about time and making the most of it. She marveled that this man who never went to church as a child and thought King James wrote the Bible, was now a Bible scholar.

When James finished, a bugler played taps, and the commanding officer presented the American flag to the widow. The mayor spoke last. His comments were short, although not necessarily sweet. He ended by saying, "I know we're in a house of worship. And I know we are to forgive. We forgive because we are a loving community. But I will not forget. Mrs. Sanders, we will not forget. And we will make sure the guilty parties do not forget. We'll make sure they get plenty of time to think about the pain they have caused. Plenty of hard time."

Despite the somber occasion, the church erupted in cheers. Doreen hoped their elation was not at David's expense.

CHAPTER 26

JADE

"Dawn, honey, you can't sit with earbuds in your ear. You need to hear what's going on," Jade said, as they sat in the station, waiting for the announcement to board the next bus to Austin.

"I can see it on the screen," Dawn replied without looking up from her phone.

"Then how about removing your earbuds so you can talk to me?" Jade asked.

"I'm sorry. This new phone is so cool. Thanks so much for getting it for me."

She and Brian had agreed to a strict budget, but Jade felt a phone was a necessity. She wanted Dawn to be able to call and she wanted to be able to call Dawn. Dawn was only going three hours away for a week, but Jade also indulged Dawn's request for two new pair of shoes, three pair of jeans, coordinating shirts, and a light jacket.

Dawn had laughed at the idea of a bra pouch when Jade showed it to her. "Mrs. Randolph taught me to keep some money pinned in a handkerchief in my bra. That advice came in handy when the Diamonds were constantly on the move," Jade recalled.

"I won't be in any big crowds where I have to worry

about pickpockets," Jade replied. "I can keep everything in my phone case."

Jade ignored Dawn's skepticism, and added it to the underwear, socks, backpack, and snacks in their cart at Wal-mart. Jade had been wrapped up in the trip preparation. Now that they were at the bus station, she was starting to feel sad. This wasn't the spring break she had envisioned.

She had planned to take Dawn with her to visit Lance in San Diego. Dawn had never been to California, or even on an airplane, and was looking forward to the trip. Jade had expected opposition from Brian. She was prepared to per-suade him this was educational for Dawn. If that didn't work, she'd shed some motherly tears about how much she missed Lance. But to her surprise, he didn't object. He said Rita wouldn't mind working extra hours.

The first change in plans came when Lance called to tell them he was being deployed and would be at sea for seven months. He wouldn't even have time to squeeze in a quick trip home before he left. Jade had been a military wife, and understood how life could change in an instant. But she was still worried and disappointed. Brian reassured her Lance would be fine and encouraged her to go on the trip anyway, since the tickets were nonrefundable. He even made her hotel reservation.

The next change in plans came during Miss Branch's last home visit. She praised Jade for the turnaround in Dawn's attitude and schoolwork. If Dawn went to summer school, she would be able to graduate next year. Dawn would turn eighteen in November and would no longer be in the foster care program. Miss Branch informed Jade once Dawn was eighteen, they would no longer receive foster care payments. Jade didn't think this was something they should have discussed in front of Dawn, but she assured Miss Branch that Dawn had a home with her and they considered her family.

Miss Branch then informed them Dawn's mother had

completed her court-ordered program, was employed, and wanted to see Dawn. She had moved to Austin to get a fresh start. Dawn's mother could initiate actions to have her transferred to Travis County. But by the time the paperwork made it through the system, Dawn would be eighteen anyway. Her mother had sent money for a bus ticket and wanted Dawn to visit during spring break.

Jade was crushed when Dawn quickly agreed to the visit. Where had this woman been the last two years? How could Dawn leap at the chance to visit someone who had abandoned her like an empty beer can? She had not called, or sent a birthday card, Christmas card, an email, or a text. Yet, Jade understood. No one wants to feel unwanted. And as much as she had tried to show Dawn love, she knew it wasn't the same. Jade also felt a twinge of jealousy. As selfish and irresponsible as Dawn's mother was, she felt enough mother love to get herself together and reach out to her child. Jade couldn't help wondering why her own mother hadn't been able to do the same.

Jade's mother showed up backstage at a Diamonds concert in Dallas. She invited her to their dressing room, to wait until they finished interviews and photos. When she returned to the dressing room, her mother was gone and so was her purse. A few months later, her mother sent a message via the Randolphs that she had been in a car accident, exhausted her benefits, and was on the verge of homelessness. Against her better judgment, Jade sent money, only to later see her mother on FriendSpace with some guy in Reno. When she discovered her mother had been the source of an unflattering tabloid article, accusing her of living the high life and leaving her family in poverty, Jade cut her off. Angel was ecstatic and said it meant they were celebrities. Jade was furious, hurt, and embarrassed. Occasionally Jade received letters from her mother, which she threw away unopened.

She hoped Dawn wasn't heading for a similar heartbreak,

but hid her concerns as they walked to the loading area. "Remember to call the minute she picks you up," Jade reminded Dawn for the tenth time.

"I will. Don't you and Brian get too freaky in the house unsupervised."

Jade laughed and stepped back as Dawn excitedly handed the driver the Navy duffel bag Lance sent her. Jade waved when she saw Dawn's head pop up in the window, and stayed until the bus had pulled out and turned the corner, out of her sight.

Jade and Brian had spent the weekend as a couple, their first time alone in years. It was a perfect spring weekend. It was late enough for trees and bushes to be fully leafed, but still too early for Houston's legendary bugs, heat, and humidity. They ordered Chinese food and ate on their patio, before going to a movie Thursday evening. Friday they even drove to Seaside in the same vehicle. Brian didn't linger after the restaurant closed as he usually did, and they were home in bed by midnight. They did something in bed they hadn't done in ages—they talked. Jade didn't realize how long it had been since they had talked about something other than their children, Dawn, bills, or Seaside. If this was a movie, they would hold hands, have passionate sex, and fall in love all over again. But this wasn't a movie, and instead of re-kindling their love, Jade discovered how different they were. Twenty years ago, Brian had seemed stable and mature. Now he seemed intolerant and boring. And even more discon-certing, he had become a Republican.

Saturday morning, the house was eerily quiet. Brian left early for Seaside and Jade lingered over coffee while she downloaded a GED study guide. Since Dawn wasn't going to San Diego, she figured she could use the trip to catch up on her studying. As she was headed to get her glasses, the doorbell rang. The doorbell rang again, followed by knocking, and when she looked through the peephole, Jade quickly unlocked the door. "What are you doing here?" she asked. "I wasn't expecting you until next weekend."

"I hope I'm not in your way."

"Dawn, you know this is your home. Get in here, girl," Jade said, as she hugged her and grabbed the black garbage bag. She wanted to ask what happened in Austin, but knew it couldn't be good.

Dawn devoured the French toast and bacon Jade fixed, like she hadn't eaten in days. Jade quietly worked on her GED study guide. After eating every crumb on her plate, Dawn asked, "Did you know Monica is pregnant?"

Jade cringed when Dawn said her mother's name. She hated to hear children refer to their parents by their first names. "No, I didn't."

"That's why she sent the ticket. She wants me to move in with her," Dawn confided. "My brothers are in San Antonio with their father, and my sisters are in a foster home in Dallas. She says if I moved to Austin with her, we could be a family again. I don't know where she gets 'again' from. We were never a family."

"Do you think you want to live there after graduation?" Jade asked.

"She wants me to come in May when school's out."

"But you can't go to summer school if you leave, and you won't graduate next year."

"She says I can get a GED," Dawn stated. "Then I can bypass the school stuff and get started on my career. I think I want to be a pilot. Flying would be pretty cool."

"Employers consider it a second-class diploma, and the

test isn't easy. GED is out," Jade declared. "There's a three-week break between the end of summer school and the fall semester. I suppose you could visit then."

"She's pregnant, and the baby is due in June. She only gets six weeks' maternity leave. If she doesn't go right back, she'll lose her job."

"So that's the deal. She wants you to babysit. Where is her husband?" Jade asked.

"You're kidding, right?" Dawn asked.

"Okay, where is the baby's father?"

"He's locked up."

Jade exhaled, struggling to contain her anger. "So, her boyfriend gets locked up, then she calls you."

"He wasn't locked up when I got there," Dawn replied. "Monica went to work, and I was asleep on the couch. Next thing I know, this bastard is naked, crawling on top of me. I screamed and kicked his little dick. He grabbed my foot when I tried to run away, and I whacked him over the head with a flowerpot. I ran in the kitchen and held him off with a butcher knife when the police knocked the door in. A neighbor had called 911. The police saw me in my night-gown and him in his birthday suit and arrested him. Since he was on probation, they automatically took him to jail. When Monica came back, she said it was my fault and I always ruin everything."

"I am so sorry," Jade said, as she wiped tears from Dawn's smooth, cream-colored cheeks.

"She spent the rest of the day locked in her room, and the next day she left for work without speaking to me. That night she came in with two steak dinners from the restaurant where she works and apologized and said they probably wouldn't have stayed together anyway. Then she said she would make it up to me and asked me to move in with her.

"I told her I was doing good here and had caught up

enough that I can graduate next year. Then she got mad and said I owed her. If I hadn't been born, my sister's father would have married her, and everything would've been different. She said if anything happened to my little brothers and sisters in foster care, it would be my fault, because I had the chance to help bring them home and didn't," Dawn said, while looking at the floor. "She accused me of picking you over her, my real mother, and said I was only a paycheck to you."

"I hope you know that's not true. I couldn't love you more if I had given birth to you," Jade said softly. Her voice was calm, but inside she was seething. *What kind of mother deliberately hurts her child's feelings?* she thought.

"I believe you. When she went to bed, I packed my bag, wrote her a note, and left. I thumbed a ride to the bus station and waited for the first bus this morning."

"Oh my God! Don't you know how dangerous that is?"

"I didn't know what else to do. Jade, I want to finish school. I didn't care about it before, but now I do. Why am I selfish because I don't want to quit and babysit for her?" Dawn asked between sobs. "I hate her."

"You listen to me," Jade said. "She's your mother and they're your siblings, but don't let her put this guilt trip on you. Don't take on the burden of hating her either. That weighs you down, while she goes on her merry way. You can do more for yourself and your family by graduating than by dropping out. You'll be an example for them and preparing to be self-sufficient. Nobody told your mother to get pregnant. She knows how to get birth control. I was hoping you'd continue your education, but at least finish high school. If you still want to leave, then go. But don't quit school. Dropping out is one of my biggest regrets."

"But once I graduate, I'll be out of the foster program—"

"I'm not here for money," Jade said. "It's a piddly amount anyway. I volunteered because I was once in your shoes and

I wanted to help someone else. Now, it's not about foster care. It's about family. You're my daughter and I want what's best for you. Do you understand?"

Dawn sniffled and nodded her head. "But what about my brothers and sisters?"

"I don't know," Jade answered. "But there has to be a solution that doesn't require you to sacrifice your future for your mother's bad choices. For now, maybe you can Face-Time them every few days. And if you want to visit them, I'll try to arrange it with Miss Branch. Are we good?"

Dawn nodded her head in agreement.

"Well, looks like we're going to San Diego after all," Jade said. "I'll go find you a suitcase."

CHAPTER 27

ANGEL

"Daddy, this is a great surprise," Angel said, as she hugged her father, inhaling his familiar Polo cologne. "You should have told me you were coming."

"I didn't want to impose. This is just a quick weekend trip," he said as they linked arms and walked through the hotel lobby to the restaurant.

"And you knew I would have insisted you stay with me."

"The hotel is fine. The view of Lake Michigan is breathtaking. After dinner, you can come see my room."

"I'll come visit, but as far as seeing your room, I've seen enough hotel rooms to last three lifetimes," Angel said, then asked the waiter to replace her water for one with no ice. They placed their orders and caught up on Crystal, her tour plans, and her nonexistent love life.

"Angela, I came to Chicago because I want to discuss something with you and I didn't want to do it over the phone."

"What is it? You're not sick, are you?" Angel asked as she put her fork down.

"No, no. Nothing like that."

"Is Mother all right? I know I'm a payment behind. I

spoke with the finance office and told them to expect a check next week. Are they hassling you?"

"No, the folks at Rainbow Village couldn't be nicer. And actually, the bill is three months behind. That's sort of what I want to discuss with you."

"Daddy, don't worry about it. I'll take care of it."

"Babygirl, there's no easy way to say this, so I'll just say it. I'm divorcing your mother."

"What?" Angel mumbled as she choked on her blackened shrimp.

"I'm not abandoning her. I'll take care of her, as I always have. But I'm retiring next year, and I can't afford to keep her at Rainbow Village. You can pretend, but I know you can't afford it either. If she were single, she'd be eligible for much more government assistance."

"I can't have my mother on government charity," Angel said indignantly.

"It's not charity. That's what it's there for."

"There has to be something we can do less drastic than divorce," Angel said.

"I met with a financial planner and we could lose the house if I don't do this. Rainbow Village wants me to mortgage the house to guarantee payments. The house is paid for—thanks to you—and I won't risk losing it. I've found a less expensive place for your mother."

"That's the least I could do, Daddy. I felt bad I didn't buy you a new house."

"Like I told you then, there was just the two of us. What would we do in some big house? Besides, you've given us more than enough. I've been to Africa and Europe, places I never imagined going. I've even been to the Super Bowl."

"You were so excited when the kicker punted and made the free score."

"You don't punt...oh, never mind. That's my point. You don't even like football and you took me to games.

You've been generous to a fault. You should've been paying off your own home. I'm not going to risk the house, because it's yours too. But there is something else."

"What else?" Angel asked.

"I've been seeing someone."

"Daddy, it's okay," she said, while patting his hand. "There's nothing to be ashamed of. Therapy is healthy. A few years ago, I was going every week. Between my ex and the record company, I thought I was losing my mind. Talking to—"

Her father cleared his throat, then interrupted, "That's not quite what I meant. I've been seeing someone special. She and I—"

Angel coughed and withdrew her hand. She tried to speak, but kept coughing, and her eyes began to water.

"Are you okay?" her father asked.

Angel nodded affirmatively and gulped her ice water.

"I know this is a shock. But I wanted you to hear it from me and I want you to meet her. She's in the room."

"You brought her here?" Angel asked in horror.

"Yes. I wanted Lydia to finally meet you."

"Finally? You make it sound like it's been going on awhile. So Lilly or Lia or whatever her name is, isn't content to be a chick on the side. Now she wants you to dump Mother?"

"Babygirl, it's not like that at all."

"So it's in sickness and health, except for Alzheimer's. I can't believe you're doing this."

"I've had almost fifty good years with your mother. We were married twelve years before you came along. The doctors told us we couldn't have children. We were content, but when you came, our lives were perfect. Now she's slipping away. Your mother barely knows me."

"But, Daddy—"

"Consider my point of view. I'll be seventy-two this

year. For a black man, I'm living on borrowed time. I'm just trying to make the best of a tough situation."

"I guess you want to get your freak on without feeling guilty," Angel stated, and threw her napkin on the table.

"Don't talk to me about being selfish. Who has been with your mother while you've been flitting around the world, sending a check or gift every now and then? I'm not blaming you. I'm happy you did those things. Now I want you to be happy for me. Can you come upstairs?"

"I'm not happy for you and no, I won't come meet your mistress. And I hope you're not planning on moving her into my mother's house." Angel grabbed her Coach bag and left.

I cannot believe him, she thought. *He probably got a hold of Viagra and is trying to make up for lost time. I won't have my mother in some raggedy old folks' home. Rainbow Village is one of the best, and my mother is not moving.*

Chapter 28

CARMEN

The time had come to make the call. Carmen sat on her bed, then scrolled through her contacts for Vernon's name. She usually relayed messages through Hope, but this conversation couldn't wait.

She and Vernon met in their college history class. To pacify her mother, she squeezed in a few classes around her Diamonds schedule. She and Vernon were in the same study group and he made sure she got class notes when she was touring. His gregarious personality and confidence attracted her. He said her curves and dimples attracted him, then he fell in love with the smart and sassy woman underneath those curves and dimples.

They got married the last time the Diamonds played Las Vegas. They initially lived on her royalty checks. However, once she left the group, her royalties were mired in a lawsuit and dwindled to almost nothing, while their family and bills grew. Vernon left school and found a job with decent pay and lots of overtime, but she found out his overtime wasn't all work-related. After one too many lies, she changed the locks, put his stuff in Hefty bags, and took it to his girlfriend's house.

She was devastated when her marriage ended, but there

was no time for regret—she had two children to take care of. She quit her job, got student loans, and attended school full-time. Even when she was on television, playing stadiums and showering her mother with gifts and shopping sprees, Gloria wanted her to attend college. Carmen had always wanted to teach. Singing was something she did for fun. So she combined the two and majored in music education.

Vernon got a job at a car dealership and given his excellent lying skills, became a top salesman. He married the owner's daughter and was now a company vice president. He was also a deacon in his church and recently appointed to the Downtown Commission. Despite his increased income, Carmen hadn't requested more child support. She had been able to take care of her children on her own. Until now. She needed his help. David needed his help.

When Officer Sanders died, the court escalated David's charges and revoked his bail. Their attorney said this was a formality and his bail would be restored after the arraignment. David had to spend six days in jail until the hearing and Carmen needed more money for legal fees.

After the bail hearing, Attorney Peters asked Carmen to stop by his office. When she got there, he spent fifteen minutes on the phone, then said, "Miss Payne, we have some decisions to make. I've been informed the other young men have reached plea deals. The driver has pled to grand theft auto and vehicular manslaughter, and the other two young men have pled guilty to an accessory charge and a drug possession charge. The two young men will probably get eighteen months and a fine up to five thousand dollars. The district attorney is offering David the charge of accessory after the fact, but I will argue for a simple drug possession charge. The sentence could range from probation to three hundred and sixty-four days in jail. But I'm pretty sure I can get it classified as a misdemeanor with probation. Of course, there's no guarantee."

"I know you didn't call me down here to tell me about a plea deal," Carmen said. "You think calling it a misdemeanor makes it more palatable? Having a drug charge on his record will ruin his future. Those boys can do what they want. David is innocent."

"I would be negligent if I didn't encourage your son to consider these options. We have seven days to respond."

"We don't need time. The answer is *no*," Carmen declared.

"Miss Payne, I mean no disrespect, but your son is an adult. This must be his decision. If he rejects this plea deal and is convicted, he could face up to six years and have a felony record."

"What are we paying you for if he's just going to plead guilty?" Carmen asked in a raised voice. "Your job is to prove him innocent, not help send him to jail."

"My job is to represent him, which includes telling him all available options."

"Mr. Peters, would you advise your son to plead guilty?" Carmen asked.

After clearing his throat, he responded, "As I said, David needs to know his options."

"And as I said, I just want you to do your job," Carmen replied, as she found her keys and walked out. She would have fired him right then, but they had already spent thousands. Hopefully, she had made herself clear. He should focus on David's freedom, not his sentence. But she was still considering a change. Vernon knew important people; maybe he could help.

"Payne residence," the housekeeper answered.

"I'd like to speak with Vernon," Carmen stated.

"Mr. Payne is in his study. May I take a message?"

"No, you may not. This is an emergency. Please tell him Carmen is calling."

"Your last name?"

"He knows," Carmen said.

"I'll see if he wants to be disturbed," the housekeeper replied curtly.

"Carmen, I don't have much time. What's the emergency?" Vernon asked when he finally answered.

"The emergency is that when Officer Sanders died, they picked David up and the judge increased his bail. I thought you were coming to the hearing."

"My schedule was crazy and then—"

"You know what—I don't give a rat's ass about your schedule. That's not why I called anyway. I need money."

"Is my payment late? I've been so busy lately, I lost track. I gave Hope some money to get her hair braided, but I know that's not technically considered child support."

"I'm not referring to the measly check you send that doesn't even cover their health insurance. I need ten thousand dollars tomorrow morning for David's bail," Carmen said. "I want to be there at eight o'clock. You can meet me at court, or stop by here before I leave, or I can come by your house."

"Whoa. I don't have that kind of money."

"Tell that bullshit to someone else," Carmen said, as she closed her bedroom door. "I have never hassled you about money because I can take care of my children. But this is an emergency. I've drawn on my home equity line, pledged the house, and borrowed from my retirement account. We're barely making it from paycheck to paycheck, and I need to pay the lawyer. Calling you was my last resort."

"Like I said. I don't have that kind of money," Vernon said.

"Then get it. Put your kids in public school. Tell your precious wife to get a job. Max out your credit cards like I did. I don't care what you do, but you need to do something, and do it quickly."

"God is the best lawyer. We just need to pray," Vernon

said. "This is only a test and God never gives us more than we can bear. Things may look—"

"I'll go to church for a sermon," Carmen interrupted. "I know you don't want me to tell reporters that Commissioner Payne won't help his own son. Are you going to help or not?"

"I'll bring you a cashier's check tomorrow."

It was almost noon when David was released, but he said he wanted breakfast. Carmen was in such a good mood, she invited Vernon to join them. Carmen fixed pancakes from scratch, David's favorite breakfast, with cheese grits, Hope's favorite. Seeing Vernon and David together reminded her of their early days and she was thankful he had come through.

When Vernon left, David went to work out and Hope went to work. Carmen did housework, called a few creditors, then relaxed in the recliner to watch *House Hunters*. But apparently, *House Hunters* was watching her, because two hours later, she was awakened when her daughter came in.

"Hey there," Carmen said, as she stretched. "This hasn't been much of a spring break, with you working every day. We'll take a big trip next year."

"That's okay, Mom. I've got almost forty hours already this week, so this will be a really good paycheck. And we've been so busy, the time goes by fast."

"Then you must be starved. I'll start dinner."

"Sounds good, Mom, but I stopped at the food court before I came home. Maybe later."

Carmen turned on the television on her kitchen counter, then searched her freezer for an easy meal to prepare. As she pulled chicken wings out, a news flash caught her attention. The board rejected the union's offer and teachers were going to strike. "Damn," Carmen mumbled.

She poured a glass of wine, sat at the kitchen table, and read through her work and union emails for updates. Two glasses of wine later, she jumped when her phone vibrated. "Hey Nathan," she said in a groggy voice.

"Wow, you sure sound sexy."

"I'm tired. Between David's case, my mother's health, work, and now a strike, I don't know if I'm coming or going. To top it off, the girls are considering a Diamonds reunion tour."

"You can't be serious. Cher and Tina Turner toured well into their sixties, but I don't think you all fit that category."

"First of all, we're a long way from sixty. And second—"

"Sorry. I didn't mean it the way it sounded."

"How did you mean it? Nobody wants to see my old, fat behind?"

"I do. I'm your number one fan."

"So I'm old and fat?"

"No. That's not what I meant either. You're mighty touchy today."

"I've got a lot going on," Carmen responded. She didn't mention one of the things she had going on was Gerald. And he was there for her, in a way no man had ever been. He fixed her leaky faucets, changed her oil, and even bought her new tires. Some women wanted furs and jewelry, but tires impressed Carmen. First, because he did it without being asked and second, because they hadn't been intimate. He insisted there were no strings, he just wanted to help her and David. For once, Hope didn't turn up her nose, which was a major endorsement, and Gloria was sold the first time she met him.

"Sounds like you need a visit from Dr. Feelgood," Nathan said. "I can't talk right now, but I just wanted to hear your voice. I'll be there this weekend. Can't wait to see you."

There was a time when her calendar revolved around Nathan's availability. But those days were gone. She wasn't in love with Gerald, but she was in serious like, and she didn't want to mess it up. Spring was a time to shed the old and it was past time to shed Nathan.

The strike news zapped her energy, so she put the wings back in the freezer and decided to go grab something from Popeyes. As she locked her door, Gerald drove up. "Thought you could use some company," he said, as she walked to his truck. "Hop in. I heard about the strike. Negotiations may go down to the wire, but I'm sure both sides will agree to a compromise."

"You've been watching too much Joel Osteen, but your optimism is one of the things I like about you," Carmen said.

"So you like me?" Gerald asked, as he leaned over the center console and pulled her toward him. They kissed as though they were lovers parting for war. "I like you too."

"That was more than an 'I like you' kiss," Carmen said softly.

"I know we said no strings, but I believe I want some strings," Gerald said, with a smile. "I see no reason we shouldn't take this to the next level. I want you to meet my mother and my daughter, and I want to stop mopping outside your classroom. I know you have some family challenges right now. Hopefully, I can make things easier."

When Carmen didn't respond, Gerald said, "I'm doing all the talking. Did I misread your feelings?"

"No. It's just that I have some loose ends to tie up," Carmen said.

"Is that what he's called?" Gerald asked. "Handle your business, and I'll do the same. Now, what's for dinner? Want me to go get something?"

"I was on my way to get chicken," Carmen said.

"I'll go. Text me what you want." As she and Gerald kissed again, a car horn startled them both, when Faye pulled in front of the house to drop off Gloria.

"Do you two need a room?" her mother teased as she walked toward the door.

"I think we do," Gerald whispered in Carmen's ear. "But I've waited this long, I'll wait a few more days. I hope you're ready."

Carmen stood in the driveway and waved as he drove away. When she went inside, her daughter greeted her with, "Ooooh, Mom has a boyfriend."

"I didn't know I had an audience," Carmen said, as she closed the door and rushed past her daughter and mother. If she had been lighter skinned, her flushed cheeks would have given away her steamy thoughts. She pulled up Nathan's number, but instead of calling him, fell back on her pillow, with a beaming grin on her face. *I'll call him tomorrow*, she thought, then exhaled.

CHAPTER 29

DOREEN

"I thought we were finished with winter for this year. I cut my jog short," James said, as he rubbed his hands together. "That harsh wind was going straight to my bones."

Doreen fluffed her pillow and turned toward the wall.

"The kids left just in time. I saw on the news it's warmer in Chicago today than in Memphis," James said, as he untied his Adidas.

Doreen pulled the sheet over her head.

"Did you have anything planned for today? How about lunch and a matinee?" James asked.

Doreen heaved a big sigh and didn't move.

"Or I could get in bed with you," James teased, pulling the sheet back. "That would be one way to generate some heat."

Doreen glared at him, then pulled the sheet back over her head.

"Since you're giving me the silent treatment, just listen. The kids are spending spring break with their father. We had him investigated like you suggested, and I visited his home and took pictures for you when I went to preach in Maywood. Sophia would want her kids to spend time with their father. There's enough love to go around."

"How long do you think Lucas will be satisfied with occasional holiday visits?" Doreen asked as she sat up.

"You're talking to me now?" James asked.

"I've been trying to talk, but you won't listen. You're on his side."

"I'm on the kids' side. Would you rather they believe their father is some deadbeat drug addict who doesn't care about them? Knowing someone else loves them can only be beneficial. The boys were so excited at the airport. You should have come."

"They aren't old enough to know better. That's why they need our protection. Paige sees him for what he is. She won't even talk to him," Doreen said.

"She's older and remembers more. Let her come around in her own way and time. Her own way means not filling her mind with stories about how terrible Lucas was."

"Am I lying?"

"No, but people can change. God can work wonders. We weren't angels, you know," James reminded her.

Doreen rolled her eyes and turned away from him.

"You can pout, but I'm not wasting a beautiful day. The usher board is having a fish fry today. I'll be at the church," he said as he left the room.

It's not that she hadn't forgiven Lucas. She just wasn't sure of his motives. She suspected after a few visits, he would want custody. Also, she didn't want Sophia's children to grow up calling another woman "Mother."

Doreen sat up in bed and drew her knees to her chest. Maybe she should have encouraged James's romantic advances. She had gotten fertility pills from her gynecologist and this weekend was her peak ovulation time. She decided to keep her eye on the goal and overlook James's misplaced kindness with Lucas.

When Doreen turned thirty, they decided they were ready for children. She got pregnant twice but suffered two second trimester miscarriages. After the first miscarriage, she got a severe infection, was hospitalized three weeks, lost twenty pounds, and became so dehydrated she had to be fed intravenously. During the second pregnancy, she developed gestational hypertension. Her blood pressure hovered in the stroke zone and she lost the baby. Her doctor instructed Doreen to let her body heal and she should not get pregnant for at least six to eight months. She and James obeyed doctor's orders and concentrated on nurturing their ministry. Then when Sophia died, and her children moved in, they knew this was God's plan. The kids were a handful and she no longer thought of them as her nieces and nephews, or Sophia's kids. They were hers. But still…

Doreen called her husband and invited him home for lunch. She searched the refrigerator and selected a menu of cheese chunks, apple slices, and made chicken salad from leftovers. She warmed croissants and brought out the good dishes and cloth napkins. Satisfied with her menu, she planned to put their gold satin sheets on their bed, then work on her CBI report a few hours before taking a long, lazy bath. Then she'd climb under the covers to wait and surprise her husband. And hopefully, in nine months they would have another surprise.

"What a special service we had today," James said. "God is so amazing. The birth of one child is a miracle. To have triplets is even more extraordinary." Blessings baptized babies on the second Sunday and today had been a first—identical triplets. "The twins were a handful. I can't imagine three new-borns."

"Do you ever wonder about our babies?" Doreen asked as she grabbed lettuce, tomato, and cucumbers for a salad to go with the catfish dinners they bought on their way home from church.

"Sometimes. I wonder what age they'd be now and what they would be doing. I take comfort in knowing they're in heaven waiting for us," James said.

"I read an article about Memphis Fertility Associates. They have a great success rate. I think we would be good candidates."

"Candidates for what?" James asked.

"To get pregnant. Their in vitro fertilization success rate is one of the highest in the country," Doreen said enthusiastically. "Despite the miscarriages, doctors say there's nothing inherently wrong. I've already seen a specialist. It's worth a try."

"What's worth a try? You don't have time for the family you have now," James stated. "I know what this is: Lucas has you spooked."

"This has nothing to do with Lucas," Doreen insisted. "I've been feeling this way for a while and I can tell you have too. I saw the way you gazed at those babies this morning."

"Those babies were adorable, but the best thing is—I can give them back. Honey, I love our family. I couldn't love Paige and the twins more if they were my own flesh and blood. I'm satisfied with our lives and I thought you were too."

"It's not that I'm not satisfied. I get goose bumps when I remember the first time Paige called me 'Mama.' But maybe we gave up too soon. They have new procedures now."

"You're feeling apprehensive, which is understandable," James said. "I miss the kids too, but we're doing the right thing. Lucas is their father and they should spend time with him."

"Even if Lucas hadn't shown up I would want to do this," Doreen confessed with a quiver in her voice. "I want us to at least try. If it doesn't happen, okay. But at least we tried."

"Are you having a midlife crisis or something? First you want to be super-banker. Then you want to go on a lark across the country resurrecting the Diamonds and that old nonsense. Now you want to have a baby. We're not twenty-five anymore."

"That's a good thing," Doreen said. "We weren't ready for a newborn then. Now we have a stable Christian home and are financially secure. I've got enough seniority at work to take a long maternity leave. I thought God was punishing us for the drugs and the abortion. I believed God could forgive everyone but me. But I don't believe that anymore. Maybe it does have something to do with turning forty. All I know is this is something I want for us. I've been praying for us to have a baby."

"You're letting emotions get in the way of common sense," James said.

"Please don't say no right away. Say you'll think about it," Doreen said, as she wiped away the mascara running into her eyes. "I know God's not through blessing us."

"Honey, we don't need a baby. Our lives are full."

"Nobody *needs* a baby. But I've always felt like I failed you," Doreen said.

"We'll talk about it tomorrow. Right now, you're in the afterglow from the baptism," James said, as he grabbed her hands. "Let's bless the food."

"If it's about me working, I can cut back," Doreen said, running her words together quickly, so James wouldn't have time to interrupt. "Better yet, I'll go on bed rest right away and be extra-careful. Please. I can do more at church if you want me to. I promise—"

"Doreen, I hate to see you working yourself up. This was never about God's forgiveness or you failing me," James confessed as he wiped the smudged mascara from her cheeks. "You never got pregnant because I had a vasectomy."

"What did you say?" Doreen asked.

"Honey, I never wanted to—"

"What did you say?" Doreen yelled, while pounding

James's chest with her fists. "What are you saying? What are you saying?"

James grabbed her wrists and said, "I'm so sorry. I should have told you, but—"

"But what, James? What can you possibly say to make this right? I've tried Reiki, tai chi, acupuncture, meditation, gentle yoga, hot yoga, aromatherapy, and other stuff I can't even remember right now. I did cleanses, took vitamin supplements, herbal supplements, and cinnamon supplements. I changed my diet, eating nasty pumpkin seeds and liver for years. I always thought the abortion was the reason I had these problems, and blamed myself for going through with it. I was depressed every month when my period came, and it was torture to watch you perform baby baptisms. I never thought that something could be wrong with you. How could you let me go through this emotional turmoil and not say a word? When did you do this?"

"Right after the last miscarriage. You were so weak. The doctor said you almost died. I couldn't stand seeing you like that, and I didn't want you to get pregnant again. The kids were small and I couldn't imagine living without you. My faith in God wasn't as strong then. Baby, I was so scared," James said, as he reached for her hand.

Doreen jerked her hand back and pushed him away. "As usual, it's all about you. There's nothing you can say to make this right, and I will never forgive you."

CHAPTER 30

CARMEN

"This looks like I'm going to work," Carmen mumbled, then took off the third outfit. She and Gerald were going to dinner, then the Corvette show. She didn't know what you did at a car show, but he seemed excited. She was excited too, or more like nervous. He said they'd come to his house after the show, and she had a feeling, tonight was the night. It had been a long time since she had a first time with someone and she wanted things to be perfect.

She had selected a lavender wrap dress, matching bra and panties, and seldom worn heels. But thanks to her weight loss, the dress hung on her like a choir gown. Her go-to black pants fit, but she wanted to wear something other than work clothes. She selected burgundy pinstripe slacks, and was pleased with the fit. But she thought the material was too winterish, and picked a royal blue skirt and floral, powder blue off-shoulder blouse. But that meant she had to iron, since the skirt had gotten smushed in her closet. She put on the blouse, so she could do her hair while the iron heated up. While humming an Aretha Franklin song, there was a soft tap at her door.

"Mom?"

"Come in."

"Here's your keys," David said, while placing the car keys on her nightstand.

"You got a haircut," Carmen said, as she emerged from her bathroom. "What's the occasion?"

"The debate club party is tonight."

"I forgot about that. You may as well keep the keys," Carmen said.

"I won't need them. Tiana is driving."

"So I'll finally get to meet the girl my baby is sweet on," Carmen said, as she reached up and pinched her son's cheek. "What time is she picking you up?"

"About ten o'clock."

"I know you don't think you're leaving my house at that time of night."

"Mom, chill. Ten o'clock isn't late."

"Where is the party anyway?" Carmen asked.

"At the VIP Club."

"VIP Club? On Beale Street? Absolutely not."

"There's plenty of security," David said. "I know how to conduct myself."

"I know, but something could get out of hand, and you don't need to get caught up in it."

"I'll be all right," David said, while rubbing the stubble on his chin.

"Did you hear me? You're not going," Carmen stated.

"Mom, this is my last year, and I don't want to miss it."

"This discussion is over. The answer is no."

"I wasn't asking. I've been locked up and survived—in an adult jail, I might add. I'll be fine," David said and walked out.

"Boy, have you lost your mind?" Carmen said, following him into the hall.

"You can't control me. I'm eighteen years old and don't need your permission."

"I don't care how old you are. You will not disrespect me."

"I could have left the house early and gone anyway. I

would think you'd appreciate me telling you the truth," David said.

"And I would think you would appreciate all I've done for you. Do you know how much money I've spent on lawyers and bail?"

"I never asked you to do all that."

"You don't have to ask me. I would go through hell or high water to protect you. And that's all I'm trying to do now," Carmen shouted.

"What's going on up there?" Gloria shouted as David rushed down the stairs, with Carmen on his heels.

"That boy is marching out of here like he thinks he's grown," Carmen said as David stormed out of the house. "He's risking everything, to go to some club."

"He's our baby boy, but he's a young man, honey. We can't shelter him," Gloria said.

"You would never have stood for me talking to you like that. And what if something happens? Doesn't he understand they're trying to send him to prison?"

"We've got to have faith. God will take care of him," Gloria said softly, as the doorbell rang.

"Oh my goodness," Carmen said. "Gerald is early. I don't feel like going out."

"Nonsense," Gloria said. "Getting out will make you feel better."

"Let me go upstairs and get myself together," Carmen said, and dashed up the stairs.

Carmen came back downstairs minutes later, for the iron. "Where's Gerald?" she asked.

"It wasn't Gerald. A letter came for you. I signed for it," Gloria said, pointing to the table.

"This is just great," Carmen said, after she opened the letter.

"What is it?" Gloria asked.

"It's from the bail bond company. I have fifteen days to

bring proof that my mortgage is current, or they'll revoke the bond. I was only a few days late."

"I can help. What do you need?" Gloria asked as the doorbell rang.

"I guess that's Gerald this time. Tell him I don't feel well," Carmen said, as she went upstairs. *How can this be happening?* she thought, and threw the letter on the floor. She kicked off her shoes, then laid across her bed. Within minutes, there was a knock at her door.

"Can I come in?"

"Gerald?" Carmen said, and quickly sat up. "My mother was supposed to—"

"I know. But in case you haven't noticed, I'm persistent," he said and sat next to her. "I hear you've had a rather stressful evening."

"It's getting to be a bit much," Carmen said, while rubbing her forehead.

"Nothing will get better, with you moping around here. Let's go," Gerald said, as he stood and picked up her purse.

"Another time. I'm drained right now," Carmen said, wearily.

"All the more reason to get out of the house. We can skip the car show. We'll pick up some Mexican food and go to my place."

"I won't be very good company," Carmen said.

"Let me be the judge of that."

"Please, don't mention judges," Carmen said.

"We don't have to talk at all if you don't want to. This will be a stress-free evening."

"Feeling better?" Gloria asked as Carmen and Gerald came in the kitchen. "Looks like someone was just what the doctor ordered," Gloria said with a wink.

"You're not very subtle," Carmen said.

Hope looked up from peering in the refrigerator and asked, "Mom, you're going out?"

"Yes and don't forget to wash the dishes, and make sure Mama's alarm is set and she has some orange juice in her room."

"You're leaving now?" Hope asked.

"I guess you think you're grown too. Is there a problem with me going out?" Carmen snapped.

"Whoa, chill," Hope said, while putting both her hands in front of her.

"If one more person tells me to chill, or everything will be all right, I'm going to scream," Carmen declared.

"I was going to comment on your interesting clothes combination. But if you want to go out dressed like you're auditioning for an episode of *What Not to Wear*, be my guest," Hope said, and marched to her room.

Carmen looked down at her burgundy pinstripe slacks, floral blouse, and house shoes. "Look at me," she exclaimed with both hands to her cheeks, feeling only one earring. "You were going to let me leave like this?"

Gerald hunched his shoulders and said, "You look good to me."

"I need to go apologize to her."

Gerald grabbed her hand. "Miss Glo will handle it. I know what you really need. Let's go."

"Make yourself at home," Gerald said, as they entered his family room. He turned on the ceiling fan, then went to let his dog out. Carmen was pleased to see no bright colors or decorative pillows on the couch, things that suggested a woman's touch. She sat on the couch and leaned her head back, as uncontrollable tears sprang forth.

"What is it?" Gerald asked when he came back in the room. "Are you okay?"

Carmen buried her face in her hands and said, "I'm so scared. Mama isn't getting better. They're messing with me at work. I have no money and they're trying to send my son to prison. Then David has the nerve to—"

"David is under a lot of pressure too," Gerald said, as he sat next to her.

"All this is my fault. If I had let him take my car, none of this would've happened," Carmen said between sobs. "I could've used my mother's car if I needed to go somewhere. I just wanted to make sure he came straight home. And his father wanted to give him a car, but I said wait until graduation. I thought I could keep tighter control if he didn't have his own car."

"You did what you thought was best, as you've done all his life," Gerald said.

"And now it's falling apart. I don't know what to do. I'm so used to being in control."

"Unfortunately, this is one of those things in life you can't control," Gerald said, while dabbing her tears with his handkerchief. "But you don't have to handle it by yourself. I will be with you every step of the way, if you'll let me."

She looked into his eyes, then placed his handkerchief on the table, cupped his face in her hands, and kissed him. Tenderly at first, until he responded with the fervor of a man lost in the desert without water. Time seemed to stop, with the whirling ceiling fan breaking the silence. Their eyes remained open throughout the kiss, until they came up for air, both smiling.

Gerald stood, then said, "Let's go to my bedroom."

She stood in front of him, pushed him back on the couch with one hand, and unzipped her skirt with the other. Gerald smiled and said, "You can control me anytime."

CHAPTER 31

JADE

Men are such babies, Jade thought. Brian had the flu and acted like he was dying. Even though he could barely talk, he had just called for the eighth time to ask for a tally on the night's receipts. Despite Brian's absence, things ran smoothly. Rita, the assistant manager, knew the regulars and kept the employees on track. Jade was surprised Rita had access to Brian's office, since it was off-limits to staff. But she could see why Brian thought so highly of her. He claimed they couldn't take a vacation, because he couldn't leave Seaside for more than a day or two. As usual, he was exaggerating, since Rita was more than capable of running the restaurant. One thing Brian hadn't exaggerated was their dire financial condition. City repairs were still hindering business and there was new competition from a restaurant that had opened across the street.

One positive: She spent the slow periods studying for her GED. Jade was so engrossed in her practice essay, that she didn't notice Rita standing in the doorway. "Do you mind if I leave early?" Rita asked. "I'd like to stop at Costco to get pickles and peppers. We're almost out."

"It's so slow, let's just close early and send everyone home," Jade said. "We appreciate your loyalty and thank you for hanging in there with us. Hopefully, the construction will be complete soon and business will pick up."

"No problem," Rita answered. "I love working here."

Jade set the alarm and ignored Brian's text inquiring about the last hour's sales. He would hear the sorry details soon enough. She did have some good news to report. Rita located a new bread vendor—their old one had cut off their credit—and Jade found a bank with reduced fees for veterans. But she knew these small steps wouldn't be enough. She was going to have to tour.

Dawn knew Jade was conflicted about the tour, and tried to reassure her that a Diamonds reunion would be a cool thing. But inside, she was worried. If the caseworker discovered Jade would be traveling, there was a chance they would move her. And even if they didn't remove her, she still dreaded being alone with Brian. He had never done or said anything inappropriate, but she still didn't like him. Hopefully, Jade was right and the Diamonds tour wouldn't even make the caseworker's radar. Brian would probably be spending all his time at Seaside as usual, and she could study.

Dawn had kept her promise to improve her grades and her teachers had been impressed by her progress. She usually stayed after school for tutoring. But not today. Painful cramps were making it impossible for her to concentrate, and she left after her second class. A parent was supposed to check her out, but Jade had a doctor's appointment and Brian didn't answer the house, restaurant, or cell phone. The secretary sent her to the school nurse, but Dawn figured her bed was as good as the nurse's cot. She called her boyfriend to pick her up.

"Thanks for coming," Dawn said, as she got in his black Mercedes. "I need to stop by Seaside. I'm not sure when Jade will be home, so I need Brian's key."

Seaside wasn't open yet, so Dawn had Marquel go through the alley to the back door. "I'll be right back," she said.

She entered the code and let herself in. Dawn heard voices and headed for the office. The door was slightly ajar, and she pushed it open. She saw the back of a woman sitting on the desk. Brian opened his eyes and met Dawn's glare. He backed away from the desk and zipped his pants. Rita hopped off the desk when she saw Dawn. Brian rushed to the door and closed it behind him as he guided Dawn to the dining room.

"Uh... Dawn, I wasn't expecting you."

"Obviously," she said, as she jerked her arm from him. "Don't touch me."

"Now, don't go jumping to conclusions. It wasn't what it looked like."

"Oh no? Then what was it?" she asked, raising her voice.

"I don't owe you an explanation," Brian snapped.

"No, but you owe Jade one. I never knew what she saw in you anyway."

"Mind your own business," Brian said, while tucking his shirt in his pants. "My wife is happy and looking forward to seeing her singing friends. You don't want to upset her, do you?"

"I'm not the one screwing around."

"That was just recreation. I love my wife and family. Why hurt her and disrupt our home? And if you do, what do you think happens to you? You return to the state and you'll be thrown in some warehouse for unwanted orphans. Be smart, keep your mouth shut, and everybody wins."

"I don't see how living with a lying, conceited prick can be a win for anybody. But you're right. Jade will be hurt and upset, and I don't want that. So, I'll keep your secret on one condition. Make it two. Stop pressuring Jade about the Diamonds tour. Maybe if you weren't screwing the help, you could figure out a way to make more money. And I have a boyfriend. His name is Marquel. Be nice to him."

"All right. Why aren't you in school anyway?" Brian asked as they walked to the back door.

"Oh yeah. I didn't feel well and was going home, but I forgot my house key," she said.

He placed his key in her outstretched hand.

"Suddenly I'm feeling much better. I think I'll stop by the mall. I need fifty dollars," she stated with her hand still outstretched.

Brian frowned and quickly counted out fifty dollars.

"You know, I read having a weekly allowance teaches teens good money management skills. This will be a good start," Dawn said, waving the money as she sauntered out the door.

Chapter 32

CARMEN

Carmen tossed her purse and satchel on the counter as she hurriedly entered the house. She hummed an Aretha Franklin tune and pulled salad fixings out of the refrigerator. The pizzas she had ordered on her way home and salad would serve as dinner. She had premade a meat loaf the night before and had planned to put it in the oven when she got home from work. But she hadn't planned on making a detour. Her car was making a funny noise and Gerald told her to stop by his house on her way home. Of course it stopped making the noise when she got to his house.

"You didn't need to make up an excuse to come over," he had teased. "But as long as you're here..." She had smiled and followed him to his bedroom, a room she'd visited frequently lately, and so much for the meat loaf.

Carmen hadn't been this giddy about sex in a long time. She figured, at forty, she was past the intense, horny stage. Was Gerald that good? Or maybe they were still in the discovery, honeymoon phase. Whatever it was, she couldn't get enough, she thought and grinned to herself. And Gerald seemed to be just as insatiable. She loved the way he stared at her body and took his time. Nathan was a good lover, but he never seemed to be fully present. He was always checking his watch, and they had planned all their encounters. She enjoyed being spontaneous for a change. She and Gerald had last-minute dates, dates with the kids, or dates where they did nothing but pop popcorn and watch a game, with no curfew. With Nathan, a quickie was because he had to get back home. With Gerald, a quickie was foreplay.

The front doorbell jolted Carmen out of her reverie. She rushed to the door and caught the delivery driver just as he and her pizzas were getting back in his car. "David, come eat," she called as she carried the pizzas to the kitchen. Garlic and oregano filled the room and reminded her she was hungry.

She called David again. He had been in bed when she got home, but she was sure he was awake by now. She figured he had on headphones and didn't hear her. It wasn't like her son to skip a meal. Carmen went upstairs and tapped on his door before entering.

To Carmen's surprise, he didn't have on headphones and the room was dark. "Do you feel all right?" she asked.

"I guess," he answered and sat upright. "Mom, I need to talk to you."

"What is it?" Carmen asked as she sat on his bed.

"Now, don't get upset."

"I'm calm as a room of monks. Hungry, but calm. So what is it?"

"I spoke with Attorney Peters and—"

"And what?" Carmen asked with an edge in her voice.

"See, you're getting upset already," David said.

Carmen stood and said, "Boy, you better not say what I think you're going to say."

"It was my decision, Mom," David said softly.

"What did you do?" she screamed, and grabbed his shoulders.

"Mom, sit down. Please," he said, looking at the floor. "I want to get this behind us. Attorney Peters said if I plead to unlawful possession of a controlled substance, they will drop the other charges. I'll just get probation and a suspended sentence."

"You'll just be a felon. You can just forget about basketball or a scholarship. You'll just be another innocent black man with a record."

"Innocent until proven guilty only exists on television, Mom. We know how a trial will end—young black man, plus dead police officer, equals guilty and prison. I'm not a punk; I can do the time if I have to and face it like a man," David said, with conviction. "I already know some guys in there. And I wouldn't be in a maximum-security type facility. It would almost be like camp. But I don't see why I should go there when I have a choice."

Carmen rubbed her forehead and paced back and forth, trying to contain her anger. "That's the advice I drew down my retirement plan for? I hope you don't believe that crap."

"He's right. He said the other guys are close to agreeing on a plea deal. The DA wants to close this case, and I'm the only reason it's still—"

"I don't care what the other guys have done, do, or don't do. And I don't care about the DA's caseload. That's his job. Now, please tell me this was only a discussion and you didn't sign anything. I should have followed my first mind and fired that lazy-ass lawyer weeks ago. We need someone else."

"Another lawyer? You can't afford that. It's not fair to you or Hope," David said forlornly.

"Who told you life was fair? When you get a bad call in a game, do you whine about the ref or keep playing? Do you quit? No, you finish the game. We are *not* quitting," Carmen declared.

"What's the point?" David asked with watery eyes. "We can't win."

"We can't win if you give up. You think going to jail and having a record proves you're not a punk? That makes you a man? All it proves is you got caught up in a system designed to entrap, incarcerate, and emasculate men without money. A man believes in himself and is the master of his own fate. Now, answer me," Carmen demanded as she got in his face. "Did—you—sign—something?"

David cleared his throat, then said, "Yes. We go before the judge Monday morning."

"The devil is a lie. Here's what *we* are going to do. *We* are going to courier a letter to Mr. Peters's residence and office informing him *we* are no longer in need of his services. And you will be a no-show on Monday, if I have to lock you in this room and chain you to this bed."

"But what if I'm convicted?" David asked, with trepidation in his voice.

"You won't be," Carmen assured him.

David stared at the floor and after a long pause said, "If you say so. Can we afford another lawyer?"

"You let me worry about that. Now let's go eat our pizza."

Carmen ignored the jeers and taunts as she walked across the parking lot. Even Lynn had stopped speaking to her. This was the third day of the strike, and she had done something she vowed she'd never do: cross the picket line. She was broke and every dime she scraped together was going to David's fourth lawyer, Craig Hawkins, who she was on her way to see. When Attorney Peters went behind her back and talked to David, she fired him. She wasn't paying him to send her son to prison.

Craig Hawkins had been referred to Vernon by one of the Kohlbergs. They were one of the largest law firms in Memphis and represented Vernon's dealership. Carmen was familiar with their commercials and was disappointed the Kohlberg law firm passed on David's case. The dreary skies matched her mood. The light April showers interfered with her GPS instructions and she kept missing her turn. She finally found the building and rushed to meet the man who was going to free them from this nightmare.

The Hawkins law office was across from the elevator and if office décor was a proxy for success, she was in the right place. If she had been here for any other reason, the plush carpet, suede furniture, and muted jazz would have put her at ease. But today even John Coltrane couldn't calm her nerves. Luckily, she didn't wait long, and the secretary motioned for her to go inside. Attorney Hawkins was much younger than she imagined, with cashew-colored skin, a shaved head, and he was wearing a Polo shirt and chinos. He looked more like David's coach than his attorney, and his youthful looks only increased Carmen's apprehension.

Her fears were quickly relieved. Carmen had emailed copies of documents and was pleased he had read them. He was familiar with David's case, and hadn't hurried through their meeting. Carmen felt they had finally found the right person to lead David's defense. "I think we've covered everything, Miss Payne," Attorney Hawkins stated, pushing back from his desk. "Any other questions?"

"I can't think of any right now," Carmen answered.

"I'm not going to sugarcoat the situation. We've got a fifty-fifty chance and things can go either way. Remember what I said. Your son needs to cut his hair, low but not bald. He should wear dark pants, white Oxford shirt, solid black tie, and loafers. Bring his letter jacket, but it will just be a prop to drape over the chair."

"Don't worry. David will be the definition of preppy," Carmen promised.

"I can't tell you how many times I've given those instructions, only to have my client show up in jeans and a T-shirt claiming they are 'keeping it real.' These little things matter. And again, as many teachers, church members, and coaches there are in the courtroom, the better. His father should sit next to you."

"Yes, sir," Carmen said, giving a mock salute. "We will follow your instructions to the letter."

"There is one more thing," Attorney Hawkins said. "My check..."

"Of course," Carmen said, looking through her purse. "This is just a down payment. I'm getting the rest together."

"We'll work out a payment plan. For right now, concentrate on helping David put his best foot forward," Attorney Hawkins said. "I know you need to return to school. I'll stop by this evening to meet David."

"Thank you for understanding. Seems like we've talked to every lawyer in Memphis, and I didn't want to take David out of school if this wasn't going to work out."

"No problem. It's on my way home. Let me get you a receipt. And here's the contract you included in the file. I leafed through it, trying to figure out what it had to do with David's case. I have a cousin that worked at Peak, so I thought maybe he sent something and it got mixed up with your documents."

"Did you look at it?" Carmen asked.

"I'm sorry. I didn't mean to pry."

"I'm glad you looked at it. What's your opinion of the proposal?"

"I'm not an entertainment lawyer, but I understand the basic points."

"Do you think it's a good deal?" Carmen asked.

"You've been offered a generous payment. But you need an entertainment lawyer."

"I can barely pay you. I don't need two lawyer bills," Carmen said.

"I don't regularly review these types of contracts, so I don't know what to compare it to."

"Well, you know more than I do. Give me an opinion based on what you know."

"You understand this is not an official legal opinion and—"

"Yeah, yeah, yeah. I won't sue you," Carmen stated.

"Okay," Attorney Hawkins said and sat back down. "First of all, the proposal lists Miss Donovan as executive producer. It usually means she would have the final say-so about fees and the schedule. You should have the position defined. Then there's a March start date. Won't you be in school? The proposal mentions sponsors. What are the terms of those deals? Also, she has incorporated and is negotiating under the name of Donovan Enterprises. You may want to do the same, otherwise you'll be personally liable if anything goes wrong. There's a licensing fee to EMG, Inc. I'm not sure what that is."

"Just as I figured," Carmen said. "That legal mumbo jumbo is a fancy way of saying she's running the show and in charge of the money." Hell was still hot and Carmen had no intention of touring. She had agreed to consider the proposal to pacify Doreen. Ironic that Doreen was the most interested, yet she had the most secure life. "Miz Donovan must be crazy if she thinks I'm going to agree to this."

"Don't be hasty. I'm sure there's room for negotiation."

"I didn't want to do it anyway," Carmen said, while searching for her keys.

"Well, there is another factor to consider."

"Like what?"

"I hate to bring this up, but there's the matter of my fee. This case will take a large amount of my time. I want to help you and your son, but I can't afford to neglect my practice."

"I just gave you ten thousand dollars," Carmen said.

"That was merely a down payment. The minimum rate for a high-profile trial involving a police officer is at least thirty thousand dollars, and usually fifty thousand."

"I don't have the money right now. You said we could work out a payment plan."

"I know and quite frankly, I took the case as a favor to Mr. Kohlberg. He has brought me in on some lucrative cases and I appreciate his mentorship. He was very empathetic to your case, and I understand why. I'm committed to you and your son, but you'll need to work with me. We don't know what twists and turns we'll encounter. The money from this contract can go a long way toward your son's case. You should seriously consider Ms. Donovan's proposal."

"Wow," Carmen said, with a look of disgust. "I guess hell just froze over."

Chapter 33

ANGEL

Angel was finally home after a long day. She still wasn't used to calling the condo home, but as of eight-thirty this morning, it was official. She had closed on the Rose Manor sale and this glorified apartment was now her home. A house had never been Angel's concern. She remembered when Carmen proudly took the girls to her new three-bedroom, two-bathroom house. They were unimpressed. Unless it was worthy of *MTV Cribs*, what twenty-year-old buys a house? She hadn't appreciated owning a home, until she didn't have one. Now she was in a rented condo, with shared walls and smells, and a snake for a landlord.

Ray was fulfilling his end of the bargain. He assured her they could tour with the Heavyweights and promised to package their bestsellers with some unreleased tracks and call it a best-of album. But he had also become a pest. Initially, it was fun reminiscing about Memphis and old times. But now, he was calling, texting, or picking her up for lunch or dinner every few days. Not that she had a busy social life, but that didn't mean she wanted to spend her free time with Ray Nelson.

Angel grabbed a bottle of water from the refrigerator and sat at the kitchen island to go through her mail. She hadn't been in her condo long, and was already inundated with junk mail. But a pink envelope made her smile. She recognized the handwriting and opened the card. Miss Glo had sent it two weeks ago for her birthday, but it had gone to Rose Manor, and was just now forwarded to her new place. It was signed Gloria and Carmen, but Angel knew Carmen hadn't signed it. *Although, Carmen had agreed to attend the planning session, so maybe she was mellowing*, Angel thought.

At the rate she was going, there wouldn't be anything to present at the meeting. She met with three companies after the closing this morning. Two said no, and Miller Hair Products, who she had done several print ad campaigns for when she first went solo, said this and next year's advertising budgets were already set. Perhaps they could consider her the following year. Angel had graciously agreed, but she wasn't concerned about two years from now. She knew old man Miller, and would have to find a way to contact him personally.

Angel was frustrated and tired when she got home, but she still needed to work out. She had put together an intense muscle-building program with hundreds of reps, to tone her arms, core, and butt. While her voice was the moneymaker, it was housed in her body, so she had to make the outside just as appealing.

She changed clothes and decided to cheat and have a small shake. Her trainer previously gave her menu choices and had Cook prepare her meals. Since they were gone, she developed her own shake recipe, with protein powder, a banana, strawberries, nuts, and a hint of cinnamon. But first, three hundred sit-ups.

Angel compared an entertainment career to having a baby. Preparation and touring were grueling, but the result was amazing. To stand on stage in front of people who specifically came to see you was exhilarating. Their faces were fuzzy, but she felt their energy. It was adrenaline, with a high better than drugs. It didn't matter if it was ten or ten thousand, she gave her best.

As a child, she sang around the house, in the school chorus, and school plays. She had been a regular on the pageant circuit and ran for Miss Teen Memphis, Miss Delta Fair, Junior Miss—if there was a Miss anything, she was there. Angel always sang for her talent competition. When she left college, she considered entering the Miss Memphis contest, but won the title of Mrs. Donovan instead. Angel thought she had given up her stage dreams, but when the opportunity to become a Diamond came along, she knew show business was her destiny.

With Rose Manor sold, she could afford to move. But spending that money would hinder her tour plans. She would simply have to stomach Ray Nelson a little longer. She grabbed her exercise mat from the closet, stretched and got busy. She had no plan B.

CHAPTER 34

DOREEN

Doreen had moved into the guest room and barely spoken to James since his vasectomy confession. This was the second Sunday Doreen had skipped church. She hadn't missed two consecutive Sundays since she had the flu, four years ago. She and James were pros at masking their feelings from their congregation. They could argue fiercely, but as soon as they turned onto the church parking lot, they donned their pastor and first lady faces. Usually by the time service was over, they had forgotten what they were arguing about. But this time she didn't even care enough to pretend, so she stayed home.

She called in sick to work three days, and wasn't answering her phone, but moping around the house made her feel worse. She figured at some point, *I'm over it*, would come. But she wasn't there yet. It was one thing to not get pregnant due to a biological issue. But to discover she'd invested so much emotion and effort into a futile fantasy was infuriating and humiliating. She was about to review her CBI reports when she heard a knock on the guest room door.

"Mom, there's a call for you," Paige said.

"Who's calling me on your phone?" Doreen asked.

"It's the hat lady from church," Paige said, while giving the phone to her mother.

"Hey, Miss Glo. How are you?"

"I'm fine, for an old hat lady. More importantly, how are you? Pastor said you were fine, but I know my girls, and you wouldn't be shutting yourself off if nothing was wrong."

"Just some things I need to work out," Doreen said.

"Translation—mind my own business. Well, you are still my business," Gloria said. "Whatever you're stressing over is probably very simple. We make things more complicated than they have to be, and give people more power than they really have. Whatever it is, God has already handled it. We can't control most things that happen to us, but we can control our reaction. Time is moving on while you're at home pouting. That's my polite way of telling you to get up off your backside."

"You're right," Doreen said. Doreen said she agreed, but felt if Miss Glo knew the whole story, she'd be less sanguine. It wasn't fair. James had taken something from her, which wasn't his to take. She'd considered leaving him, but there was no way she would uproot the children. She briefly thought of telling him to leave. But if James left, Blessings would be in an upheaval and Lucas would have an excuse to increase his foothold in the kids' lives. Doreen felt trapped.

Even though Miss Glo didn't know the whole story, she was right about one thing: Doreen couldn't control what had happened, but she had the power to make herself feel better. James had been wrong as two left shoes, and self-centered. But she was being self-centered too. The kids had been through enough trauma. She would never have a baby, but mourning that loss was keeping her from nurturing the three children she did have. It was time to move on.

"I guess I can't hibernate forever," Doreen said.

"So I'll see you on Sunday?" Gloria asked.

"Yes, ma'am."

"Good. Wear a hat. You can't help but smile when you're wearing a hat."

With renewed vigor, Doreen moved back into their bedroom. As she returned clothes to her closet, she noticed a dusty box on the top shelf. She pulled it down and removed her mother's favorite white hat. *This will do just fine for Sunday*, she thought. Next, she grabbed her phone and Googled *housekeepers*—no more superwoman. Then she found the envelope from Angel, called and left a message confirming her participation. She was taking her power back.

CHAPTER 35

CARMEN

The week began badly and went downhill from there. On Monday, Carmen's principal placed a reprimand notice in her personnel file, due to excessive absences. Her principal understood David's situation, but Carmen had used all her personal days and there was no leave category for fighting bogus court charges. She had bundled her car and home insurance, and Tuesday she received a notice that both rates were increasing due to the drop in her credit score. Hope cracked a filling on Wednesday, and on Thursday they learned someone had broken into Gloria's house.

Ten minutes after the bell rang Friday afternoon, she was summoned to the office. She locked her room and headed to the principal's office, thinking, *What now?* She was surprised when the secretary pointed to a vase of two dozen yellow roses. The card was signed *Can't wait to see you.* She found a box to put the vase in, then headed out the door.

"Looks like you had a special delivery," Gerald said, as she walked to her car.

"I guess that's your way of asking who sent them."

"Only if you want to tell me."

"They're from Nathan." Carmen had committed a cardinal dating sin—discussing past relationships. He had talked about his daughter's mother and a few other exes. Carmen had confessed her complicated relationship with Nathan and other dating disasters. She had advised him on what women wanted and Gerald tried to defend the male perspective. At the time, their conversations were friendly battles of the sexes. Today it wasn't so friendly.

"Did he think it was your birthday or something?"

"No. I called him and he—"

"What did you call him for?" Gerald asked. "Have you been still seeing him?"

"No," Carmen replied.

"I'm supposed to believe he sent you flowers just because?" Gerald asked.

"So you think I'm lying?"

"I'm not sure what to think. Have you been seeing him?"

"I already told you no," Carmen said, with a heavy sigh. "I think he may have misinterpreted my phone call."

"What did you say to him?"

"I asked him to meet me—"

"You asked to see him?" Gerald interrupted.

"I wanted to tell him I'm not going to see him any-more."

"I thought you did that already," Gerald stated. "And what sense does that make? You need to see him to tell him you're not going to see him? You could have said that on the phone."

"I believe it's better to do those things in person," Carmen replied.

"Well, I don't. If you don't want to tell him on the phone, text him."

"Are you telling me what to do?" Carmen asked, with an edge in her voice.

"I shouldn't have to tell you. But if you resent me telling you, then we aren't as close as I thought we were."

"You're jumping to conclusions and I don't like being interrogated."

"I tell you what, you don't have to worry about me jumping to anything," Gerald said and turned and walked to his truck.

Carmen placed the flowers in her back seat, then got in her car. When she looked up from fastening her seat belt, Gerald had pulled into the parking space beside her and motioned for her to lower her window.

"I apologize for my tone, but not for what I said. Either you're through with him or you're not, and I don't want to waste my time or yours."

"Nothing is going on. I just want proper closure," Carmen explained.

"If you want closure, you don't want me. Take care of yourself," Gerald said, then drove off.

CHAPTER 36

ANGEL

"Mr. Nelson will see you now," the secretary said and stood behind her desk.

"You can sit. I know the way," Angel said. *I probably paid for all this furniture*, she thought.

"Angel, what a welcome surprise," Ray said, as he met her at the door.

"I won't stay long. I know you're busy, and I have to get ready for the girls' arrival. We're having a planning session this weekend," Angel said, as she handed Ray an envelope. "My attorney has reviewed everything and other than the changes we've already discussed, the documents look great. I want to tell you again how much I appreciate this. You won't regret it."

"You can show how much you appreciate it by having lunch with me."

"How about a rain check? I still have a few things to do before this weekend. But I wanted to personally deliver the contract and get it signed so I can have copies for the girls." She also wanted Ray to cut her advance check as soon as possible. Rainbow Village had sent a final payment notice, with a Monday deadline.

"We'll take care of that later," Ray said. "Let's celebrate."

Angel and her benefactor went to Everest for a five-course lunch and stunning view of Chicago's skyline and Lake Michigan. She then rode with him out to the north side to check on an apartment building, then he asked her to accompany him to the Bulls playoff game. Angel insisted she wasn't dressed appropriately and needed to get home. Rather than take her home, he took her to Giorgio Armani and told her to pick anything she wanted. When he finally brought her home, to her dismay, he parked, rather than drop her off.

"It's been a long day, Ray, and—"

"Make that a perfect day," Ray said. "Just a little nightcap?"

He asked the question, but meant it as a statement, since he was already turning off his car and grabbing his phone. Angel reluctantly followed and once they were in her living room, he got two crystal glasses from her cabinet and grabbed a bottle of wine. She winced when he uncorked the bottle. It was a 1989 vintage she had been saving to share with a special someone, which he was not.

"Let's toast to our new partnership," Ray said, handing her a glass. "We've pulled off the impossible in less than five months. The paperwork is complete, and my company is on board as a sponsor for the Diamonds Encore Tour. I told you I could make it happen," he boasted and grabbed the remote and searched for a music channel. When he heard Luther Vandross, he pushed the glass sofa table to the side, then did a grand bow. "May I have this dance?"

Angel stood, and they stepped to the first song. Then "Here and Now" came on and Ray pulled her close. Ordinarily she loved to slow dance. She loved being held by a man and feeling as though the song was written just for them. But it was hard to feel romantic when she was staring down at his balding head. When the song was over, Angel finished her second glass of wine, then turned to CNN.

"You got anything to eat?" Ray asked as he went to the kitchen.

"No," Angel said, looking at her watch.

"You're right," Ray said, as he emerged from the kitchen with two more glasses of wine. "Not much of anything in there, but what I want is right here," he said and sat beside Angel on the couch.

Angel attempted to stand, but he pulled her back down and tried to kiss her. "What are you doing?"

"I'm going to make love to a beautiful woman. Is there a problem?" Ray asked as he stood and reached for her hand.

Angel wanted to shout, *Hell yes there is a problem. There's lots of problems. They're called tuition, IRS, and Rainbow Village.* She didn't make the mistake most women make—equating sex and love. It was just a feeling and she had no qualms about exchanging that feeling for something tangible. It was business. She picked up her wineglass, drained it, and hoped for a wham-bam-thank-you-ma'am, and followed him into her bedroom. He slowly undressed her while planting sloppy kisses on her neck. He sat on her bed, pulled a condom out of his wallet, then beckoned for her to join him. He massaged her feet, then her back and shoulders. Ordinarily, she relished a man that knew how to use his hands, but Ray was not the one. She became the aggressor, straddled Ray, put his hands on her butt cheeks and did her best Donna Summer impression.

"I knew you wanted me, mama," Ray said, grinning like a Cheshire cat.

Angel shuddered and closed her eyes, wondering how a man so savvy in business could be so clueless. Even though she tried to speed things up, time was moving in slow-motion. Each sound he made stretched and echoed like a horror movie soundtrack. Some things didn't get better with age. Finally, the longest four minutes and thirty seconds of her life were over. He fell asleep with his arm across her stomach. She wondered how she would get rid of him before her eight o'clock appointment, but she needn't have worried. He got up around four o'clock, dressed, and left. She pretended to be asleep, but the minute he was out the door, she hopped out of bed.

Ray had left a note apologizing for leaving, saying he had an early meeting. He also thanked her for last night, saying it was like old times. Ray appeared ready to pick up where they left off. But those days were gone. She wasn't a protégé that needed molding or fashion tips anymore. She viewed them more as equals and considered their arrangement a business deal. Last night had been unavoidable, but those four-and-one-half miserable minutes would buy time for her plan to come together. Angel balled up the note and threw it in the trash.

CHAPTER 37

CARMEN

Carmen turned onto Cherry Street and parked in front of her mother's house for a meeting with her siblings. Coming to their mother's house usually meant peach cobbler, card games, and side-splitting laughter. Unfortunately, today's visit offered none of those.

"Hello Miss Murray," Carmen said to their mother's neighbor as she walked up the front walkway.

"How's your mother?"

"Feisty as ever," Carmen said. "The break-in made her want to return to her house even more."

"You work hard for your stuff and some lazy low-life comes along to take it. I try to watch out as best I can," Miss Murray said.

"Hopefully, the new alarm system and cameras will help," Carmen said.

"Not many of us old-timers left over here. Seems like just yesterday, you girls were practicing on her porch and marching up and down the street with books on your head. Hope she gets better soon."

"Me too," Carmen said. "I'll tell her I saw you."

"Hey," Faye said as her sister entered their mother's

living room. "Sonny couldn't leave work. He said to call and put him on speakerphone," Faye said.

"I'll call him later," Carmen replied.

"So, what is it?" Faye asked. "I've been a nervous wreck since you called yesterday."

"Mama's doctor called me," Carmen said. "He said she hasn't returned her paperwork, and he's concerned valuable time is slipping away."

"What paperwork?"

"That was my question. The doctor told Mama a month ago he's recommending more aggressive treatment for her foot ulcer and he needs to amputate three toes."

"Oh no," Faye said, and sat on the couch.

"There's a sore on her heel that hasn't healed. She's been hiding it from us," Carmen said. "I missed so many days of work with David's case, Mama told me I didn't need to go with her to the doctor. I'm thankful I was named as a contact, otherwise we might not have found out until it was too late."

"I wondered why she wore sling-back shoes to church. I was worried about her catching cold with her feet getting wet in the rain. I thought she was trying to be cute," Faye said. "I'll go with her to her next appointment. Let's schedule it as soon as possible."

"It's not that simple. Because of her age and the stage of her diabetes, she needs a wheelchair during her recovery," Carmen explained.

"Mama, in a wheelchair? There must be another way," Faye said.

"And there's another problem," Carmen said, while wiping dust off the coffee table. "My house isn't wheelchair accessible. It needs major renovations, which I can't afford."

"I could kick myself for having all my bedrooms upstairs. And the steps here are so steep, she can't stay here either,"

Faye said. "This is our slow season until Mother's Day and wedding season kicks in. Why don't you ask Doreen for a loan?"

"She claims she can't approve a loan for me because I don't have any collateral or money in the bank. And I've borrowed the limit on my retirement plan."

"I'll see if there's room on any of our credit cards. I can also get Mitchell to call the contractors we used," Faye said.

"Mama won't ever be able to move back in this house, will she?" Carmen asked softly.

"Let's not think the worst. I've seen people with a prosthesis walk better than you and me," Faye said.

"Let's get Mama's stuff and get out of here," Carmen said. "It's spooky with her not here."

Carmen and Faye hugged each other and headed to their homes. Carmen drove up to her house, just as Gerald was walking to his car. He waved as she pulled into her driveway.

"I came by to talk," he said, as she got out of her car. "I don't like the way we left things the other day. I haven't changed my mind about you talking to that guy, but if you say it's over, I guess I have to trust you. So was that our first fight? When do we get to make—Is everything okay? You look like your dog ran away. I would like to flatter myself and say it's because we haven't talked in a couple days, but somehow, I don't think that's it."

"Not really. I hate to keep burdening you with my problems. I don't want to run you off."

"I don't scare easy. Let me take you to dinner," Gerald asked.

"How about we stay here, and I'll cook?"

As the pork chops simmered, she and Gerald examined her house. "Inclines are needed for the front and back doors. You should replace your doorknobs with levers too," Gerald advised.

"This is what will cost the most money," Carmen said, as

she flipped on the hall bathroom light. "This space is so tight, I'll need a new vanity and sink so a wheelchair can fit underneath. Faye's checking with the contractors they used for her shop. Or maybe I'll get Sonny's friends to do some of the work."

"No disrespect to Sonny or his friends, but when dealing with major plumbing work, it's best to use licensed tradesmen. You may want to sell the house someday, and these modifications must meet building codes. I know reputable guys who do district jobs, so I'm sure they're licensed and familiar with Americans with Disabilities code. I'll talk to them and get you a fair price. And instead of remodeling the bathroom, it will be easier and cost about the same to add on. It would also increase your home's value."

"Sounds wonderful, but expensive. Your friends don't work for food, do they?"

"You're a good cook, but I think they prefer cash," Gerald said.

"Then I'm back where I started," Carmen stated, with a heavy sigh.

"I have an idea," Gerald said, as he checked the potatoes.

"Don't even think about it. No way could I borrow that much money from you."

"That's not what I had in mind," Gerald said. "Didn't you mention a possible Diamonds reunion? Why don't you reconsider the tour?"

"You too? Mama, Doreen, and David's attorney have said the same thing. But I can't leave town with David's case in limbo and Mama's health so fragile."

"Why not? School will be out soon. You need money, there's money waiting to be made. It's up to you, but it seems like an easy solution to me."

"Touring with Angela? There's got to be another way," Carmen insisted.

"So, it's not David's case or your mom's health that's the

issue. Don't take this the wrong way, but I think you're being a little childish."

"Don't take it the wrong way? What other way is there to take it? You're supposed to be on my side," Carmen stated. "You don't know Angela. What you see on television is not what you get. That woman added the *b* to the itch."

"There are two sides to every story—make that three. Each person's version, and then the truth. But assume everything you say is true," Gerald said, and turned off the stove. "You're going to hold your son's freedom and your mother's health hostage because of someone else's issues? Seems to me you can keep your eye on your goal and over-look anything Miss Angel dishes out. The Carmen Payne I know can hold her own."

For almost two decades, she had handled more than her share of undisciplined preteens and obnoxious parents, so she knew she could deal with Angela. But she was always proud that the Diamonds went out on top. She'd moved on and made a life for herself and her children, content to let the Diamonds be the answer to a pop history trivia question. She pitied has-been singers, way past their prime trying to hold on to the past. She didn't need the Diamonds to maintain her sense of self. But she realized her children did need the Diamonds. Carmen knew how the justice system was sup-posed to work, but with young black men it was too often a crapshoot, and she needed to do all she could to put the odds in David's favor. Attorney Hawkins wasn't pressuring her, but she had mortgaged their future, and if she didn't do the tour, how would she resurrect her finances? Her van was on its last leg, her house was only weeks from foreclosure, and David and Hope's college money was gone.

"I guess you're right. The tour earnings would be a life-saver."

"The time will pass quickly, and we'll all come see you. I'll bet Faye wouldn't mind bringing Miss Glo and Hope to one of your concerts. David and I can hang out here. Then I'll come a couple weekends, to make sure those groupies keep their hands off," Gerald said, shaking his finger at her. "I'm sure Angel has mellowed by now. And even if she hasn't, we won't let her spoil our fun."

"Mr. Wells, you're right again. It looks like I'm going back on the road."

"Glad to be of service. What would you do without me?" he asked, as he kissed her on the forehead.

Carmen was beginning to wonder the same thing.

CHAPTER 38

DOREEN

"I thought this was a weekend trip," James said, lifting Doreen's suitcases into the trunk. "You've got enough clothes for a month."

"I wasn't sure what to pack. Chicago's weather can be quirky," Doreen said, while emailing last-minute instructions to her assistant. A month had passed since James's vasectomy confession. She returned to their bedroom, but brought with her a new attitude. They also decided to follow their own advice and seek counseling. Their marriage had taken a back seat to everything else and needed work. She already saw benefits, as James was being more considerate and flexible. When she told James she was attending the planning meeting, he didn't fuss and even upgraded her ticket to a sleeping car, when he learned Carmen wouldn't fly.

"There's a lot of new development down here," James said, as they arrived at the station. "I remember when this area was desolate."

"Our CBI initiative will underwrite similar investments in other parts of the city."

"If you're on the case, I know it will happen," James said, as he grabbed his wife's hand.

"Thanks, honey," Doreen said. "And thanks for being understanding about the trip."

"Don't thank me because I don't understand. I'll be prayerful, but I still don't see how you can justify leaving with so much going on at church. I guess you're trying to get back at me."

"This isn't about you," Doreen said with a sigh. "I'm just curious and want to see what Angel is proposing. I think it would be fun to spend time with the girls again."

"Blessings is full of girls who need you to spend time with them. Rachel is always soliciting volunteers."

"Call it an early midlife crisis. Some women cut their hair, others get younger men. All I want to do is spend time with old friends—sober this time."

"I certainly don't want you looking for a younger man. If hanging with your old friends makes you happy, then enjoy yourself."

James and Doreen entered the train station like celebrities. Doreen spotted Carmen, but they were stopped several times by church members and other well-wishers. She left James talking to a security guard and headed in Carmen's direction. "Miss Glo, this will never do," Doreen said, pointing to the walker.

"The doctors want me to use this contraption until my foot heals," Gloria said, as she adjusted her hat.

"I hope you're following doctor's orders. We may be needing a chaperone," Doreen said.

"Touring wouldn't be the same without you standing in the wings, motioning for us to stand up straight," Carmen said.

"And I need you to keep the men away from my wife," James said, as he joined them.

"Pastor, you know you have nothing to worry about.

Doreen was always a good girl," Gloria said. "You were both good kids."

"Even though you chased me out of their room?"

"I had forgotten that," Carmen said.

James had always been like a young, old man. As the Diamonds' drummer, he insisted the guys not use profanity around the girls, though Carmen could out-cuss most of them. He made the guys carry the girls' bags and he helped Gloria run off male groupies. While he was watching out for the Diamonds, he was watching one particular Diamond.

"You kids thought I didn't know you were sneaking in there," Gloria said, with a chuckle.

"Carmen was supposed to be the lookout," James said.

"Sorry," Carmen said in a singsong voice. "I fell asleep. You lovebirds were taking too long."

"We had some good times," Doreen said. "Remember when—"

"You two have all weekend to walk down memory lane. I'm getting one last smooch," James said, pulling his wife to the side. "Be careful, and remember I love you."

Doreen nodded and planted a tender kiss on his lips.

"Before we leave, I want to say something. I apologize for how I acted when I came to your office. This whole trial business has me so worried," Carmen said.

"We're all concerned. It's taking longer than it should, but I'm sure this whole mess will be resolved in David's favor," Doreen said as she reached for and squeezed her friend's hand. "Besides, you know I never pay any attention to you. Now, let's get this show on the road."

Carmen and Doreen boarded the train and found their roomette. The train left on time and by daybreak they would be in Chicago. For the first time in twenty years, the Diamonds would be together.

CHAPTER 39

THE DIAMONDS

"Can you believe what that cab charged to take us six blocks?" Doreen asked.

"They charge extra for each piece of luggage. Why did you bring so much stuff? This isn't a vacation," Carmen said.

"It's a vacation if we make it one. We won't be cooped up in the hotel the whole time. I wonder if that pizza place we liked is still here. And we must go to Michigan Avenue," Doreen said eagerly.

"I did not ride ten hours to go shopping and eat pizza. Let's see what pipe dream Angela has concocted, and head home. We could've done this with a video chat or conference call."

"Ummmhmmm."

"And what does that mean?" Carmen asked.

"I saw Gerald with you and Miss Glo at the station. Maybe that's why you aren't interested in shopping and pizza. In a hurry to get back, are we?" Doreen teased.

"You know Gerald?" Carmen asked.

"Sure. He's one of my clients. You two make a nice couple."

"Seems like everyone knew Gerald except me," Carmen said.

"I knew it," Doreen said with a clap. "I said you two make a nice couple, and you didn't deny you were a couple. This is great. You deserve a nice guy."

"Now you sound like Mama. She's got us practically walking down the aisle."

"If Miss Glo likes him, he's passed the ultimate test. I can tell from the way you talk about him you really like him."

"I'll admit, Gerald checks all the boxes. They're always great in the beginning, but eventually they show their true colors," Carmen said.

"Don't write him off already, but it doesn't hurt to take things slow," Doreen said. "This weekend will be a chance for him to miss you, while we catch up. I'm looking forward to hanging out with everyone."

"Goes to show, people always want what they don't have. You have an adoring husband at home, and you'd rather spend time with some moody women."

"Things aren't always what they seem," Doreen said, as she gave the doorman a ten-dollar bill.

Carmen and Doreen checked into the hotel, dropped their luggage in their rooms, then went to their meeting room on the first floor. Before they could knock, the door opened. "Welcome, I'm Brooke Watson, Ms. Donovan's manager," Brooke said, ushering them into the suite.

Jade jumped from her seat. "Group hug," she exclaimed with her arms outstretched. "It's so good to see you. If Miss Glo had come it would be perfect."

"She's recuperating from surgery, but sends her love," Carmen said. Carmen then filled them in on her mother's health challenges. The three Diamonds also caught up on children, husbands, ex-husbands, and careers. Carmen had an envelope of old pictures and newspaper clippings Gloria had saved. They looked through them and reminisced, sometimes laughing so hard they had tears in their eyes.

"That life seems so long ago," Jade said. "Sometimes I forget I even lived it."

"I don't care if we don't sing a note. I'm just happy to be with you both. No matter what happens, we must stay in touch," Doreen said.

"The gang's all here," Jade said. "All we need is Angel."

"Do we really?" Carmen asked, with a raised eyebrow.

"Be nice," Doreen admonished.

Brooke stepped into the room and said, "Miss Angel will be here shortly. Her breakfast appointment ran long."

"Some things never change. She always has to make an entrance," Carmen said.

"Hello all," Angel said, as she burst into the room. "Forgive my tardiness."

"I stand corrected, some things do change," Carmen whispered. "Madam seems to have graduated from a B cup."

"We were busy gabbing and didn't mind," Doreen said, as she nudged Carmen in the side.

"So you and James are big-time preachers," Angel said, and stepped back with her hands on her hips. "I sure didn't see that one coming. I guess you traded one stage for another."

"You haven't changed a bit," Jade said. "Television doesn't do you justice."

"I always liked this girl," Angel said, as she grabbed Jade's shoulders with extended arms. "Hmmmm, you're not blond anymore. I guess I can get used to it."

"Carmen dear, it's good to see you," Angel said.

"Hello Angela," Carmen stated as she walked to the snack table.

"I assume everyone has met Brooke," Angel said. "She's been with me twelve years, and has wonderful ideas for us. For years, promoters have asked me to reunite the Diamonds. The timing wasn't right, until now. Brooke is better at the legal lingo than I am, so she'll explain everything."

"Thanks, Miss Angel. First, let me say how delighted I am to finally meet you," Brooke said, passing out folders. "This may not be professional, but I have all your records. I was a huge Diamonds fan, and that's why I jumped at the chance to—"

"Save the fan speech and get to the point," Carmen said, as she placed a blueberry muffin on a saucer.

For the next ninety minutes Brooke and Angel recited details of a media blitz worthy of the queen. "To start, this is not a reunion tour. *Reunion* sounds like broke has-beens trying to relive their youth," Angel said. "This is an anniversary celebration and will be called the *Encore*. Details haven't been finalized, but the Peak Records homecoming on Labor Day will be our opening show and we'll end in New York in December. We'll be touring with the Heavyweights. And there are wardrobe sketches in your folders."

"Mr. Nelson has already talked to BET about taping the tour, maybe doing a reality show," Brooke said, as she passed around a tentative itinerary. "Of course, nothing is final."

"Ray Nelson?" Carmen asked. "He already screwed us once. Why would we ask for more?"

"We were rookies then. Things are different now," Angel stated.

"We're meeting him for dinner," Brooke said. "He can't wait to see all of you together again. Promoters are begging for the show, but Ray suggests we limit it to fifteen cities. This will increase demand for the concert TV show."

"So ladies, what do you think?" Angel asked, smugly crossing her arms.

"We always toured to promote a new album," Jade said. "Will we be recording?"

"People don't buy albums anymore," Angel said. "They download new music, but the streaming services barely pay pennies per song. So right now, we need to concentrate on making this tour unforgettable. Well, if that's it—"

"I know you've worked hard on all this," Doreen said. "But I can't work with Ray Nelson. You know how he mistreated my sister."

"Aren't Christians supposed to forgive and forget?" Angel asked.

"Forgiveness doesn't mean I have no standards," Doreen said, opening a bottle of water.

"You don't have to explain yourself to her," Carmen said. "I don't want anything to do with Ray either. She'd work with the devil if she could get top billing."

"Another thing, Tunica and Vegas are on this list. I can't sing in casinos," Doreen said.

"You don't have to gamble," Angel said, with exasperation.

"But I can't do anything to encourage gambling either. And I see Wednesday shows on this list. I can take a Friday off here or there, but not Wednesday, Thursday, and Friday."

"You have a job?" Angel asked. "Isn't James—or excuse me, Pastor Golden—a big-time preacher now? Why are you still working?"

"James meets people's spiritual needs. And I help meet their financial needs."

"I guess it all works together. The church can't function with broke members," Angel said, as she sipped from her Perrier bottle. "We could even add a couple non-churchy church songs to the set. It would open up a whole new audience for us."

"Angel, you're missing the point," Doreen said, grabbing napkins to fan herself.

"Girl, don't try to explain anything to her," Carmen said. "Ray is a ruthless bastard and I won't work with him either. I can only do weekends too unless you move it to summer. Besides, I thought we would have a tour bus like we used to."

"Since this is for a short time, we thought it would be

more cost-effective to fly. We're trying to get an airline as one of our sponsors," Brooke said.

"Then you need to book cities within a half-day's drive of Memphis or that have Amtrak. I don't fly anymore," Carmen announced.

"You don't fly?" Angel asked. "How can you not fly?"

"I haven't been on a plane since 9/11."

"That's absurd," Angel said, throwing up her hands.

"Call it what you want. If it worked for Aretha Franklin, it's good enough for me."

"That could be a problem," Brooke said. "This is only preliminary—that's why we didn't put anything in your information packet—but we're negotiating with a promoter in Dubai. They love black women over there."

"Bye-bye to Dubai, you'll go without me," Carmen stated.

"You'll change your mind when you hear the money they're offering," Angel gushed.

"Everyone is not ruled by the almighty dollar," Carmen said.

"As usual, Carmen, you're being—"

"I have a concern also," Jade interrupted. "I thought this was a summer tour. I need to be home when school starts."

"Aren't your kids out of high school?" Angel asked.

"They are, but we have a foster daughter."

"Can't your husband watch her? It doesn't matter. You'll make so much money on this tour, you can get round-the-clock day care."

"She's a teenager, she doesn't need day care," Jade replied.

"Then she should be able to stay home alone," Angel said.

"It's complicated."

"You don't have to explain," Carmen said, grabbing

another muffin. "And speaking of all the money you say we'll be making, I've been looking through this folder and I only see the promotion contract with Nelson Enterprises. What about our individual contracts?"

"And is the money guaranteed?" Jade asked. "How certain is any of this?"

"Negotiations are ongoing, but potential partners want to know everyone is on board," Brooke said.

"But you still haven't answered my question," Jade said. "Will we get paid no matter how many tickets are sold? What if no one shows up? I can't leave my family for a maybe."

"Once we have signed contracts with everyone, we can move forward," Brooke said. "Most of those details are outlined in the documents we sent you."

"I thought that was a draft," Carmen said. "Are all the contracts the same?"

"They are standard contracts. Everything is in order," Brooke stated.

"Miss Watson—that's your name, right?" Carmen asked. "You are Angela's employee. Please don't insult my intelligence by telling me what you think is or is not in order. I asked if everyone's contract and formula was the same?"

"Not exactly," Brooke said.

"Explain 'not exactly,'" Carmen demanded.

"Miss Donovan is one of the tour producers, so her formula includes repayment of her seed money, performance fees, and a reasonable return on her investment."

"Ummmmm. I'll take a copy of everything, including Angela's contract. I'll have my attorney review them and get back to you in a couple weeks. That gives you time to replace Ray Nelson," Carmen said.

"Ray isn't one of my favorite people either, but there isn't a line of producers clamoring to underwrite our tour," Angel said.

"A few minutes ago you said promoters were begging for the show," Carmen said.

"Promoter and producer are not the same. Ray is the only one willing to invest on the front end," Angel said. "You can't let emotions rule you. Sometimes you do what you have to do until you can do what you want to do."

"That's the same thing the ladies down on Lamar say as they flag down a john," Carmen said, grabbing a handful of grapes.

"What are you trying to say?" Angel asked, flipping her hair behind her shoulder.

"I'm not trying to say anything. There's a name for women who do things for money and we all know what it is."

"Look," Angel said, as she stepped toward Carmen. "I've put a lot of work into this tour, and I will not let you disrupt my plans with your grumpy, petty, ghetto attitude."

"You talk a lot of shit for somebody who's basically homeless. Think we don't know you lost your house and recording contract? You probably had to screw Ray's troll ass to get him to back this tour. Well, I'm not interested," Carmen countered. "Not one damn bit."

"Must you use profanity?" Angel asked with a heavy sigh. "I see college didn't expand your vocabulary."

"Your conversation is primarily feces—is that better?"

"Carmen, this isn't productive. I didn't bring you here to listen to one of your tantrums," Angel said, shaking her head.

"I believe Carmen's request is reasonable," Doreen said. "If we can't get copies now, you can email them to us."

"We don't have time for attorneys and such. Do you realize how much work we have to do?" Angel asked. "We have to rehearse the songs, put together choreography—"

"I know you're not asking us to sign anything right now," Doreen said.

"An attorney has already reviewed the contracts," Angel stressed.

"*Your* attorney. I made that mistake once and ended up losing writing credit on 'Summer Blues,'" Carmen said. "My attorney will review the contracts, thank you very much."

"Carmen, please don't bring up all that history," Angel said.

"I am not interested in Angela get-over-on-us version 2.0," Carmen said, as she placed a handful of potato chips on a saucer. "He, or should I say, she, who doesn't know his history, is doomed to repeat it. I learned that in college, by the way—George Santayana, nineteenth- and early twentieth-century philosopher."

"She has a point," Jade said. "I'm not saying you would do anything unfair, Angel, but we need time to digest the information, talk to our families and—"

"I can't believe how ungrateful you all are," Angel said, raising her hands in frustration. "I've offered you the opportunity to make more money in five months than you probably have in five years. You act like I'm trying to swindle you. If that's the way you feel, forget it."

"Then thanks for the trip. I have time to visit my cousins," Carmen said, checking her watch.

"This is such an exciting project. Surely we can work something out," Brooke said.

"Listen here, Lois Lane, if it's not in writing, I'm not hearing anything you have to say," Carmen said.

"Brooke, don't try to reason with her," Angel said, as she pushed loose strands behind her ear. "Some people never grow up."

"I've had about enough of you," Carmen said, with one hand on her hip. "Just shut the f—"

"Let's all calm down," Jade said, stepping between them.

Brooke stood and patted Angel on the back. "It won't hurt for them to review the contracts with their families and attorneys. We want everyone to feel comfortable. Mr. Nelson is a busy man and I'm sure his involvement will be limited. We can try to ensure all dates are weekend dates if school is a problem. And we can consider other options for Las Vegas and Tunica. If I email documents, can you get back to me within a week?"

"I prefer you mail them to my post office box," Jade said.

"And send different wardrobe choices. Unlike Angela, I have hips and those short, tight dresses won't look good on me," Carmen said.

"I didn't know you had gained so much weight. You must be terribly uncomfortable. Maybe you can lose a few pounds in the next few months," Angel said.

"Maybe if you gained a few pounds, you could carry a tune," Carmen said.

"What did she say?" Angel asked Brooke with a look of fire in her eyes.

Jade and Doreen said goodbye, pushing Carmen into the hall. Playing referee was second nature, since they had plenty of experience from their Diamonds days. Carmen and Angel never could hold a conversation without it escalating into a catfight. They sang beautiful harmony together, but once the music stopped the chords became dissonant.

This meeting lasted three hours. How would they survive six months together?

ACT IV

PLAYING BY EAR

CHAPTER 40

ANGEL

As they left the airport, Angel was having second thoughts about coming to Memphis. She had been a featured performer at the National Beer Bottlers Association convention in New Orleans, and at Crystal's urging, agreed to a short visit before returning to Chicago. But her daughter had pulled a fast one, and it was her father that picked her up. She hadn't seen him since his divorce announcement, and they had only spoken briefly. As it turned out, Lydia was only news to Angel. Crystal knew all about her, and urged her mother to be more understanding.

"Being a caregiver is demanding and Pops has devoted his life to Grandma," Crystal rationalized, when Angel expressed her disapproval. "But what more can he do? Don't you want him to be happy? You've got to accept that Grandma, as we knew her, is gone."

"It doesn't seem right, but I'll try," Angel promised.

Now she was trapped in the car with her father and his mistress. She couldn't remember when she had been more uncomfortable. Thankfully, he dropped his sidepiece off, and Angel could relax. But her distress returned when they drove up and she saw the FOR SALE sign in her parents' front yard.

Her visits with her mother had been even more unsettling. As part of her payment arrangement with Rainbow Village, her mother was moved to a less expensive double room with a roommate. As soon as Angel entered, she was startled by how much weight her mother had lost. Her father said her mother was becoming a finicky eater, but Angel hadn't been prepared for this. Next, she noticed the bulky bracelet on her mother's frail wrist. It could be mistaken for a large smartwatch, but it was a tracking device. The nurse told Angel her mother had been disoriented by the move, and would wander the halls. The device was for her safety. This year it had been taking her mother longer and longer on each visit, to recognize her daughter. But on this visit, her mother never spoke Angel's name. Her mother sat and gazed at the television, withdrew her hand when Angel tried to hold it, and turned away when Angel hugged her. When Angel tried to brush her soft hair she became combative and wouldn't sit still. She let the nurse's aide take her to the restroom, but wouldn't budge for Angel. On the last evening, a Motown playlist was piped in the dining room and her mother's face lit up. She snapped her fingers to the beat and ate all her food. They walked arm in arm, back to her room, where she hugged her daughter, then got in bed and went to sleep.

Angel polished her mother's fingernails, then gently greased her mother's scalp and cornrowed her hair. Her mother briefly awoke, raised her hand to inspect her nails, smiled, and went back to sleep. Angel dozed off in the stiff chair next to her mother's bed, but was jolted awake by her mother's roommate's outburst. She rang for an attendant but was told the outbursts weren't unusual and to ignore them. Her mother turned her head and never opened her eyes. *I've got to get her back in a private room*, she thought.

Angel spent most of her last night at Rainbow Village and at dawn, went to the house to change clothes for her flight. She called a cab to take her to the airport, tiptoed in to plant a kiss on her father's sleepy forehead, then quietly left.

Even though she had spent her visit sitting around, she was exhausted. So when she finally got to Chicago, she was thankful Brooke had offered to pick her up.

"Am I glad to see you," Angel said, when Brooke arrived.

"You may not be so glad when I tell you the news."

"I can't take any bad news," Angel said.

"It's not exactly bad news. I tried everyone I could think of and couldn't find another sponsor. But I think Mr. Nelson heard we were still shopping the deal, and he raised his offer. I know how the others feel about him, but—"

"You know what, I don't care. Call Doreen, tell her we'll delete the casinos, and tell Carmen and Jade we'll try to schedule some dates before school starts, and the rest on weekends and during their winter break."

"What about Mr. Nelson?" Brooke asked. "Carmen and Doreen said—"

"Just set it up," Angel ordered. "I need this tour to get started."

CHAPTER 41

CARMEN

Mother's Day was coming, but the mood was not cheerful. Gloria was not responding to her medicine and what was supposed to be a minor outpatient procedure had turned into a four-day and counting hospital stay. There was no movement on David's case. Hope's store was closing and she was laid off. Carmen was broke and most of her coworkers weren't speaking to her. The only bright spot was Gerald. He was patient with her moods, generous with his time and money, and he was the toe-curler her mother had predicted she would find. Her son became a permanent fan, when Gerald suggested David drive his Corvette to prom, rather than Carmen's car or a rental. Hope was relieved her mother finally had a good-looking guy in her life. And Gloria let him see her cornrowed head without a wig—a privilege reserved for a handful of family members. Sometimes she wondered if Gloria forgot he was coming to see Carmen, not her.

He had been over every evening this week, trying to finish the bathroom addition before Mother's Day. He had planned to come Saturday morning, but when they learned Gloria wasn't being discharged, Carmen asked him not to. She said her children needed some Mommy time, and she planned to cook their favorite breakfast, then visit Gloria.

Gerald said he understood and would take his daughter out for the day.

After their pancake brunch, she washed dishes while Hope dried and put them away. David swept and mopped and for a brief time, they were a carefree family again. She told them to be ready to leave in one hour. She grabbed the items Gloria had requested she bring on her next visit. As she was headed upstairs, the doorbell rang.

"What are you doing here?" she asked through the screen door.

"What kind of greeting is that?"

"I guess that was a little rude," Carmen stated.

"Are you going to leave a brother on the porch?" Nathan asked. "I drove six hours, dropped the boys off at my mom's, then came straight here. I wanted to tell you my good news in person."

"I'm sorry," Carmen said, and opened the door. "I'm a little off-kilter; my mother is in the hospital."

"I hope she's okay," he stated.

"She had a setback last week but the doctors say she's much better."

"Glad to hear it. Sooooooo, we have the house to ourselves?" Nathan asked as he grabbed her waist. "Hey, what happened to all my junk in the trunk? Are you on one of those crash diets?"

"I'm not dieting. And no, we don't have the house to ourselves, but sit for a minute," Carmen said, while stepping away from him. "I need to talk to you."

"That doesn't sound good," Nathan said, as he sat on the couch. "Whatever I did, didn't do, said or didn't say, I'm sorry. Does that cover it?"

"How can you apologize for something, if you don't know what you did?" Carmen asked. "That's just an insincere statement to shut me up."

"Okay, I'm sorry, I said I was sorry. So what did I do?" Nathan asked.

"I didn't say you did anything."

"Then what is the problem?" Nathan asked, raising his voice. "What's going on with you?"

"Nathan, this relationship or whatever you want to call it, has run its course. It's time—"

"After all this time, you can't give up now," Nathan said, as he stood. "That's my good news. I'm being transferred back to Memphis. We'll be able to see each other again."

"Is your wife moving with you?" Carmen asked. "You know what—it doesn't even matter. I'm ready to move on."

"Move on in general—or move on to someone else?"

"I've said all I have to say," Carmen said with a sigh, wishing she had called him as Gerald suggested.

"So you are seeing someone else. I thought you were my girl."

"This conversation is over," Carmen said, as she pulled her ringing phone out of her pocket.

"I suppose that's him."

"Nathan, this is David's attorney. I need to take his call. See yourself out," Carmen said. She answered her phone while rushing upstairs.

"Hey, what's going on?" Carmen asked.

"Miss Payne, there's been a change. Judge Gray is retiring, so they are moving David's case to Judge Haynes's court."

"So is this judge better?" Carmen asked.

"Not better, just different. We need to reassess our defense plans. I'd like to meet with David as soon as possible. Can I come over now?"

"We're going to the hospital to see my mom, but I can move that back. Come on over."

As Carmen headed to David's room to tell him the news, she heard voices downstairs. As she descended the stairs, she was surprised to see other visitors in her living room. Gerald and his daughter stood in the doorway. "I didn't know you were here," Carmen said, while tightening her housecoat.

"I know you were having work done and I saw the company name on the truck, so I let him in," Nathan said, and sat back in the recliner. "I hope that's okay, babe."

Carmen avoided Gerald's eyes, wishing she could disappear into the floor.

"I should have called first. Didn't mean to interrupt," Gerald said, as he guided his daughter out the door.

"Wait," Carmen pleaded, following Gerald out the door. "Don't go. I don't want you to misunderstand—"

"I understand very well," he said, as he opened the truck door for his daughter.

"It's not at all what you think," Carmen insisted, following Gerald to the driver's side of the truck.

Gerald stopped, turned around, and asked, "Then what is it?"

"I promise to explain later," Carmen said, while checking her watch. "Something critical has come up and David's attorney is coming over. I'll come to your place as soon as he leaves."

"Don't bother. I don't need closure." Gerald got in his truck and drove off, leaving Carmen standing in her driveway.

CHAPTER 42

JADE

As a foster child, Jade never had a birthday party. Brian thought that was so sad, so he hosted an annual barbeque for her birthday. She considered the gesture sweet in their early years. Now, she'd prefer a quiet evening at home, especially since most guests were Brian's friends and relatives, and a few Seaside employees, so he could deduct the expenses on their taxes.

Ever since she agreed to tour, Brian had been so jovial, she almost forgot how grouchy he could be. He even splurged and ordered a cake from her favorite bakery. He usually said they had a chef on payroll that could bake anything—why pay someone else? The birthday cake wasn't the only splurge. Earlier, while looking through his bag for an extra phone charger, she found a jewelry box. She peeked inside and saw a gold bracelet with two emerald charms, and an eleven-hundred-dollar Visa receipt. She figured her usually tight-fisted husband was trying to cheer her up because Dawn was leaving.

Three weeks after she signed the tour contract, their caseworker called and said the state would remove Dawn if Jade traveled for an extended time. Jade guessed they heard about the tour on television. By then it was too late to back out, plus their finances had deteriorated further. She assured the caseworker it was only a few weekends and Dawn could join her. Brian even got his sister to promise to stay at the house, but the agency denied their appeal. Jade appreciated the effort, but jewelry wasn't going to make her feel better, and she planned to get him to return the bracelet tomorrow. The tour money was to rebuild their savings and help Seaside, not pay for jewelry and parties.

She tried to enjoy the festivities, but all she saw was the forlorn look on Dawn's face when she told her about the tour.

"That's pretty cool. I'll be able to tell everyone I stayed with a celebrity," Dawn had responded when Jade told her.

"If I had known they wouldn't let you join me I never would have agreed to it," Jade said.

"It's a fantastic opportunity. You'd be crazy to pass it up."

"I hate to leave you, but Brian says we really need the money. It's only for a few months."

"Jade, let's not pretend. We know this is where we part ways, but I'll always remember your kindness."

"Quit talking like this is permanent. Brian has been a good provider, and I owe him this. I hate for you to leave, but I'll be back before you know it."

"I'll be all right. I'm moving in with Marquel."

"Dawn, I think that's a mistake."

"He's already paying rent, so he's not looking for money from me. I'm going to finish school, like you said. But I'm not returning to a group home," Dawn declared.

"I know you don't want to, but it's just temporary. Brian promised to keep in touch with you, so call if you need anything."

"I'll believe that when I see it."

"Things haven't always been smooth, but you and Brian are in a good place. He even let you drive the Camaro. He never let Lance drive that car. The choices you make now affect the rest of your life. Staying with Marquel isn't in your best interest," Jade cautioned.

"Seems to me you should take your own advice."

"What are you talking about?"

"Jade, you're such a nice person. I hate to see you getting played. Tour if you want to, but don't do it for Brian. You don't owe him anything."

"I suppose it's hard for you to understand, but I was alone until I met Brian. You don't know what he's done for me," Jade explained.

"You're right, I don't know what he's done for you," Dawn said. "But I do know what he's doing behind your back. He's only being nice to me because I caught him with one of your employees."

"What do you mean?" Jade asked.

"Brian and that Rita lady have been messing around for months."

"You must have misunderstood."

"Believe that if you want to. I'm just glad I told you. What you choose to do or not do with the information is up to you. At least I told you."

"Brian and I may have had our problems, but I know he loves me, and I'm sure there's an explanation for whatever you think you saw. He's trying and when we get this money, things will be better for all of us. You'll see."

Scary-looking clouds rolled in, hastening the party's end. After a quick Stevie Wonder "Happy Birthday" rendition, Jade opened her cards and gifts. The last gift was a big, beautifully wrapped box from Brian—a new laptop computer.

"This one is faster and has more memory," he said. "That'll help you study while you're on the road."

Based on the hugs and accolades they received as everyone left, the party had been a success. Their assistant manager, Rita, was one of the last to leave, and Jade thanked her for coming, but then something caught her eye. As Rita pulled keys out of her purse, a gold bracelet dangled from her wrist.

"That's a lovely bracelet," Jade said. "Are those emerald charms?"

"Thank you. They're my birthstone," Rita responded. "We share a birthday month. This was a gift from a friend."

Jade needed a new laptop, but had wondered about the bracelet in Brian's bag. Now she had her answer.

CHAPTER 43

DOREEN

"Sure you can't stay for a celebratory toast?" Doreen's boss asked. "Don't worry about professional protocol. It's the weekend, and it's almost noon."

Doreen and her team had just attended the monthly Chamber of Commerce brunch and her CBI presentation was a roaring success. The chamber president and four CEOs pledged their support with mentors, contracts, and dollars.

"I can't stay today," Doreen replied.

"I'm sorry. How insensitive of me. Sometimes I forget you're a preacher's wife. You can get a nonalcoholic beverage."

"That's not it. My husband has meetings this morning and we promised the boys we'd take them to the new Spider-Man movie this afternoon." Doreen also figured she had time to catch the last hour of his meeting and the luncheon.

James had been upset when she said she couldn't attend today's district quarterly planning meeting and luncheon. During counseling, he said they were supposed to be a team and her absences showed a lack of support. She promised to attend the next meeting, but that was before she knew it conflicted with the chamber meeting. She tried to explain to James, but he just slammed the door and left. The bank was open weekdays from nine to five, but Doreen knew the deals were made at events like today's brunch, and she had to be present. Now that the project was off to a sound start, she could reduce her overtime.

Doreen rushed to the Hilton Hotel, which wasn't far from her chamber brunch. When she went to the lobby, the district meeting wasn't on the events board. The hotel concierge confirmed that no meeting was scheduled. She called the church to get the location and learned the bishop was ill and had canceled the meeting.

Her call to James went to voice mail, so she texted to remind him of the movie time and asked him to call her. She called the boys to remind them to do their chores, then pulled out of her fourth-floor parking space. But when she drove through the second level, she saw James's BMW. The *real men love Jesus* bumper sticker left no doubt. Instead of exiting, she circled the floor and drove past his car again, then backed into a spot on the same row. She rolled her window down and waited, though she wasn't sure what she was waiting for. James's ministry took him all over the city, at all times of day and night. Until his vasectomy admission, she had never known him to lie to her, and in his convoluted way, that lie of omission had come from love. She had never questioned him or felt the need to check up on him. But based on what she saw next, maybe she shouldn't have been so trusting.

James got off the elevator, but he wasn't alone. Devoted Sister Rachel was by his side.

CHAPTER 44

ANGEL

Angel strained to pull her Louis Vuitton suitcase off the baggage carousel. At times like this, she missed her personal assistant. Now she had to get her own luggage, ride in a cab rather than have a limo waiting, and learn how to tip. Most cabdrivers didn't even get out to open her door. But she figured these hardships were temporary. She would not be a "where are they now" footnote in some magazine. The reunion tour was just the first part of her plan. The tour would get her recognized by some record company, who would sign her to a contract. But this time, she had the wisdom of years in the music business. She'd insist on having publishing rights and sing her own songs. That's where the money was. She would be smarter with her money and invest in something other than husbands. And since her baby would be a college graduate, Crystal could be her business manager. It would be good to have family handling her money. Her records and concerts weren't selling like they used to, but she had made enough money to last a lifetime. *Where did it all go?* she often wondered. Angel learned too late that most of it had gone in Ray Nelson's bank account. Million-dollar contracts sound impressive, but the advance was just a loan against future earnings in a system where the accounting was rigged. The limos, studio time, designer wardrobe, even the fresh fruit in the dressing room had been charged against her account. All she had to show for her travails were designer clothes, pictures, and memories. One thing she had done right was educate her child, and seeing her princess walk across the stage tomorrow would make it all worth it.

Angel felt someone pull her arm. She was used to fans touching her, and turned around ready to speak, quickly make apologies, and move on. It was her favorite fan. "Mother, I'm sorry we weren't here when you landed. We ran into traffic. I'm glad we found you, but you're never hard to spot in a crowd."

They walked over to the next curb and a pearl white SUV pulled up. Angel was stunned when Preston got out and walked toward her. While they had spoken occasionally on the phone, she hadn't seen her first husband in six years, at Crystal's high school graduation.

"You look lovely as always," he said, as he hugged her. He opened the door for her and Angel stepped in, not sure what to say. Angel stole glances at him as he drove. His hair was still cut short with slight waves, but the hairline was a little farther back, and gray specks in his beard complemented his creamy caramel skin. His chino slacks and powder blue button-down shirt looked like they were tailor-made for his fit six-foot frame.

Angel had turned down a lucrative engagement in Las Vegas. She needed money, but couldn't miss her daughter's graduation. Crystal had started at Stanford, changed her major every year, and seemed destined to be a professional student. But her daughter transferred to the University of Memphis, and settled on finance. She was studying for her CPA exam.

They arrived at Preston's house and he had to park three houses away. Cars filled the driveway and the street. "My mom and dad are staying with me. My brother and his wife also came for the graduation," Preston said.

"Aunt Ivy arrived yesterday and you'll also get a chance to meet Ahmad," Crystal said.

"Is that the boyfriend? It's about time you let me look him over. Preston, have you met him? Do you like him?" Angel asked.

"He seems like an intelligent young man. Of course, no one is good enough for our baby, but if Crystal is happy, I'm happy. I hope he plans to cut those plaits off his head when he starts job hunting."

"Those are dreads, Daddy."

"That's an appropriate name. They look dreadful," Preston said, shaking his head.

"So that's why you stopped fixing your hair," Angel said.

"I fix my hair. I just don't fix it the way you've been conditioned by Western society to expect. Anyway, Ahmad doesn't want a job. He's already been accepted by the Peace Corps and I've applied too."

"What?" Preston asked.

"The Peace Corps? Don't they send you to places without running water or electricity?" Angel asked.

"What better education than working in the world? The selection process can take over a year, so I'll still start my accounting internship. I'll give you the details later. Some of my friends have also been accepted. They're coming over too."

"Sounds like a full house; you should've let me reserve the Imperial suite downtown. I must tell Ellen how much I appreciate her hosting my baby's celebration."

"She won't be there," Crystal said.

"Oh? Did she have to go out of town suddenly?"

"We've separated," Preston said. "She moved out."

Angel noticed for the first time, he wasn't wearing a wedding ring. She never thought Preston and Ellen made a good couple. Ellen was clingy and jealous and dressed like she shopped at the Walmart clearance rack.

"So sorry to hear that. You made a lovely couple," Angel said.

Aunt Ivy and Angel's dad must have been standing in the window, because they came outside to greet them before Preston even had his keys out of the ignition. "I'll help you with the bags. I know my daughter packed enough for a month."

Aunt Ivy and Angel locked arms and walked up the driveway. "Just think, your baby is going to be a college graduate. Such a shame my sister can't be here. Your mother would be so proud of her. So what do you think about the news?"

"It's wonderful. I know I'm biased, but Crystal is amazing," Angel said.

"She is, but that's not what I'm talking about." Aunt Ivy then whispered, "You know Preston is getting divorced from that woman."

"I heard. What a shame."

"A shame? More like perfect timing. He's available, you're available..." Aunt Ivy said and nudged Angel with her elbow. "Now's your chance."

"What are you talking about? Preston and I are ancient history."

"Tell that to someone else. My sister can't tell you, so I'm speaking for her. You can't find the right one, because you already had him. You've seen the world and made your mark. It's time for you to settle down. Don't blow it this time."

Preston's brother and sister-in-law greeted her as she entered the house. Angel remembered Preston bribing him with candy and quarters to keep him from tattling when he found Preston and Angel kissing. She was relieved her father had not brought his new woman, and the two of them found a spot to eat together.

"Angela, there you are," her cousin Margie said, when she found Angel getting a second helping of ribs and corn. "Let me go tell these amateurs that you and I got next." Angel and her cousins played cards, joked and talked trash as though they hung out every weekend. No one wanted the day to end, but the mosquitos were chasing them inside and they had to get up early for the graduation. Angel and Aunt Ivy were going to Rainbow Village after the commencement, then Angel was taking a late flight back to Chicago.

Crystal's apartment was near downtown, in an arts district that had been abandoned warehouses when Angel was growing up. Angel remembered decorating playhouses and castles in Rose Manor for her daughter's visits. Now she was visiting her daughter's place. It seemed she had grown up overnight, Angel thought as she ran a bath. Angel was lighting candles when her phone rang.

"Brooke, hey girl. How's it going?"

"You sound mighty chipper. Sorry I have to spoil your good mood."

"You worry too much. What is it?" Angel asked.

"Jade called and said she wants to do the tour. But Carmen's attorney said she won't tour unless everyone is paid the same."

"That's ridiculous. If it weren't for me busting my butt the last twenty years, people would have forgotten about the Diamonds long ago. What about Doreen?"

"I called her, and she said it wouldn't be the same without Carmen. But she would think about it," Brooke said.

"How ungrateful. I'm sorry I asked them," Angel said.

"We have to submit signed contracts next week, otherwise I wouldn't have bothered you at your daughter's graduation. Should I request more time?" Brooke asked.

"No. Go ahead and get the contracts changed," Angel replied.

"Are you sure?" Brooke asked.

"We don't have much choice. I've got to move my mother, and move out of Ray's condo as soon as possible," Angel said. *Like yesterday*, she thought, as she poured her daughter's Skin So Soft bath oil in the tub.

Angel found a Whitney Houston playlist, put her phone on speaker, then stepped into her daughter's tiny bathtub. It had been a lovely day, and even Brooke's news couldn't spoil her high spirits. There were no A-listers, wannabe A-listers, or paparazzi, other than cell phones. She learned line dances, drank beer—from a glass of course—and ate more than her share of hot wings. She had even let a *y'all* or two slip into her conversation. These were people who didn't care if she had a record contract, a song on the charts, or lived in Rose Manor. When she was younger, she thought success was adoring fans, sold-out concerts, and hit records. Now she knew people's adoration was conditional, but having caring friends and family were the real measures of success. She smiled while scrolling through the pictures on her phone, savoring the family outing, and lingering over the selfies she had taken with Preston and Crystal. Aunt Ivy's advice about Preston stayed in her thoughts. They had been so different then and were even more different now. But were they really? Today, she was just Angela, and for the first time in a long time, that was enough.

CHAPTER 45

CARMEN

It had been ages since Carmen had been inside a mall. Before they signed with Peak Records, Gloria scheduled mall promotional dates for the Diamonds. The girls thought they were really big stuff then. Carmen just smiled and shook her head.

She didn't shop often, and what shopping she did, she did online. Today she was exchanging the two pair of yoga pants she had ordered for a smaller size. She needed them for her trip to Chicago and didn't have time to ship them back. Her mind and memory were telling her not to tour, but her bank account said yes. Angel agreed to the contract changes David's attorney suggested and agreed to delay their meeting date to accommodate Carmen's school schedule.

Carmen finished her exchange, then stopped by Hope's new job. There was a line of customers, so she just waved to her daughter and headed to the parking lot. On the way, she browsed in a few stores. She had lost three dress sizes and shopping was fun again. But with David's legal bills sucking up all her money, new clothes weren't in the budget. She resisted Macy's call, but couldn't resist the smell of almond brown sugar, cinnamon-coated pretzels as she passed the food court. When she set her purse on a table to check how much cash she had, she spotted a familiar face. He was at the next table, engrossed in his phone.

"Hey stranger," Carmen said.

"Hello," Gerald said, as he looked up. "How are you?"

"Who says men don't do malls?" Carmen asked. They hadn't spoken since he left her house, three weeks earlier. He hadn't answered her calls or texts and Carmen eventually gave up. She thought she was fine with it, until now. Hearing his sexy, smooth voice made her smile, contradicting the nonchalant facade she was aiming to portray.

"I'm waiting on my daughter and a friend. Her shopping with my credit card, and me waiting is her idea of us spending time together. How is David?"

"Doing as well as can be expected. Thanks for the graduation card. Although David has to go to summer school to graduate. We thought he could test out, but he missed too many days. We're hoping this nightmare will soon be over." After a painfully long twenty second silence, Carmen said, "You know, we never really talked after that day at the house—"

"Carmen, I know you like closure, but let's leave it alone. We had a few fun dates, then moved on. No drama or hurt feelings," Gerald said, as he stood. "You take care of yourself and tell Miss Glo I said hello." He walked to the escalator, where his daughter grabbed his arm and a Nia Long look-alike greeted him with a peck on the lips. Carmen watched as they disappeared into Macy's.

A few fun dates? If that's all it was, why did she feel so bad?

CHAPTER 46

JADE

"It's getting hot in here," Dawn said. "I guess I should go inside."

The van had idled so long, the air conditioner was no longer cooling. It wasn't officially summer, but the heat was already stifling, and condensation had formed on the windshield. Jade had prolonged their parting as long as she could. "Did you memorize the number I gave you?"

"It's in my backpack," Dawn said, as she popped her gum.

"You need to memorize it. Call me any time, for any reason. Miss Branch said you'll have liberal phone privileges."

"I want you to know I appreciate everything you've done. You've been real decent."

"You're welcome," Jade replied. "But why are you talking like you won't see me again?"

"I've been through this before. I know you're not coming back, but it doesn't matter. I'll be eighteen in a few months, then I can go on my own."

"Dawn, I'll have everything set before your birthday. This is for us. I'll earn enough from touring to leave Brian and get an apartment. What can I do or say to make you believe me?"

"Come back," Dawn said softly.

Jade was headed to Chicago for the first official Encore Tour rehearsal. She couldn't wait to get started. The sooner she started, the sooner she could straighten out Dawn's situation. She had made the painful decision to let Dawn be placed in a group home while tour preparations were in process. Once she got her advance, she'd get an apartment and could come get Dawn.

She had also made another decision—to leave Brian. Jade felt like she had emerged from a fog, and had spent the last few weeks putting her plans in place. But that meant letting Brian think she had forgiven him. She had spent the last few years trying to figure out what was wrong between them and how she could fix it.

Mrs. Randolph would have said she needed more Jesus, so she joined a church. The services were uplifting, but she still felt adrift. Next, she loaded up on negligees, scented oils, and sex toys in an effort to resurrect her libido—but that didn't help either. When Brian refused to attend marriage counseling, she attended therapy alone. The therapist asked what made her happy—and what were her life goals? Questions she had never asked herself. She realized she regretted not finishing high school, so she began GED classes. They discussed her childhood and her ambivalence about her mother and Native American heritage. Jade believed she was making progress, but Brian denounced it as psychobabble and said they couldn't afford her "whine" sessions.

But just as you can't un-ring a bell, she wasn't comfortable bottling up her feelings anymore. She wasn't even mad about Rita. His affair was the catalyst she needed. It had taken her twenty years to learn security and happiness were not synonymous.

"Hello, ladies," Miss Branch said. "Dawn is just in time for lunch. Follow me."

Jade picked up a suitcase, but Miss Branch stopped her. "We'll take her things. In our experience, we've found it's best you say your goodbyes here."

Jade hugged Dawn and whispered in her ear, "I will be back. Think of it as a horrible summer camp. Use the time to study for the ACT. Miss Branch said they will take you to the library so you can keep your Saturday tutoring appointments. I'll be back in time for you to start school. I promise."

"Goodbye," Dawn said, and turned to follow the caseworker.

"Not goodbye—see you soon," Jade promised.

After she dropped Dawn off, she went home and finished packing. She was fixing lunch when Brian came in the kitchen.

"Want a grilled cheese sandwich?"

"No time to eat. You need to come with me to the bank this afternoon," Brian said, as he grabbed a bottle of water.

"Did you forget? My flight is at four o'clock. I'll go when I get back next week," Jade replied.

"That's too late. I told the bank officer we would clear the overdraft and bring the loan current today."

"How are we going to do that?"

"I told him we'd use your advance check to catch up on the past-due payments and he agreed to release our savings account and instead take an assignment of your contract as collateral."

"You shouldn't have made that commitment without asking me," Jade said.

"Well, what's your plan?" Brian asked. "We won't make payroll if we don't clear the overdraft."

"You should have thought about that before you bought your girlfriend that fancy bracelet."

"What are you talking about?" Brian asked.

"You know what I'm talking about. I was going to wait, but now is as good a time as any. I'm doing something I should have done a long time ago. I'm leaving you," Jade announced, as she flipped the sandwich.

"What has gotten into you?"

"Give it up, Brian. I know everything. Maybe not everything—but enough. You and Rita can worry about Seaside. I'm through and I'm certainly not signing over my advance."

"I guess Dawn told you some wild story. She blames me for having to go to a group home and this is her revenge. She's making this up," Brian said.

Jade turned the stove off, then turned to face her husband. "This has nothing to do with Dawn. The truth has been yelling at me for years. I've just refused to listen."

"Then listen to this," Brian said, pointing his index finger barely an inch from Jade's nose. "No homeless bitch whose own mother didn't want her is going to ruin my household. And I'm not going to lose my restaurant because you're jealous over some waitress."

"Don't flatter yourself. She's welcome to you, and since it's *your* restaurant, you pay for it." Jade stormed to their bedroom, slammed her suitcase shut, and grabbed her purse. Brian followed her and grabbed her arm as she tried to walk past him. "Let me go," she demanded.

"I've carried your sorry ass all this time and now you think you can walk out?"

"You carried me? Now who's making things up?"

"Rita means nothing to me," Brian confessed as he let her arm go. "I'll make it up to you. But don't do this."

"Brian, it's too late."

"It's never too late baby. I shouldn't have said those things. I love you and I know you love me. This is just a rough patch for us. Let's go to counseling, like you suggested."

"All right," Jade said, as she rubbed her arm. "But I'll follow you to the bank. I'll sign everything, then you stay and finish whatever else needs to be done. I don't want to miss my flight. I'll text you the location where I park the van, and you and one of the guys can pick it up."

"Anything you say, baby," Brian said. He picked up her suitcase and carried it to her van.

Brian pulled out of the driveway and Jade followed him for fifteen minutes. But when they got to the freeway, Brian got on and she stayed on the frontage road. Her phone rang and she pushed the *speaker* button.

"What happened?" Brian asked. "Did the light catch you?"

"Yeah, the light of common sense," Jade replied.

"I thought we had this all worked out," Brian said. "I don't have time to listen to your whining."

"Then listen to this. I'm taking my sorry ass to Chicago and when I return I'm taking my sorry ass and my advance check to a lawyer to get rid of my sorry ass husband."

"Go ahead. You'll be back," Brian shouted. "You're nothing but poor white trash. Wait, you ain't even that good. I should say poor half-breed trash. The next time—"

Jade disconnected the call. He called back three times, but she didn't answer. Her heart was beating so hard, she pulled into a parking lot to catch her breath. She hadn't felt an adrenaline rush like that since her first time onstage as a Diamond. Today was the day she had lived on eggshells trying to avoid. Now that she had finally left Brian, she couldn't wait to move on.

The plane arrived in Chicago, but traffic was so congested it took her as long to get from the airport to her hotel as it did to fly from Houston. When she finally made it, her first order of business was to call room service. No plain grilled cheese for this free bird. She ordered an appetizer, entrée, and dessert. She also ordered a bottle of Pinot Noir to celebrate. The waiter thanked Jade profusely for her generous tip. She took a shower, then toasted to her emancipation.

She fell asleep watching a Bette Davis movie and the room phone awakened her. The pale teal light peeking through the curtains confused her. Jade couldn't remember the last time she had slept eight hours straight. She started not to answer, thinking it was Brian with some lame apology, but reconsidered, since it could be Angel, checking to make sure she had arrived.

"Good morning," the cheerful voice said. "This is the front desk."

"You have the wrong room," Jade said, in a groggy voice. "I didn't arrange a wake-up call."

"This is Mrs. Anderson, isn't it?"

"Yes."

"I apologize for waking you, but we have a matter we need taken care of. We place a hold on guest credit cards for incidentals, but our computers were down when you checked in. Your card was declined when we ran it this morning, so we need another payment method."

"Maybe your computers are down again. Try again later," Jade stated, then hung up. Jade turned over and pulled the sheet over her shoulder just as the phone rang again. She turned back over and snatched the phone off the stand. "What?"

"Mrs. Anderson, I'm so sorry to disturb you again, but we—"

"How is this my problem?" Jade asked as she sat up in the

bed. "Your computers weren't working and now you're harassing me. What is your manager's name?"

"I am the manager, Mrs. Anderson. Please accept our apologies, but it's hotel policy that we have a credit card on file. Miss Brooke Watson made the reservation; perhaps that's who we should have called."

"I'll take care of it. Can it wait until later, or do you want me to come to the lobby in my nightgown?"

"No, ma'am. We just wanted to make sure you were aware."

"I have an appointment at nine. I'll stop by the front desk on my way out."

"Thank you, Mrs. Anderson. Any time before noon will be fine."

Jade put on her glasses and grabbed her purse. She found the Visa card and tried to call customer service, but her phone was dead. She plugged it into another outlet, then used the room phone to call. She was bewildered when the recording said the card had been reported stolen and was suspended. She called to talk to a human and was told the same thing. When she asked about getting a replacement, they said she was just a signor, and the primary cardholder would have to initiate the request. She checked on her American Express card and was told the same thing. Her card had been reported stolen and the account closed. She called her cell phone and the recording said the number was no longer in service. It didn't take Sherlock Holmes to figure out what had happened. Brian had canceled the cards and her phone. She emptied her wallet and counted three hundred sixty-seven dollars, and there was six hundred in her personal bank account. Her first thought was to phone Brian and call him the profane names she had left out the day before. But she wasn't really mad. His actions were confirmation that she was doing the right thing.

Jade devised a plan to stall the hotel clerk until Monday, when she could have money wired. Angel said their first payment would be direct deposited within ten days and she would use that money to find an apartment and an attorney. The reunion tour would be the seed money to start her new life. Twenty years ago, the Diamonds had been the source of her independence. She needed that support one more time.

CHAPTER 47

THE DIAMONDS

To avoid the front desk clerk, Jade had exited through the parking garage. And to conserve cash, she walked the six blocks to the address Angel had sent. The building appeared to be under construction and Jade double-checked the address. She tentatively opened the door and two men with tool belts and paint-splattered overalls pointed to the elevator. She exited on the sixth floor and met Brooke, who escorted her to the room serving as their rehearsal studio. She, Doreen, and Carmen squealed like schoolgirls when they saw each other.

"Can you believe we're doing this?" Doreen asked.

"As usual, Mama was right—never say never," Carmen said.

Diamonds songs were playing in the background and they laughed as they tried to re-create their choreography. After Doreen suggested a bathroom break, Carmen checked her watch and said, "Don't take this wrong, I love seeing you, but it's almost ten o'clock. Where is Miss Thang? By the time she arrives, I'll be ready for lunch."

"Sorry I'm late," Angel said, breezing into the room. "I misjudged my time this morning, then my cabdriver got stuck behind an accident."

"You contacted us," Carmen said. "The least you can do is be on time."

"Must you be such a nag? It's barely been two minutes and you're griping," Angel said.

"Two minutes for you, an hour for us. I do believe we live in the same time zone. That's central standard time, not Angela standard time."

"Let's get started," Doreen said, while fanning herself. "I thought you lived in this building."

"Ray is still renovating this building. My condo is closer to the lake."

"Miss Angel, I told you to rent a car," Brooke said. "It would be more reliable."

"Oh no, she didn't suggest Angela Donovan drive a car like a mere mortal?" Carmen said, under her breath.

Jade poked Carmen in the side.

"Girl, hush," Doreen snickered.

Angel quickly stepped out of her skirt and strapped sandals. She wore a black bodysuit and her hair was pulled into a sleek ponytail. She removed four candles from a small velvet bag and placed them on the table.

"Are you trying to set a romantic mood or something?" Carmen asked.

"These are magnolia-scented tea candles. Feng shui principles state placing four candles in the center of any meeting room promotes harmony."

"Being on time promotes harmony too," Carmen said. "And that smell is too sweet for me."

"You are determined to spread your bad karma," Angel said, with both hands on her hips. "I can't function with negativity. If you don't want—"

"All right, you two," Jade interrupted. "I left my referee whistle in Houston, so play nice."

The songs were easy. Everyone remembered the lyrics and their harmonies were tight. There was friction when

Angel complained Carmen was spending too much time on her phone, but otherwise the morning went smoothly. They had a working lunch and discussed tour details. The first topic was wardrobe.

"We'll come out in black, form-fitting, strapless dresses of varying lengths, with lace-up gladiator stilettos, then change to diamond-studded leather outfits for our upbeat dance songs," Angel said. For the finale, Angel passed around drafts of a shimmering, silver gown with a plunging neckline, thigh-high slit, and deep V in the back.

Carmen laughed when she saw it. "I know you don't think I'm wearing that. There's no support. Some of us do have breasts that haven't been artificially modified."

"Cups are built into the dress," Angel replied, as she opened a bottle of green tea.

"I don't know…" Jade said slowly.

"This material looks the most like Diamonds, so we should stick with it," Angel said, while collecting the sketches. "I picked the slit design, so we could show our tattoos. But that won't work with Carmen's lumpy cellulite. Maybe we can use the same material and vary the styles."

"We're not falling for that," Carmen argued, turning to Doreen and Jade. "Remember how we'd plan our outfits, then Angela would show up wearing something totally different? Who's going to pay attention to us if she's got her titties and ass hanging out?"

"We don't have to wear tents just because you've let yourself go," Angel said.

"It's a little revealing," Doreen said, while fanning herself. "Especially the slit. I am a preacher's wife, you know."

"Another thing," Jade said. "I don't wear high heels anymore. I've got a bad back."

"And I have a bunion that gives me the blues whenever I wear heels," Carmen added.

"You sound like senior citizens," Angel said, shaking her head.

"I have another idea," Doreen said. "Let's include a tribute to Sophia."

"People are coming to have fun," Angel said. "We shouldn't bring up anything negative."

"If it wasn't for Sophia, you wouldn't even have joined the group," Carmen said. "Doreen and I were against it."

"I never met her, but I don't see the harm," Jade said. "There could be a hologram during one of our songs. They can make it look so real."

"That's too nostalgic, and a little creepy," Angel said.

"Well, we say yes. You're not the HNIC," Carmen said.

"It's hot in here," Doreen said, as she grabbed a bottle of water. "This isn't cold. Is there a refrigerator in here?"

"Cold drinks and ice contract your vocal cords," Angel said. "I drink water at room temperature."

"Hooray for you," Carmen said, and clapped twice.

Brooke cleared her throat and asked, "Are there any other preliminaries to discuss?"

"We didn't include a hairdresser in the tour budget, but looks like we may need one," Angel said, tapping her bottom lip. "Jade, you'll need to lighten up a shade or two. And Carmen, have you thought about what you'll do with your hair?"

"Nope," Carmen replied.

"Mario has been with me several years. He has the Midas touch and his potions and perms make your hair grow."

"I don't do perms," Carmen stated.

Angel sighed and said, "Of course you don't. Well, Mario can create anything we want. He uses Malaysian human hair and—"

"No, thank you," Carmen replied. "I like the human hair on my head."

"And I stopped coloring my hair years ago," Jade said.

"Your color is okay, could use highlights. And definitely another style," Angel said.

"Brian never liked me to cut my hair."

"You can't be serious," Angel said. "Are we back in the 1950s?"

"I'm considering going natural," Doreen said.

"That's okay for plodding around Memphis, but onstage, the audience wants glamour."

"The audience wants talent, not hair," Carmen said.

"I've been doing this awhile and I think I know what people want," Angel said. "We're talking about the professional stage, not some church or school production."

"We've all performed professionally, so please don't talk to us like we're amateurs," Doreen stated.

"You're the one with the career slump," Carmen said. "The Diamonds went out on top, so we're doing you a favor."

"We can resolve these things later. I'll email more wardrobe choices to everyone. Why don't you take a break?" Brooke said, looking at her watch. "Nico will be here in twenty minutes to go over the choreography. I'll find some ice."

Twenty minutes later, Nico bounced into the room with enough energy for them all. Carmen was answering a phone call and told them to start without her. Jade and Doreen stumbled through the first song and the results weren't any better once Carmen returned.

"You guys were supposed to practice at home," Angel complained. "You act like you're learning these steps for the first time. We have less than two months to get this together and it's almost June."

"I didn't realize I was so out of shape," Doreen said, as she wiped her brow.

"Me either," Carmen agreed.

"That's why I work out," Angel said. "I know you've

lost weight, but you need to exercise too. Although, it's probably those cancer sticks you puff that have you out of breath."

"Let's just use the steps we had before," Carmen stated. "It wouldn't take us long to brush up on those."

"Surely you don't expect us to go onstage doing the vogue and the running man?" Angel said. "If you weren't so *busy* with your phone calls, maybe you could keep up."

"I'm not auditioning for *Soul Train*," Carmen said, as she sat. "As long as we sound good, we don't need fancy steps."

Doreen sat too and fanned herself with a newspaper.

"You must be having a hot flash," Carmen said.

"I'm not that old," Doreen insisted.

"It can start in your thirties," Jade said. "I saw it on *The View*."

"It's not menopause. It's hot in here," Doreen said.

"I don't know what the big deal is," Carmen said. "I'll be glad to eliminate pads and tampons from my shopping list. Shut this baby-maker down."

"About five years ago, Brian and I considered having another child," Jade confided.

"You've got to be kidding," Carmen said. "I couldn't imagine myself with a small child at this age."

"I'm getting nervous," Angel said. "Carmen and I agree on something. I think it's selfish to have a baby at an older age."

"Men do it all the time," Doreen said, as she opened another bottle of water.

"And we all know men are selfish. So, I rest my case," Carmen said.

"I said five years ago. It's not like I was forty."

"Forty isn't old," Doreen argued.

"It's too old to be having a baby," Carmen said.

"Women keep having them, so God must not think it's too old," Doreen said. "Look at Madonna and Halle Berry. Janet Jackson was fifty."

"As much as I love to stay trendy, I'll pass on that one. I worked too hard on this body," Angel said, patting her flat stomach.

"Me too," Carmen said and laughed as she answered her phone.

Nico returned to the room and clapped his hands for them to restart as Carmen left the room to take her call.

"Okay, this is ridiculous," Angel blurted. "We all have outside responsibilities. If we can clear our calendars, Carmen can too."

"Time is money, girls," Nico said, tapping his watch.

Carmen returned to the room and announced, "I have to leave."

"Now what?" Angel asked.

"Is something wrong?" Doreen said.

"Another case settled, and the judge has an opening in her schedule. David's trial has been moved up to next week."

"Trial? What trial?" Jade asked.

"He was in a car accident last summer, and it turns out the car was stolen, and had drugs and guns in it. David was a passenger, but they claim he had something to do with the car theft, the guns and the drugs," Doreen stated. "The other driver died. He was a police officer."

"That's crazy," Angel remarked. "How was he supposed to know the car was stolen? And he certainly didn't tell the driver to have an accident."

"Hopefully, the jury agrees," Carmen said, while gathering her things.

"A jury trial? For a car accident?" Jade asked.

"So much for our color-blind justice system," Carmen said. "That's why I agreed to this tour. I need money for David's legal fees."

"All the more reason for us to do our best and put together an outstanding show," Angel said. "Nico doesn't come cheap. Let's finish up with him, then—"

"Didn't you hear me? I have to go. They're trying to send my baby to prison."

"I need a break," Doreen said, breathing heavily and holding on to the back of a chair.

"You don't look good," Jade observed.

"I'll be fine. Just let me go outside and get some air. Did we ever get ice?"

"Why don't we all take a break?" Jade asked. "Carmen can check on David. Doreen can cool off. Then we'll—"

"You all are making this impossible," Angel complained. "You couldn't leave home, so we recorded the routines for you to access online, and said we'd do a marathon weekend practice. You didn't practice at home and can't understand why you aren't catching on to the steps or why you're so tired. We've cut it to two days and you can't even work a full day. It takes hard work and sacrifice to be successful."

"I think you forgot one more ingredient for your success—you need knives to put in people's backs," Doreen said, as she walked toward the door. "Lord forgive me. I've tried to remain civil with you, but don't try to act all brand-new, as the young folks say."

"And I know you're not lecturing me about hard work and sacrifice. At least I raised my children and didn't spend the last twenty years sleeping with every Tom, Dick and Eric," Carmen said.

"That's where this attitude is coming from? You think I had something to do with you and Eric breaking up? He really wasn't my type. I should have let you have him."

"You don't *let* me do anything. We were going to break up anyway, but you sure helped speed it up. You were supposed to be my friend," Carmen said.

"She's right. You were dead wrong, Angel," Jade said. "Carmen, I wanted to tell you, but I was new. I didn't want to rock the boat."

"Nobody asked you anything," Angel snapped, as she

pushed a stray strand behind her ear. "You couldn't carry a tune in a bucket. If you weren't white with big boobs, you wouldn't even be here."

"I'm going out with Doreen, before I say something I can't take back," Jade said.

"You have something to say? Say it. All of you have carried a grudge against me for no reason. You're just jealous because you quit and I didn't."

"I wouldn't call getting my sister kicked out of the group, no reason," Doreen stated. "Then you didn't have the decency to come to her funeral."

"If it makes you feel better, go ahead and blame me. But we all know Sophia was strung out and missing rehearsals and shows. I loved Sophia, but she had plenty of chances to get clean. I couldn't come to the funeral, but did all I could for her while she was alive. Who do you think paid for her last rehab stay? She called me because she wanted to get her kids back and said you wouldn't help her."

"Sophia knew I'd do anything for her," Doreen insisted, while wiping sweat from her brow.

"That's not what she told me," Angel said. "She said you sold your mother's house, without giving her a dime. And now you want to honor your beloved sister. Please. That's just to ease your conscience."

"That's a lie," Doreen shouted.

"Keep telling yourself that. We both know the truth. And Carmen, I didn't take Eric from you. I didn't know you were serious about him."

"This isn't about Eric. And as far as your comment about hard work and sacrifice, I work hard every day. Try being in a room all day with thirty teenagers and see how you do."

"I wouldn't do well at all. I admire teachers, mostly because they work for so little pay. I demand a lifestyle that teaching won't provide."

"It's not always about money. I wanted to raise my own

children and be home with them every night," Carmen said. "My children have always come first."

"We see how great that's worked out. I guess if I had stayed in Memphis, my child could be on trial too," Angel said.

"I knew this was a mistake," Carmen said, with eyes of fire. "You are the same self-centered, shameless bitch you always were. You're lucky I teach peer mediation. Back in the day, I would've slapped the silicone out of your fake titties and hung you with your weave."

"All this animosity about some guy who couldn't kiss or screw. Eric was a sweetheart, but we were just fooling around," Angel said.

"I told you this wasn't about Eric. What about Ray? I suppose you were just fooling around with him too. Sleeping with the boss is the oldest trick—and I do mean *trick*—in the book to get ahead. And if I recall, didn't you have a husband?" Carmen said.

"What? You slept with Ray too? Wasn't he rather old for you?" Jade asked.

"We had an understanding. And you," Angel said, pointing to Jade, "should be glad because Ray planned to drop you when the group broke up. He said they overdubbed everything, but I convinced him to extend your contract when we moved to Chicago."

"So, we owe you a debt of gratitude? You were looking out for everybody? You looked out for Angel. I thought it was strange you got a solo deal," Jade said, and moved to stand next to Carmen.

"I worked hard and earned a solo deal."

"Yeah, and we know what you were working," Doreen said and hi-fived Carmen and Jade.

"I'll admit, I've done things I'm not proud of. I was young. If I were a man, you'd say I was a player and slap me on the back."

"I'd like to slap you, all right," Carmen stated.

"Well, I'm not going to lie and say I wouldn't do it again. I kept my eyes on the prize and I used what my mama gave me to get it."

"The ends justify the means—no matter what? You are so lost. All I can do is pray for you," Doreen said.

"Please stop that high-and-mighty first lady act. I know you. You and James smoked crack almost nonstop. But when you got clean, rather than help Sophia, you deserted her," Angel said.

"That's a lie and this reunion charade is over. You're just using us to resurrect your played-out career. Kiss my black ass," Doreen said, as she grabbed a bottle of water and walked out.

"This is the bottom line. You can bicker about who did what to who and when on your own time," Angel said. "I gave everything for this group, and I won't let your bitterness and laziness spoil our legacy. I can easily get some no-name background singers. They'll be glad to work."

"I wish you would," Carmen said. "Doreen and I are the original Diamonds. If you try to do a reunion tour with someone else, we'll tie you up in court so long, you'll have to roll onstage with a walker by the time everything is resolved. My mother treated you like a daughter and you betrayed her. I would expect something low-down from Ray; we knew he was a snake. But my mother helped you every way she could. It's taken all my strength not to tell her what you did. She loves those cheap trinkets you send, but I know you're only easing your guilt."

"She said she was tired of the road and wanted to take things easier for a while," Jade said.

"My mother loved this group and to avoid discord, she resigned. When I found out, I quit."

"The new managers had already negotiated increased performance fees and better perks. You quit just as we were about to make big money," Angel said.

"Everything's not about money, and there is a way to do things," Carmen insisted. "You should have consulted my mother about your concerns."

"As usual, you don't have a clue. Miss Glo and I worked that out a long time ago."

"What are you saying?" Carmen asked.

"I'm saying—"

"Ladies!" Nico interrupted as he entered the room. "Miss Angel, it's Miss Doreen. She's in the hall—"

"Tell her I'm ready to go too. This has been a total waste of time," Carmen said, with disgust.

"Miss Doreen is in the hall. She's passed out," Nico said hysterically.

Angel, Jade, and Carmen knocked over the coffee table, as they rushed to the hall and found Doreen sprawled facedown on the floor. Jade kneeled next to her and gently turned her head. "Call 911," she shouted.

"I'll call them," Nico said. "And I'll go downstairs to flag them down when they get here."

"Let's turn her over," Carmen said.

"We shouldn't move her," Jade said. "There's no blood, but something might be broken. I hope the paramedics get here quickly. She kept saying she was hot. I thought she was just—"

Angel's scream interrupted their conversation. "I was getting a pillow to put under Doreen's head, but when I moved it, the couch cushion burst into flames," Angel said breathlessly.

"Get something to smother the flames," Carmen ordered. "And call the fire department."

Angel reached for her purse, then said, "Great. My phone was on the couch, and it's burning. You call the fire department."

Carmen ran to the sink and opened the cabinets, then shouted, "The water works, but there aren't any containers in here."

"These windows are sealed shut," Angel said, fumbling with the blinds.

"Unless you plan to jump six stories, leave them alone," Carmen shouted. "Opening a window increases oxygen and fuels the fire. We need to get out before the fire spreads."

"Did you say there's a fire in there?" Jade asked as Angel and Carmen rushed to the hall.

"Yes. Let's go now," Carmen said.

"How are we going to get Doreen out?" Jade asked.

"We'll have to carry her," Angel said, as she pressed the elevator button.

"You can't take an elevator during a fire," Carmen warned.

"The fire isn't out here," Angel said.

"Not yet, but wherever the fire is, it can mess with electrical wiring and cause the elevator to stop, or the elevator shaft can fill with smoke. I'm a fire drill captain at my school, and we stress not to get in an elevator."

"Then what do you suggest, Miss Einstein?" Angel said.

"Now you want my advice. I would have suggested you find somewhere other than this half-finished firetrap for us to practice."

"Anything is a firetrap if you knock over lit candles. You still haven't learned to control your temper. I don't know how you can teach someone's child when you can't control yourself."

"Will you two stop?" Jade shouted. "Look, smoke is seeping beneath the door."

"We'll have to take the stairs. I'll hold her under her arms. Jade, grab her legs and Angel, walk sideways and hold her waist," Carmen directed. "Let's go."

CHAPTER 48

JADE

Jade had stalled the hotel clerk and promised to straighten out her bill on Monday, but with rehearsals canceled, there was no reason to stay. Carmen's train had left, and James and Angel remained with Doreen at the hospital. Jade had said her goodbyes last night. She knew with no money or credit to pay her bill and probably no advance check either, she needed to leave as soon and quietly as possible. Tina Turner may have found a hotel that gave her a complimentary room, but Jade doubted she would be so lucky.

Despite setting the alarm clock, Jade was terrified of oversleeping, so she was up at dawn, and at the complimentary breakfast across the street when it opened. She returned to her room to get her bags, took the elevator to the second floor, then stairs to the parking garage, and slipped out the side door. It wasn't easy since the wheels on her suitcase seemed to have their own mind. But she made her way to the El station and figured out how to take it to the airport. The nine-thirty flight was full, but another flight was boarding, and she was able to get on. There was a two-hour layover in Dallas, but at least she was on her way.

By the time Jade arrived in Houston, she was exhausted and hungry. The free hotel breakfast had been her only meal all day. She savored the peanuts they gave her on the plane like they were caviar and requested a second bag. The food court beckoned as she walked toward baggage claim. But she needed cash to get her van from the parking lot; a van almost on empty, so she ignored her hunger pangs. Also, she was running out of time to get to the foster agency before closing.

She stopped at a gift shop to ask where was the nearest pay phone. The clerk said those were removed years ago, but let her use the store phone. She called Dawn's phone, but Brian had cut it off too. She had to empty her purse, but finally found the agency's direct phone number.

"May I speak with Miss Branch?" Jade asked.

"She's not in, would you like her voice mail?"

"This is Dawn Faber's foster mother and I would like to begin the process to release her into my care."

"Miss Branch has left for the day. She'll be back Monday."

"Okay. I'll just come in for a quick visit with Dawn."

"Ma'am, you should speak with Miss Branch. I'll put you through to her voice mail and she'll call you Monday."

"I don't have a call-back number right now. My phone isn't working. It won't take me long to get there," Jade said.

"You should talk to Miss Branch before you come in."

"Miss Branch is familiar with my case. I'll be there shortly." It would take her almost an hour to get there. In Houston traffic, "shortly" didn't exist.

Dawn and I can start apartment hunting tomorrow, Jade thought, as she tried to turn her air conditioner up. She hadn't figured out how she would support them. But she would find a way. Jade used the hour in traffic to plan her strategy. She would find a cheap hotel that took cash and stay there a few days. Monday, her first stop would be a lawyer's office. She didn't want the house or Seaside, so hopefully things could be resolved quickly. All she wanted was a small settlement to tide her over until she found a job. Brian would think he was winning, but she was winning something more important— her freedom.

Jade pulled into the Family Services parking lot and dashed inside. "I called Miss Branch to make an appointment, but got a recording," she told the receptionist.

"Mrs. Anderson, I tried to call you back. Miss Branch is out for the day. I'm sorry you've made an unnecessary trip."

"My plans changed, and I won't be out of town after all. I can fill her in on the details on Monday, but I just couldn't wait to see Dawn."

"Dawn isn't here."

"Did the girls go on a field trip?"

"We spoke with your husband. Didn't he tell you?"

"Tell me what?"

"When the driver went to get Dawn from tutoring yesterday, she never came out."

"That's over twenty-four hours ago," Jade said, with alarm. "Have you called the police? Anything could have happened to her."

"We searched her room and her things are gone. She's run away."

Jade sat in the agency parking lot for two hours. She couldn't go home. She didn't have a working credit card, so she couldn't check into a hotel and her bank was already closed. The desperation of her situation hadn't bothered her when she thought she and Dawn would be together. Jade figured Dawn was with Marquel, but she didn't have his phone number. She rushed to the library and waited for a public computer, then looked up her cell phone bill online. She knew the account passwords and realized she could reverse Brian's cancellation. Then she printed the pages of numbers Dawn called. She was sure one of the numbers was

Marquel's. But then what? At least Marquel had an apartment. Jade had nothing. The tour was off and the Diamonds would return to their annual phone calls and Christmas cards. Her marriage was over and she had nowhere to go in one hour when the library closed. She was back where she started twenty years ago—alone.

The cell phone chimes startled her. The librarian gave her a stern look, but it was a welcome sound to Jade. She was connected to the world again. "It's Angel. I've been trying to reach you. Where are you?"

"I'm back in Houston," Jade said, as she walked to her van. "I saw no reason to hang around. Whoever said, 'Diamonds are forever' wasn't talking about us."

"I'm not giving up," Angel insisted. "Carmen has made her position clear. After yesterday's rehearsal, I don't think we could work together anyway. And Doreen isn't up to it right now. But you and I can still tour."

"How?"

"Hire my background singers. We don't have to pay them as much, so we'll make more money," Angel gushed. "They know the songs and have already told Brooke they're interested."

"I don't know, Angel. It doesn't seem right."

"People do it all the time. Look how many members the Temptations have had. You and I are the main ones anyway. I sang most leads and..."

"And I was the token white girl."

"That's not what I was going to say. But you're what made us unique. And the bottom line is, I need the money and I know you do too. The hotel manager called Brooke. He said you skipped on your bill."

"Angel, I am so embarrassed. It seems my credit card—"

"I spared you my long story, spare me yours. The bottom line is we both need this payday. What do you say?"

Jade didn't want to tour without Carmen and Doreen, but she couldn't ignore the fact that she was in a library parking lot with no place to go. Having a source of income would make things easier with the foster agency and help her find an apartment. There wasn't much demand for a forty-year-old former singer with baking skills and no diploma. Carmen had her family to fall back on. Doreen had a husband and a church full of members. Jade had Jade.

"Angel, I say yes."

CHAPTER 49

ANGEL

Angel stepped off the treadmill and grabbed her keys, hand sanitizer, and water. She could have done another thirty minutes, but a young man had come in and she no longer had the room to herself. Her building had a workout room. But Angel disliked exercising in public, and was used to having her own workout room and private trainer. She was pleasantly surprised how easily she adjusted to living in a smaller space. But she did miss her workout room.

She had missed three texts and two calls from her daughter. Her phone vibrated as soon as she entered her condo. "Preston, what's going on?" Angel asked. "Is Crystal all right?"

"Yes. She just needs some information to complete her Peace Corps application. There were some questions I couldn't help her with."

"That's a relief," Angel said. "When I saw your phone number, I thought maybe there was a problem."

"Well, I hate my number to be associated with problems. I guess I need to call more often. I told Crystal you were probably in bed. You always did sleep late," Preston said.

"For the record, I've been up two hours. I was working out."

"So that's how you keep your sexy shape."

"I'll take that as a compliment," Angel said, drinking in her ex-husband's sexy drawl. "So what does Crystal need?"

"The application requires names and dates of foreign countries she's visited."

"That'll take some digging. Most of my stuff is packed away. Between moving and getting ready for the tour, I'm a little disorganized," Angel said.

"So, the tour is really going to happen? I never see Carmen, but I see Doreen occasionally at the bank. It will be good for you ladies to get back together."

"Doreen and Carmen won't be on the tour."

"Why not?"

"We ran into complications. But Jade will be touring and my background singers are fantastic."

"You're the main attraction anyway," Preston said. "Maybe I'll come to one of your shows."

"I don't remember you being a Diamonds fan."

"Just one Diamond in particular," Preston said.

"Do you know when she needs the list?" Angel asked. She wondered if Preston and his wife were still on bad terms. He wasn't talking like someone with a wife nearby.

"Pretty quick. Most applicants probably don't have this problem. There aren't many young people who've had the opportunities you've given Crystal."

"I guess that was another compliment," Angel said. "I know you never gave me high marks for motherhood."

"True, you aren't the traditional mother. But that's what makes you special and has made Crystal special," Preston said. "Can you believe our little girl is a college graduate? I'm so proud of her. And I can't thank you enough for paying for her tuition. I'm so grateful she didn't have to take out student loans."

"Wow. You didn't get a bad report from the doctor, did

you? Are you trying to get right with God or something?" Angel asked with a chuckle.

"I hope I live every day in a way that pleases God. Can't I say something nice to the mother of my only child?"

Angel, who interacted with the public for a living, was uncharacteristically at a loss for words. "Speaking of mothers, how is your mother?" Angel asked, after an awkward silence.

"She's fine, lively as ever. I wish I could package whatever she has and sell it."

They say you can tell how a man will treat you by watching how he treats his mother, and Preston adored and pampered his mother. When they were married, Angel had accused him of being a mama's boy. But now, she appreciated his attentiveness and understood his mother's concern.

"Speaking of Mother, she's calling, can you hold?"

"That's okay, I need to call Crystal. You take care and thanks again for calling." Angel wondered if she would have been better off being a regular person and staying with Preston. They probably would have had more children and she'd be thirty pounds heavier. Their insurmountable differences now seemed unimportant, especially after his call today. But she couldn't help wondering if she was reading too much into his comments.

Ray sent a good-morning text, as Angel was texting her daughter. She was grateful for his help with the tour, but she needed to put more space between them. Shelley and Keisha, the new Diamonds, were arriving tomorrow. Ray had a furnished model on the first floor of her building they were staying in for the next four weeks. They would immerse themselves in the songs and learn the choreography and "spontaneous" banter for the show. Jade couldn't come right away, but they agreed to set up a webcam so Jade could participate in the rehearsals from Houston. At that moment, Angel had an idea. *Why not turn something I'm doing anyway into an online exercise platform? The cost is minimal, but the upside potential is huge,* she thought. The new generation of entertainers knew how to control their fate and monetize their brand. 50 Cent had water, JLo had perfume, and everybody had clothes. Maybe Carmen not participating was a good thing. Angel couldn't promote getting fit with Carmen's big behind covering half the screen. Between Preston and a possible new business venture, things were turning out even better than she planned.

CHAPTER 50

JADE

Sweat beads rolled down Jade's neck as she trudged up the steps to her apartment, with the last of her purchases. The tour was confirmed, but she wasn't sure when she would get paid again so she was still guarding every cent. But today she splurged. Dawn was coming home. So even though she was planning to move, she spent some of her nest egg to upgrade her apartment. She had been to Walmart, Target, and Family Dollar to get groceries, bedding, towels, and a fire stick, so Dawn could watch movies. Things finally seemed to be falling in line.

Jade had panicked when she returned from Chicago and couldn't find Dawn. Her daughter Tiffany tracked down Marquel at his family's funeral home. They contacted Dawn and convinced her to return to the agency. Dawn had wanted to just come live with Jade since it was only a few months until her birthday. But Jade pleaded with her not to jeopardize her benefits. If Dawn aged out of the foster system, she was eligible for a college tuition waiver and health insurance. Dawn reluctantly agreed to go back, while Jade got things in order.

This was the first time Jade had lived on her own, and

even though she wasn't in the best part of town, it was a step up from the nasty motel she had stayed in when she returned from Chicago. It took ten days for her advance to arrive and clear the bank, and then she had to wait until the first of the month before she could move into an apartment. After three weeks that had seemed like an eternity, she was finally settled and tomorrow morning, she and Dawn would be together again. But Jade couldn't wait, and called the agency to ask to pick her up this evening. *Dawn will be thrilled*, Jade thought as she called the number, and maneuvered through the phone instructions to get to the right department.

"Miss Branch, I wondered if I could just come on over this evening," Jade asked.

"Mrs. Anderson, I'm so glad you called. I meant to call yesterday, but got busy. We've run into a problem with Dawn's placement."

"What do you mean?"

"I wasn't aware you weren't living with your husband," Miss Branch stated.

"We've separated. But that has no bearing on Dawn. If anything, it's positive, since they didn't always get along."

"That may be, but we completed the documents as though Dawn were returning to the same living situation. If circumstances have changed, the process is different."

"I can give you my address. What else do you need?" Jade asked.

"It's more involved than that. I have to open a new case, and it will take several weeks—"

"Several weeks? She's already been there too long. Dawn is my daughter; the paperwork is just a formality," Jade protested.

"The state doesn't see it that way. You were approved as a couple with a home and stable income. Being in an apartment with erratic income is quite different."

"Wait a minute. How do you know I'm in an apartment and that my husband and I separated?" Jade asked while pacing back and forth.

"That doesn't matter. The bottom line is, we have to open a new case. I'll do my best to expedite it. I know you're disappointed, but my hands are tied," Miss Branch said.

"Does Dawn know?" Jade asked.

"I believe Mr. Anderson spoke with her when he was here yesterday."

"My husband was there?"

"Yes, his name is in the visitor log. I realize the process can be frustrating, but we must follow procedures. I'll call in a few days to let you know what to do next."

"All right. I'll look forward to hearing from you," Jade said, as she grabbed her purse. She had already wasted too much time and had no intention of waiting for the state.

CHAPTER 51

DOREEN

"Wake up, Mrs. Golden, your lunch is here." Doreen didn't understand how anyone rested in a hospital. If they weren't drawing blood, giving her a pill, or bringing her bland food, the automatic blood pressure cuff was squeezing her arm. After the fire, she was in the hospital in Chicago for three days until she was stable enough to travel to Memphis. She was home ten days, then fainted while under the dryer at her hair appointment and ended up back in the hospital. They took several tests and finally figured out the problem was her thyroid. While not a minor diagnosis, she and James were relieved it wasn't more serious.

She was tired of being poked and prodded, but wasn't ready to return to her life. James seemed to think she had moved on, but his betrayal still stung, and she felt she had let everyone down. The Diamonds tour was off. Rumors were circulating around the church. The kids were staying with Lucas three extra weeks while she recuperated, and the CBI project was on hold.

Doreen heard a tap on the door and quickly tightened her head scarf, then said, "Come in."

"Hello, honey."

"Miss Glo. What a surprise, I thought you were a nurse."

Doreen was taken aback by Gloria's appearance. She was in a wheelchair, at least thirty pounds lighter, with scraggly gray roots sticking out of her satin turban, and oxygen tubes in her nostrils.

"Sorry to disappoint you," Gloria said, while maneuvering her wheelchair in front of the window. "Your view is better. My window faces the parking garage."

"Carmen told me about your surgery. How are you?"

"Blessed and highly favored. I'm not ready to do the Electric Slide, but the doctors say I will walk again. I would have visited sooner if I had known you were still here. Carmen said you had been discharged."

"I could have gone home Monday. But since I'd have to return every day for breathing exercises and blood work, my doctor gave me the choice of staying or going home. It was easier to just stay."

"Child, always go home when you get the chance. I know too many instances of hospital mix-ups and infections," Gloria said. "I was supposed to go home two days ago but the doctors want to watch my foot longer and changed my discharge date. The only good thing, here I've got this digital gadget, and don't have to prick my fingers. But if I could, I'd be gone faster than a hot knife through butter."

"They've just figured out the best dosage to give me. I was either jittery or sleepy. I'm getting better, but I need a few more days to rebuild my strength," Doreen said.

"Well, you can't hide here forever," Gloria remarked as she took a piece of hard candy out of her pocket. "The sooner you go home, the sooner you can begin your real healing."

"I feel so bad, Miss Glo. When we were in Chicago, Angel said Sophia told her I took her kids and wouldn't help her. I should have let her stay in the house, and my last words to her were horrible. I thought tough love was what she needed. But instead, I took away her hope and she gave up. I've always blamed Lucas, but I was the one who let her down."

"You're giving yourself too much credit," Gloria chided. "Sophia was sweet as can be, but she was also headstrong. Everyone has regrets. You can't let regret about the past, take away your present and future."

"That sounds good, but it's not that easy."

"Your mother and I didn't agree on everything. But if she were here, I bet she'd tell you to get over yourself. Everyone has problems. But you have a good husband, a good job, your family is healthy, your bills are paid, you've traveled the world, and you wear a size seven. So quit whining and go home. A lot of good sisters are just looking for an excuse to 'comfort' their pastor, and I don't mean bring him soup."

"I *was* a size seven. That medicine has made me gain twenty pounds. And I don't know how good James is either. We've seen lust and women sidetrack many great ministries. James said he would never fall into that trap, but now I'm not so sure."

"He's a great minister, but he's still a man. Although I don't think you have anything to worry about."

Doreen turned and looked out the window, then said, "Maybe he'd be better off with someone else. He could have had children by now. You know I lost two babies."

"Did you ever think maybe the Lord wanted you and James to take care of Sophia's children and the children of the church?"

"Miss Glo, my marriage is in trouble and I'm not sure it can survive. James is seeing someone," Doreen confided, as she adjusted her bed.

"The way some women throw themselves at preachers, even the pope would have a tough time resisting," Gloria said. "You just need to be more visible, and let the hussy know she's wasting her time. She'll give up and go prowling at another church."

"It's not that simple. It's not a woman in the congregation."

"Is it a man?" Gloria asked with raised eyebrows.

"Nooooo," Doreen said, with a smile.

"You never know these days. Not that I'm judging."

"It's someone on staff—Rachel."

"Sister Rachel, the youth leader? She is cute and she does spend a lot of time at the church. But I haven't heard one rumor," Gloria said. "I think she just wants to help out."

"She wants to help him, all right. That's not the only issue. He let the kids go stay with Lucas. He knows how I feel about it. He treats me like his secretary. And speaking of secretary, Sister Mayes is sooooo helpful, but I can tell she thinks I should be helping James more too."

"Minnie Pearl Mayes? Don't concern yourself with anything she says," Gloria said, with a dismissive wave. "Messy is her middle name."

"Well, James certainly values her opinion. Whatever I say means nothing, and if my opinion differs from his, it's like I'm going against God," Doreen complained.

"Sounds like the counselors need counseling."

"We've already been to counseling. I thought we were making progress, but now I don't know."

"Everyone goes through valleys from time to time. I'm sure you'll climb out of this one," Gloria said.

"I don't know if I can. And I feel bad about it, because I know I'm supposed to be forgiving and practice what I preach. I was really looking forward to the Diamonds tour. Hanging with the girls again would've been fun."

"I know you wanted to do the tour. I wanted you girls to reunite too. But as always, God knows best. Right now, I think you need to focus on forgiveness."

"You're right. Angel's words hurt, but I was pretty ugly to her too. And James has been—"

"I'm not talking about forgiving them," Gloria said. "You have to forgive yourself. The babies, Sophia, nothing you can do about that now. Once you accept that, I believe things will be much clearer. You have everything you need to be happy. But happiness is not having what you want, but wanting what you have."

"You're right," Doreen said, with a sigh.

"We both have family who care about us and a reasonable portion of health and strength. These are the most important things. This wheelchair won't stop anything. It just means I get the good parking spot."

"You're right as usual."

"So, we're going to get ourselves together and break out of this joint. And so what about the tour? We can still do a girls' trip. Maybe we can go to Biloxi for a weekend and hang out at the beach. I think I can use my casino points for free rooms."

"I'll need to lose weight first," Doreen said.

"Child, please, I wish I could gain my weight back. You look fine to me."

"But none of my clothes fit."

"Then look on the bright side. You'll have a reason to shop," Gloria said. "When all things seem over your head, remember, they are still under God's feet."

"I'm the minister's wife. I should be giving you spiritual advice."

"Having your body parts sliced off will make you think. The Lord has blessed me to see sixty-two years, and I plan to enjoy whatever time I have left. Part of enjoying it is being positive."

"Don't talk like that, Miss Glo. You're not going anywhere for a long time."

"I hope you're right, but you never know," Gloria said,

shaking her head. "If something does happen, I want part of my insurance money to go to the church. And make sure Sonny gets my house."

"You're supposed to put your wishes in a will. You might consider a revocable trust."

"I thought that was for rich folks," Gloria said.

"Anyone with assets or children needs a will at a minimum. But why are we talking about wills and beneficiaries? I'll have someone from the bank discuss all that with you. Now, let's talk about something else."

"Baby, we'll have to talk later. Wilson said he would be here at one o'clock, and I don't want to keep my man waiting. I suggest you call your man too," Gloria advised as she backed up her wheelchair, readjusted her nasal oxygen tubes, and rolled into the hall.

CHAPTER 52

CARMEN

Carmen pulled a gel pack from the freezer to place on her ankle, then sat to tackle the dreaded bill-paying task. She pulled out bills to see which ones she'd pay, which would get a letter, and which she wouldn't even acknowledge. To save on her electric bill, she sat in the living room under the ceiling fan, rather than turn on the air conditioner.

Carmen pushed aside the get-well cards on the coffee table to make room. She didn't like clutter and didn't usually save greeting cards, but most were from her students, and at times had been the highlight of her day. Several were hand-made, and some students had written letters. Sometimes she couldn't tell if she was making a difference. But occasionally she got validation of her efforts. Like when a former student flagged her down at the grocery store or when she received a playbill from a former student who was in a Broadway musical cast.

Carmen had sprained her ankle and back carrying Doreen down the stairs at the ill-fated rehearsal. She couldn't put weight on her left foot for a week and the back pain was so strong, she lived on extra-strength Tylenol the first ten days. It had been a month since the fire and each day got a little better.

Despite the sprained ankle, some good things came from the incident. Smoke inhalation made her throat so sensitive she stopped smoking. And she was home to supervise her mother's rehab. Gloria had three toes amputated and was in a wheelchair. The doctors said she wouldn't be in the wheelchair long if she kept up with her therapy. She and Gloria had spent the past few weeks like best friends on vacation. Her mother massaged her ankle and Carmen made sugar-free versions of her mother's favorite recipes. She showed Gloria how to use the internet and Gloria shared hilarious stories about their family back in Eden, Arkansas. They watched the soaps, played gin rummy, and laughed at the trifling people on the court shows.

"Hey old lady, how are you feeling?" Carmen asked, as the driver helped her mother in from dialysis.

"Blessed and highly favored," Gloria replied. "Where's the remote? It's time for *Judge Mathis*. And turn on the air. It's hot in here."

"Let's watch something else. The only court I want to see is the one downtown when they declare my baby innocent," Carmen said.

"Honey, we can't stress about things we can't control. Besides, I know things will work out. Just like I know you and Gerald are going to work out."

"Mama, that's old news."

"You looking through your cards? I saw the one he sent you," Gloria said.

"They made an announcement at work. Some of the teachers and staff sent a card," Carmen explained.

"But he didn't sign the group card. He sent his own. That was your cue to call."

"Give it up," Carmen said, shaking her head, not divulging that she had indeed called him. "You and I did fine these last few weeks."

"I love spending time with you, but baby, you need a man in your life. Wilson can't half see or hear, but if I asked him to bring me a pop or rub my back he'd be here. David and Hope are growing up and will be gone soon."

"Why do I need a man to complete my life? All they bring is drama. I like sleeping in the middle of my bed, controlling the remote, and passing gas when I feel like it."

"I worry about you," Gloria said softly. "You're not getting any younger, you know, and I won't always be here."

"Well, you're here now and I'm ready to spank you in gin rummy," Carmen said, as she hobbled to the cabinet to get the cards.

"Your ankle should be getting better by now," Gloria observed. "What did the doctor say?"

"He said to elevate my leg as much as possible, and time is the best medicine."

"I told you what to do. I'll tell Wilson to pick up some Icy Hot cream on his way over. Massage your ankle with it and wear two pair of socks. You'll be better before you know it. But you'll always be able to tell when it's going to rain," Gloria said, while surfing through the channels. "Hey look."

"She didn't waste any time," Carmen said, as an entertainment show host reported on the Diamonds reunion tour. "I understand why those cubic zirconias signed on, but I never thought Jade would sell out. As soon as this ordeal with David is over, I'll handle them. There's got to be a law that prohibits them from passing themselves off as the group."

"Jade probably needed the money," Gloria said. "And Angel's whole identity is tied up in her career. You've always been too hard on her."

"How can you say that? I know she and Ray forced you out."

"They were right. I had taken you as far as I could. It was time for someone with more experience to take my girls to the next level."

"That should've been a group decision. We were family and didn't need a contract, but they took advantage of that. And Angela went behind our backs and helped Ray put you out. Then lied about it," Carmen said, as she adjusted the ice pack. "I never confronted her. The decision was done, so I quit. When we were in Chicago last month, I guess twenty years of anger bubbled out and I told her about herself. She said they talked to you and you were okay with everything. I told her that's because you put the group ahead of your feelings. I said a few more things, but out of respect for you, I won't repeat them,"

"Why in the world were you talking about that history? And is that why you quit?" Gloria asked. "You wouldn't ever talk about it. I figured you were feuding over that Eric you both liked. Then you and Vernon got together, so I thought maybe they were fooling around. She was always flirty and Vernon did have a roving eye."

"Eric and I were over right after we toured with his band. And she wasn't Vernon's type. I just couldn't work with someone so low-down. You had done more for her than anyone."

"I'll admit, I was angry and hurt when I learned her role in my dismissal," Gloria said. "But I let that go long ago. Besides, they actually did me a favor."

"I know you believe in turning the other cheek. But I just—"

"Child, I'm not talking about turning no cheek. I'm talking about getting paid. Ray may have been slick as snot on a doorknob, but your grandmama didn't raise no fool. There's a reason it's called show *business*, and I knew to get legal advice. I told Ray we had an implied contract and threatened to sue. He was shocked to learn I had trademarked the group name, and incorporated as EMG, Inc. That's Gloria Mae Ellis, backwards," Gloria said, crossing her arms and flashing a smug smile. "Whenever anyone uses the Diamonds name, I get paid."

"You're kidding," Carmen said, with widened eyes.

"I didn't reach sixty without learning a few things along the way. Whenever Angel worked, I got paid. It's not a big check, but it has helped pay my bills and I paid cash for a couple of my cars. Although the checks would be bigger if you girls had done the reunion tour."

"You never cease to amaze me," Carmen said, shaking her head. Her mother's nonchalant demeanor and forgiving attitude about being replaced, now made more sense. At the time, Carmen was upset enough for both of them. Angel casually mentioned their plans while the group was stranded in Minneapolis.

"This is ridiculous," Angel complained, upon learning their flight had been postponed again due to a snowstorm. "Who books a show in Minnesota in the winter? And the least that cheapskate Ray could do is get us a hotel. We shouldn't be stuck in this airport."

"How do people live here?" Jade asked, with a shudder.

"Our records are always on the radio, and we seem to live on the road. Yet, what do we have to show for it?" Angel asked. "We need to make some changes."

"You think we should change labels?" Doreen asked. "Fine by me. Ray Nelson is basically pimping us. Sophia saw through him from the start."

"I heard the company is for sale, and Ray may not be head honcho much longer anyway. Maybe we'll get a better deal with the new owners," Angel said. "We should wait before making a move."

"How do you know that?" Carmen asked.

"I have my sources. But there is something we can do right now. We need new management."

"What are you saying?" Carmen asked, as she pulled her coat tighter around her.

"Miss Glo has been great. None of this would have happened without her. But it's time to get a professional company," Angel stated.

"Carmen, we can make so much more money," Jade said.

"So you knew about this? What about you, Doreen?"

"Angel set up a meeting with representatives from Artists Services Agency," Doreen said, staring at her nails.

"And no one told me?" Carmen asked, with a raised voice.

"We thought Angel told you," Jade said.

"I guess my invite is in the mail," Carmen quipped. "So when will I get to hear this great presentation?"

"The contracts should be in Ray's office by now," Angel stated. "Initially he wasn't crazy about the idea, but ASA has already delivered on some of their promises."

"I'm not crazy about the idea either. I'll need time to think about it," Carmen said.

"It's a done deal," Angel stated. "We've already voted."

"Voted?" Carmen asked. "Who voted to let your treacherous ass in the group?"

"Just listen," Angel said, moving to the seat next to Carmen. "Did you know Miss Glo had us sign a three-sixty deal? Peak Records controls our likeness, our publishing, and we owe them three more albums, with no specific release date. I'm not blaming her. She did her best. But ASA says they can get us out of that contract because Jade wasn't eighteen when she signed it. We've been busting our butts for years and what do we have to show for it? That seven-figure contract we thought would put us on easy street, has put us on barely okay street, after taxes, production expenses, and splitting it four ways. We could be doing so much better."

"You could've been busting your butt in that beauty shop you came from. You've done pretty well, I would say," Carmen said.

"I'm grateful. We all are. But it's time to make a change," Angel said. "Miss Glo has taken us as far as she can. It's not personal."

"The numbers are hard to ignore," Doreen added. "James says—"

"I don't care what the numbers say, and I don't care what James says. Just because he's screwing you doesn't give him a say."

"Carmen, I would think you'd be the most concerned with financial security. Think about little David's future," Angel said.

"Don't pretend you're so concerned about my baby. Remember what you said when I told you guys I was pregnant?" Carmen asked.

"This is not productive," Angel said, changing her seat. "We're all crazy about David and only want what's best for him. Miss Glo still uses a Rolodex, for God's sake. Besides, Ray has already sent your mom the letter."

"Letter? You didn't have the decency to tell her in person?" Carmen asked.

"I thought we were going to meet with her," Doreen said.

"This is not right," Carmen said, with tears in her eyes. "I expected better from you, Doreen."

"Can you lower your voice, please?" Angel asked, looking around. "Ray talked to her and said she was cool with everything."

"Well, I'm not. If you don't want my mother, you don't want me," Carmen declared.

That was the first time Carmen quit. But Gloria advised her daughter, "This is God's way of telling me to slow down. I can watch the baby when you're traveling. We had a good run. Now it's time for you girls to reach even higher. I'll be fine," Gloria had said while hugging her daughter. Instead of Carmen comforting her mother, Gloria was comforting her. "Now, you walk into rehearsal tomorrow with your head held high and act like nothing has happened."

Carmen did as her mother ordered. But things weren't the same. Six months later, when ASA representatives showed up for the gold record presentation, Carmen quit, for good.

"A Diamonds reunion would've been wonderful. Such a shame you couldn't work things out," Gloria said. "I'd love more money, but more than that, I'd really love to see my girls back together. Angel and I are fine with each other. She's a little prissy and high-strung, but you're no walk in the park yourself."

"Maybe I've been too hard on Angela. I guess anyone that loves you can't be all bad," Carmen said.

"Let's call her," Gloria said, joyfully.

"She'll probably have a heart attack if she hears my voice," Carmen chuckled.

"Wait—she might be getting ready for a show," Gloria said. "Let's call in the morning."

"All right. So what do you feel like eating?" Carmen asked, opening the freezer.

"Fix what you like," Gloria said. "I'm leaving shortly."

"You're going out?"

"Wilson has tickets for the Temptations revue at the casino."

"I thought we'd watch the playoffs this evening," Carmen said.

"We're going to the show, then the seafood buffet, and then drop a few coins in the machines. They're giving four times bonus points since it's Father's Day weekend."

"Should he be driving at night? You just said he can't half see or hear."

"He does fine. We go the speed limit and let everyone

else pass us. I know Hope is at Vernon's and David is out. Why don't you invite Gerald over? Call him and apologize. He was such a nice man."

"Apologize? What makes you think I did something wrong?" Carmen asked.

"Because I know how stubborn you can be. And if you didn't do anything, apologize anyway. Men like to think they're in charge. They can be a hassle, but sometimes they're nice to have around."

"That sounds so sexist. But it doesn't matter. He's seeing someone. I saw them together at the mall."

"He's not married, is he? You can still call him," Gloria said.

"Mama, let it go," Carmen said, as she shuffled the cards. Carmen and her mother played four hands of gin rummy until Mr. Wilson rang the doorbell.

"Here's your liniment, darling," he said, when he came in. "I got you a bag of sugar-free Jolly Ranchers too."

"Thank you, sweetie." Gloria grabbed her purse and wheeled her chair toward the door. "Remember what we talked about. Make the call, Carmen."

Carmen recalled their conversation as she watched Mr. Wilson help her mother to the car. Her mother was right; she wasn't getting any younger. Her mother wasn't letting a wheelchair slow her down. Hope worked almost every evening. David was meeting with a tutor and working with a trainer to boost his prospects of walking on a team. Carmen had to admit she was tired of being alone, and tired of pursuing men who did not want to be with her. She would make the call—to Nathan.

Carmen saw a pale light peek through the drapes and sat straight up in the bed. She glanced at her watch and was alarmed to see it was almost six o'clock. Nathan had left about midnight and she meant to leave shortly after. But the three glasses of Asti had eased the pain of her throbbing ankle, but it also made her sleepy. Her ankle felt fine when she left the house. But the walk across the hotel parking lot reminded her that her ankle looked better than it felt.

Nathan was in town for a quick house hunting trip and was glad she changed her mind about seeing him. But she was disappointed that he couldn't get away until ten o'clock. And while driving to the hotel, she realized how nice it had been to have a man actually pick her up.

They arrived within minutes of each other, and Atlanta seemed to agree with him. He ordered room service and a pay-per-view movie that they didn't watch. After a passionate hour of lovemaking, Nathan announced he had to go. "You're kidding," Carmen said.

"The boys were playing video games when I left and I know my mother won't make them go to bed. I don't want to come in too late."

"I stayed late with you plenty of nights. You were never this considerate about appearances with my children," Carmen said.

"Your situation is different from mine," Nathan said, as he zipped his pants.

"And this is what I'm supposed to be excited about returning to?"

"Don't spoil our good time," Nathan said, tying his shoes.

"You mean your good time. This was just an upscale booty call," Carmen said, struggling to move. "I can't believe I've wasted so much time waiting for a sliver of your time."

"I don't think you've been sitting around waiting. What about your janitor boyfriend?" Nathan asked, buttoning his shirt.

"You have a wife, remember?"

"You seem to be the one that forgot that fact."

"This is some first-class bullshit," Carmen said, as she sat up and swung her legs to the floor. She winced when her foot touched the floor.

"Are you okay?" Nathan asked.

"I'm fine and if I wasn't I guess it would just be my tough luck, since you have to get home."

"I wasn't planning on leaving home last night. Remember, you called me."

"My mistake. I should go home too. Mama doesn't always set her alarm and Hope may forget to check on her."

"I'm sure everything is fine. The room is paid for. Stay and enjoy it," Nathan said.

"This is the part where you tiptoe out and leave a one-hundred-dollar bill on the nightstand." Carmen said.

"Why are you doing this? If I wanted drama, I could stay with my wife. You're tripping," Nathan said, and lit a cigarette. "I'll call you later."

Carmen wanted to tell him "don't bother," but she didn't want to prolong his exit. She didn't want him to see her limp to the bathroom to get a warm towel for her ankle. His fake concern would only further infuriate her.

Once he left, she hobbled to the bathroom and turned on the vent to erase the lingering cigarette smell, then warmed a towel with the hair dryer. *How could I have been so stupid?* she thought. Carmen propped the pillows against the headboard and sat up with her ankle wrapped. This was supposed to be until the towel cooled off, but six hours had passed. She quickly dressed and checked her phone as she dug her keys out of her purse. She had missed ten calls from Faye, three from home, and one from Nathan. She called Faye and called home, but didn't get an answer. She figured Nathan could wait...a long time, then deleted his number.

She limped to her car and headed home. She caught every light and was almost home when she glanced in her rearview mirror and saw flashing red lights. As she pulled over to let the ambulance pass, she thought about Gerald, who either picked her up and brought her home, or followed her home if she was driving at night. He would surprise her with small gifts on her desk and always filled her car. Her mother had been right. He had been a keeper and she let him go. Based on their encounter at the mall, he had moved on. But it couldn't hurt to call him one more time. His tools were still at her house. The least she could do was offer to return them.

Carmen turned onto her street and was surprised to see flashing red lights on her block. Then she realized they were at her house. She parked on the street and hobbled up the driveway. The ambulance door was open, and she caught a glimpse of her mother's cornrowed head peeking out from a white blanket with an oxygen mask over her nose and an IV in her arm. "What's going on?" she shouted. The paramedic waved her back and closed the door. Carmen rushed to the driver's side and cried, "That's my mother." Carmen saw her sister in a housecoat and slippers getting in the ambulance front seat. "Faye, what happened?"

"How could you be so irresponsible?" Faye shouted. "I can't believe you'd stay out all night, knowing her condition."

"She was gone when I left, and she was fine the last time I saw her," Carmen explained.

"Well, she's not fine now."

"Please close the door, miss. We need to go," the driver said, then turned on the siren. The ambulance whipped out of the driveway and sped away with sirens blaring. David and Faye's husband followed them in Faye's truck.

Carmen ran to the front door as the ambulance drove off. "Hope, what happened?"

"Mom, where were you?"

"What happened?" Carmen asked, shaking Hope by the shoulders.

"Gram fell in the bathroom. She said she was calling me, but I didn't hear her. By the time I heard her, she could barely talk. I screamed and David ran in. We tried to ask her some questions, but she just coughed and closed her eyes. He called 911, told me to call you and started CPR. When you didn't answer, I called Aunt Faye. She and Uncle Mitchell got here not long before the paramedics. They told me to give you this card," Hope said breathlessly.

"Put some clothes on. We've got to get to the hospital."

"Mom, this is my fault," Hope stammered as she wiped tears with the back of her hand. "I was in bed when Gram got home, and I forgot to check her alarm and take her some orange juice. Will she be okay?"

"This is not your fault. I should never have put that responsibility on you. This is just one of those things. Gram will be fine." Carmen wasn't sure if she was reassuring her daughter or trying to convince herself.

Carmen was exhausted. This was the second day she and David had spent at the courthouse. The attorneys were going through voir dire, selecting or more accurately, rejecting potential jurors. At school, Carmen moved constantly and never realized how tiring sitting all day could be. She was taking notes and had her own list of keepers and rejects.

She had never served on a jury, and these candidates weren't impressive. Some didn't even seem to be paying attention. If it weren't her son, she probably would have been bored too. Whenever she received a jury duty summons, she found an acceptable excuse. Her mother took pride in serving and nagged Carmen about shirking her civic duty. Carmen vowed she'd never make an excuse again.

One of several changes she had pledged to make once the trial was over.

Voir dire was the first phase of her day. When she left the courthouse, she had to go to the hospital and sit some more. Doctors said Gloria was rebounding well from this latest low blood sugar episode, but warned she had come dangerously close to having another stroke. They had removed her IV and expected to release her by the weekend. This was great news, but Carmen didn't feel like celebrating. The trial was starting next week.

There was a whole team of attorneys and paralegals working with Attorney Hawkins. She appreciated his thoroughness, but he was also very blunt. He told them they had a 75 percent chance of winning. That was progress, considering he had said 50-50 when she hired him. But it also meant there was a 25 percent chance her son could be found guilty. Carmen needed a sure thing.

Chapter 53

DOREEN

Paige and the twins sang a silly song, while Doreen blew kisses. Today they told her about their swimming lessons and trip to Six Flags. Even Paige seemed to be enjoying herself. Doreen was grateful she could FaceTime them and keep up with their daily activities, but she was still counting the days until they came home.

Today had been her first day back at work. Everyone was glad to see her, but she could tell from their reaction they were surprised she had gained so much weight. Since she was getting stronger, she hoped to be able to exercise and lose the weight.

"How did it go?" James asked.

"Okay. I could tell everyone was surprised by my weight gain."

"I'm sure you're more conscious about it than others are. You're a little bigger than you used to be, but plenty of people would love to be your size. Besides, I kind of like the little extra on top," James confided with a wink.

"All this eating out and ordering in hasn't helped," Doreen said. "Since the kids have been gone, I can count on one hand the times I have cooked."

"Enjoy the break. You deserve it," James said.

"I'm not complaining. But I do miss the kids."

"We see them almost every day, and they seem to be having a ball. I'm comfortable they're being well taken care of."

"I won't be comfortable until they are in their rooms upstairs," Doreen said.

"School will be starting before you know it. How about taking a short vacation before the kids come back," James suggested.

"That's a great idea. My boss may not like me taking off so soon after returning, but that's too bad. Why should I work like a slave to make Southern Federal shareholders rich?"

"The Diamonds will be in Nashville next month. I thought we could catch a show. I know you'd like to see the girls."

"That's sweet of you. Although it's strange to think of Angel and Jade onstage without me and Carmen."

"I guess it wasn't meant to be. I hope you're not too disappointed."

"I still think it would've been fun, but not at the expense of my family and my health. Those are the most important things."

"You are so right," James said, as he walked behind his wife and began massaging her shoulders. "You're letting your hair grow. I like it."

"I missed my appointments while I was sick and it grew out. Decided I would try something different."

"Ummmmm, hmmmmm," James said. "That's not all I like…"

"Honey, I know it's been a while, but I'm exhausted."

"I know. I was just going to give you a massage."

"Is that all? Usually you want that to lead to something else."

"Just a massage. But if you have other things on your mind, I won't object," James admitted.

"I knew it," Doreen said, playfully waving her finger at him.

"I can't help it if I find you irresistible," James said and kissed her neck.

"Hmmmmmm, maybe I'm not that tired. But are you up to it? No pun intended."

"Only one way to find out."

"James, wait," Doreen said, as she gently pushed him away. "I want you to know how much it means to me that you had your vasectomy reversed. Although I should be mad at you for not discussing it with me. I didn't even know you were considering it."

"There are no guarantees, but I didn't want to be the barrier to you achieving one of your dreams. I never realized the stress and disappointment you went through every month when you weren't pregnant. You seemed so wrapped up in the bank, I never imagined you would take off for maternity leave," James said. "And I thought you loved liver and spinach and pumpkin seeds. I didn't know you were eating that stuff to increase your fertility. I had the vasectomy because I couldn't bear the thought of losing you, but I was wrong."

"Okay, we can't change the past. But you just did the same thing, when you had the reversal without telling me," Doreen said. "What if something had happened?"

"I figured God would take care of me, and I didn't want you to worry. So let's make this our last secret. Think of the unnecessary worry, stress, and pain we've gone through," James said. "And another thing. How in the world could you think something was going on between me and Rachel? Why didn't you just ask me?"

"So much was going wrong, I guess I was afraid of the answer."

"See, more unnecessary worry and stress," James said, shaking his head. "If you had asked me, I would have told you we were evaluating sites for the district conference. And if you had come on in, you would have seen the entire site committee in the lobby."

"I feel pretty silly about it now," Doreen admitted.

"I thought you knew me better than that. I'm still hurt," James said, with a fake sniffle. "But I know how you can make it up to me." He pulled his wife toward him, kissed her neck, and cupped her behind. Just as Doreen put her arms around his neck, her cell phone ring interrupted their caress.

"Let me turn the phone on *silent*," Doreen said, as her phone rang again. "I'm sure whatever it is can wait a few minutes."

"A few minutes? I'm insulted," James said.

As Doreen grabbed her phone, it rang again. "It's Carmen. She's probably calling about the lawsuit. She has been bugging me about suing Angel and Jade for touring without us. I've told her I'm not interested," Doreen said, as she put the phone on the dresser.

Ten seconds later, James's phone rang. "It's Carmen," he noted when he took his phone out of his pocket.

"Go ahead and answer it," Doreen said, while unbuckling her husband's pants. "If we don't answer, she's liable to show up on our doorstep."

"This had better be good," James said, when he answered. "When? We'll be right there."

"What is it?" Doreen asked.

"It's Miss Glo. She had a stroke this morning and is in intensive care."

ACT V

THE SHOW MUST GO ON

Chapter 54

ANGEL

Angel sipped Chablis as the plane glided through the clouds. It was nice to be back in first class. They had just completed the first six shows. Ticket sales were respectable and Ray had spared no expense on travel, promotion, wardrobe, or set design.

The tour opened in Memphis and Angel was overwhelmed by her hometown's welcome. The mayor presented them with the key to the city. They did interviews on all the local news shows, visited her old schools, and were awarded a note on the Beale Street Walk of Fame. Doreen brought Gloria to the greenroom before the first show. Even in a wheelchair, she was bossing everyone, telling Angel not to favor her right side as she tended to do and reminding Jade to stand up straight. She lectured the new girls, giving them a group history lesson and warning about the pitfalls of the road—before insisting on a hug from each of them. The audience loved everything they did and gave them three standing ovations.

After the show, autograph seekers lined the corridor, just like in the old days. Angel graciously signed and posed for pictures as she made her way to her dressing room. She heard a knock and was about to send the person away when she recognized Preston's voice.

"What a surprise," she said, opening the door.

"For you," Preston said, handing her a dozen gardenias.

"Thank you." Angel sniffed the flowers and moved clothes to make a place for him to sit.

"I don't know how you're still on your feet after that performance. I see how you keep your curves."

"Thank you again. You were in the audience?"

"Row three. That's the first show I've ever attended of yours."

"I know," Angel said.

"I guess I didn't want to see what you loved more than me."

"I didn't love it more than you. There was room for both. But thanks for coming. That means a lot to me, Preston. I know how you've felt about my career."

"And I was wrong. I said you were selfish for wanting to leave our family. But I was selfish for wanting to constrain you, and I hope you'll forgive me. Your gift should be shared. There were thousands of people there tonight, who knew the words to all your songs. There were all races and ages, singing as one. Too bad we can't bottle that feeling and sprinkle it around the world. I've watched you on television some, but live was totally different. You were mesmerizing."

Angel had to admit the shows had been even better than she predicted. The new Diamonds had caught on and Jade was singing like her life depended on every note. They were getting flattering reviews and Ray wanted to add more cities to the tour. But the review that meant the most to her was Preston's.

"Wow, you should be the president of my fan club."

"I already am," Preston admitted as he pulled her toward him and kissed her. Not the dry pecks they had been exchanging over the last fifteen years. But the real thing.

"Wow again," Angel said, as she stepped back. "Look, I have to attend this after-party that Ray set up—"

"I know you're busy, although I would like to see you before you leave town."

"Why don't you come with me?" Angel asked.

"I don't like those types of things," Preston said.

"How do you know? Besides, I don't like them either. Being with you will make it tolerable. My contract requires me to stay forty-five minutes, then we'll leave."

They showed up at the party and Ray whisked her away to mingle with DJs, producers, and investors. It turned out Preston knew more people than she did, and she didn't see him until it was time to leave the party. Many former Peak Records artists who had settled down to regular lives in Memphis had come. Preston and Jade met for the first time and Jade gave Angel a thumbs-up when he wasn't looking.

Crystal also gave them a thumbs-up. "Mother, your show was awesome," she said, as she entered the dressing room. "I had to show the bodyguard our picture before he would let me back here. He's definitely on his job. He should be...Dad, what are you doing here?" she asked when she spotted Preston sitting in the corner.

"Visiting my two favorite ladies," he said, with a wide smile.

"I'll be ready in ten minutes," Angel said.

"Take your time, Angela. You should be exhausted," Preston replied.

"Okay, this is weird. Is somebody sick? Did somebody die?" Crystal asked.

"Of course not. Don't be so dramatic," Angel replied.

"I wonder where she gets it," Preston said.

"I thought you liked my theatrical side," Angel said, flipping her hair behind her shoulder.

"I'm not complaining. I wouldn't have you any other way."

"You probably say that to all the girls."

"Only the ones I really like," Preston said, with a wink.

"Is this a prank? Are you two flirting with each other?" Crystal asked.

"Don't be silly," Angel said, and stepped into the bathroom.

Crystal followed her mother into the tiny bathroom. "Sooooooo, what is going on here?"

"How about a little privacy?" Angel asked, reaching for a towel.

"Are you and Dad...?"

"Do I interrogate you about your friends?"

"Actually, you do. But this is not just any friend. This is you and Dad, and you two looked mighty comfy in there."

"Why shouldn't we? We *were* married at one time."

"Emphasis on past tense. I always wondered how you ever got together. You're so different. But after seeing you two in there, there's undeniable chemistry."

"Crystal, we're just—"

"Mother, please. We both know Preston Donovan wouldn't be in downtown Memphis at ten o'clock on a weeknight without a strong incentive. I think you're the incentive, and I ain't mad at either of you. I'll leave so you can get dressed to hang out with your *friend*."

Preston had also met her in Dallas and last week in New Orleans. Angel didn't do repeats. Once she was finished with a man, she didn't go back. But he seemed familiar and new at the same time. Maybe they were both different. He had mellowed enough to appreciate her drive, and she had matured enough to value his reticence. He wasn't jealous, didn't want her money, and wasn't trying to manage her career. And while she had had plenty of sexual encounters, it had been a long time since someone made love to her. Preston had moved from her past to her present and she wondered if he was her future.

Preston mentioned the same misgivings over dinner on a riverboat cruise in New Orleans. "This has been like a mini-vacation for me. But we need time in a more normal environment to see if we have something here, or if this is just a fling."

"This fling—as you call it—has been nice, but it's pretty scary. I've been wrong so many times," Angel said.

"That's why we need to spend more time together," Preston said, gazing into her eyes and reaching for both of her hands. "I'm not pressuring you, but we're not kids. I don't want to spend a lot of time if this isn't going to work."

"Don't want to waste your time, huh?"

"I didn't say that," Preston said, pushing a lock of hair from her face. "I can't think of a better way to spend my time. But everything seems great when you have room service, laundry service, and people tripping over themselves to meet your every need. We need to get somewhere where we can be real. I need to see if you've learned to cook."

"And I can see if you've started snoring in your old age," Angel added.

"Only when I'm really worn out, and hopefully you will continue to wear me out," Preston said, with a sly smile.

"Come to Chicago next month. I have a three-week break."

"I have a better idea. Why don't you come to Memphis? I want us to spend more than an occasional weekend together, but I can't leave my business or the school board very long," Preston said. "Finish your tour, then come stay with me a few months. I know your career can be fickle and if you can't spend time with me, I'll understand and back off."

"I don't want you to back off," Angel said, reaching for her ex-husband's hand.

"Sounds good. That gives me time to get things in order, so we can spend as much time together as possible."

Angel replayed their conversation over and over in her mind and couldn't believe how well things in her life were going right now. The pilot announced their descent into O'Hare Airport, and she made a mental list of things to get in order. Ray Nelson topped the list. Now that the tour was underway, she could reduce their interaction. The new girls enjoyed his Svengali-like attention, but Angel and Jade didn't need his oversight. He had come to their St. Louis and Louisville shows, but Angel talked him out of visiting them on the rest of the tour. She had a three-week break before the next tour segment and wanted to spend as much time as possible with Preston.

The top of Ray's bald head was the first thing Angel saw as the escalator reached the bottom. "What are you doing here?" she asked.

"Meeting you, of course," he said, as he grabbed her Givenchy tote and led her to the baggage carousel. "Baby, you're a genius. I'll admit, I wasn't convinced about this tour, especially since you only had a couple months to put it together. But you pulled it off. Enjoy this break because you're going to have more work than you can handle. You won't believe the offers we're getting."

"We?" Angel asked.

"Of course. You know you're my number one."

"Ray, if I didn't know better, I would almost believe you," Angel said, as she pointed out her luggage.

"Well, believe this: I'm negotiating with twenty more promoters at twice the price. We'll miss most of the state fair season, but we can hit the states with festivals after Labor Day."

"That's bad timing for me, Ray."

"Why? Are you lining up jobs I don't know about?"

"I'm not looking for more work right now. I have plans for after the tour."

"Wasn't this our goal? I'm talking major money. And I know you've already spent your money from this contract."

"How do you know what I do with my money?" Angel asked. "And what concern is it of yours?"

"It's my business to know as much as possible about the people I do business with. I understand wanting to take care of family, but I think you've been too generous."

"I didn't ask for your opinion or permission."

"I know, that's why I didn't say anything. If you want to play Santa Claus, fine with me. But Santa needs money too," Ray said.

"There are more important things than money."

"Uh, excuse me. You must be an imposter. The Angel Donovan I know would never say that."

"Maybe you only think you know me. I've been on this whirlwind for twenty years. I think it's time for a change."

"Could your new—or should I say old—boyfriend have something to do with this change of heart?" Ray asked.

"Again, why are you all up in my business?" Angel asked, flipping her hair behind her shoulder. "Don't you have some young rapper to rip off?"

"I'm looking out for you. Preston hasn't changed," Ray said. "If anything, he's probably more set in his ways."

"Let me worry about that."

"Just looking out for my favorite client. Not client. We're more like family," Ray said, and put her luggage in a cab and paid the driver.

"Ray, you need to quit," Angel said with a slight smile and punched him in the shoulder. "I hope you haven't spent too much time on the tour dates. I'm serious about taking a break."

"Go home and rest. We'll talk tomorrow about extending the tour," Ray said, as he held the cab door open for her.

"I already told you, I can't."

"You'll feel differently once you've gotten a good night's sleep in your own bed. And, once you see what kind of money we're talking about."

Angel shook her head and waved as they pulled away from the curb. Ray was right, it wasn't like her to turn down a good gig. But the tour would only be a few months. Preston sounded like he was ready for life.

CHAPTER 55

JADE

After a restless night, Jade arose before dawn. She loaded up her van, grabbed a pack of Pop-Tarts, locked her apartment door, then headed to her van. Her flight didn't leave for four hours, but her drive to the airport would be longer since she was taking the back streets. Her van had been running hot, and it would be easier to pull over if she wasn't on the freeway.

Jade wasn't sure when she would be paid again, so she pinched every penny. She paid two months' rent, had gotten a cheap phone, had no cable or internet, and bought generic everything. Brian had handled the finances and paid the bills, so she didn't know how much things cost. Her first electric bill was almost a third of her rent. After that, she bought a box fan and ran the air conditioner sparingly. The next sticker shock came when she tried to hire a divorce lawyer. Because a business was involved, the fee would be much higher than the amount advertised on TV and their websites. She didn't understand, since she didn't even want Seaside. The next jolt came when she learned they required a sizable down payment. When she explained her situation and her erratic income schedule—most had been Diamonds fans and gushed with compliments—they repeated their request for a down payment. She finally found a lawyer who agreed to take her case and wait for payment. It was a new firm and the attorney had been very empathetic when she told him about Dawn, and even offered to help Jade hire a private detective to locate her. It took a little longer to get the divorce moving since she didn't have documents and couldn't get them. But he finally said he had what he needed, and she'd hear from him soon.

Tonight's show was in Minneapolis, Milwaukee on Saturday, and Chicago on Sunday. Jade felt like a traveling salesman, and was already tired of airports and airplanes, and this was just the third week. While flying was quicker, she missed the tour bus. They had so much fun back then. These gigs were nothing like those days, and she had never imagined being onstage without Carmen and Doreen.

Jade parked in the farthest, cheapest airport parking lot. She placed a blanket over her back seat to hide the few belongings she didn't want to leave in the apartment. There had been two recent break-ins in the complex, so each week she went through the ritual of loading up her van and unloading it when she returned. Her phone rang and she recognized the number. She started not to answer, but thought it might concern the kids, or Dawn.

"Honey, I've been trying to reach you," Brian said, barely letting her say hello. "The kids wouldn't even give me your phone number. I didn't have a number for you until I got this divorce thing."

"Great. So you got the petition," Jade said, with a lilt in her voice.

"This has gone too far, and we need to talk. You can't throw away twenty years of marriage."

"I don't know how we were supposed to talk, when you cut off my phone," Jade said, dragging her suitcase, which was missing a wheel, to the shuttle pickup stop.

"I shouldn't have done that, but I was so upset. Anyway,

your phone is back on," Brian said. "When can we get together to talk?"

"I'm leaving town. Talk to my lawyer."

"We can settle our own disagreements, and don't need lawyers. This has gone too far," Brian pleaded. "I know what this is. You got your little Diamond thing going again, and you figure you don't need me. Angel never did like me, but this music thing won't last. Then what will you do? I hope you don't think there's some big divorce settlement."

"My lawyer will handle those details."

"Jade, you're not listening. You are tearing our family apart. What about Lance and Tiffany?"

"All my life I wanted my own family," Jade said. "So I bought your version of what a family was. I wanted my children to have the stable home I never had. It was stable, but it never felt right. The kids are young adults now, and will be fine. I'm divorcing you, not them."

"You don't know how sorry I am. I can change. Let me make it up to you."

"What are you sorry for?" Jade asked, as she juggled her phone, suitcase, and purse.

"I told you, Rita doesn't mean anything to me."

"You're just sorry you got caught," Jade said, rolling her eyes. "Yes, I was furious about you messing with the help. But the tipping point was your callous treatment of Dawn and disregard for my feelings."

"So you won't even give me a chance? I said I was sorry. What do you want me to do?"

"I want you to sign the papers, and return them to my lawyer."

"And that's it?" Brian asked. "We're done?"

"That's it," Jade said, noticing peach streaks across the sky as the sun rose, prelude to another scorching, muggy day. "Well, there is something—have you heard from Dawn?"

"Maybe I have and maybe I haven't."

"Asshole." Jade closed her flip phone.

Jade called Miss Branch every other day to see if they had located Dawn. The response was always the same: "We haven't had contact with Miss Faber. We will pass on your information if we do." Although, she wasn't convinced they were trying to find Dawn. They probably hadn't even kept the information she had given them. She worried once she left her roach-infested apartment, there was even less hope of finding Dawn. Especially since Dawn didn't have her new phone number. *Damn Brian*, she thought. While it hurt to think of Dawn struggling on her own, Jade decided to focus on things she could control. That meant making as much money as she could and getting divorced.

Jade also did something she had been considering for a long time—she reached out to her mother. Brian had always discouraged her, saying her mother wouldn't be a good influence on their children. It was time to let the past go, and her resentment toward her mother was part of that past.

The plane landed on time, and the lady in the window seat was nudging Jade so she could get by. Jade had fallen asleep during takeoff, and slept soundly throughout the flight. This was the third week of the tour and her lower-back soreness was finally easing up. They did three shows in three cities in three nights each week. Once upon a time, back-to-back shows didn't faze her. But time had moved on and so had her stamina. Things happened so fast, she didn't have time to get in shape, and since leaving Brian, she had been living on junk food.

Jade checked into the hotel, then went straight to the theater. She dressed and went for the mic-check. Angel was speaking with the band, giving orders as usual. Jade and the new girls made small talk. She glanced at her watch, anxious for the show to start, so it would be over. The tour was everything Angel had predicted. Ticket sales were great and the audiences had been energized. Performing was still fun, but the rest felt like work. The first time around had been an adventure, with friends. Tiffany had joined her last weekend, in North and South Carolina, turning it into a mini-vacation. Now it was just a job with coworkers. The new girls were nice enough, but there was no camaraderie among the four of them. She was almost old enough to be their mother, or at least aunt. A record company wasn't sponsoring them, so there were few perks, and everyone had cell phones now, so lights were constantly flickering during the show. Everything was so computerized and the sound seemed louder. But Jade wasn't complaining. This tour had been a lifesaver.

The stage lights went low and the girls filed onstage, while singing "My Baby Just Cares For Me," accompanied only by a piano. The curtain went up slowly and for the next ninety minutes the Diamonds put on a terrific show. The new girls were great dancers and had strong voices. Angel led most songs, which was fine with Jade. They ended with "The Best Is Yet to Come," and left the audience cheering for more.

After the show, they were scheduled to attend a reception hosted by the local radio station, and the new girls invited Jade to a party after the reception. Jade declined both. She remembered partying until daybreak after shows. But not anymore. She had been looking forward to climbing in that plush hotel bed ever since she landed. Being on the road was drudgery, but one thing she did enjoy was the comfortable bed, cable television, and unlimited air-conditioning. In her apartment, she had a pullout couch with a terrible mattress, and never slept well. Although there were four locks on her apartment door, she was paranoid about someone breaking in. She felt vibrations whenever one of her neighbors shut their door, and they came and went at all hours. Her plan was to order a sandwich from the Subway next to the hotel, go to her room, bathe, eat, and collapse into that heavenly bed.

As she walked to the dressing room, she heard someone call her name. "Dawn," she exclaimed when she turned around. "What are you—how did you—"

"I snuck in the freight entrance. They kicked me out of your dressing room, so I hid in the ladies' room and waited."

"But how did you get here?" Jade said, hugging her.

"Marquel bought my ticket. I tried to catch you last week, in Charlotte, but the bus had mechanical issues and I missed my connection. By the time I got there, you were already gone."

"You've been doing all this riding alone, on the bus?" Jade asked incredulously.

"Yeah, it was a long ride, but I liked seeing other parts of the country," Dawn said. "You guys were really good. You're like a real celebrity. I almost didn't recognize your short haircut. It's cute. And look at your fancy dress."

"Are you okay?" Jade asked, wiping away tears. "I am so glad to see you."

"I'm glad you're glad. I was afraid you wouldn't want to be bothered," Dawn said softly.

"Are you kidding?" Jade asked. "Touring just became fun again. Come with me to a reception. I want everyone to meet you."

CHAPTER 56

ANGEL

Angel rolled the last suitcase out of the elevator and thanked her neighbor for holding the door despite the annoying alarm. They had a three-week break, and she was spending a few days in Chicago before going to Memphis. She had appointments with Mario, her manicurist, and her old trainer. As she put her key in the door, the knob turned from the other side.

"Welcome home."

"What are you doing here?" Angel asked.

"Being your landlord has its perks," Ray said, as he held her door open.

"You can't just come in here. How did you get in?"

"It's my building, and I can enter any space that I need to. And today I needed to, so I could have a welcome-home dinner waiting for you. It's the least I can do since I had to leave the tour. I want to hear all about it," Ray said, rolling her suitcases into the living room.

"I'm really tired. Can we talk tomorrow?"

"Sure, I understand. Go ahead and get comfortable. I ordered your favorite shrimp dish from Louie's when I saw the cab drive up. It shouldn't be long."

"That was thoughtful, but I'm not up for a dinner."

"You don't have to eat now. You must be exhausted. Why don't you take a long bath, then climb into bed? Get some rest, because in a few hours, I plan to join you," Ray said, and poured himself a drink.

"Ray, what I meant was, I've been around people for weeks. I'd really like some me time."

"Is that what you mean? Or do you really mean, I've gotten what I needed from you, now get the hell out."

"Ray, not now," Angel said, as she stepped out of her shoes.

"You got that right. You're not fixing to play me now or ever. This is my place and I'll leave when I get good and damn ready."

"What are you talking about? I'm the one who insisted I sign a lease, so everything would be legal. Brooke said you wouldn't accept my rent checks. You yourself said this was a business arrangement," Angel said.

"Who do you think you're talking to? Now that you've made a little money—thanks to me, I might add—you want to claim this was a business arrangement. You owe me, and I intend to collect," he declared, as he grabbed her waist.

"Get your hands off me. I should have known better. Get out before I call the police."

"Go ahead. You call the police and I'll make some calls too. Your little tour will be over," Ray countered.

"You can't do that. Besides, you may be slimy, but you still love money. We're making you lots of money right now."

"I don't need you to make money for me. You're the one who was being put out on the street," Ray said.

"I'm a survivor. I would have made it with or without you."

"But my money made it easier, didn't it? Don't fool yourself, you're just a pretentious whore."

"Too bad your money can't buy you some class, or some inches. And I don't mean just height." Angel laughed as she picked up her phone. "Get your dwarf ass out of here."

Ray picked up the remote control, turned on the television, and turned up the volume. Then he walked over to Angel and snatched the phone out of her hand with his right hand and backhanded her across the face with his left.

"Are you crazy? You won't get away with this," she shouted, as she tried to get her footing.

Ray slapped her again, then shoved her backward. She fell into the table before she hit the floor. "I don't hear you talking so much now," he said. He leaned over and pulled her arm behind her back. "What did you say?" he asked as he pulled harder and grabbed a fistful of her hair. "Tell me you're sorry."

Angel glared at him but didn't say a word. Ray got on one knee and pressed his other knee into her stomach. "Tell me you're sorry," he sneered and jerked her head back again. "Damn," he said, as he looked at the fistful of hair in his hand. "This is your real hair. I always thought it was a weave. Now, I'm giving you one more chance to tell me you're sorry."

"I'm bleeding," Angel cried, as she touched her head.

"You should have thought of that before you disrespected me. I'm not spending my money so you can have a fling with your ex," Ray said, and extended his arm to help her up.

Angel pushed him back and stood on her own. "I don't know what type of women you're used to dealing with, but I am not for sale."

"Since when? Here, take this," Ray said, as he handed her a wad of paper towels. "Now that we understand each other, things will be much better between us."

Angel pushed his hand to the side. "Get out," she hissed, and spat in his face.

"Bitch, are you crazy?"

"Crazy for ever getting mixed up with you again," Angel said, dialing her phone.

Ray jerked the phone out of her hand, then pushed her to the floor. "You think I'm playing with you?" he fumed and pulled her head from behind. "Didn't your crazy mammy teach you it was bad manners to spit on people? You owe me an apology."

Tears rolled down Angel's cheeks and her eyes burned as the glue from her false eyelashes ran into her eyes.

"I don't hear you," Ray said, as he cupped his ear with his left hand and jerked her blouse with his right hand.

"Screw you," Angel snapped.

"That's what I had in mind," Ray said, and unbuckled his belt. He straddled her squirming body, pulled her skirt up over her knees, and ripped off her panties. He grabbed her wrist and held it over her head as he leaned over her. "You have one more chance to say you're sorry."

"I'm sorry," Angel whimpered.

"I can't hear you."

"I'm sorry," Angel said, a little louder.

"I thought so." Ray stood and wiped off his knees. "I'm tired of your old-ass pussy anyway. You've got twenty-four hours to get out of my building." He stomped on her phone and walked toward the door. "One more thing. Find another sucker to finance your tour."

"You know that's impossible," Angel said.

"Ask your baby daddy. I'm done. Bye, Felicia," Ray said, and walked out.

Angel sat up, pulled her knees to her chest, and rocked as tears of rage streamed down her face. She didn't expect much from men and figured the trifling gene was in their DNA. A year or so after her divorce from Preston, she had gotten engaged. Weeks away from her dream wedding, she found her fiancé in bed with another man. A woman had come backstage during a show in Detroit and announced that Angel's second husband was the father of her baby. Lorenzo was the latest in a line of men who had used her fame to make money. But no man had ever put his hands on her, and she vowed Ray Nelson would pay.

CHAPTER 57

CARMEN

Carmen took a bite of her third slice of pecan pie and scanned the Memphis Community College website. She was supposed to be scheduling an orientation visit but couldn't focus. David had missed so much school, he needed to make up two classes in summer school, just to graduate. It wasn't supposed to be like this. They had stacks of Division One and SWAC college recruiting letters. That all ended when this nightmare began.

David was eligible to attend the community college for free, and planned to try to walk on the basketball team. Community college was a big step down from the schools that had been recruiting him. Carmen didn't care much about basketball, other than the scholarship. But she knew it meant a lot to David. She was glad he was still focused on basketball. That meant he wasn't dwelling on his case. She was worrying enough for them both. But even these scaled-back dreams depended on the jury doing the right thing and rendering an innocent verdict.

The prosecutor presented the state's case for three days and made David sound like some callous gangbanger from a single parent home. He asked David what were the Crips' colors, and did he know the Vice Lords' signs. Most kids knew that stuff, which didn't mean they were gang members. He even insinuated David's pierced ear had some coded message. Then the prosecution assassinated their family. He asked David about his relationship with his father, or rather his lack of relationship. He asked about his relationship with his godparents, then just happened to mention they had been drug addicts. The state's star witness was the slain policeman's widow. Even Carmen's eyes watered during the testimony about how much her husband loved his job and family. Then, finally, it was their turn.

Hawkins questioned each young man and got them to state when they got the car, where and when they picked David up, and who was driving the car. Carmen had been afraid the cross-examination was harmful when they answered questions about their criminal records and their friendship with David. But Hawkins said their testimony was critical to establish they had gotten the car before they picked David up.

Coach Jones, Pastor Golden, and David's principal testified on his behalf. Carmen had wanted to call more character witnesses. But Hawkins said juries don't like to hear redundant testimony. They did call two expert witnesses who revealed that the police car was not following established procedure. Based on the skid mark length, the police car had not slowed down at the intersection as they were trained to do. Hawkins had hired a dedicated paralegal and together they researched precedents and identified a pattern where black passengers were charged as accessories more often than white passengers in similar circumstances. The judge disallowed some testimony, but the information was already out there. And with five black people on the jury, Hawkins knew those facts would be difficult to ignore.

David was the last witness. Hawkins hired a communications coach to work with David and he was poised on the stand. Carmen knew she was prejudiced, but she didn't see how anyone could believe her son would knowingly participate in a crime. She hoped the jury saw what she saw. Both sides presented thirty minutes of closing arguments and then it was over.

This was the jury's third day, and Carmen was getting nervous. *What could they possibly have to deliberate?* she thought. Their attorney said not to worry, but Carmen watched the court cable channel and knew long deliberations were a bad sign.

She fixed a big breakfast, then she, her mother, Hope, and David played cards. Carmen sat next to Gloria and helped her play her hand. Her mother's dexterity and speech hadn't fully recovered since the stroke, and this was a good way to get her to exercise without calling it exercise. Her mother didn't like physical or speech therapy and was a stubborn patient. The game took longer, but they didn't mind; it was a good distraction. And even though Gloria's speech was slower, she still had plenty of trash talk. They played until Hope had to go to work. David went to his room to play video games, and Carmen went to the kitchen to prepare her mother a snack. Carmen washed some grapes and surrounded them with a few Wheat Thins. But when she returned to the dining room, Gloria was asleep in her wheelchair.

Carmen placed a shawl over her mother's shoulders, then did forty minutes on her exercise bike, then cleaned out her file cabinet. She shredded old checks and bills. She shredded not-so-old bills too. *I won't be able to pay them anyway*, she thought. She dusted, then mopped and waxed her floors. But even the airwaves were conspiring against her. She heard a Diamonds song when she turned on the radio, and Angel, Jade, and the cubic zirconias were doing an interview when she turned on the television.

Carmen remembered a time when she relished a quiet day at home. Now the house was too quiet. In times past, she would have called Nathan, but she had finally come to her senses. Maybe she was meant to be alone. Even Wallace, her old standby, had moved on. He was engaged and sent a wedding invitation. Gerald had seemed promising, but that was over too.

This was the first summer in years that she hadn't taught summer school. While taking care of her mother and the trial had kept her busy, the last three days were the longest of her life. Hope had been to work, and Gloria had been to dialysis, but Carmen and David had not left the house since the trial ended. Thankfully, they were in the home stretch and soon their thirteen-month nightmare would be over. Luckily, Hawkins hadn't asked for more money. With the tour cancellation, she didn't know how she would have paid him, but figured she had plenty of time to worry about that.

She rummaged through the freezer and decided to try a new salmon recipe. Maybe she could dress it up enough that Gloria would eat it. Her mother didn't have much appetite since her stroke. As she placed the microwave on defrost, her phone rang. It was Attorney Hawkins. The jury had reached a verdict.

CHAPTER 58

ANGEL

"Angel, I received a direct deposit of one hundred thousand dollars. I thought it was an error and contacted the bank and they said it's from Donovan Enterprises. Is this right?" Jade asked.

"Didn't you get my text? I told you to expect a big check shortly."

"I didn't know you meant this big. We didn't even finish the tour," Jade said.

"Girl, forget about that tour. Those shows whetted the promotors' appetites. I'm putting together an even better deal."

"I don't know how to thank you. Brian claimed we were bankrupt and wouldn't give me a dime. I could have fought him, but I just wanted to be done. I didn't know divorces were so expensive. No wonder you ran out of money," Jade remarked.

"Well, I won't run out of money again. I'll be set for life. For real this time."

"This must be some tour you're planning."

This income stream didn't have anything to do with the tour, at least not directly, Angel thought. She was mortified, furious, and embarrassed when Ray left the condo. She had been cheated on, used for money, and slandered on social media. But no man had ever put his hands on her. She broke her arm when she fell, but even worse, he committed the ultimate sin against a black woman. He pulled out her hair. She got a restraining order and an injunction that gave her ninety days to find a new place. Angel accused him of unlawful entry, aggravated assault, and attempted rape, and wanted him put under the jail. But her attorney advised her to let him plead to a misdemeanor assault charge. He explained that in a trial she'd be subjected to as much negative scrutiny as Ray. Then he gave examples of questions she'd be asked. "Have you and Mr. Nelson had consensual sex? How many times? Weren't there sexual encounters during his marriage? Aren't you living rent-free in his property? How long have you known Mr. Nelson?"

Angel complained her answers would make her sound sleazy, and Ray attacked her—why would she be on trial? Her attorney explained society shames the victim, and that's just how the system works. Angel reluctantly agreed to a small settlement and payment for her medical expenses and loss of income. She was now a testament to one of Miss Glo's sayings: *If you lay down with dogs, you get up with fleas.* But she did get some satisfaction since Ray was "encouraged to retire" when Peak Records legal department found out. But her real payday had nothing to do with the courts.

After Ray's attack, Angel remained on the floor, with her knees to her chest, crying and cold. Mario arrived for her hair appointment, and found her door ajar. He pushed the door open slowly, then rushed to her side. "What happened?" he asked. "I'm calling the police."

"Just get me to a doctor. I'll file a police report later," Angel said, while rubbing her arm, and telling Mario what happened.

As Mario was helping her get dressed, he noticed the large gash in her head and put his hand over his mouth to muffle his scream. "And they call me a sissy. What man pulls a woman's hair?"

"So, what can we do?" Angel asked.

"You can go with the flower, like Billie Holiday. Or you can go with wigs like Whitney Houston. But I have another suggestion. Cut it."

"You're not serious," Angel said.

"I am very serious."

"I don't have the face for short hair."

"How do you know? When has your hair ever been short?" Mario asked.

"My hair is part of my brand. It says glamour and sex appeal," Angel said, while stepping over broken glass.

"It also says pretentious and played out. You want to revive your career, change your look. Give the people something different. What's the worst that could happen? You don't like it, you wear wigs and hats until it grows out."

Angel let him cut her hair, and the world didn't end. To her delight, the short, natural upswept hairstyle made her look younger. Mario used his products and within six weeks, her hair had already grown almost two inches. The executive she had been meeting with at Miller Hair Products, to sponsor the tour, noticed her hair growth and offered to mass-produce the product, with Angel as the spokesperson. Angel thought this was a great idea until she talked it over with Crystal.

"Why peddle someone else's product? Cut out the middleman, and you and Mario start your own hair-care line."

AngelHair was born, and Angel Donovan added *business tycoon* to her résumé. Preston found a warehouse in a Memphis redevelopment zone, and Doreen arranged a small business loan. She and Mario did infomercials and online demonstrations, and hit the hair show circuit. Customers may have initially stopped at their booth because of her singing career.

But they all left with bags of blue bottles, and spread the word about AngelHair. Walmart and Target asked to carry their products. Black women spent billions on hair care products, with a fraction going to black-owned companies. AngelHair was an effective, safe product, but also satisfied customers' desire to support their community. Her bank account was higher than it had ever been, and she and Mario had even been interviewed for *Black Enterprise* and *Inc.* magazines.

Her personal life was also prospering. Angel and Preston were officially a couple. They bought a house with a mother-in-law wing and moved her mother in with them. She paid for twenty-four-hour care, and her mother seemed less confused and withdrawn. After seeing her mother's positive reaction to music, and learning how therapeutic music can be for individuals with Alzheimer's, dementia, and other cognitive issues, she became an ambassador for the nonprofit Music & Memory, an organization that distributed personalized playlists to these individuals and caregivers. She made a generous donation to Doreen's church, and a few other donations. Otherwise, her money was invested. Seeing numbers with zeroes behind them, now gave her more satisfaction than red bottom shoes and designer labels.

In the last year, she had lost her recording contract, gotten divorced, left her beloved Rose Manor, the tour had been canceled, and had to cut off her pride and joy—her hair.

Who knew you could win by losing?

CHAPTER 59

CARMEN

After Attorney Hawkins called to tell them the jury had reached a verdict, Carmen and David hurriedly changed clothes and rushed to the courthouse. She barely paused at each red light and parked in a no-parking spot in their haste to get inside.

On the elevator, she told David, "It's almost over. Stay strong, and I'm treating you to the biggest steak you can find when we leave this purgatory." Attorney Hawkins was waiting when the doors opened. She squeezed David's hand before he left. Her hand was sweaty, his—cold.

Another case finally finished, and the doors opened. She paced the hall, praying and making deals with God. She promised the Lord she would sing in the choir, tithe, and remain celibate, if he would please send an innocent verdict.

She then marched in and sat behind her son, next to Vernon. As the jury filed in, she tried to read their faces for clues about her son's fate. They seemed more relaxed than usual. She didn't know if that meant they were pleased to help an innocent young man go free, or if they were just happy to be finished.

Everyone rose when the judge entered, and Carmen noticed the judge's chipped nail polish. These life-and-death issues were so mundane to her, she didn't even bother to get her nails done.

Carmen watched the jury foreman hand the paper that held her son's future to the bailiff. Her heart stopped when the judge unfolded the paper, nodded her head, and handed the paper back to the bailiff. She felt like a slave waiting for 'massa' to read the Emancipation Proclamation. She tried to read the judge's face. But the judge's expression remained the same, no hint of the life-changing decision she had just read.

"Ladies and gentlemen of the jury, have you reached a verdict?"

"We have, Your Honor," the foreman announced. "We find the defendant, David Vernon Payne, not guilty."

The judge stated instructions, which Carmen didn't hear, struck her gavel, and left. Carmen was so drained, she couldn't even stand when the judge rose to leave. The band of family and friends clapped and cheered and swarmed to hug David. All Carmen could do was lean her head on the banister in front of her and cry. These weren't cute tears. Her nose was running, and she was blubbering like a baby. Hope rubbed her back and handed her Burger Barn napkins. David made his way through the crowd and helped his mother stand. Carmen buried her head in his chest, unable to stop the tears.

"Everything is okay, just like you said. Don't cry, Mom."

She looked up into the face of the child she used to tell the same thing. "I've gotten your shirt all wet," she said, as she raised her head and wiped her face.

"Use this."

Carmen looked over her shoulder as a monogrammed handkerchief was placed in her hands. David grinned and stepped back as his mother leaned into another set of arms.

"I didn't know you were here," Carmen said, in a cracked voice.

"I'll always be here," Gerald said. Carmen buried her face in his chest and it was his turn to get a wet shirt.

Carmen may have been broke, but she spared no expense on David's celebration party. She invited everyone she knew and bought top-shelf liquor, decorations, new patio furniture, and so much meat, her shopping cart was running over. She wrote checks rather than use her debit card. *My checks are going to bounce like a rubber ball*, she thought as she smiled at the grocery store cashier. *But I'll worry about that later.*

Sonny had gotten his settlement and paid for the renovations to Carmen's house. Gerald supervised the renovations, and cleaned and manicured her yard. Handyman tasks were initially an excuse to visit Carmen every day. But sometime between new drywall and installing the walk-in tub, he and Carmen become a couple again.

Everyone had shown brave faces during David's ordeal. Now they could finally exhale. The party was for David, but everyone was ready to celebrate. Gerald was in charge of grilling, and greeted guests as though he was the man of the house. Doreen and her family, Miss Murray, Mr. Wilson, the Sexy Seniors, David's coach and teammates, and some of David's teachers were there. Even Vernon and his family were welcome today. When Attorney Hawkins entered, Carmen gathered everyone and toasted him as the man of the hour. After her toast, she pulled him aside.

"The words *thank you* don't express my gratitude. I can't tell you how much I appreciate you hanging with me, even after the tour was canceled. I promise to pay every cent I owe you."

"You don't owe anything."

"No, I'm going to pay my balance. It's the least I can do. It may take a while, but—"

"Miss Payne, it's been paid."

"What? When? Who?"

"My secretary received a phone call from someone requesting to know the balance. I remember because I reprimanded her for disclosing confidential information. I immediately returned the call and insisted I couldn't accept the payment without your knowledge. She said it was money she had owed you for a long time and she wanted to surprise you. She told me to put on the type of defense Johnnie Cochran would have presented and money was no object. I was doing my best, but that money made the difference. That's how I hired the paralegal and paid the expert witnesses. I thought you knew."

"But who was it?"

"It was Angel Donovan. Again, I apologize. I think my secretary got a little starstruck."

Carmen hadn't spoken with Angel since they took Doreen to the emergency room. She hadn't answered Angel's calls or texts. She didn't attend their show opening, or the Beale Street award ceremony. Once again, her mother had been right, and now her grudge seemed petty. *How in the world can I thank her?* Carmen thought. She grabbed her phone and was scrolling for Angel's number when Gerald grabbed her hand. He then called everyone into the living room. He hushed everyone, then turned toward Carmen and got on one knee.

"Carmen Marie Ellis Payne, would you honor me by becoming my wife?"

Carmen put her hands over her mouth and stifled a scream.

"She says *yes*," Gloria and Faye shouted.

"Do you have an older uncle or cousin somewhere?" Miss Murray asked. "But not too old."

Instead of winding down, the party resumed with a new reason to celebrate.

Chapter 60

THE DIAMONDS

Mother Nature was reminding Memphis residents who was in charge. They had come through the driest spring in years, and now summer was setting rainfall records. Storms the last few days had brought howling winds and tornado warnings. But today was picture-perfect. The sun had come out of hiding and it was as though the heavens were welcoming Gloria into their fold.

Gloria's health had been declining for months, but her death was still a gut punch. She was full of energy at the party after the verdict. But she was weak the next morning, and Carmen rushed her to the hospital. They kept her overnight, changed her prescriptions, and sent her home, but she had another stroke a few weeks later. She came home, but spent most of her days in bed and her recovery time between dialysis treatments got longer. She stopped attending church but insisted on going the first Sunday Carmen sang in the choir. Gloria appeared to be getting better with summer's blooming crepe myrtles and longer days. The family gathered at Gloria's house for her birthday. She was so rejuvenated she began making plans to move back to her house by summer. She was researching home health-care options and had Gerald draw up plans to make her entrance wheelchair accessible. But then a few weeks later, Hope went to her grandmother's room to ask what she wanted for breakfast and found Gloria on the floor near the bathroom. They called the paramedics, who rushed her to the hospital. She spent six days in various stages of consciousness, but on the seventh morning, Gloria was gone.

Doreen was dressing for Sunday school when they got the call. The doctor had given Carmen a sedative, and she was asleep when they arrived. Sonny and Mr. Wilson were inconsolable, and James tried to comfort them. Doreen told Faye to go home, she'd call the usher board president, who would make sure the family was taken care of. Doreen called Angel and Jade. They canceled their next two performances and booked tickets to Memphis.

Gloria would've been proud to see the ushers bringing chairs for the overflow crowd. Faye ensured elaborate floral arrangements covered the front of the sanctuary. Several Peak Records artists came and James delivered a humorous and inspiring eulogy. Hope led the choir and Angel closed the service with a solo. Ladies were asked to wear hats, in honor of Gloria. Doreen had remained strong throughout the service, but her eyes welled with tears during Angel's solo. She mourned for Miss Glo, but some tears were for her sister. It was the same song Carmen had sung at Sophia's funeral.

The ride to the cemetery was somber and Mr. Wilson was despondent as they walked to the burial site. "Ashes to ashes and dust to dust," James said, then read a Bible passage to end the graveside service. Sunbeams reflected off the golden coffin and it looked like God's finger was touching Gloria's tomb, welcoming her home.

Mourners began to mingle and spoke in hushed tones about the beautiful service and complimented her children on how nicely their mother was "put away." Carmen nodded and said "thank you," but the credit went to her mother. Gloria had chosen and paid for her own casket and burial plot. She shopped for months like she was choosing a new car. She often asked Carmen's opinion, but Carmen tuned her out and changed the subject. She showed her daughters which dress to bury her in, and told them to be sure she was wearing one of her salt-and-pepper human hair wigs, and her red fascinator hat. She had even purchased the headstone and had the caption, *Loving Mother, Humble Servant* inscribed. Although there was nothing humble about Gloria Mae Ellis. The tombstone did provide the answer to one of life's biggest mysteries. Her birth year was inscribed on the tombstone. Gloria had guarded this secret like the gold in Fort Knox. She left instructions about which funeral home to use, the order of service, and she requested Angel sing "I Won't Complain." She believed the other girls' voices were richer than Angel's, but she knew that would impress her friends.

Carmen was glad this ordeal was almost over, with one more ritual to endure. They got in the hearse and returned to the church for the repast. The processional finally made it back to the church cafeteria. Carmen had hoped the crowd would have thinned out, but the prospect of a free meal kept the parking lot full. Carmen could hear the laughter and conversations as they entered the cafeteria. The mood was almost festive. "They act like they're at a party," Carmen complained as they walked in behind the funeral director.

"You know Mama would not have wanted a glum, sorry affair," Faye insisted. The serving table was packed with dressing, greens, yams, macaroni and cheese, salads, green beans, ham, and chicken. Every type of pie and cake imaginable were on another table. Although for once, Carmen didn't feel like eating.

A photographer interrupted Carmen as she picked over her food and asked if she would pose for a picture with the other Diamonds. She hadn't spoken to any of them today and wanted to particularly thank Angel and Jade for coming. They hadn't all been together since the last disastrous rehearsal. She had written Angel a two-page letter thanking her for helping with David's legal fees and letting her know how much Gloria loved her. Angel called when she received the letter and they cried, talked, and laughed for two hours. They would never be best friends, but were more like close cousins. You accept them as they are and love them because they're family, and even though they get on your last nerve, they are there in time of need.

"Thank you for coming," Carmen said, as she took off her hat to fan herself.

"Of course we'd be here. Miss Glo was the fifth Diamond," Angel stated.

"Can everyone look this way?" the photographer asked.

Carmen, Doreen, and Jade had worn black. But leave it to Angel to stand out, with a fitted violet dress. The photographer asked her to stand in the center. The brim of her hat was so wide, the others had to stretch to be in the picture, and as usual, she was the sun the other Diamonds orbited.

After he took the picture, several church members asked for Angel's autograph and pictures. Once upon a time, that would have aggravated Carmen. She now knew craving attention was just part of Angel's DNA. But the fan club of Gerald, Hope, and David was enough for her.

While sitting down to comfort Mr. Wilson, Carmen heard Faye's voice over the microphone. "Thank you so much for coming and for honoring my mother's request to make donations to the Memphis Dialysis Center. But before we leave, my mother had one more request. She was a renaissance woman, able to manage a McDonald's as easily as a houseful of hardheaded children. But as proud as she was of her children, there was something else she managed that gave her a major source of pride—the Diamonds. All the girls are here, and what better way to memorialize her life than for them to sing together?"

The hall burst into applause, but Carmen wanted to crawl under the table. She did not feel like singing. Carmen lowered her head as the applause grew and she saw three pairs of feet. Angel, Doreen, and Jade stood in front of her with their hands extended. "Baby, you can do this," Gerald urged as he wiped her tears with his handkerchief. Something overtook her body, and Carmen rose and followed them to the microphone.

Doreen began, "*God be with you 'til we meet again,*" as she grabbed Carmen's hand. Then, as though they had rehearsed for the occasion, Angel's melodic soprano, Jade's perfect pitch, and Carmen's soulful alto joined, "*by his counsels guide uphold you . . .*" The girls ended with a group hug as everyone stood and applauded.

Dawn rushed to congratulate them. "That was awesome."

"Maybe it's the acoustics, but we did sound good," Angel said.

"The Lord was with us today," Doreen added.

"It definitely had to be the Lord, because there was no way I planned to ever sing with you again," Carmen said, as she looked at Angel. "As far as I was concerned, the Diamonds were history."

"Don't be mad. I needed the money," Jade said.

"I'm glad you went ahead with the tour. How have things been going?"

"They're going okay, but it's not the same without you and Doreen," Jade admitted.

"After hearing us today, I know we can do it," Angel gushed. "And you won't believe the money we can make, especially with all four of us."

"We had a good run, maybe we should leave it alone," Carmen said, shaking her head. "We've been off the scene a long time."

"Are you kidding? We didn't fade out like some groups. We quit at our peak and left them wanting more," Angel said. "We just took a long intermission, and everyone knows the part after intermission is the best part of the show."

"What about the new girls?" Jade asked.

"Yeah, what about the cubic zirconias?" Carmen asked.

"Don't worry about them. I can work something out," Angel said, pushing her bangs out of her eyes. "And I was thinking, we should add a tribute to Sophia."

"That would mean a lot," Doreen said.

"How about it, Carmen?" Jade asked.

"We had to get a new sponsor, so we have over half the tour left. We'll finish this fall because I start rehearsals for *Forty Acres*. I got the lead and we open on Broadway next spring."

"Congratulations, Angel," Doreen said.

"Plus, Dawn and I start college classes this fall, so we'll only be traveling on weekends," Jade said.

"If you're bringing Dawn, I'll bring Paige. James and the boys can hang out at home. I think it would be fun."

"Carmen, it's three to one," Angel said.

"Good try, but I'm not interested," Carmen replied. "Besides, aren't you still under the doctor's care, Doreen?"

"Yes, but I'm sure I can get cleared. Although I can't do any rigorous dance moves, and I need to wear flat shoes," Doreen said, while patting her stomach.

"We can work around that," Angel said. She was looking for her phone, then looked back up at Doreen. "Is there something you're not telling us?"

Doreen grinned. "As Carmen would say, my old behind is having a baby."

"Girl, don't pay any attention to me," Carmen said, as she hugged Doreen. "I'm happy for you. Your hair is growing; that means it's a girl."

"That sounds like something Miss Glo would say. We'll really miss her at Blessings," Doreen said.

"Mama would've loved spoiling your baby," Carmen said. "Enjoy it. Time is so precious."

"I've already left the bank, so the timing is perfect for me."

"I don't blame you," Jade said. "Start your maternity leave and pamper yourself."

"It's not maternity leave. I'm leaving the bank. Blessings is opening a credit union and I'm heading it up. We should be open this time next year."

"You've been holding out on us," Angel said. "Now I know where to come for a loan."

"I think someone else has been holding out on us," Jade said, grabbing Carmen's left hand. "Does this blinding rock on your finger mean what I think it means?"

"Gerald and I got married last week in Mama's hospital room. James conducted the service, and she gave me away. As weak as Mama was, she insisted on wearing a hat," Carmen said, flashing her dimples for the first time today.

"I'm happy, if you're happy," Angel said. "But me and marriage don't mix."

"Maybe seven will be your lucky number," Carmen teased.

"I've only been married four times, thank you very much."

"You're a newlywed and I'm getting divorced," Jade said.

"I didn't know," Carmen said. "I'm sorry to hear that."

"Don't be. I don't know what took me so long."

"What about the restaurant?" Doreen asked. "I know you invested a lot of time and money."

"I like to cook, but if I never see another restaurant kitchen, that'll be fine with me. I signed over my Seaside interest to my children. I feel like I've been released from prison."

"Freedom is grand. You won't regret it," Angel said. "I hated being tied down."

"You didn't look like you were trying to be free to me," Jade said. "Preston has been tracking us like a bounty hunter."

"What happens on the road, stays on the road," Angel said, clearing her throat.

"Being tied down is okay, if you're tied to the right one," Carmen said, raising her left hand and wiggling her ring finger.

"You got that right," Doreen said, as she gave Carmen a high five.

"So, we all have something to celebrate. Come on, Carmen," Jade said. "It's like being nineteen again, except with Spanx and earplugs."

"Wouldn't it be great to reboot your savings and start married life with a healthy bank account?" Doreen asked.

"We know the business, and we've got more talent than these booty-shaking, lip-synchers out now," Angel said. "I bet we sell out everywhere. You know that's what Miss Glo wanted."

"Wow, way to play the guilt card," Carmen said. "Let me think about it…"

Microphone static interrupted conversations as attendees were gathering their belongings and to-go plates. "We thank everyone for coming to celebrate our mother's life," Faye said. "We have honored my mother's memory with class and reverence. But anyone who knew Gloria Mae Ellis, knows she liked having a good time. I know we're in a church, but I don't think the Lord will mind if we leave on a festive note.

Her favorite song was, "The Best Is Yet to Come." Can we get the Diamonds to sing a couple verses? I can't think of a better send-off for our mother."

Doreen, Jade, Angel, and Carmen joined hands and the Diamonds sang one more song. And they knew Miss Glo was smiling down on her girls, and reminding them to stand up straight.